#1 *New York Times* Bestselling Author

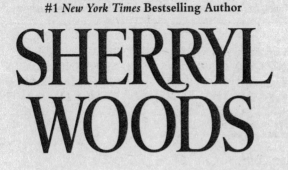

SHERRYL
WOODS

Twilight

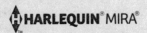

HARLEQUIN® MIRA®

Recycling programs
for this product may
not exist in your area.

ISBN-13: 978-0-7783-1512-4

TWILIGHT

Harlequin MIRA 2013

First Published by Zebra Books

Copyright © 1997 by Sherryl Woods

For questions and comments about the quality of this book, please contact us at CustomerService@Harlequin.com.

Printed in U.S.A.

www.Harlequin.com

Dear friends,

Every now and then a story pops into my head and simply won't go away. *Twilight* was like that for me when it was first written a number of years ago. I still feel the powerful emotions of a woman whose faith in God has been tested by tragedy.

Add in an unlikely and very much unwanted attraction to a man she holds responsible for her husband's death, and there's plenty of conflict and a healthy dose of mystery in the story.

I hope you'll feel the same emotional tug that I felt when this book was first written, and that you'll turn the last page and give a thought to what you'd do if your faith were ever tested.

All best,

Sherryl

Twilight

Prologue

The brilliant late afternoon sun could only do so much. The orange blaze shimmered on the Gulf of Mexico like a scattering of gemstones. It warmed the wide stretch of sandy beach. But it couldn't touch the cold place deep inside Dana Miller's heart.

She had never felt so totally empty, so thoroughly alone. Even with her sons whooping and hollering and splashing a few feet away at the water's edge, she was gut-deep lonely. Even knowing that her parents were there for her—that they shared her anguish and understood her pain—couldn't erase the horrible sense that she was facing a bleak and empty future.

Her husband, her sweet, gentle, kind husband, was dead. Murdered by a person, or persons, unknown, according to the cryptic police report that she read over and over, alone in her room at night, trying to make sense of it, trying to find acceptance of the cold, hard truth.

It had been over a month since that terrible January night, and there were still no answers—not for her, not for the Chicago police, who seemed to dread her daily calls almost as much as she hated making them. But she couldn't stop. She desperately needed answers, and no one had them. Until she did, there could be no tears, no healing.

"Put it out of your head," her mother had pleaded more than once. "You may never know why it happened. What does it really matter, anyway? Knowing won't bring Ken back. The boys need you. You have to move on for their sake."

Dana wished she could do as her mother asked. The boys did need her. If only she had something left to give.

Every night she prayed for some sort of peace, some small measure of the kind of serenity she had always felt in Ken's arms. He had brought so much into her life. As a private investigator, she had seen a lot of ugliness. She had seen people at their worst, but Ken had changed that. He had shown her how to find the goodness in everyone. He had taught her about joy and laughter and the kind of oneness with God that few mortals ever felt. Ken had felt it, though, and he had known how to communicate it to others—even a doubter such as she had been before they'd met.

Her lips curved into a sad half smile as she remembered how he had loved the church, the rituals and the hymns and the prayers. He had loved ministering to his congregation, loved sharing his strength and his beliefs with those whose faith had been tested by tragedy. Rich or poor, saint or sinner, Ken had been there for them, generous with his time and with his unconditional love.

And now that he was gone, Dana had no one to bolster her shattered faith as her husband would have done. From the moment the police had come to her door, from the moment they had tersely described Ken's senseless slaying in the middle of Chicago gang turf, her faith had been destroyed. A benevolent God could not have allowed that to happen, not to Ken, not to one of His most ardent believers.

And since Ken was very much dead, Dana bitterly accepted the fact that God had abandoned him and her and their three precious boys. If there was some sort of divine purpose behind such an act of madness, she couldn't discern it. She doubted she ever would.

She shivered as the sun ducked behind a cloud and the sensation of emptiness returned. Where once there had been hope and happiness, now there was only this huge, gaping wound where her soul had been.

Time promised to heal eventually, but Dana had never been a patient woman. She'd always been decisive and quick and instinctively curious. She'd had daring to spare. Those traits had made her one of the best private investigators in the Midwest, but she'd given it all up when her first son was born. The same danger that brought a satisfying rush of adrenaline also came with a warning: do not mix with parenting.

She had made the sacrifice willingly and never looked back. Ken and the boys—first Bobby, then Kevin and finally Jonathan—had fulfilled her in a way she'd never imagined possible. The challenges had been vastly different, but just as rewarding. After a surprisingly brief period of adjustment, she had been thoroughly content with her decision, as fiercely protective of their safety as she had once been lax with her own.

Until now. Now those old urges to pursue truth taunted her late at night, when the loneliness was at its worst. She needed answers, and the police weren't getting them. She had the same investigative skills they had, but more important, she had the passion for this particular hunt. She wouldn't relegate it to some cold case file drawer, content to let it remain unsolved until, years from now, some street thug confessed or some witness uttered a tip from his deathbed.

With the boys already settled in a new school for the

rest of the year to give them time away from Chicago to heal, with her plans half made to move to Florida permanently, as her parents wanted, there was only one thing keeping her from making the decision final. She had unfinished business back home.

More and more, she saw going back to Chicago, taking charge of her life and the search for the killer, as the only way she would ever be at peace again. Staying in Florida now without knowing was as good as quitting, and she had never been a quitter.

She dreaded telling her parents, though. They were already worried sick about her. She was too quiet, too lifeless, even for a woman in mourning. She'd caught the troubled glances, the whispered exchanges, the helpless sighs. They would be terrified that in her state of mind she would take dangerous, unnecessary risks. She doubted she could make her reassurances convincing enough to soothe their fears.

Yet she knew, if she asked, that they would keep the boys with them, give them a sense of stability that she couldn't with her heart in turmoil. They would protect them and love them while she went home to do the only thing she could. The only thing.

She would find the cold-blooded, violent person who had ripped her heart and her life to shreds. She would find answers for the unceasing questions asked by her sons, answers they all needed, if they were ever to move on.

And though the police claimed to have followed up on, then dismissed, her repeated suggestions, she thought she knew exactly where to start.

1

The blasted sofa must have belonged to the Marquis de Sade in another life, Rick Sanchez thought as he shifted his body in a futile attempt to find a more comfortable position. Between the oddly solidified lumps and protruding springs, he was lucky he hadn't gouged out a vital organ. He was very careful to avoid lying on his stomach.

This was the fourth night he'd gone through this same torture, and he was beginning to wonder if he was wasting his time. Whoever had been breaking into the Yo, Amigo headquarters either knew he'd moved in to guard the place or had simply decided that there was more fertile turf for theft elsewhere.

Lord knew, that was true enough, he thought as he cautiously rearranged his body once more on the worn-out, too-short sofa. The program he'd founded two years earlier was perpetually short of funds and equipment. The sole, ancient computer he'd hoodwinked a friend into donating had been an early victim of daring neighborhood thieves. Now about the only things of value lying around were the TV and DVD player in the lounge. They were bolted down, though not so securely that anyone intent on nabbing them couldn't manage it with a little time and diligence.

They were also in pathetic condition, but at least they'd been obtained legally, unlike the collection of state-of-the-art electronic equipment a few of the boys had offered him the week before. He'd really hated turning them down, but Yo, Amigo was all about taking a moral stance and teaching values. Accepting stolen property would pretty much defeat the very message he was trying to send out.

Exhausted but wide awake, he closed his eyes and tried counting confiscated weapons instead of sheep. He'd turned over a dozen to the police two days earlier, another seven the week before. It was a drop in the bucket, but each gun or knife he managed to get out of gang hands and off the streets was a small victory.

Rather than putting him to sleep, though, the mental game left him more alert than ever. Images of boys killing boys, of babies being shot by accident in a violent turf war crowded into his head. He wondered despondently if the program he'd founded would ever be more than a tiny, ineffective bandage on the huge problem.

Such thoughts led inevitably to memories of Ken Miller, the decent, caring man who had been his friend and, some said, had lost his life because of it. Rick knew he would never have a moment's peace again if he allowed himself to share that conviction. His conscience, which already carried a heavy enough burden of guilt from the sins of his youth, would destroy him, if even indirect responsibility for Ken's death were added to the list.

He shifted positions and felt the sharp jab of a metal spring in the middle of his back. He muttered a harsh expletive under his breath and sat up.

Just as he did, he thought he heard a faint whisper of sound, an almost imperceptible scratching from the back of the old brick firetrap that had been condemned until he took it over and began restoring it room by room with the help of the boys in his program. He went perfectly still and listened intently.

The second subtle scrape of metal against metal had him on his feet in an instant. He grabbed the baseball bat he'd kept by the door and eased from the office.

Slipping quietly through the shadowy rooms toward the increasingly persistent sound, he wished for a moment that he hadn't sworn off guns. He also wished the budget had been large enough to pay for a cell phone, rather than the lone, ancient phone that suddenly seemed very far away on his desk. He might as well have wished for a fleet of shiny new vans to transport the teens to the job assignments that were a part of the program. All were out of reach on the shoestring Yo, Amigo budget.

Just as he closed in on the back door, he heard the heavy-duty lock give. Whoever had conquered it was skilled with lock-picking tools, he concluded with grudging admiration. It hardly narrowed the field, since most of the kids he knew had been breaking and entering since they could reach a door handle or heave a rock through a window. Most, however, didn't have the finesse or patience to work at a lock with the tedious determination that this person had.

The heavy steel door inched open silently on its well-oiled hinges. Pressed against a wall, Rick waited in the shadows. There was no point in risking his neck until he knew exactly what he was up against. One thief. Two. Or a whole gang, in which case his goose was cooked and he could kiss the TV and DVD player goodbye.

To his relief, the lone person who slipped inside was

slightly built and dressed in black from head to toe. Black baseball cap, long-sleeved black T-shirt, trim black pants, even black sneakers. Vaguely taken aback, he concluded it was the working gear of a pro, not some daring kid intent on mischief. The kids he knew wore the baggy clothes and colors of their gangs. Solid, formfitting black like this would have appalled them.

More on edge than ever, and itching for action, he studied the person creeping slowly and unwittingly toward him in the narrow hallway. Rick figured he easily had a fifty-pound advantage over the intruder, plus several inches in height. Even so, he forced himself to wait patiently and watch for accomplices.

When none appeared, he bit back a sigh of relief and considered his options. The bat seemed unnecessary. He propped it cautiously against the wall. Then he slipped up behind the increasingly confident and fast-moving thief and, without uttering a word, slammed the jerk onto the hardwood floor in a full-body tackle that knocked the breath out of both of them.

Rick recovered from the fall first, latched on to a pair of skinny wrists and brutally wrenched the would-be thief's arms behind him.

He received a blistering earful of curses for his trouble. The words didn't shock him. He'd heard far worse. Used far worse, for that matter.

What flat-out stunned him, though, was the fact that the voice uttering such foulmouthed language was so evidently and self-righteously outraged. More startling yet, it was also very clearly feminine.

"If you don't let me up right this instant, I will slap you with a lawsuit that will take away this building and every dime you have to your name," the woman vowed furiously.

Rick was intrigued despite himself. Not intrigued enough to let her go, but fascinated enough to pursue the conversational direction for a bit.

"Is that so?" he asked, unexpectedly amused by her gambit. "And how do you figure you're the injured party here?"

"Because I've been attacked by an idiot with more muscle than sense. I wouldn't be at all surprised if half my ribs were cracked."

"You did break into private property," he reminded her.

"A technicality," she insisted.

"Some technicality. You a lawyer?"

"Sweet heavens, no," she said with such heartfelt distaste that Rick grinned.

"I'm not overly fond of them myself. I guess that gives us something in common, doll face."

"Doll face?" she repeated with more of that misplaced indignant outrage. "No one calls me doll face or honey or sweetheart."

"Too bad," Rick said sympathetically. He decided he could really enjoy deliberately aggravating this woman. "Mind telling me why you dropped by, doll face? Since you chose not to use the front door or to come during business hours, I have to assume your mission is less than legal."

"That's not true," she said.

"The facts say otherwise."

"To hell with your so-called facts. Are you going to let me up or not?"

"Not just yet," he said, wondering abruptly if the decision was the security precaution he wanted to believe or merely an attempt to prolong the distinctly provocative contact. Worry over his motives kept him silent for so long that his captive jumped back in with her two cents.

"If you're figuring on copping a feel, you'd better think again," she said in that imperious way that amused him so. "I'll slap you with sexual battery charges while I'm at it."

. Rick chuckled. "Doll face, I do not need to get my kicks from accosting total strangers. In case you've missed the point, I am subduing a thief who broke into this building. I'm within my rights, believe me."

"I am not a thief," she retorted.

"Maybe not technically, since you never got a chance to lay your hands on anything of value," he agreed. "But you seem to be in deep denial of the seriousness of your position. Now, how about giving me some answers?"

She hesitated for a very long time, probably evaluating her alternatives, before asking, "Such as?"

"Who are you and what are you doing here?"

"Who are you?" she countered. "For all I know, you're just a thief who got here first."

She had audacity. Rick had to give her that. She was the kind of smart-mouthed handful who'd drive a man crazy. He wished he could get a better look at her to see if she'd be worth the trouble, but the lighting in the hallway was virtually nonexistent. The only thing he knew for sure was that she wasn't local. She had no accent. All of the girls in this neighborhood—and some of them were indeed tough as nails—were Latinas.

Based on her shape, though, this one definitely had promise. His own body had picked up on that without his brain even having to kick in. Another couple of minutes of close contact and he'd be dangerously aroused. Hell, he was already aroused. For a man who'd vehemently sworn to remain celibate through all eternity after his very brief and ill-advised marriage had gone sour, it was a troubling turn of events. He'd better settle this nonsense in a hurry and extricate himself from a dangerous situation.

"Let me assure you, doll face, I belong here," he said. "I run the place."

The announcement had an odd effect on her. Though she'd remained relatively still since he'd taken her captive, it now seemed that the remaining breath whooshed right out of her. She was utterly and absolutely motionless. That didn't strike Rick as a good sign.

"Doll face?"

"You're Rick Sanchez?" she asked in a broken whisper.

Rick couldn't tell if her voice was choked by tears or was shaking with some inexplicable anger, but he definitely got the feeling she knew a whole lot more about Yo, Amigo than he'd assumed. He also realized that he was the very last person she'd expected to encounter here tonight.

"That's me," he told her. "Which leaves us with you. Who are you, doll face?"

Several seconds ticked by before she answered.

"I'm Dana Miller."

She said it in a tone so stiff and cold that it sent goose bumps chasing over Rick's body. Dismay slammed through him as the name registered. Ken's wife? Dear God in heaven, he'd tackled Ken's wife as though she were a common criminal. Which, of course, at the moment she appeared to be, but that was beside the point.

He released her wrists at once and leaped to his feet, holding out his hand to help her up. She ignored it and rose with a grace and dignity that belied the situation.

"I'm sorry," he said, trying to convey a month's worth

of emotions in those two simple words. "For everything. For Ken. For just now."

"Save it," she said harshly. "Save it for someone who'll buy your phony sympathy."

Anger radiated from her in almost palpable waves. Rick had known she blamed him for Ken's death. A half-dozen people had told him exactly how bitter she was toward him and Yo, Amigo. In fact, he had stayed away from the funeral for that very reason, out of consideration for her feelings, justified or not. He'd figured Ken's graveside was no place to force a confrontation. Later he'd tried to see her, but she'd been gone, off in Florida to recover from the tragedy, her best friend had told him.

Now he realized that he should have seen her sooner, should have gone at once to offer his condolences, to explain how deeply he, too, was grieving over the death of her husband. He doubted she would have believed him any more then than she did now, but he knew how wounds could fester unless they were cleansed right away. This soul-deep wound was no different than one to the flesh. It had had more than a month to worsen dangerously.

Ironically, he had anticipated that sooner or later, she might come after him. He just hadn't expected it to be in the middle of the night.

Gazing into her bleak expression, he tried to tell her now what he would have said weeks ago, if he'd had the opportunity.

"Your husband was the best friend—"

He never got to finish the sentence. Her open hand connected with his face in a stinging slap that rocked him on his heels.

"Don't you dare say that," she said. "Don't you dare."

Rick fell silent, uncertain how to cope with such anguish and outrage. Used to coping with broken teenaged dreams with words and hugs and timeworn platitudes, he could think of nothing that would touch Dana Miller's hurt, or calm her fury. Obviously, she needed to lash out at someone and she'd picked him.

Since the topics of Ken Miller and his death were clearly off-limits, despite their obvious connection to tonight's break-in, he decided to focus on why Dana Miller was at Yo, Amigo headquarters in the middle of the night. It didn't take a genius to figure that one out.

"You expected to find answers here, didn't you?" he asked softly.

The direct question seemed to surprise her. Her gaze clashed with his. "It's the obvious place to start."

"The police thought so, too," he reminded her. "They've searched through every file, talked with every one of the kids who comes here regularly, questioned every potential eyewitness. They've almost destroyed the program in the process." He regarded her defiantly. "I won't let you start the whole thing all over again."

"You don't have a choice in the matter," she told him coldly. "I will do whatever I have to do to find Ken's murderer. You can't stop me."

He found her resolve chilling, but it bolstered his own commitment to salvage Yo, Amigo, at any cost. "Oh, but I can. These kids need a safe haven. They need one person who believes in them. That's me. They had Ken, too, but he's gone now."

"Because of you," she accused bitterly.

"Not because of me or these kids," Rick insisted. "I'd stake my life on that."

"Then you're a blind fool," she said. "He was here, in this neighborhood, because of you. Week after week, he risked his life by coming here. Eventually the odds caught up with him." That said, she turned her back on him and headed for the door.

Rick couldn't let her go, not like this. "Dana?"

Her determined footsteps faltered, but she didn't look back.

"I will do anything to help you find Ken's killer, but I will not let you destroy Yo, Amigo. There's too much at stake."

"You can't stop me," she said again.

"I'll report what happened here tonight, if I have to," he said, catching her attention. Her eyes blazed when she turned to face him. He went on with his warning, hoping to scare some sense into her. "I will let the police know that you're on a vigilante's mission. They'll stop you."

She choked back what sounded like a sob, but her voice was steady when she said, "Do what you have to do, Mr. Sanchez. And I will do what I have to do."

Before he could think of anything to say to that, she slipped out into the night and vanished even more quietly than she had arrived.

More shaken than he'd ever been by an encounter with a rival gang, Rick sighed at her leaving. She was a handful, all right, everything Ken had ever described her as being.

And he had a terrible feeling that tonight had just been the first skirmish in what was likely to turn into all-out war.

Dana climbed into her car a half block from Yo, Amigo and leaned back against the seat. Her whole body was shaking, not from the very real danger that existed all around her in this neighborhood, but from that face-to-face confrontation with Rick Sanchez.

How could she have been so stupid, so careless? Ob-

viously she'd lost not only her mind, but her touch. She'd
been so anxious to begin her search for answers, so determined not to stay away from the boys one second longer than necessary, that she'd gotten off the plane and
plunged ahead on her first night back in Chicago. She'd
done it without thinking things through, without so much
as a day's surveillance of how the stupid program operated or who was likely to be in the building. She'd just
assumed it would be empty at night. Assumptions had
been the downfall of more than one private eye. She knew
that, and she'd acted impetuously anyway.

Now Sanchez knew she was after him or, if not him
directly, then one of those precious criminals he defended
so arduously.

"Blast it all," she muttered, hugging herself to ward
off the chill that came from getting caught on her very
first attempt to gather information.

She drew in a deep breath and made a promise to herself that tonight's foolishness would be the very last mistake she'd make. She couldn't afford another one, not with
a man like Rick Sanchez. Ken wouldn't have admired
him so if he'd been anything less than brilliant and committed. That meant he would be every bit as passionate
in his defense of his boys and his program as she would
be in her search for the killer.

His offer to help echoed in her head. Of course he
wanted to help. He wanted to steer her as far from Yo,
Amigo as he possibly could. She couldn't afford to be
taken in by the compassion or the sorrow he'd expressed.
He had his own agenda and it was not the same as hers.
Far from it, in fact.

For a moment she allowed herself to wish it were otherwise. The next days and weeks promised to be lonely,
albeit frantically busy. It would have been nice to have

someone with whom to share theories, as she once would have with Ken.

But Rick Sanchez was not that man. She thought of the powerful, barely leashed strength he'd radiated, the taunting arrogance as he'd held her down before he'd learned who she was. The memory made her shiver, this time with unwanted awareness of just how dangerous a man he was.

She shook off the sensation that she was flirting with disaster. She couldn't afford to be scared off now. Tomorrow, when she'd had some rest, had a chance to compose herself, she would plot out her strategy. And no one— not even the formidable Rick Sanchez—would stand in her way.

2

The greatest act of courage Dana had ever performed wasn't breaking into Yo, Amigo. It wasn't fighting off an assailant that had turned out to be the man she held responsible for her husband's death. It was walking back into the house she and Ken had shared for most of their marriage.

With her heart thudding dully, she hesitated on the tiny cement stoop, unable to push the key into the lock. Her fingers, so nimble earlier, felt stiff and awkward now. Her key ring seemed to have tripled in weight, as if every key had been coated with lead.

"Come on, Dana, it's just a house," she told herself sternly. "A few walls, a roof, some putrid gold carpeting you never liked anyway. How can you be scared to face that?"

Because with Ken there, it had been home. It was as simple as that, proof positive that it wasn't the appearance of a place that turned it into a home, but love. She had felt it every time she had walked through the front door.

Now she faced only emptiness. For one brief second she regretted leaving the boys in Florida. They would have filled the place with noise and laughter. Their presence would have kept loneliness at bay, at least until the darkest hours of the night.

How pitiful was that? she thought ruefully. How pitiful was it to even consider using her kids to buffer the pain? Besides, she had come home for one reason and one reason only: to find Ken's murderer. That was the best thing she could do for all of them, the only thing that would give them any peace. She couldn't afford any distractions if she intended to solve things quickly so that they could move on with their lives.

That reminder was enough to stiffen her resolve. Revenge is a powerful motivator. Even though her hand shook, she managed this time to get the key into the lock, even to walk through the front door.

Perhaps it was better that it was the middle of a moonless night, pitch-dark so that she couldn't see the collection of family photographs sitting on top of the upright piano that Ken had played with more enthusiasm than skill, couldn't see the eclectic stack of books beside his favorite chair, or the notes he had been making for his last sermon, still scattered across his desk.

But even though the room was cast in shadows, she could imagine it all, could visualize it as clearly as if every light blazed. It was as if he had just stepped away for a moment or an hour, not forever.

She dropped her luggage inside the door, tossed aside her jacket. Guided by pure instinct, she made her way to his chair, the overstuffed one where she had often sat cradled in his lap, content just to be held as the strains of Brahms or Beethoven surrounded them at the end of a long day.

She reached out, traced the butter-soft leather, and smiled at the memory of how appalled he'd been by the indulgence when there were so many more practical things they could have used. It had gone against his frugal nature to waste money on luxuries. But even as he'd protested, he had settled into the chair, sinking into the deep cushions, caressing the leather as sensuously as he might have traced the curve of her hip or the weight of her breast. He had fallen in love with it, just as she'd known he would.

It was a wonderful memory, one to cherish, she thought as she plucked an afghan from the back of the nearby sofa and settled into the chair. The coldness of the leather was a shock, snapping her back to reality like a slap. Even this, it seemed, would never be the same. The warmth was gone.

Still, she craved the sense of connection that sitting in Ken's favorite chair gave her. It was personal, something he'd used daily, yet it lacked the intimacy of their bed. She wasn't sure when she'd be able to sleep there alone, if ever. From the night she had learned of his death until she had left for Florida, she had slept in this chair. It had brought her a small measure of comfort.

Now, once again, she wrapped the afghan around her and curled up, cradled by leather now, instead of Ken's strong arms. Even so, the restlessness that had plagued her in Florida eased. For better or worse, her journey to find the truth behind Ken's murder had begun.

Finally, as dawn turned the sky gray, then mauve, and at last a pale, winter-weary blue, she slept, more soundly than she had in weeks. It was as if her body were preparing for whatever lay ahead.

Her dreams, though, were disturbing. They were not of the man she'd loved so fiercely, but of a shadowy gunman, his face tantalizingly obscured.

Dana awakened at midday to find her best friend staring down at her, hands on generous hips, a worried frown puckering her brow.

"How'd you get in?" she muttered groggily.

Kate Jefferson waved a key ring under her nose. "I found these in the front door. Even if I hadn't, I have the one you gave me so I could bring in the mail, remember? When did you get home? You were due in at eight. The plane was on time. I checked. I called until all hours, but you never answered. I finally decided you'd changed your mind or missed the plane."

"I got here in the middle of the night," Dana said without elaborating. She struggled awake. Her back ached. Her neck was stiff and she was freezing. She'd forgotten to turn the heat up when she'd come in the night before. It couldn't be much more than fifty-five in the room, the temperature her father had decreed would at least keep the pipes from freezing.

"Where are the boys?" Kate asked. "Didn't they come with you?"

"No. I enrolled them in school in Florida for the rest of the year. They're with my parents."

Kate stared at her in shock. "You've enrolled them in school? Have you decided to move to Florida, after all?"

Dana sighed. "No, not for sure. I haven't decided anything definitely. I can't think that clearly. I just wanted them to get some sense of normalcy back into their lives." She stood up and headed toward the kitchen. "Any more questions will have to wait until I have coffee."

"It's already made," Kate said, proving once again that she had an admirable, take-charge attitude. Dana had often told her it should have been put to use running some company, instead of being wasted on her often unappreciative friends or two typically rebellious teenage daughters.

"An hour ago, in fact," Kate added pointedly. "I've been banging pots and pans ever since, hoping to stir some sort of a reaction from you. I thought maybe you were planning to sleep into the next century."

"Would if I could," Dana told her as she filled a mug with the gourmet blend she hadn't been able to give up, despite Ken's conviction that instant served the same purpose. Leaning against the kitchen counter, she carefully avoided looking outside toward the small church where Ken had preached and beyond to the cemetery where he was buried. She drank deeply, one long swallow, then another. Finally she met Kate's worried gaze. "Stop frowning. Aren't you glad to see me?"

"Of course I am. You just gave me a fright when I found the keys in the door and you didn't answer after I knocked or rang that awful, screeching bell."

Dana figured it was a testament to Kate's anxiety that she'd touched the bell at all. The sound was more appropriate for some creaky Addams Family domicile than a parsonage. Kate shuddered every time she was forced to ring it. Dana had always thought it was a hoot, which probably showed just how perverse her sense of humor was.

"If the boys are in school in Florida, why are you here? I thought you'd be down there a few more weeks at least," Kate said. "I thought the plan was for you to get some rest before you came home to tackle everything that needs to be done here."

Dana shrugged. "Plans change."

Kate's brow puckered again. "Meaning?"

"There are things that can't wait."

"What things?"

"The house, for one thing. Sooner or later, I'm going to have to get out of it. It belongs to the church."

"Lawrence Tremayne told you it was yours for as long as you needed it," Kate reminded her. "Local pastors are taking services for now. If they hire a new pastor, they'll make temporary arrangements for him, if they have to." She gave Dana a penetrating look. "So, what's really going on?"

"You know, you'd make a great private eye," Dana observed. "You poke and prod with the best of us."

"I thought you'd retired."

"I did."

Kate's frown deepened as she apparently guessed what was going on in Dana's head. "Dana, you can't investigate Ken's murder," she protested. "Leave it to the police."

"Who said anything about me investigating?"

"I know you. You're impatient. You're frustrated with the lack of answers. Anybody would be. But it's harder for you, because you think you could do the job better. Plus, you've been evading every question I've asked. How am I doing so far?"

Dana thought about denying it, but couldn't find the energy. "On the money."

"Bad idea," Kate shot back. "You're too close to this one. I know you were one of the best private eyes in the business. That's how we met, remember? You found the proof I needed to take that low-down ex of mine back into court and show that he had hidden assets in half the states in the country, even though he claimed he couldn't come up with child support. I know you have contacts up the wazoo, but this is personal. You can't be objective. You won't be cool and rational, the way you need to be. You won't be able to analyze the risks. You can't very well sashay around gang turf asking questions. You'll stand out like a sore thumb."

Dana wasn't about to be dissuaded. "I'll just have to

work even harder to keep my emotions out of it...." The way she had done it last night, busting into the Yo, Amigo headquarters without a plan, she thought dryly. If Kate ever heard about that, she'd be muttering "I told you so" for the rest of Dana's days.

"What about the boys?" Kate demanded.

"What about them? They're perfectly safe with my parents," she said. "They like the new school well enough. Best of all, there are no sad memories for them in Florida. They're adjusting, better than I am, as a matter of fact."

"That's all lovely, but they need you. I don't care how well adjusted they seem."

Dana sighed. "I know, Kate. And they'll have me, they'll have my full-time attention just as soon as things are taken care of here."

Kate clearly wasn't satisfied. She leveled another of those penetrating looks straight into Dana's eyes. "This could wait. They should be with their mother so they won't start to worry that they've lost her, too."

That last one cut. It stirred guilt that she'd worked hard to bury. "You've made your point," Dana said tightly. "Now drop it."

Kate was a wonderful friend—compassionate, thoughtful, levelheaded. She was also tenacious. Dana figured she was wasting her breath trying to shut her up. Kate's next words proved it.

"I will not drop it. You can't put yourself in danger, Dana. It's not fair to your sons. What if something were to happen to you? Their sense of security is already shaken by losing their dad. As for your parents, they're great people, but they're older. How long will it be before three rambunctious boys get to be too much for them?"

It wasn't as if she hadn't considered everything Kate was saying. She had, over and over again. In the end, all those things had been outweighed by her conviction that finding Ken's killer was the first step in healing for all of them. She would be no good to her children if she weren't at peace with herself.

"It's not fair to Ken that he's dead and that no one knows who did it," Dana retorted stubbornly. "Look, you can fight me on this, but it won't do any good. I've been over every single argument, time and again. Believe me, my mother and father repeated most of them morning, noon and night, up until the minute I got on the plane. The bottom line is that I have no choice."

"We always have choices." Kate stepped closer and wrapped her arms around her. "Sweetie, I know how much all of this hurts, but getting yourself killed isn't the answer."

Dana returned the fierce hug, then stepped away. "I'm a professional. I know how to minimize risks."

"Oh, really?" Kate retorted skeptically. "Is that why I got a call at the crack of dawn from Rick Sanchez, telling me to keep an eye on you, suggesting that you were behaving irrationally?"

Obviously she'd been saving that little tidbit for its shock value. It worked, too. Astonishment left Dana speechless for thirty seconds. Then her temper kicked in. She snatched up the wall phone, glanced at the list of numbers posted next to it and punched in the one for Yo, Amigo headquarters. Kate reached over and cut off the call. Dana whirled on her, furious.

"What do you think you're doing?"

"Keeping you from making a fool of yourself. He called me because I asked him to let me know if you showed up there."

Dana's mouth gaped, unsure which stunned her more, Kate's foresight or her betrayal. "Why?"

"Because I know you. It was only a matter of time before you decided to charge in there, demanding answers. Of course, even I didn't expect you to sneak in in the middle of the night like a common thief. It's nice to know you haven't lost your touch with a set of lock picks," she said with more wry humor than genuine admiration.

"Thanks," Dana responded anyway, recalling the surge of adrenaline rushing through her as she'd felt that lock give way to her touch. She hadn't realized just how much she'd missed living on the edge until that moment.

"I'd feel better, though, if you hadn't gotten caught." Kate scowled. "What is wrong with you? Didn't that prove you're too rusty or muddleheaded to be doing this?"

"Rusty, maybe," Dana conceded. "Right now, though, I'd prefer to know just how cozy you and Rick Sanchez have gotten in my absence. I didn't even know you knew him."

"I didn't. He came around looking for you one day when I was here to bring in the mail and water the plants."

"What the hell was he doing here?"

"I imagine he came to offer his condolences."

"Yeah, right."

"I liked him," Kate said. "I also thought he was being sincere. He thought a lot of Ken. I could tell. He walked out to the cemetery and stayed for the longest time. When he came back, he had tears in his eyes."

"Big deal!" she said, adding an expletive for emphasis.

"Dana!" Kate protested.

She was clearly as shocked at hearing such language as Dana was at having uttered it. She'd learned to temper her tart tongue the day she'd fallen in love with a minister. Ken had never voiced his disapproval of her tendency to curse, but she'd seen the disappointment in his eyes whenever a particularly foul word slipped out.

She'd been home less than twenty-four hours and she'd been cursing a blue streak ever since. She doubted that Kate had ever said anything harsher than darn in her life.

"Okay, I'm sorry," she apologized. "I can't help it. It's just that the thought of Rick Sanchez brings out the worst in me. He got Ken killed."

Kate was shaking her head before Dana could complete the sentence. "You know better than that. Ken was at Yo, Amigo because that was the kind of compassionate, caring man he was. He saw the good in those kids. He wanted them to have a chance. You wouldn't have loved him if he hadn't tried to live up to his own ideals, if he hadn't put himself on the front line, no matter the cost to himself. Ken believed in that program. He believed in Rick Sanchez."

"And he died because of it," Dana repeated. "I can't forgive Sanchez for that. I won't."

"Is he the one you can't forgive, or is it yourself?" Kate asked quietly. "Are you sure you're not taking risks to punish yourself?"

Dana's eyes brimmed with stinging tears, and her throat clogged up at the softly spoken question. That was the trouble with having a friend who knew your deepest, darkest secrets. All those confidences could come back to haunt you, Dana thought.

"I should never have told you," she whispered.

"Yes, you should have," Kate contradicted, automatically handing Dana a pristine hankie from her pocket. "If you hadn't told me that you and Ken had fought that night, it would have eaten away at you. You have to forgive yourself, sweetie. Ken was going to Yo, Amigo that night, whether you two had argued or not. He'd made up his mind, and he was every bit as stubborn as you are. It wasn't your fault he got killed."

"No," Dana agreed, clutching the handkerchief and ignoring the tears that streaked down her cheeks. "But I shouldn't have let him leave when he was so angry. Maybe that's what made him careless. Maybe that's why he didn't see that there was someone there with a gun."

"And maybe he just got in the way of some drug-crazed kid," Kate said. "That's what the police think."

"One of the kids Rick Sanchez protects," Dana countered bitterly, bringing the argument full circle.

Kate sighed. "There's nothing I can say to talk you out of this, is there?"

"Nothing," Dana agreed.

Kate's expression turned resigned. "Then tell me what I can do to help."

"Just be my friend."

"No, I want to do something constructive. You helped me when my life was a mess. Now it's my turn. I can work a phone with the best of them. You've always said I could talk anyone into doing anything I wanted. Let me put those powers of persuasion to work for a good cause. We'll be a team."

Dana laughed at the excitement sparkling in her friend's eyes. "Kate, you are not a private investigator," she pointed out.

"Technically, neither are you."

Dana was taken aback for a minute, until she realized that Kate was right. She had long since let her license lapse. Hopefully her skills were a bit more up-to-date, though after last night's disaster, she had to wonder. Not that she'd ever admit to such a thing.

"What about your kids? What about the risks?" she asked, throwing Kate's earlier arguments right back into her face.

"One's seventeen, the other's nineteen," Kate said dismissively. "They barely know I exist, anyway. Besides, I'm just going to be chatting on the phone, like I always do. How much danger can there be in that?"

"Famous last words," Dana retorted. "Are you really sure you want to help?"

"I really want to help. Just tell me what you want me to do."

"I will," Dana promised. Unfortunately, without any of the clues she had hoped to find at Yo, Amigo, she had no clear-cut idea just yet what the first step ought to be.

3

Rick couldn't decide whether he'd done the right thing by calling Kate Jefferson first thing in the morning. Obviously, she and Dana Miller were close friends. He had found the slightly plump, angelic-looking blonde at the Millers' house when he'd finally worked up the courage to stop by to see Ken's wife and try to make peace with her. Besides, she had made him promise to call the minute Dana turned up.

Knowing how Ken's widow felt about him and about Yo, Amigo, at first he hadn't expected Dana to come anywhere near him—not for a long time, anyway. Only after careful thought had he realized that she was not the type of woman to let things lie. Obviously Kate knew her friend very well.

Even now his lips curved as he thought of the audacity Dana Miller had shown, first in breaking in, then in accusing him of assault when he'd tackled her. She was a handful, all right. Ken had always told him that and now he'd seen her in action firsthand.

She was going to be trouble. He knew that, too. She had the same sort of passion for her particular cause that he had for his, which put them at cross-purposes, for the moment. Oddly enough, they both wanted to find Ken's murderer. She would destroy Yo, Amigo in the process, if she had to. He was convinced that no one connected to the program had had anything to do with the shooting.

The kids he worked with weren't saints. Far from it. They'd been handling knives and guns and wearing gang colors starting at a frighteningly early age. Most of them had been touched by tragedy and violence more often than white, middle-class America could imagine. They'd responded the only way that made sense to them, by seeking protection in numbers, by arming themselves. Only a few had learned the lesson that violence only spawned more violence. It solved nothing. As injustices mounted and anger deepened, the violence only escalated, unless they learned another way. He'd tried to teach them that.

Even so, even knowing that his message had convinced only a handful of the teens he worked with, Rick knew in his gut that not one of them would have harmed Ken Miller. They had respected the *padre,* as they called him. The youngest ones had clustered around him, desperately seeking the warmth and love he radiated, the father figure he represented. The older boys grudgingly admired his straight talk and his jump shots. Ken had run circles around them on a basketball court, playing with a ferocity that had been startling in a man normally so placid.

Rick hadn't relied solely on his gut in reaching the conclusion that no one he knew would have harmed Ken. He was a little too cynical for that. He'd asked questions, gently most of the time, forcefully when necessary. He'd laid it all out for these tough kids who were trying to find their way. One of their own was down, and he wanted to know the names of the people responsible. The future of Yo, Amigo, their future, was on the line. He believed so strongly that any one of them would have ratted out his best friend for Ken's sake, that he would have staked his reputation and his life on it.

When no one had stepped forward with so much as a whiff of innuendo—much less a solid clue—it convinced him that his kids were innocent. That left a whole lot of unanswered questions. He was as frustrated as Dana Miller had to be. He was also convinced that the answers had to lie outside the hood.

The difference was, she was going to tear his fragile grasp on the souls of these boys to shreds trying to find those answers. She was going to put herself at risk by poking and prodding and turning up in every dangerous nook and cranny until she found something. For every boy in the program who'd respect her for trying, there were a dozen on the streets who would take advantage of her. Some would only take her money for leads that would merely take her down blind alleys. Some were capable of doing far worse.

Rick figured either he was going to have to trail along behind, protecting her, or he was going to have to find some way to join forces with her—for the program's sake and for hers.

Of course, that meant seeing her again, trying to cut through the pain and the hatred and the anger to convince her that they were on the same side. His pulse raced predictably at the prospect. His quick rise to any challenge was both a blessing and a curse. After the way he'd responded to the woman struggling in his arms the night before, he figured this time it was downright suicidal. His body apparently didn't have the same high moral standards his head did, standards that said a man shouldn't be intrigued by his best friend's wife. Ken's death hadn't

changed that. In his eyes, Dana Miller still belonged to
her late husband.

"*Que pasa,* Señor Rick?"

At the sound of the softly spoken question, Rick's gaze
shot up. "Maria, you have to stop sneaking up on me,"
he told the teenager with the huge brown eyes and shy,
dimpled smile. "My heart can't take it."

The shyness faded, replaced by a knowing twinkle.
"Oh, I think your heart can take quite a lot, Señor Rick."

"And how would an innocent girl like you know a
thing like that?"

"The others talk," she said, then shook her head. "As
if you didn't know that already. They think you are *muy*
sexy, a how-do-you-say-it, a chunk?"

Rick laughed. "That's *hunk,* as if you didn't know
that already. Your English only fails you when it suits
your purposes."

"No, no," she protested. *"Para me, anglais es muy
difficile."*

"Maria, you were born right here in Chicago."

Her chin rose a defiant notch. "But my parents, they
speak only Spanish at home," she protested, her expression all innocence. "I heard no English until I went to
school."

It was a common enough story in certain immigrant
neighborhoods, including this one. Rick happened to
know, however, that Maria could speak and understand
English like a native, unless it seemed inconvenient to
do so.

"The way I hear it, you were a quick study. I've seen
all your transcripts. Straight As. That's why the *padre*
was trying to help you get a scholarship to college."

At the mention of Ken, she immediately sketched a
cross across her chest and her eyes turned sad. "I miss

him every day," she said softly. "He was very good to me and the others, especially my brothers."

"He loved you all. He wanted you to succeed."

Maria perched uneasily on the edge of the chair opposite Rick's desk. She folded her hands in her lap in the pose of a proper young lady, but it was only seconds before she began to fidget nervously. "What do you think will happen now? Will they find the person who killed him? They don't seem to try very hard anymore."

Rick couldn't deny that. It was one reason he could understand Dana Miller's determination to take matters into her own hands. "I don't know whether the police have given up," he told Maria honestly. "But I haven't."

"Do you have any leads?"

"No, but I think someone knew exactly what he was doing that night." It was the first time he had voiced that particular opinion, but he was forced to temper it by acknowledging the other possibility, the one Dana Miller and the police shared. "On the other hand, if the killer is from the hood, I'll find him."

Maria looked shocked. "You think one of us could have harmed him?"

"No one in the program," he said firmly. "But others, who knows? Others believe anything is possible here. The only way to prove them wrong is to find the person responsible. Have you heard anything, Maria? Anything at all? Is anyone bragging a little."

"Who would brag about such a thing?" she demanded indignantly.

"We both know there are people who would like to see the program fail, who would gloat if we lost our funding. They might even commit murder to bring us down."

"But why? What you do here is good."

"Not for those who want to recruit every young child into a gang. They're afraid we might cut into their power."

"They are fools!" she declared dismissively. "And I have too much work to do to waste time on them."

As she left his office, Rick smiled at her vehemence. There was no chance that Maria would become one of the lost souls. Raised by two strict, doting, Catholic parents, she and her brothers had been taught right and wrong. Unlike so many others, they had been surrounded by love. They had been taught the value of hard work, grit and determination. There would be no shortcuts, no straying from the straight and narrow.

When Juan Jesus, the youngest, had gotten too friendly with members of the toughest gang in the area, the entire family had come to Rick for guidance. Dollars had been scraped together for the tuition to a private school in Ken's suburb. A family in Ken's congregation had taken Juan Jesus in as one of their own on weekdays. Ken had brought him back to his family on Friday afternoons and picked him up again at dawn on Monday mornings for the trip north of town. Those days away from the hood had been the boy's salvation.

Only Maria knew that the small pittance the family had raised was a fraction of the actual tuition. Had the others known, they would have been too proud to accept the arrangements.

Ever since discovering that Rick and Ken had chipped in to pay the rest, Maria had been coming to the program headquarters every morning to do whatever jobs needed doing. She typed. She answered phones. She cleaned. She bullied Rick into eating, when he would have forgotten. She stayed as long as he did, sometimes longer.

Unofficially, she counseled the teenage girls who trusted her with secrets they might never have shared with Rick. All in all, Rick knew he'd gotten the better end of the deal when he'd made the contribution to Juan Jesus's education. And when Maria had her college scholarship, he guessed she would study psychology or social work and make an even greater contribution to his program, or another like it.

Now and again, when he saw the flash of passion in her eyes for Yo, Amigo's goals, when he heard her sweet voice of reason working its magic on a potential backer, he could envision her in the state capital or in Washington, making a difference for all of the teens who seemed intent on sacrificing their youth, or their lives, to gangs. For now, he might be the brains and the drive behind Yo, Amigo, but Maria and a few others like her were its heart. Ken Miller had been its soul.

Not a day passed that Rick didn't miss him. Not an hour passed that he didn't contemplate his own inadvertent complicity in bringing Ken into the barrio, where he died. Not a minute passed that he didn't want to avenge his friend's death.

Thinking of that brought him full circle, back to the fury he'd read in Dana Miller's eyes the night before. She was trouble, all right, and it was way past time he faced it. His warnings last night weren't nearly enough to make her back down.

"Maria, I've got to go out for a while," he said as he passed the desk where she was trying to make sense of the piles of paperwork that accumulated on a daily basis, paperwork that Rick had no patience for, even when he understood the necessity for it.

"I'll be here," she told him with a wry expression. "You haven't touched this in a week. It will take me most of the day to see which is important and which could have been tossed into the trash, if only you'd bothered to read it."

"*Gracias*. What would I do without you?"

She shook her head. "I cannot imagine."

"Neither can I, *nina*. Neither can I."

"Then it is good you won't have to find out."

"Until next fall," he reminded her. That was when he was convinced she would have the full scholarship to Northwestern that she deserved.

"Even then, I will be here to worry you every day," she insisted.

It was an old argument and one they wouldn't resolve today or even tomorrow. Maria Consuela Villanueva was a woman who knew her own mind, probably had from the time she was two, Rick guessed. There had been times he regretted the age difference between them. She was barely eighteen to his thirty-four. Had she been a few years older, she might have been a good match for him. As it was, he thought of her only as the kid sister he'd never had. Even when she was at her nagging, pestering worst, he would have protected her with his life.

"When will you be back?" she asked.

He thought of the likely battle that lay ahead. Either Dana would slam the door in his face and he'd be back in no time, or she'd listen. He was counting on the latter. He held no illusions, though, that he could persuade her easily to accept his help.

"I'm out for the day," he said, "unless there's an emergency."

"What constitutes an emergency this time? Fire? The arrival of the mayor? A delegation from the capital?"

"Those would do," he agreed.

"Where will you be?"

"With Ken's widow." He shrugged, then added realistically, "Or nursing my wounds beside Lake Michigan with a hot dog in one hand and a beer in the other."

"Better you should take bandages," she retorted.

Rick stared at her suspiciously. Something in her tone alerted him that she knew something about what had gone on here the night before. "Why would you say that?"

"People talk," she said enigmatically.

"Maria! Spit it out. What are people saying?"

"They say that bruise on your cheek is the work of Mrs. Miller. Since it was not there when I left last night, I assume you've seen her since then." She tilted her head and studied his face. "She must not have been glad to see you."

"I'm sure she wasn't," Rick agreed.

"And you think today will go better?"

"Probably not."

Maria opened a cabinet behind the desk and plucked out a handful of Band-Aids and a bottle of peroxide from the stock kept on hand for the multitude of kids with minor wounds who turned up on their doorstep nearly every day. They were all too practiced at coping with major wounds as well, at least as long as it took to send for an ambulance.

"Then these may come in handy," she said. "Of course, people say she is also a trained private eye, like Magnum." Maria was a very big Tom Selleck fan. She thought he was even "chunkier" than Rick.

"She was a private detective," Rick corrected. "What does that have to do with anything?"

"She knows how to use a gun, yes?"

"Very amusing, Maria. You seem to forget that I have at least a vague familiarity with guns myself."

"The difference is that you have vowed never to touch another one. Can you say the same for Mrs. Miller?"

Rick could only say that he knew, with relative certainty, that she hadn't had one with her the night before. She would have found some way to use it on him.

Of course, that didn't mean she wouldn't grab a gun the second she realized who was on her doorstep. Another adrenaline rush raced through him at the prospect. Disarming her could prove to be absolutely fascinating.

4

The screeching of that damnable doorbell brought Dana to her feet at once. It had to be a stranger. No one she knew liked the sound of it any better than Kate.

"Want me to get it?" Kate offered.

"I'm still capable of answering the door," Dana said dryly, pushing aside the virtually untouched slice of the pecan coffee cake that she had made when she could no longer sit still. "I haven't lost all my wits yet."

She stepped into the foyer and paused. She could see the large shape of a man through the glass panels on either side of the door. Tall, broad-shouldered and wearing an ancient football jacket from one of the Catholic high schools in Chicago, Rick Sanchez was unmistakable.

"Oh, boy," she muttered under her breath.

"Dana, who is it?" Kate whispered, slipping up behind her.

"Rick Sanchez."

"*Oh, boy,* is right. Has he brought the police with him?"

"I doubt that Mr. Sanchez is any fonder of the police than I am at the moment."

"Were you counting on that when you broke into the Yo, Amigo headquarters last night?"

"No, I was counting on not getting caught," Dana said, keeping a wary eye on the man outside.

He seemed to be growing more agitated by the minute. When he turned and leaned on the doorbell, filling the house with the squealing sound, she decided there was no point in postponing the inevitable. He was here to see her and he'd probably break down the door, if he had to. She was in no position, at the moment, to complain about a little breaking and entering on his part.

"Okay, okay, I'm coming," she shouted as she unlocked the door. When it was open, she glared at him and said, "Mr. Sanchez, you really need to work on your patience."

A twinkle lit his brown eyes, softening his hard, unyielding expression. "Isn't that the pot calling the kettle black?"

Standing squarely in the doorway, Dana refused to concede the point. "Why are you here?"

"To talk."

"I'd say we both made our positions completely clear last night. Anything we said today would be a waste of breath."

"Then I guess you haven't seen the error of your ways," he said with exaggerated regret. "Too bad. I was hoping this was going to be easy." He glanced over her shoulder. "Hello again, Mrs. Jefferson. Good to see you."

Dana shot a warning look at Kate, whose love life was such that a potent man like Rick Sanchez might be able to charm her with little more than a smile. "Don't think you can use my friend to get to me."

"I wouldn't dream of it. I'm an up-front kind of guy. My friends say I'm direct."

"And your enemies?"

"They say quite a lot of things about me," he conceded.

With his hands shoved in his pockets and his hair tousled by the wind, he had a look of pure innocence about him. Clearly it was deceptive. "I can imagine," she said.

"I'm hoping you and I will become friends."

"Not in this lifetime," she said fiercely.

"That's what Ken would have wanted," he added with quiet conviction.

Dana wanted to hit him for dragging Ken into the conversation, even though he was obviously the reason Rick Sanchez was here. "Do your friends know that you hit below the belt, Mr. Sanchez?"

He didn't look half as insulted as Dana might have liked. In fact, he looked her squarely in the eye.

"I'm a product of the streets," he reminded her. "I fight any way I have to for what I believe in."

The penetrating, brown-eyed gaze, the softly spoken words sent a chill washing through her. For the first time, she fully accepted just how dangerous an adversary Rick Sanchez could be. Knowing the enemy could sometimes be as important as arming against him. With that in mind, she stepped aside and gestured toward the kitchen.

"Kate and I were just having coffee, if you'd care to join us."

There was nothing gloating in his expression, no hint of smug arrogance. In fact, if she'd had to describe what was going on inside him, she would have had to say he looked relieved. Obviously, he hadn't expected her to capitulate so easily. Good. That meant she'd thrown him off guard.

In the kitchen, she poured him a cup of coffee, then refilled her own and Kate's. She deliberately didn't offer him any of the coffee cake. It didn't matter. His gaze landed on her slice, then lifted hopefully. "Aren't you planning to eat that?"

"No," she said resignedly and pushed it toward him. "There's more on the counter."

"I can smell the cinnamon and nuts. Just baked, isn't it?" he asked, sounding as eager as a kid.

"Yes."

"Why'd you bother if you didn't intend to eat it?"

"For something to do. What difference does it make?"

He shrugged. "None, I guess. Just making small talk."

"Don't waste your time."

He accepted the advice without comment and pulled out a chair. When he was seated at the round oak table, Dana suddenly wished that she'd suggested the living room instead.

This table, bought at an auction the first year of her marriage, had been at the heart of her family's life. Every breakfast and every dinner, they had gathered here, no matter the other demands on their time. This was also where she and Ken had discussed the future, made plans for vacations, argued over finances. It was at this table, lit by the soft glow of candles, that she had first told him she was pregnant on three different occasions.

It was also where they had lingered over coffee, gazing into each other's eyes with yearning, both of them regretting for just a moment that there were boys underfoot to keep them from acting on the desire that always simmered just beneath the surface of their relationship.

Seating Rick Sanchez here, of all places, seemed to defile the memories. She had never wanted this man to touch the intimate portions of her life with Ken. That was why she had stubbornly refused for so long to include him in family dinners, in holiday celebrations. Ken had accepted her decision, had even understood its roots, but it had been clear that he thought less of her for her inflexibility.

Even then, she realized, Rick Sanchez had found a way to come between them. Now he was doing so by replacing her memories of Ken sitting across from her with his own powerful and very masculine presence. She added that to the list of things to hold against him—the fact that he was so virile, so alive, while just outside her husband was cold in his grave.

She could feel the patches of angry color burning in her cheeks as she scowled at him. "Why are you here?" she asked for the second time that morning. There was nothing gracious or even polite in her tone. Kate glanced at her sharply, subtly warning her to back off. Dana sighed and forced a smile. "That is, what did you want to talk about?"

"You and me," he said.

She scowled at that. "Oh?" she said, her voice a lethal warning against assuming any kind of intimacy was possible between them.

His perfectly sculpted lips curved ever so slightly. "*That* was not what I meant, Dana."

Despite the denial, her name on his tongue was like a caress. Heat crept up her neck and inflamed her cheeks again. "Of course not," she said stiffly. "But I think you'd better explain exactly what you did mean."

Without answering, Rick pushed himself away from the table and stood. Half of the coffee cake remained. Obviously, his appetite had fled, too.

Still silent, letting her demand for answers hang in the air, he moved toward the window, as if he couldn't stay away. She knew precisely what he was seeing—the cold, barren earth, the simple marker, the place where Ken would rest for all eternity.

"He deserves to rest in peace," he said so quietly that she had to strain to hear him.

When the words registered, she realized it was as if he had read her mind. For a brief second, there was a connection between them, a fragile thread of understanding that she hadn't expected. It shook her to discover that she could feel that, despite the overwhelming hatred she felt toward him.

When he finally turned back, his eyes glistened with unshed tears. As Kate had warned her, it was a devastating sight in one so strong. Dana had to steel herself against that image, as she had against so many others lately. She couldn't afford to feel any compassion for this man. None. Ken had been nothing to him, nothing more than someone to be used for the good of his cause. She believed that of Rick Sanchez, because she had to. The hatred, the need for revenge, was all that anchored her these days.

Rick leaned against the counter, propped one sneaker-clad foot on the rung of a chair and cradled his coffee mug in hands that, despite their nicks and scars, looked somehow graceful. Sure and competent hands. Hands that could caress a woman's body and bring it alive.

Dear heaven, where had that last come from? She glanced at Kate and saw that she, too, was fascinated with Rick Sanchez, fascinated the way a woman would be with a devastatingly attractive man who radiated sexuality from every pore.

That, of course, was his single most potent weapon, Dana realized. If she weren't careful, if she weren't strong, he would weave that easy magic over her, as well. She was lonely now and, like too many lonely women, she was vulnerable. She could not, *she would not,* allow anything to happen between her and this man. She would keep the hostility alive as protection, as a duty.

"I'm waiting," she said, keeping her voice icy, her expression remote. "Unless you have something specific to discuss, I'd like you to go."

His lips curved again. "Patience, Dana."

"I don't have time to be patient. I have things to do."

"Planning more break-ins?"

She scowled at him. "Possibly."

"Not at Yo, Amigo, I hope."

"If that's where the answers are, then I'll be back."

"I've already told you that the program and its boys are not the key to Ken's death."

"How can you possibly be so confident of that?"

"Because everyone at Yo, Amigo loved Ken," he said.

The simple declaration shook her as more vehement statements might not have done so. For just a moment, she wished she hadn't remained so adamantly opposed to what Ken had been doing. She wished that she had accepted one of his repeated offers to take her with him, to let her see for herself why these lost kids mattered so much to him.

Instead, she had clung to the long-ago betrayal of a boy very much like those in Rick's program. She had been trying to help him and his lawyer fight armed robbery charges he claimed had been unfairly brought. She had believed in him. Only after they had successfully fought off a conviction had she discovered he was guilty, that he had played on her sympathy and used her clever investigative skills to win his case.

Weeks later, released from jail, he had shot and killed another storekeeper in yet another robbery attempt. A scared sixteen-year-old boy had been his accomplice. He had been shot by police arriving at the scene. She had vowed right then never to trust her instincts again, never to trust vows of innocence and remorse from the very kind of boys Ken and Rick believed capable of change.

Had she put aside that vow and gone with Ken, would she have shared Rick's belief that his teens were incapable of harming Ken? She doubted it. Her own experience would have warned against it.

In fact, she would have grabbed on to any possible motive, any possible suspect, just as she was doing now. She was too desperate for answers to exclude anyone on blind faith alone.

"What do these kids know about love?" she countered.

"Precious little," Rick agreed. "But they experienced it with your husband. Ken showed them what it meant to be accepted unconditionally, to be forgiven. He taught them they were worthy of God's love. Every one of them was blessed to have known him." His gaze locked on hers. "And they knew that."

Dana shuddered under that unwavering gaze. In his own way, Rick Sanchez was as fervent in his beliefs as Ken had been in his. She, to the contrary, believed in nothing anymore, not even in the generous, compassionate, forgiving God who had guided her husband.

Despite their opposing views of his boys, she couldn't help being swayed just a little by Rick's faith in them. "Okay, Mr. Sanchez. Say I were to take your word for the moment that no one connected to the program had anything to do with Ken's death. Where would you start to look for answers?"

"Closer to home," he said at once.

He said it with such quick certainty that she was startled. "What on earth does that mean? Surely you don't think that I...?"

"Of course not. I was talking about the people Ken

dealt with right here, in his own congregation, in his own community. He told me there was a faction who wanted him removed."

Dana stared. "If there was, this is the first I've heard of it."

"It had just come up. He didn't want to worry you. He told me it was the sort of nuisance thing that arises every now and then. A few people don't like the way their minister thinks, or they respond to some imagined slight. In Ken's case, he suspected there were some who disapproved of his work with Yo, Amigo. They feared he was already dragging the gang problem into their backyard."

It was easy enough to make the connection, then. "This came up after he brought Juan Jesus here to live with the Wilsons, didn't it?" she asked.

Rick nodded. "That would be my guess."

"But he is such a sweet young man. How could anybody fear him?" Kate demanded.

It was the first time she had said a word in so long that both Dana and Rick turned to stare at her. Rick smiled at the fiercely protective tone of voice. Obviously, all of her motherly instincts had been aroused. And unlike Dana, she hadn't been a holdout, fighting Ken's commitment to the kids in the barrio. She had gotten to know Juan Jesus and any of the others he had brought around from time to time. Kate's soft heart hadn't been touched by the kind of tragedy that had made Dana so terribly wary.

"Taken individually, most of our boys are just like Juan Jesus," Rick responded. "They're tough on the outside, but if you look beyond that, you find a scared, vulnerable kid. Put him in the right environment and he will flourish."

"Put him in a gang, he becomes dangerous," Dana pointed out.

"Yes," he said. "Some do."

"Most," she countered.

He studied her intently, assessing her. "Would you have joined with the faction who felt threatened by Juan Jesus's presence in the community?" Rick asked.

Dana didn't like the immediate response that formed. She bit back the instinctive yes that formed in her gut. She and Ken had argued over that very subject more than once. They had argued about it again on the day he had died. She had wanted their boys to live in a safe environment. She hadn't wanted outside influences to change their protected world. It was petty and selfish of her, but there it was. She was a mother first and she'd seen firsthand the very real danger that came with trusting a kid with a record.

Intellectually, she had understood that boys like Juan Jesus deserved a chance. Give them their chance, she had argued—just not here. Not here, where a failed experiment could be so terribly costly to their own children. She hadn't realized there were others in the church who'd said the same thing.

Nor had she considered that such feelings might run hot enough to do harm. For a brief moment, with Rick's knowing gaze studying her, she allowed herself to feel ashamed at her unwitting complicity with narrow-minded, hurtful people, who would have ruined her husband's career out of fear.

"Would you?" Rick asked again.

"I would like to think I'm better than they are, more open-minded, fairer, but the truth is I had said many of the same things to Ken myself," she confessed reluctantly.

"Dana, you hadn't!" Kate protested.

Dana nodded. "Yes, I had. I didn't want that kind of influence around my kids. I'm sorry, but that's the truth, and you know why I feel that way. I've seen firsthand just how destructive an influence kids like that can be."

Rick regarded her with disturbing intensity. He seemed to be weighing something.

"You know, Dana, I've changed my mind. I think the best place for you to start this investigation would be at Yo, Amigo," he said eventually.

She stared at him in amazement, torn between gratitude and suspicion. "You'll open the doors to me? Let me look at your files, talk to the kids?"

He nodded.

"Why? You said the answers weren't there."

"Maybe not to Ken's murder," he agreed. "But I think you might learn quite a lot about your husband."

She found the suggestion that she hadn't really known Ken to be insulting, but she couldn't afford to turn down the offer. Once again, she and Rick Sanchez would be operating at cross-purposes. But whatever his motives in offering, she had to take advantage of the opportunity.

"I have no idea what made you change your mind, but thank you. I will be there first thing in the morning," she said, meeting his gaze evenly.

"Why not now? You could come back with me."

The prospect of being confined in a car with this man rattled her, but she could see the sense of taking him up on this offer, as well. Despite her determination to take whatever risks were necessary to get answers, there was no point in being foolhardy. Going into that neighborhood in broad daylight with Rick Sanchez as her escort made sense. His acceptance of her presence might smooth the way for her, might make others speak to her more openly.

"I'll get my purse."

"Just your keys," he countered. "You won't be needing your purse."

"What if I get a hankering for something to eat?"

"I can afford to treat you to lunch, Dana. Dinner, too, for that matter."

Something in his eyes, a flash of heat, a suggestion of sensuality, told her she would be wise to stay away from cozy meals for two with this man. He'd persuaded cold-hearted politicians to part with city money for his pipe dream. He'd sweet-talked tough, streetwise kids out of their weapons. If he put his mind to it, would he be able to convince her to leave Yo, Amigo out of her investigation?

Hell would have to freeze over first, she vowed silently, her gaze clashing defiantly with his. To her regret, he looked amused, not intimidated.

He would learn, though. She vowed that he would discover very soon that Dana Miller was a formidable enemy.

5

Rick had regretted his impulsive offer to take Dana into Chicago the instant the words were uttered. Was he out of his mind to consider giving Dana Miller full access to Yo, Amigo? He'd seen no evidence of a kinder, gentler side to her. Yet for some reason, perhaps Ken's frequently expressed faith in his wife's essential goodness, Rick had to believe that her ingrained attitude of distrust wouldn't come back to haunt him.

Still, what would the kids think when they realized she was there to investigate Ken's death, when they saw that they were the target of her suspicions? It could unravel every shred of progress he'd made with them over the past couple of years. It could shatter their trust.

He couldn't renege, though. One way or another, she would be underfoot, snooping. He owed it to Ken to keep Dana where he could watch over her, where he could protect her. Somehow he'd have to make the kids understand that.

Maybe it wouldn't be as difficult as he imagined. They were bright. Maybe they would see how much pain Dana was in and would cut her some slack, especially if she managed to keep that tart tongue of hers in check. Maybe it would be a good lesson in tolerance for all of them.

And maybe they'd hang him for bringing the enemy into their midst, he thought wryly.

Oh, well, there was nothing to be done about it now. Dana was upstairs, probably tucking some sort of wire into her blouse and a gun into her back pocket, if he read her correctly. She might leave her purse at home, but she wasn't about to go with him unprepared for her own style of battle. She had the determination of a pit bull. As angry as she was, she was also likely to be oblivious to real danger.

He glanced across the kitchen table to find Kate Jefferson studying him intently, a frown knitting her brow. "What?" he demanded.

"If you allow anyone to harm one hair on Dana's head, I'll come after you, personally," she warned. She leaned closer and repeatedly jabbed a finger into his chest. "I may look like some sweet, innocuous, little suburban homebody to you, but nobody is more ferocious than a woman like me when someone we care about gets hurt."

Because she sounded so serious, Rick held back the grin that threatened to emerge. "I don't doubt it," he said solemnly and fought the urge to rub the spot she'd been assaulting. He'd probably have a bruise there to match the one Dana had left on his cheek. "Believe it or not, I want her to find what she's looking for."

"Ken's killer?"

"That," he agreed, then added, "and peace of mind."

Kate sighed heavily. "I'm afraid the last won't come easily."

"Where I come from, Mrs. Jefferson, very little comes easily."

* * *

Rick's car was old and battered and nondescript. The outside seemed to be held together mainly by beige paint and rust. It would be an unlikely target for young thieves, Dana concluded. Inside, however, it was immaculate, and it ran like the car of a man who tinkered possessively with its engine.

"How fast does it go?" Dana asked as they made their way into Chicago.

He slanted a look in her direction. "Fast enough. Why?"

"Just making small talk, Mr. Sanchez," she said, mimicking his earlier claim. The truth was that a part of her wondered if he'd tuned it for quick getaways, but for once, she managed to keep the deliberate insult to herself. Somehow she had to find a way to meet the man halfway.

He glanced over at her. "Can't you call me Rick?"

Dana debated before answering. That would mean taking one brick out of the wall of defenses she'd built between them. She wasn't sure she dared risk it. Refusing, though, seemed churlish. Not that he had a particularly high impression of her, anyway, but she hated to add to the negatives. For the time being, she needed his cooperation and goodwill.

"I'll try to remember," she said eventually.

He seemed to be fighting a smile. "That'll do," he said, then added pointedly, "For now."

Dana let that remark go unanswered. He was only trying to provoke her, a trait that obviously came naturally enough to him. Perhaps, if she failed to rise to the bait a few times, he'd give up and settle for the uneasy truce they'd reached. She still wasn't exactly sure why he'd suddenly agreed to her meeting the kids at Yo, Amigo. Clearly he had a point of some sort to make.

As they neared the Yo, Amigo headquarters, the signage in the neighborhood was more frequently in Spanish than English. The *taquerias,* the *bodegas,* the promise that those inside spoke Spanish made Dana feel as if she'd unwittingly entered a foreign land. This world of immigrants, who clung to the past, to old ways and their old culture, seemed totally alien.

"Are most people here from Mexico?" she asked, her natural curiosity stirring.

"Most. Many are Cuban, a few from Central America."

She nodded, absorbing that and the fact that in broad daylight, the streets seemed less menacing. Bundled up against the freezing wind and bitter cold of early March, people were simply going about their daily business, pausing only briefly to chat with neighbors, their breath visible in the icy air. Strains of rapidly spoken Spanish filtered through the car's windows. Latin music blasted from passing boom boxes, the salsa beat cheerful and provocative.

It seemed so… She searched for the right word, then settled for *normal.* Except for the language, the street could have been any other ethnic neighborhood in Chicago, rich with color and surging with life. Where was the danger in this? she wondered.

"It changes at night," Rick said quietly, once more displaying that uncanny knack for reading her mind. "These people stay inside after dark, even in summer. Kids aren't allowed to play in the streets because of the threat—no, the certainty—of drive-by shootings. Children here see more violence up close than yours will see on TV. They'll know it as a reality, as the loss of a brother or sister or a friend. It's no way for a kid to grow up."

Dana thought of Juan Jesus, whose presence in her

neighborhood had stirred such controversy and wrath. As worried as she'd been about his influence on her kids and others, would she have wanted this life for him, instead? He was just a boy who'd already seen too much, experienced things no child should have to endure. Gazing around her, she gained a tiny bit of insight into Ken's perspective.

And Rick's, she conceded reluctantly.

Leaving her to her thoughts, he turned the corner into the alley behind Yo, Amigo. Dana recognized it. She had crept down it just the night before, staying in shadows, filled with determination and rage. She was calmer now, but no less determined.

Rick stopped the car just a few feet from the back door in a spot clearly marked as his by the scrawled name in bright yellow paint on the brick wall of the building. It was surrounded by fading graffiti. If she'd been paying attention, as she should have been the night before, would she have spotted his car there? She thought back carefully. She couldn't summon a single image of any car being in the alley. Surely she would have noticed it and checked it out. Her skills weren't that rusty.

"Where were you parked last night?"

He regarded her innocently. "You were in a very big hurry. Are you so certain I wasn't right here?"

She thought about it once more, then nodded with more certainty. "I'm positive."

"Very good," he praised, though his tone was mocking. "Actually, I left the car at home and hitched a ride over."

"Why?"

The question seemed to make him uncomfortable for some reason, so she asked it again.

"Because we've had a few problems."

She could see that the admission cost him. "What sort of problems?"

"Unwelcome visitors," he said tersely.

"Other than me?"

He smiled at that. "I wasn't expecting you, at least not last night."

"Truthfully, you weren't expecting me at all, were you?"

"Your friend seemed all but certain you'd turn up here eventually."

Dana persisted. "But you didn't believe her, did you?"

"No," he admitted. "At least, I didn't think you'd have the guts to come creeping around here in the middle of the night, since you'd never been inclined to show up with Ken during the day."

"I didn't stay away out of fear," she protested.

"Just disapproval," he guessed.

She realized that in his eyes that was far, far worse. Compared with her compassionate husband, she had to seem cold and hardhearted. She didn't want Rick's opinion to matter, but oddly enough, it did. Even so, she refused to waste time right now trying to change it. Even if she'd explained about the boy she had once trusted, would he have understood? Or would he have said that was just one boy, that others shouldn't be condemned for his mistakes? Ken had said that often enough, but it hadn't swayed her. She hadn't had his capacity for forgiveness or his willingness to risk a second, more dangerous betrayal.

Now, though, she needed to get inside, to start looking at files and talking to people. She had to do something, find at least one solid piece of the puzzle. The compulsion that had brought her back from Florida was stronger than ever. Once again, she had allowed Rick to deliberately distract her. She wondered how many more times she would come up against the tactic as he tried to protect his precious program.

"Are we going to go in or are we going to sit here all day analyzing my psyche?" she inquired testily.

"Analyzing your psyche might be fascinating," he said. Before she could respond, he added, "But you're clearly too impatient to get on with your agenda to cooperate."

She reached for the door handle, but before she could open it, his hand closed over hers. The shock of his touch, the heat of it, stilled her. He waited until she turned to look at him before he said a word.

"One bit of caution—proceed slowly in there. If you go in like a private detective, they won't talk." His gaze locked with hers. "I've taken a huge gamble by bringing you here. I won't let you hassle them."

"You promised—" she began, only to be cut off.

"I promised to bring you here, to let you get to know what we're all about. If you get answers as a result of that, fine. If you can't live with that, I'll take you back home right now."

She didn't like the rules. Nor was she certain how she would operate within them. "How will you explain me?"

For a moment he seemed to be weighing the alternatives. "I'm going to tell them who you are," he replied eventually.

Her gaze narrowed. There was more. She could read it in his eyes. "And then what?"

He smiled. "And then I'm going to say that you're here to take up where your husband left off."

She stared at him, aghast by the suggestion—no, the command—that she was going to become a part of the Yo, Amigo program in some way. She felt manipulated, though no doubt the signs of his intentions had been there from the moment he uttered his invitation.

"I can't do that," she protested.

"You will do that," he corrected, then added more gently, "It's the only way to find the answers you're after. You'll have to blend in, become one of us."

"I don't shoot hoops," she grumbled.

"Then tutor them in reading, teach the girls to sew. We have a kitchen here. You can teach them to cook. It won't matter what you do. It'll matter more that you're here."

Dana didn't like the gender-based suggestions. More importantly, she wanted to move her investigation along far faster than the snail's pace he was suggesting. And yet, she conceded reluctantly, she could see the sense of what he was saying. She knew just how distrustful these toughened street kids were likely to be. If she came on too forcefully, demanded too much, they would walk away without a backward glance.

But Rick's way would also risk getting involved, putting her emotions on the line. She didn't want to know these ex–gang members. She didn't want to take a chance that she might actually come to feel something for them as Ken had felt.

No, she didn't like his plan at all, but she would do as he was demanding. She could tell from his unrelenting expression that he wasn't giving her a choice.

"Let's go," she said through gritted teeth.

This time he didn't try to stop her from getting out of the car. But when they reached the door that she had used the night before, he blocked her way. Once again, she felt the power of his presence, the heat of his body, his taut strength.

"If you find out anything, anything at all, you will tell me about it first," he said, his gaze locked with hers.

"You told me I wouldn't find anything here," she taunted.

"I don't believe you will, but there's always an outside chance I'm wrong. I don't want you tearing off half-cocked and getting yourself killed."

"Why? You'd be rid of a serious thorn in your side."

"No," he corrected. "I'd have one more death on my conscience. Ken's already keeps me awake at night."

There was just enough torment in his voice that Dana had no choice but to believe him. She knew all about that kind of guilt and anguish. She hadn't had a decent night's sleep herself since the murder.

Even so, she was far from ready to forgive him, even further from being willing to trust him. He was a means to an end at the moment. He was giving her entry into a world that she might never have been able to penetrate on her own. She would use him, as he had used Ken. If she destroyed him and Yo, Amigo in the process, it still wouldn't be enough to compensate for the loss of her husband.

6

Apparently it was too early in the day for a big crowd. Inside the Yo, Amigo headquarters, Dana spotted only a handful of boys and even fewer girls. Perhaps it was part of Rick's tactic to bring her here when there would be only a few people to talk to.

But it was a starting point, she reminded herself sternly, and, right now that was all she needed.

She watched as Rick strolled through the cavernous building with the confidence of a man who was in charge. She overheard him tease and taunt in a surprisingly light-hearted manner, saw the playful exchange of punches and handclasps. There was respect here and trust.

There was none of that in the hard, cold gazes that turned on her. She was eyed with obvious suspicion. Even when Rick explained, first in quiet Spanish, then in English, who she was, there was only the slightest softening of attitudes, the faintest mellowing of distrust.

The boy Rick had called Marco was the first to speak directly to her. With chiseled features and thick black hair, he had classic good looks, plus plenty of attitude. He surveyed her with an insolent, assessing gaze, then muttered something in Spanish that had his friends chuckling, until a stern look from Rick cut them off. He spoke sharply to them in such rapid Spanish that Dana caught only an occasional word, and even then, her long-ago lessons in the language failed her.

Whatever he'd said, though, seemed to alter the charged atmosphere. First one girl and then another smiled and shyly introduced herself. There was Rosa with the huge dark eyes and curly hair and the thickening waistline of pregnancy. Then came Ileana, with the tattoo of a scorpion on her wrist and half her head shaved. Dana forced herself not to react to the eccentricities, but to the hesitant welcome in their eyes.

There were more, but Dana knew she would never keep the names straight and apologized for it. She added in faltering Spanish that she was glad to be there, glad to meet them.

Her attempt to speak their language gained her another grudging point or two. She could see the first vague hint of acceptance in their eyes. She knew, though, that it was only a beginning. There would be many more steps before she could ask the questions that plagued her, that much was clear. One wrong step and the distrust would return, stronger than ever.

She had tiptoed through many an awkward interrogation, smooth-talked her way around deep suspicions in the past, but she was out of practice, and no one she had ever encountered was as deeply distrustful as these kids clearly were. How had she ever imagined that she could blithely waltz in here and demand answers? The past few minutes had shown her the folly of that thinking.

When an awkward silence fell, Rick stepped in. "You guys can spend time with Mrs. Miller later. We have a few things to take care of first in my office."

Dana knew he was right to hustle her along, to give

them time to absorb the idea of her presence, but she
hated the prospect of even so minor a delay. Still, she
said her goodbyes and dutifully followed him to the open
door on which his name had been painted by the same
artistic hand that had inscribed it on the wall out back.

When they walked inside, a beautiful, dark-haired teen
looked up from the piles of paper in front of her, started
to say something, saw Dana and gaped. She had barely
recovered when Rick's introduction had her gaping again.

"You are the *padre's esposa?* I mean, his wife?"

There was such awe and reverence in the girl's voice
that Dana could do no more than nod.

"This is Maria Consuela Villanueva," Rick said. "She
keeps things in order around here."

Dana surveyed the chaos doubtfully.

"I know, *señora,*" Maria said with a shrug, "it does
not look as if I have achieved much, but you should have
seen it before I came."

Dana could not imagine it being worse than it was
now. File folders lined the walls in stacks that were waist
high. There were no file cabinets to hold them. A rick-
ety table in the corner held a coffeemaker, a mismatched
assortment of mugs and some sort of pastries. All of it
looked ready to topple to the floor if so much as a breeze
stirred.

Then there was the general decor. It seemed to Dana
as if someone had gotten a deal on seconds at the paint
store. The old metal desk with its fresh coat of bright red
paint looked incongruous against the buttercup-yellow
walls. The backbreaking metal chair in which Maria sat
was a vivid blue. Even the trash can had received a coat
of new paint—lime-green.

"Who's your decorator?" Dana inquired.

"That would be Maria," Rick said with obvious pride. "She thought it was too dull around here before."

"It was gray," Maria said, wrinkling her nose in disgust. "Everything gray. It was enough to make a person depressed."

Dana glanced at Rick. "I assume the gray had been your choice."

"No, it was here when we took over the building from the county. Institutional gray. Very bland and nonthreatening."

"And your office? Did you allow Maria to change the decor in there? Or were you happy with your bland environment?"

Rick opened the door. "See for yourself."

Dana stepped inside and promptly had to hide a chuckle. His walls were fire-engine-red, his desk yellow. His chair was lime-green. Those for his guests were a startling shade of purple.

"It's very…" She hesitated, then settled for "…bright."

"Cheerful, yes?" Maria said, gazing around the room happily. "Everyone helped. We did it as a surprise."

Dana searched Rick's face. "And were you surprised?"

"Stunned is more like it," he muttered. "I'd really grown rather fond of that gray."

"Too boring," Maria said, ignoring his plaintive expression. "This is better. People leave this room feeling happy."

"Or dizzy," Rick countered.

Maria's brow crinkled worriedly. "You hate it?"

Dana waited to see just how diplomatic Rick Sanchez could be when the situation required tact. Sure enough, he reached out and gave Maria's hand a quick squeeze.

"It's a beautiful office," he reassured her. "Everyone who comes here says so."

She gave a nod of satisfaction. "We could do something wonderful with your apartment, too, if you would just allow us." She glanced at Dana. "Beige, floor to ceiling, nothing but beige and brown. It is worse than the gray, I think. It feels as if you are already in your grave with the dirt closing in."

Dana shuddered at the imagery.

"It is not beige," Rick protested. "It's Navajo-white. I picked it out myself."

"Call it what you like. I know beige when I see it. And the carpet is brown, yes? And the sofa? And that disgusting chair you love so much?"

Rick threw up his hands. "Okay, yes. But I'm not wasting money to change any of it. It's livable. Besides, I'm never there."

"True enough," Maria agreed, "especially since..." A warning glance from Rick silenced her. "Never mind. Would you like coffee, Señora Miller?"

Dana shook her head.

"Okay, then. I will leave you to your meeting." She retreated hurriedly.

Dana had listened to the exchange with fascination. She had watched the casual, affectionate teasing and wondered if there was more to their relationship than boss and secretary. Maria seemed to know an awful lot about Rick's home.

"If she's not crazy about your decor at home, maybe you should let her change it," Dana said when Maria was gone.

Rick stared at her blankly. "Why would I do that?"

"If you expect her to spend any time there..."

Rick's immediate chuckle stopped any further speculation. "My, my, you do have a vivid imagination, don't you? I thought private detectives were supposed to look for evidence, not jump to conclusions."

"In this case, the facts add up."

"What facts?"

"She's a beautiful young woman. You're a healthy male. Both of you are single and unattached. She knows exactly what your apartment looks like, so obviously she's spent time there."

His gaze locked with hers. "I *am* a healthy male," he confirmed softly. The mood suddenly shifted as he stepped closer. "You're a beautiful widow." One finger stroked lightly, provocatively along her jaw. "I know exactly what your house looks like, so obviously I've spent time there."

Dana swallowed hard, but she couldn't seem to make herself look away. She knew he was just trying to make a point, but she was too caught up in unexpected sensations to reason out what it was.

"So, Ms. Private Detective, would you say you and I are having an affair?"

She should have anticipated it, but she hadn't. The taunting, softly spoken suggestion shocked her. Dana scowled at him, even as a traitorous tingle of awareness and anticipation shot through her. She forced herself not to back away, not to show any sign at all that he had shaken her with that slight caress.

"Touché," she said, her voice husky and uneven, despite her best efforts. "Sometimes the facts may not add up."

"Maybe it would be best if you and I stick to the things we can prove," he suggested, his tone astonishingly casual considering the level of electricity that had been humming through the air just seconds before.

Dana could only nod.

"Have you thought about what you'd like to do here?" he asked as if the conversation up until that moment had been about nothing more consequential than the weather.

For once, she was grateful for the quick change of subject. "Poke through the files," she said readily.

"I meant with the kids."

She sighed. "You're really going to make me go through with this, aren't you?"

"It's part of the deal. Reading, cooking, sewing, whatever. It's up to you."

She thought over the choices he'd offered and rejected all of them. She wanted something that would potentially reveal more of their personalities. "How about photography?" she said impulsively. "I have some experience with that." Of course most of it had been snapping shots of errant husbands in the arms of the other woman. She supposed she could translate that and her two formal classes into an impromptu course of some sort.

Rick looked doubtful. "I don't know."

His lack of enthusiasm only fueled hers. "Why not? It's a skill that they might be able to use."

"But to get the equipment they'll need, they might resort to theft," he said realistically. "We can't afford to buy the digital cameras."

Dana wasn't sure whether it was real enthusiasm for the idea or just plain perversity that made her say, "I have several old cameras at home and I can pay for the supplies."

"You would trust these kids with your cameras?"

His doubting expression had her hesitating, but only for an instant. She didn't want him to think she wasn't willing to put herself on the line in exchange for the information she so desperately wanted. "Until they give me reason not to," she said firmly.

A grin spread across his face. "Well, well, Mrs. Miller, now you're beginning to sound just a little like your husband. There may be hope for you yet."

The hard-won, if somewhat mocking, compliment pleased her more than it should have. She forced an indifferent shrug. "One small step at a time. What should we do? Put up an announcement of some kind?"

"Just set a time for the start of classes and tell Maria. Believe me, word will get around."

"And if no one shows up, do we still have a deal?"

He shook his head. "You have to win them over. That was the deal. If photography doesn't work, I guess you'll just have to come up with something else, won't you?"

The challenge was unmistakable. Dana resolved then and there that she would make the photography class work. She would teach these kids the skills they would need to take first-rate snapshots. Maybe, with a little luck, she'd even find one who could become a professional. Catching herself, she realized she was actually getting carried away. She saw how easy it was to become excited about possibilities.

She was also, once again, getting distracted. She eyed Rick suspiciously. Was that what he really intended? Had he hoped that she would get so caught up with these kids, so emotionally attached to them, that she'd forget all about the little matter of identifying her husband's murderer?

"It won't work," she said quietly.

"What won't work?"

"I won't forget about Ken's death. I won't drop the investigation."

His unblinking gaze stayed level with hers. "Never thought you would."

Either he was being straight with her, or he was a masterful liar. It was too soon to lay odds on which.

"When do you want to get started?" he asked.

"The sooner the better, but I'll need my equipment."

"Tomorrow, then."

She nodded. "I'll be here first thing in the morning."

"Better wait till afternoon. These kids are supposed to be in school in the morning," he said dryly.

"But those in there—"

"Dropped out or were suspended. We're working on getting them reenrolled. I don't want to reward them by offering a special class in the morning. Make it four o'clock. That way, more kids will be here and I'll have time to get some work done before I come out to pick you up and bring you in."

"That's not necessary. I can drive myself in."

He shook his head. "I thought we'd settled that. On my turf, I make the rules."

"I'm not one of your strays."

"No, but you are here because I've made it possible," he reminded her in a way that reaffirmed who held the power.

"It's a public building," she countered defiantly.

"You think you can get these old bricks to talk, go right ahead and try," he retorted smoothly.

Dana sighed. "Okay, you've made your point. Four o'clock will be fine. Am I expected to sit in the corner until you're free, or are you taking me home now?"

"No, I am not taking you home now. I'm taking you to lunch. You've lost too much weight. You're obviously not eating."

"How would you know a thing like that? You've never seen me before today."

Before she realized what he intended, he reached out

and snagged a chunk of material at her waist and tugged. There was at least an inch or better to spare.

"Evidence, Dana. Solid, irrefutable evidence."

"Maybe I just like to wear my clothes loose."

He grinned. "Give it up. You're not going to win. Ken was very proud of your fashion sense. He often wished he could persuade you to teach these girls a thing or two about style."

He had expressed the same wish to her on several occasions, but she had always dismissed the idea with one excuse or another. She had never realized that he'd shared those thoughts with Rick.

"He said you were too busy with other commitments," Rick said, though it was clear he hadn't bought the excuses.

"Okay, okay. Maybe I have lost a couple of pounds," she conceded. "I haven't felt much like eating."

"Today you will," he assured her. "I'm going to stuff you with black beans and rice, maybe a few enchiladas, maybe a taco or two."

Despite herself, her mouth was watering. "Spicy?" she asked.

"If that's the way you want them."

"Is there any other way?"

He nodded approvingly. "See there, you and I do have one thing in common."

"Don't let it go to your head," she warned.

"Hey, I've always believed that the path to victory was to find the first little chink in your opponent's armor."

"Is that what we are? Opponents?"

"Aren't we?"

For some reason that she didn't care to explore too closely, Dana suddenly regretted the accuracy of his assessment, but she couldn't dispute it.

"Yes," she said softly. "I suppose that is exactly what we are."

It was too bad, too. What she was in desperate need of these days was an ally.

7

Rick leaned back in the booth at Tico's and studied the woman opposite him. He'd waited for disdain to fill her eyes all morning, first when she had met the kids at Yo, Amigo and minutes ago, when they had entered the tiny, unpretentious neighborhood restaurant. So far, she had surprised him.

She had been polite, if guarded, with the teenagers. Inside the door of Tico's, she had drawn in a deep breath, and a positively rapturous expression had crossed her face. Once they'd found an available booth in the crowded room, she had grabbed the typed, laminated menu eagerly. For five minutes after that she had pestered him with questions about unfamiliar items.

She had ordered with such abandon that even the unflappable Tico had been startled. She would be stunned to discover that her meal would be enough to stuff a truck driver. Tico's place might not be much for atmosphere, but he never stinted on his portions, especially not for a customer who demonstrated so much enthusiasm. Rick had had to hide his amusement at his friend's bemused expression.

What a complex woman Dana Miller was, he thought,

a little bemused himself as he watched her. This side of her was far too alluring, far too dangerous, when he was already having difficulty resisting the effect she had on his body.

"Didn't anyone ever teach you that it's not polite to stare?" she inquired, squirming just a little under his gaze.

He liked knowing that he could rattle her. "Not that I can recall," he said, enjoying her uneasiness. She had caught him totally off-guard the night before. He figured it was only fair that he return the favor. "I don't think it applied to circumstances like this, anyway."

She regarded him quizzically. "And what circumstances would these be?"

"Two people each trying to figure out what makes the other one tick."

"Is that what you're trying to do?"

Rick smiled. "Aren't you?"

"I already know what makes you tick, Mr. Sanchez," she said with evident bitterness. "You have a passion for just one thing—that program that you have poured your heart and soul into."

It was essentially true, but Rick was vaguely insulted just the same. No man liked to hear himself described as so one-dimensional. "You see no more in me than that?"

"Is there more?"

"Maybe we should let you discover my other passions as we go," he said softly, and watched the color climb into her cheeks.

The taunt came as naturally as breathing, before he could stop himself. It drew a spark of pure fire in her eyes that intrigued him, despite his best intentions. Dana Miller was a woman with passions of her own. Whatever they might be, though, they were off-limits to him. Honoring his friendship to Ken demanded it.

"This isn't personal between us," she said, her teeth clenched.

"Oh, no? You blame me for the death of your husband. You want to destroy something I love, something I've worked hard the past few years to get off the ground. I'd say that makes it pretty personal, Dana."

"I meant—"

He couldn't resist trying to shock her. "You meant there would be no sex, isn't that right?"

The pink in her cheeks deepened. "How crude of you to put it so bluntly."

"I don't waste a lot of time dancing around the obvious, if that's what you mean." He leaned forward. "As for the sex, I think it's a little too soon to rule anything out."

She glared at him. "You are every bit as despicable as I'd imagined, Mr. Sanchez. My husband is—"

"Dead," he reminded her, then cursed himself when the color washed out of her face. "I'm sorry," he said, and meant it. "I should never have said that."

"I think we should go now," she said, her eyes shadowed with unbearable pain. "I've suddenly lost my appetite."

Rick wondered only briefly whether he should accede to her wishes. Perhaps if she remained very angry with him, if she thoroughly despised him, she would stay away from Yo, Amigo, after all. He knew better, though. She wouldn't allow anything—not even her dislike of him—to get in her way. She might avoid him, but she would be back.

He met her gaze squarely. "Suit yourself, but my appetite is just fine, and I'm not about to let Tico's food go to waste."

Their meal arrived as if on cue, plates loaded down with fragrant, spicy concoctions that blended meat and cheese and chili peppers in ways that fast-food chains had never imagined. As furious as Dana was with him, she eyed the plates avidly. He wondered if she would be stubborn enough to leave the food untouched to spite him.

For a moment or two, she did exactly that, hands folded primly in her lap, her chin tilted defiantly, her gaze fixed on some distant point beyond him.

But as he continued to eat, slowly and deliberately savoring each mouthful, he could see her wavering. Finally, with a soft sigh of resignation, she picked up her fork.

She took one tiny, tentative bite at first, still resisting the idea of enjoying her meal. That bite was quickly followed by another, larger one, and then another.

"Oh, my," she whispered, more to herself than to him. "This is heavenly."

Rick grinned. "See, not even I can ruin the taste of Tico's enchiladas."

She ignored the comment. "Do you think he would give me the recipe? What's in this mole sauce? How many chilis?"

"I have no idea, and I doubt if he'd tell you. I think he would rather you came here often," Rick said, and immediately regretted his own foolhardiness. He was practically begging to make things more personal, more intimate between them. How many meals could they share without the undeniable sparks between them leading to something neither of them wanted? Her violent response to his taunting comment just moments earlier proved that she was not half as immune to him as she wanted to be. No doubt she believed that such a significant spark of attraction made a mockery of her mourning, whereas he believed it was simply a life force exerting its pull.

"For more of this," she said, holding up a forkful of savory meat, "I would spend time with the devil himself."

For one brief second, Dana Miller was just an attractive, intelligent woman, a woman whom his body responded to, even when his head told him nothing could ever come of it. There were depths to her that it would be fascinating to explore, depths he would never know. That being the case, it was better to remind them both of why they were together at all.

"Ken always loved it here, too," he said.

Rather than pain at the mention of her husband's name, though, something soft and wondering lit her eyes. "He came here?"

It was as if he'd offered her an unexpected connection to the man she had lost. "Often," Rick said. "He loved the food and the people. Tico was one of our first success stories when we began four years ago."

Astonishment spread across her face. "Tico was in a gang?"

"He led one of the gangs," Rick corrected, then added somberly, "until one of the members of his own gang killed his little brother, claiming he was a snitch."

She gasped at that. "How horrible!"

"But out of that tragedy came some good. Tico was ready to listen to what Yo, Amigo had to say, to what Ken had to say. His mother was an excellent cook. Tico took her recipes and began to experiment with them. He fixed several suppers for everyone at Yo, Amigo. Everyone was wildly enthusiastic. Ken found a few people in the restaurant business, invited them over one night and, after tasting some of Tico's wizardry with Mexican food, they came up with the money to back this place."

"It was a wise investment, wasn't it?" Dana asked.

Rick nodded. "He repaid all of the loans in the first year and he's been in the black ever since. Four of his younger brothers and sisters work here now. His mother comes in to act as hostess in the evening. It's truly a family enterprise."

"You must be very proud," she said with obvious sincerity.

"Not me. Ken had the foresight to see what Tico could be. I was worried only about getting him off the streets. It takes more than that. I can rescue kids every day. I can talk until I'm blue in the face about opportunity and dreams and success. It takes people like Ken to make them a reality, to keep these kids from drifting back to their old ways. Your husband offered more than a moral compass. He offered hope."

He met her gaze evenly. "Can you see now that even though my loss is very different from yours, it runs just as deep?"

He could see the struggle in her eyes, the unwillingness to acknowledge that he might be suffering because of Ken's death, just as she was. Eventually, though, she was too honest to lie, even to herself.

"I think I'm beginning to see that," she conceded, albeit grudgingly. "But don't you see that it was because of that very need you had for him that he's dead?"

Ah, Rick thought, there was the rub. He fought that acknowledgment, denied it. When he did allow it, he could see his responsibility so clearly it kept him awake nights.

"I'm sorry," he told her once more. "But even if I'd known what the outcome was going to be, I wouldn't have stopped him from coming. Yo, Amigo, the kids there, kids like Tico, needed him."

"So did I," she said fervently, visibly choking back a sob.

Rick reached across the table and took her hand in his. It was cold as ice, but she didn't pull away.

"I know, Dana," he told her quietly. "I know."

She wasn't through with him yet, though. "Because of you, my kids will grow up without a father."

He could have told her there were plenty of kids here in the barrio who would grow up without a father, as well, but it would have brought her no comfort. He thought of her going home to that empty, silent house in the suburbs and, for once, he didn't envy the life she and so many others had.

Once, not so very long ago, he would have dismissed her as an uncaring, pampered housewife. He had kept that opinion to himself, even when Ken had sung her praises and ignored her shortcomings. Now he was glad that he had. She had loved her husband and her kids. With her misguided notion that she could insulate them from the world, she had wanted nothing more than to protect them. How could he fault her for that? It was exactly what he wanted for so many others.

"I'll take you home now," he said at last.

From the despondent look in her eyes, he suddenly realized that it was a trip neither of them was looking forward to.

With every mile that brought them closer to home, Dana felt the tension inside her mount. It was worse in many ways than what she'd felt only hours earlier, when she had made the reverse trip into Chicago. She had gone to Yo, Amigo filled with rage and, perhaps, if she were totally honest, just a modicum of fear of the uncertainties ahead.

Coming home, where she knew exactly what to expect, she felt only this vague tightness in her chest, the far more devastating threat of more emptiness. Even though the winter sky was darkening, it was barely four in the afternoon. A long, lonely evening stretched out ahead of her.

When they pulled into the driveway, Rick glanced at her knowingly. "Are you going to be okay here by yourself?"

"Of course," she said, denying the truth. "I've lived in this house for nine years. It's home." For how much longer? she wondered. She couldn't drag out the move forever. Sooner or later, the board's patience would wear thin.

"I'll be fine," she insisted.

He regarded her with obvious skepticism. "Maybe you should call Mrs. Jefferson."

The thought appealed too much. Kate's cheerful ways and common sense would chase away the shadows. She forced herself to shake her head. "No, this is the way it's going to be. I have to get used to it."

"Not overnight."

"Yes," she said. "The sooner the better." Changing the subject, she asked, "What time will you be here tomorrow?" Only after she'd asked did she wonder if she'd sounded too anxious to escape.

"Two-thirty, maybe three."

"Or maybe later," she said, imagining him to be the kind of man who lost all track of time.

"I said two-thirty or three," he corrected. "That's what I meant."

She shrugged. "Whatever."

He regarded her with a direct look that commanded her attention. Only when he had it, did he say, "Dana, I know you don't want to trust me, not even in so small a detail, but I mean what I say. You'll see."

"It's not important."

"I think it is. Would you like me to come in with you?"

She almost smiled at that. "To chase away the ghosts?"

"In a manner of speaking."

"No," she said too quickly. She didn't want him inside again, in Ken's space. He was the kind of man who could far too quickly overshadow memories. They would fade fast enough without the competition. "I'll be fine. I'll see you tomorrow."

She left the car in a rush, then hurried up the front walk. She fumbled the key in the lock and then she was inside. She closed the door quickly behind her, blocking out the view of Rick Sanchez still sitting in her driveway, his gaze worried as he stared after her.

She didn't want his worry or his concern. The only thing she wanted from Rick Sanchez was entry into the world where her husband had died.

She peeked out from behind a curtain and saw that he was still there. Eventually, though, he started the car and backed out of the drive. Only then did she release the breath she had unconsciously been holding. Relief followed, relief that didn't bear too close an examination.

Fortunately, just then the phone rang. Switching on a light as she crossed the room, she grabbed the portable phone eagerly, glad for anything that would push Rick Sanchez and the disturbing afternoon they'd just shared from her mind.

"Mom?"

She wasn't prepared for her son's whispered voice. It was thick with tears and enough to break her heart. Her oldest prided himself on never crying. Since Ken's death, Bobby had taken his role as man of the house far too seriously. Except at the funeral, he had remained stoically dry-eyed. He had been the one to comfort his younger brothers, to try to explain the inexplicable, when Dana's words had failed. This afternoon, though, he sounded more like a scared and lonely little boy.

"Mommy?"

"Yes, sweetheart, I'm here."

"Why can't we come home? We miss you."

"Oh, baby, I know. I miss you, too. How's school?"

"Awful. It's not like home."

"I know it's an adjustment," she said with a sigh. "But we talked about that. You all said you wanted to stay in Florida for the rest of the school year, remember? You wanted to see if you liked it better there than Chicago."

"Well, I already know. I don't," he said emphatically.

"You haven't given it a chance. I'll be back soon and we'll talk about it some more, okay? In the meantime, aren't you having fun with Grandma and Grandpa?"

"They make us go to bed too early."

"How early?"

"Eight o'clock, like I'm some baby," he said with disgust.

The privilege of staying up until nine had been hard-won. They'd negotiated it on his eighth birthday. She wasn't surprised that he was chafing at an early bedtime.

"I'll speak to Grandma."

"They won't order in pizza, either," he said, apparently encouraged by her response to his first complaint.

"Now, that's something with which I totally agree," she said. "We did that too much."

"But they won't do it *ever!*"

She noticed that her little diplomat was quick to switch tactics, seek a compromise. There was no mistaking his father's influence in him. Dana chuckled despite herself. "Okay, I'll see what I can do about that, too. Anything else?"

His already low voice dropped another notch. "Jon wet the bed and Grandma yelled at him."

Dana closed her eyes against a sudden rush of guilt. What had she done by leaving the boys behind? At five, Jonathan was way past bed wetting—or he had been until his world had been rocked by the loss of the father he idolized. That first week, when she'd found it almost impossible to explain why Daddy wasn't coming home ever again, there had been accident after accident. By the time she'd left Florida, though, she had thought the problem solved. Obviously her departure had caused him to regress and her mother's patience to wear thin.

"I'll talk to Grandma about that, too."

"Kevin's acting weird, too. He just stares at the TV until Grandpa makes him do something. It's like he's not even here or something," Bobby said. "I think maybe you'd better come back and get us."

The image of rambunctious, six-year-old Kevin sitting for endless hours in front of the TV brought on the salty sting of tears. She couldn't let it sway her, though. She simply couldn't. "I will, very soon."

"How soon?" Bobby persisted.

"I can't put a time limit on this, sweetie, but I'll talk to you every day."

"It's not the same as you being here."

Dana sighed. "I know. I'll try to finish up here as fast as I can. Now, where's Jon?"

"He and Kevin are with Grandpa down at the pool. Kevin cried, but Grandpa made him go. He said we should have a swim before dinner to work up an appetite."

"Where's Grandma? Is she fixing dinner now?"

"No. She's playing cards with her friends."

The thought of Bobby in her parents' condo all by himself frightened her. There was too much mischief he could get into. What had her parents been thinking? Of course, it was entirely possible—no, it was likely, she concluded ruefully—that they had no idea he'd come inside. He was probably supposed to be at the pool with the others.

"Bobby, go back to the pool with Grandpa before he misses you and starts worrying. I'll call this evening."

"Promise?"

"Cross my heart."

"No," he wailed unexpectedly. "Don't say that."

Dana was stunned by the outburst. "Bobby? Sweetie, what is it? What's wrong?"

"Don't you know the rest of that? Don't you remember?"

Dana couldn't imagine what had upset him so about something they'd been saying to each other for years. "What?"

"It's 'cross my heart, *hope to die,*'" he said, sounding teary again. "Don't say that ever again, Mommy. Please. You'll make it come true, just like Daddy. That's what he promised the night he got killed."

His anguished logic stunned her. "Oh, no, baby, it's just a saying. I'm not going to die."

"Daddy said it," he repeated brokenly. "And he died."

"Not because of that," she reassured him. "Bobby, you know what happened to Daddy wasn't because he said some silly words, don't you?"

He gulped back a sob. "A bad guy shot him," he said in a tiny voice.

"That's right. It wasn't because of anything Daddy said or did. It wasn't his fault."

"But why would anyone shoot Daddy?" Bobby asked. "Why would God let it happen?"

Dana couldn't think of how to answer that one. It was a question she had repeatedly asked herself. That bullet that had felled Ken had done more than kill her husband and destroy her life. It had destroyed the faith that had been central to their lives.

If she couldn't see the sense of Ken's death, how could she make an eight-year-old see it?

"I don't know why, baby. Maybe God is just testing us to see how strong we are."

"Mommy?"

"What?"

"Sometimes I don't feel very strong at all."

"Me, neither, sweetie. Me, neither." Shaken by the whole conversation, she tried to figure out how to reassure her son long distance. The answer to that, too, eluded her. "Bobby, go on back outside with Grandpa, okay? I'll talk to you tonight."

"You won't forget to tell Grandma about bedtime, will you?"

She smiled, despite the previously somber mood. "I won't forget. Now, scoot. Love you, Bobby."

"I love you, Mommy."

The phone clattered back into the cradle and left her listening to the faint buzz of a disconnected line. Tears slid down her cheeks, as finally, slowly, she hung up on her end, as well.

Had she been wrong to leave the boys? Had she been wrong to come back here to find the answers the police were unable to find?

The part of her that was a mother said yes. She belonged with her children. They needed her, now more than ever. Her parents had told her that. So had Kate. A conversation like this one only reinforced what she already knew in her heart.

But the part of her that had been a wife, a lover, a friend, said otherwise. She had no choice but to use all of her skills as an investigator to solve her husband's murder. There would be no real adjustment for any of them until the murderer was behind bars.

8

The sweat was pouring down Rick's back as he squared off in front of Tico under the hoop on Yo, Amigo's indoor basketball court. Gazing straight into the other man's eyes, he kept his body loose as he tried to outguess him.

Tico dribbled the ball slowly, deliberately, between them as if he had all the time in the world. Without the rules of a game, in their one-on-one contest it was a test of patience as much as anything. For two habitually impatient men, it was a real struggle to wait each other out.

Despite the fierce concentration in Tico's eyes, he managed to keep up a steady stream of chatter, alternating between English and Spanish. So far, most of the remarks had been focused on Dana Miller. Tico had more questions and observations than a reporter on a deadline.

"*Que pasa?* Are you two going to become a hot ticket? I saw the way she looked at you. Pure lust."

"Pure hatred is more like it," Rick said, listening to the rhythm of the bouncing ball, even as he kept his gaze steady. These late-night contests had become a welcome ritual, relieving stress with pure exhaustion. Rick had really been counting on its effectiveness tonight, but Tico's remarks were having the opposite effect. Dana's image was staying front and center and growing more provocative by the second.

"Love, hate, sometimes it is all the same, *mi amigo,*" Tico commented.

"Her husband just died," Rick protested. "The only thing Dana really cares about is finding the person responsible and getting even. Since she hasn't found that person yet, I'm the target of all of her rage."

Shock spread across Tico's face, but he never once lost his concentration. "She blames you for Ken's death?" he asked incredulously.

"She doesn't think I pulled the trigger, but she blames me, yes."

Tico's expression turned thoughtful. "And yet she shared a meal with you today. It could be that she is beginning to see reason." He grinned. "Or she has been charmed by that great wit of yours."

"She ate with me because it suited her purposes. I've promised to help her find the killer."

Tico feinted left, then swiveled to the right and shot. The ball swished through the net. Rick grabbed the rebound.

"Six-four, you son of a bitch," he said.

Tico grinned. "You should pay closer attention, *mi amigo.* Your mind is elsewhere tonight, eh?"

"No," Rick said adamantly, but he doubted he convinced his friend. He certainly wasn't convinced himself. Dana had been preying on his mind ever since he'd left her. She'd looked so lost and alone as she'd walked up the driveway and into the house earlier.

"Not so long ago you feared she or the police would bring down Yo, Amigo with all of their questions," Tico reminded him. "What's happened to change your mind?"

"I haven't changed my mind," Rick declared, alternately dribbling the ball with his left hand, then his right. "That's exactly why I agreed to help."

"Was that the reason or was it those sad, blue eyes of hers?"

Rick's hand faltered at that and Tico seized the opportunity to steal the ball, pivot and shoot. Another perfect shot. Two, if the remark about Dana's eyes counted.

"I could really grow to dislike you," he muttered.

Tico laughed, unoffended by the threat. "It is because I see so clearly that which you do not wish to see."

"It's because you beat me every time we walk onto this court. I give up," he said, reaching for a towel and mopping his face.

"So soon?" Tico taunted. "You usually last until midnight."

"My concentration's shot."

"Something else for you to hold against the lovely widow, no doubt." Tico shot him a wry look. "It will not be enough, *mi amigo.* Once a woman is under your skin, blaming her for it accomplishes nothing."

"She is not under my skin. She's my best friend's widow. I even thought she was the wrong woman for him."

"But right for you," Tico said knowingly. "It happens that way sometimes."

Rick scowled at him. "Give it a rest, will you? This so-called alliance of ours isn't personal. She made that perfectly clear over lunch today."

Tico's amusement returned. "I know. I heard."

"You know, my friend, you could do me a lot more good if you would eavesdrop on the conversations on the street and help me find Ken's killer."

For once Tico's expression sobered. "I have heard

nothing, not since the night it happened. There has not been so much as a whisper."

"Does that make sense to you?"

"No. Frankly, it worries me. There should be more talk. Someone should be claiming credit, gloating."

"What do you think it means, that no one has?"

"That for once the gangs had nothing to do with it," Tico responded readily, confirming Rick's own opinion.

"How can it be that no one saw a stranger, though? Wouldn't word have spread about that? A lot of people here cared about the *padre*."

"I did not say it was a stranger. I said it wasn't gang-related."

Rick's head shot up at that. "Meaning?"

"Some of those involved in the gangs have ties to important people."

"Such as politicians," Rick said at once, thinking of the voter drives that had been organized and paid for with political money and operated by neighborhood insiders, gang leaders who craved clout at City Hall. The streets had never been safer than they had been on Election Day. It was an angle he had never once considered.

But what had Ken Miller to do with Chicago politics? Nothing, so far as he knew. It was a link that made no sense. He shook his head.

"I think we're reaching."

"You'd rather believe it was some kid high on drugs or a stray bullet meant for one of our own?"

"Those would be the obvious answers," Rick said, echoing the police with whom he'd spoken.

"Too obvious," Tico insisted. "I prefer subtleties."

Rick tried to reason it out, but he still couldn't accept what Tico was suggesting. "Ken was from a suburb north of town. Why would he be the target of some Chicago politician?"

"Not Ken, but through him, Yo, Amigo. His ties to the program were well known. Killing him might be expected to create such an outpouring of rage that those in power would be forced to shut the place down. It could be seen as proof that nothing had changed in the barrio."

That, unfortunately, made a terrible kind of sense. And when it came to politicians who disliked the program, there were more than enough to choose from.

Oh, on the record, they said all the right things. They didn't dare publicly decry a program that was already making a visible difference in the neighborhood. But privately they didn't like handing over funds to an ex–gang member with an arrogant streak and unorthodox methods. They didn't like Rick Sanchez, period. He had tangled with them too often, shown too many of them up for the corrupt fools they were. He never groveled for their money, never sang their praises to the media when they did the right and just thing.

Tico was studying him curiously, clearly aware that his suggestion had struck a chord. "Will you tell Dana what we discussed?"

"Not just yet," Rick said. "Not until I have some kind of proof."

"The smoking gun, so to speak?"

"Exactly."

"I'm afraid any smoking gun is probably at the bottom of Lake Michigan by now."

Rick's expression turned grim. "Then I'll just have to find out who's been out boating lately."

Dana spent another restless night in Ken's leather chair. She was up at dawn, putting together a ragtag assortment of photographic equipment, including every single camera she had in the house. She found Bobby's cheap child's version.

Holding it, she paused to recall their second conversation the day before. It had been no less troubling than the first. To her frustration, her mother hadn't been back from her card game, either, so Dana hadn't been able to share Bobby's complaints and work out a reasonable compromise. She considered calling again now, but a glance at the clock changed her mind. It was too early. Instead, she returned to the hunt for cameras.

She found Ken's far more expensive and complex Nikon, plus several of the moderately priced ones she had used on stakeouts. She included her own telephoto lenses, too. She would run out for memory cards and perhaps a few of those disposable cameras as soon as the nearby drugstore opened.

In the meantime, she sat at the kitchen table with a fresh pot of coffee nearby and thought about Rick's comment the day before that perhaps the murderer was closer to home. In other words, someone Ken knew, someone in the neighborhood, perhaps even in his own congregation.

As badly as she wanted to dismiss the notion out of hand, she couldn't. She wouldn't be thorough and objective if she didn't consider each and every possibility. Hadn't that potential lack of objectivity been the very thing Kate had warned her about?

She grabbed a notepad and made a list of places to check, including Ken's office at the nearby church. She would go over before his secretary came in, so no one would realize that she'd been in there snooping. Not that she didn't have a perfect right to collect his personal things, but that wouldn't explain why she was going through church files.

She considered other places to look. Perhaps the morgue at the local paper. Though she read it regularly, it was possible she had missed any articles on people vehemently opposed to Ken's program to bring gang members into suburban homes. She'd check the *Tribune* and the *Sun-Times,* too.

She sat back. There, she'd done it. She had a starting place now, aside from Yo, Amigo. That ought to satisfy both Kate and Rick that she was being totally objective. It didn't matter that the list was probably a waste of time. She was all but certain that the answers were right smack in the middle of the gang turf that surrounded the program. The best way to prove that, though, would be to eliminate these others.

Invigorated by having a sense of purpose, she took a quick shower and dressed in jeans, a thick sweater and sneakers for the short jaunt across to the church. She tossed a jacket across her shoulders. She could be in and out easily before anyone showed up at nine.

Or she could have been, she thought with a sigh as she spotted Kate on the front stoop. She opened the door before Kate's knock.

"Eager to see me?" Kate said, then caught sight of the jacket. "Or were you just going out?"

"Actually, I was."

"Where? It's not even seven."

Dana was too exhausted to come up with a quick, evasive retort that would be believable. The truth would have to suffice. "Ken's office. I want to clear out some of his things."

Kate eyed her skeptically. "You want to snoop. I heard what Rick said yesterday. You've been thinking about it, haven't you? You're wondering if someone here could have been behind Ken's murder."

"I have to at least explore the idea," Dana conceded. "But can you see Mrs. Davis or Mr. Worth sneaking into Chicago with a gun and shooting their pastor?"

Mrs. Davis was a seventy-year-old retired school-teacher with a cherubic face and twinkling eyes. Mr. Worth, also retired, had been a librarian at Northwestern. He still had the scent of old books about him. They barely went beyond the corner grocery anymore. Kate knew them both, as well as most of the other regulars at the church.

"It's not as if all of Ken's parishioners were old," she pointed out. "You picked the two people least likely to harm a flea. Now, that Mr. Nelson, I wouldn't put anything past him. He has shifty eyes and the build of an ex-boxer."

"He *is* an ex-boxer," Dana said dryly. "His eyes were injured in a fight."

"I still don't trust him."

"Since you seem to have such superior insight into the members of Ken's congregation, would you like to come along and help? Maybe we can sift through the files and get out of there, before we get caught."

Kate's expression brightened. "Really? Let's go."

With startling eagerness, she whirled around and headed back down the steps. A light layer of snow had fallen during the night, then iced over. It crunched underfoot as they took a shortcut across the lawn to the door leading to the office and parish hall portion of the church complex.

Added years after the original church had been built, it was a modern brick structure with a handful of class-rooms for Sunday school and other meetings. The parish hall had a small stage facing a cavernous room that was empty now. Folding tables and chairs were set up once a month for a potluck supper and twice a year for pancake breakfasts. They were also used for wedding receptions and other events. Sometimes rows of chairs were lined up instead for a performance by the choir or the various children's Sunday school classes.

Their sneakers made no sound as they hurried across the open space to the set of offices closest to the church. Even so, Dana could feel her heart thumping unsteadily. She couldn't be certain whether it was caused by the fear of discovery or merely dread. This would be the first time she had been into Ken's office since his death. She used to run across once or twice a day to bring his lunch or simply to look in on him.

At the door to his secretary's office, she hesitated. She felt the pressure of Kate's hand on her shoulder.

"You okay?" Kate asked. "We don't have to do this."

"Yes, we do," Dana insisted. She drew a deep breath. "I'll be fine."

She plucked a set of keys out of her pocket and unlocked the door. Kate flipped on the light.

Mrs. Fallon kept her office neatly organized. Dana thought of the chaos in Rick's outer office, despite Maria's valiant efforts, and almost smiled. Perhaps she should lend him Mrs. Fallon for a few weeks. Between her and his lovely Maria, they would make short work of the mess.

Kate glanced around. "No files in here."

"She mainly answers the phone, types and keeps Ken's schedule," Dana said. "Ken liked to keep the files under lock and key with him. Even though Mrs. Fallon was probably in and out of them a dozen times a day, he thought it preserved the illusion of strict confidentiality."

"What the heck's in the files?" Kate asked. "Did he make notes on confessions?"

"Nothing so private, I'm sure. Birth records, marriage records, business stuff, I suppose." She hesitated. "Now that I think about it, I'm not really sure what he would have filed away. Right now, all I'm looking for is a list of church members as a starting point."

At the door to Ken's actual office, Dana halted again. This time before Kate could offer her another excuse for leaving, she forced herself to step across the threshold. She fumbled for the light switch, found it and flipped it on.

"Oh, my," Kate murmured, mirroring Dana's own gasp of shock.

The place had been ransacked. It had to have happened very recently, overnight, perhaps. Mrs. Fallon would never have tolerated such chaos for long.

Dana exchanged a look with her friend.

"Do you think Rick could have been right?" Kate asked in a hushed voice. "Was somebody in here trying to cover his tracks?"

Before she could reply, Dana caught sight of a smashed picture frame on the floor. A choked sob welled up in her throat. Being careful of the broken glass, she picked it up. The picture inside was unharmed. It was a family portrait, taken just last Christmas. Ken had kept it on his desk so he could glance up as he worked and catch a glimpse of the family he loved.

Dana clung to the frame so tightly she could feel the silver digging into her palms. Suddenly the room swam and her knees felt weak. She swayed, but Kate caught her and guided her to a chair.

"Sit. Head between your knees," she instructed briskly. She nodded when Dana complied. "Good. Feel better?"

Dana sat up slowly. "I don't know what came over me."

"Too much stress. Too little sleep. Not enough food.

That's just for starters," Kate said. "I think we should get out of here."

"Not without that list," Dana said stubbornly. "It's more important than ever."

"Okay, you sit. I'll find the list."

"We should call the police."

"Let Mrs. Fallon deal with the police. She'll be in her element bossing them around."

Dana glanced around the office. "This will be terribly upsetting for her."

"No," Kate corrected. "It will infuriate her. She'll consider it almost as much of a desecration as if someone had stolen the cross from the altar."

"True," Dana agreed eventually. She still felt terrible about leaving the secretary to deal with the ransacking. "I just don't know—"

"Well, I do," Kate countered firmly just as she reached into a drawer of the desk and nabbed a stack of pages that had been stapled together. She waved it triumphantly. "The list. Now let's get the heck out of here."

Dana reluctantly followed her. They slipped through the parish hall and back outside. Not until they were back in her own yard did she breathe a sigh of relief. The cold air wiped away the last of her queasiness. With that list in hand, she suddenly felt rejuvenated. Okay, it was in Kate's hand, at the moment, but they had it. Kate was demonstrating a remarkable alacrity for investigating. Driven by loyalty and indignation, the woman had absolutely no fear.

"I should have forced you to get your P.I. license years ago," she told her as they sat down at the kitchen table with coffee and the rest of the pecan coffee cake Dana had made the day before. "You're a natural."

Kate's eyes sparkled. "I've been looking for a new ca-

reer goal. Maybe I've found my niche. That was invig-
orating. A real adrenaline rush. I haven't felt this good
since the last time I had sex."

Dana chuckled. "And exactly how long ago was that?"

"Never mind," Kate said primly.

"That long, huh?"

Kate made a face, then held out the packet of papers.
"Okay, now that we have it, what do we do with it?"

Dana stared at the names and addresses blankly for
the space of a heartbeat. It was doubtful that there would
be an asterisk by any of the names suggesting he or she
was a possible murderer. They were just going to have to
use their instincts and some good old-fashioned detective
work to discover if there was any suspect at all on the list.

"You've been a member here ever since we met,
right?" she asked Kate.

"Yes. I transferred from my old church as soon as I
found out your husband was the minister. I liked Ken the
minute you introduced us. So did the girls."

"And Ken and I have been here for nine years. Between us, surely we know something about most of the
people on that list. How many are there?"

Kate flipped through the pages. "Looks like four or
five hundred."

"Holy cow!" she exclaimed, daunted by the unexpectedly high number.

Kate's spirits never wavered. "I guess we'd better get
started," she said eagerly. "Shall I read the names aloud?"

"Uh-huh," Dana murmured distractedly. She couldn't
stop thinking about the size of the task. "If there were
that many members, how come Sunday services never
drew more than a couple of hundred?"

"Lapsed believers," Kate suggested. "Maybe some of
these are dead."

"Mrs. Fallon updates that list once a month. If they're on there, they're alive."

"Maybe some just drifted away and never said anything. Or showed up once every couple of months or at Christmas. They'd still be considered active members, right?"

"Right. Or maybe they split very recently when they disagreed with Ken about the gang members," Dana said. "He might have told Mrs. Fallon to leave them on, in the hope they'd be back. We can probably eliminate anyone that neither of us is familiar with. That should narrow the list down to half, anyway, don't you think?"

"Only one way to find out," Kate offered briskly. "Ready?"

"I suppose so."

"First name, Richard Adams."

It didn't ring any bells at all for Dana. "Do you know him?" she asked.

Kate shook her head.

"Neither do I. Put a question mark next to his name."

They were still at it, with only a handful of recognizable parishioners so far, when Dana glanced at the clock and noted that it was past noon. If Rick kept his word, he would be here for her in a couple of hours.

"Let's get some lunch and call it a day," she suggested. "We've made it through almost half the alphabet, anyway."

Kate stared at her. "Why not finish the rest? Are you going out?"

"Back into Chicago, as a matter of fact," she said, forcing a blasé note into her voice.

"Oh, no. Not again. You cannot be thinking of going back to Yo, Amigo."

"Actually, I am. Rick's coming for me. I'm going to be teaching a photography class."

Kate's mouth dropped open. "You're not!"

"I am. Care to come help?"

"My, my," Kate murmured. "He's even better than I'd imagined."

Dana stared at her. "Meaning?"

"Just that I thought you'd be a tough sell. I'd given him forty-eight hours to work his magic."

"I'm not doing this by choice," Dana protested.

"Yeah, right. He twisted your arm and begged."

"No," Dana said. "He made it a condition of my talking to the kids at the center."

"Then by all means, go, talk."

"I will, but first I'm going to call Mrs. Fallon and see if the police have been there. I haven't seen any squad cars cruising by, have you?"

"No," Kate said. "That seems a little odd, now that I think about it."

"I was thinking the same thing," Dana said as she dialed the familiar number. At the sound of her voice, Mrs. Fallon immediately began clucking sympathetically.

"Oh, you poor darling. I saw the car in the driveway and guessed you were back. How are you?"

"I'm just fine, thanks. Mrs. Fallon, about Ken's office."

"Oh, you saw that, did you? I'm so sorry. I thought I'd have it tidied up before you came over. That's why I didn't call earlier."

"Then the police have been there to investigate."

"Investigate, my eye," she said with disgust. "The police are the ones who left it that way."

9

"Dana, what on earth? Where are you going?" Kate demanded as Dana hung up the phone and grabbed her jacket.

"Back to the church."

"Why?"

"That mess we found over there was caused by the cops."

"You're kidding." Kate reached for her own coat and followed Dana out the door, jogging to keep up with her.

Dana had never been so angry in all of her life. It had been one thing to think that the destruction in Ken's office had been caused by an intruder of some kind. It was quite another to realize that the people responsible for it were supposed to be the good guys.

There was nothing surreptitious about the entry she made this time. She slammed open the door and ran across the parish hall. Mrs. Fallon was waiting for her, her distress plain.

"See, there, I've gone and upset you," she murmured apologetically. "I never meant to do that."

"You're not the one who upset me," Dana reassured the flustered old woman. "Did the police give you a card?

Do you know which officers were here? How many were there?"

The barrage of questions only added to Mrs. Fallon's already visible distress. "Now, wait a minute," she said. "Let me think. This whole thing has me so rattled I can't string two words together that make any sense."

"I'm sorry. Let's sit down," Dana suggested.

"No, no, I'll be okay. There were two of them," she said eventually, "though now that I think about it, one of them looked as if he were from Chicago. I was so frantic when they came barging in here, I didn't focus on that at the time. I'm almost certain he wasn't wearing a local uniform." She opened her desk drawer and nabbed a card. "Here, this is the card the one from our department gave me. He wasn't in uniform. I believe he was a detective."

"Dillon O'Flannery," Dana read aloud. She glanced at Kate, who'd grown up right here in town. "Have you ever run across him?"

"Not me. I try to stay as far away from cops as I can. They make me nervous, especially when I'm behind the wheel. One more speeding ticket and they'll take away my keys. What about you? I thought you knew most of those guys."

"So did I," Dana said grimly, punching in the number on the card. It looked as if it might be a direct line, rather than the central switchboard.

"O'Flannery."

His voice was deep, his manner terse. Dana took an immediate dislike to him. Of course, her reaction at this point wouldn't have been any more positive if he'd sung his greeting like Pavarotti.

"Officer O'Flannery," she said sweetly, deliberately downgrading his rank.

"It's Detective O'Flannery."

"Not if I get my way," she retorted. "I'd suggest you get your butt over to St. Michael's pronto, buster, or I'll have your badge before the day's out."

"Now, wait just a minute! Who the hell is this?"

"This is Mrs. Dana Miller. You recently ransacked my husband's office. I'd like you here with an explanation and a cleanup crew, on the double."

She slammed the phone in his ear before he could respond, then smiled grimly. "That ought to do it."

Mrs. Fallon looked stunned. Kate appeared worried.

"Do you think, maybe, you were just a little too abrupt?" Kate asked. "Maybe the situation called for a little diplomacy and friendly persuasion. He is the one with the badge, after all."

"Men like Detective O'Flannery do not respond to persuasion. You have to match their Gestapo-like tactics to get their attention." The police station was only blocks away. The sound of a siren's blare getting closer by the second proved her point. "I believe that would be Detective O'Flannery now."

Kate and Mrs. Fallon stared toward the door, as if waiting for a vision to appear. Sure enough, a man wearing black slacks and a gray tweed blazer came charging through like a lineman for the Chicago Bears. He was a vision, all right, the epitome of seething male.

He pulled up short at the sight of the three women. He seemed to zero in on Dana at once as the culprit behind the phone call. She wasn't quite sure what that said about her appearance. Maybe she was the one who looked as if she were about to flip out.

"You would be Mrs. Miller," he guessed.

"And you're Detective O'Flannery," she said, then added pointedly, "For the moment, anyway."

Blue eyes the color of a very deep lake locked on her. He seemed to be struggling with his temper.

"I know what a strain you've been under," he said eventually.

His tone was so patronizing she wanted to slug him. "You have no idea," she shot back. "Finding that my husband's office was leveled by two cops hasn't improved my mood any." Hands on hips, she squared off in front of him. "Exactly what did you hope to find in there?"

"Something that might help the Chicago police with their case," he said. He turned to Kate, as if to appeal to her more reasonable nature. "We like to cooperate with other departments whenever we can."

"Assuming that a search of my husband's office was critical to the investigation," Dana shot back, "do you have any idea why it took them over a month to get around to it?"

"They didn't share that with me. They sent an officer and I came along for the ride."

"What a prince," Dana said sarcastically. Between this man and Rick Sanchez, her normal good nature had taken a serious beating. She was turning into a first-class bitch. Unfortunately, this wasn't the time to worry about correcting that shift in her personality. She had a hunch getting a few straight answers would eventually take care of the problem, anyway.

"Tearing things up around here must have made your day," she accused.

Mrs. Fallon swallowed hard and sank into the chair behind her desk. She looked as if she feared Dana's arrest was imminent. After working for a man as even-tempered and gentle as Ken, seeing Dana in action had to be a shock.

Dana glanced at Kate and saw that she looked just

the teensiest bit shell-shocked herself, although her state seemed to have more to do with the detective than with Dana's behavior. She took her own survey of O'Flannery. She supposed that someone with eyes that blue and mussed hair the color of coal might have that sort of effect on some women. It was a pity Kate was one of them.

"Did you find anything?" Kate asked in a breathy voice that Dana had never once heard come out of her mouth before.

Detective O'Flannery was either a sucker for a smitten woman or just plain relieved to have someone address him in a friendlier tone than Dana had. He beamed at her.

"Why don't we all sit down?" he suggested. "Let's talk about this."

"Did you find anything?" Dana snapped.

"Sweetie, I think he was just about to tell us," Kate soothed. She latched on to Dana's hand with a warning grip so tight Dana's wedding ring dug into her finger.

"Fine," Dana said, but she refused to sit.

Her stubbornness seemed to amuse the detective. He and Kate exchanged commiserating glances. Dana concluded she was going to have to fire her new assistant investigator, since her hormones seemed to be getting in the way of her better judgment.

"Did you find anything in my husband's office?" she repeated in a more patient tone.

"Nothing conclusive," he equivocated.

"Meaning that you found nothing or that you found something, but you just haven't figured out yet what it means?"

He seemed taken aback by the question. Maybe he hadn't figured she had the intelligence to realize there was a difference.

"Very good, Mrs. Miller," he praised.

There was that condescending tone again. Dana gritted her teeth and forced herself not to fly off the handle again. "Which is it?" Just in case he couldn't manage to answer a direct question, she tried another angle. "Did you remove anything from the office?"

"Your husband's calendar," he conceded grudgingly.

There was no need to ask why. If Ken had had meetings in the hours or even days immediately preceding his murder, it was entirely possible that one of those might point toward a killer. She should have thought of that herself right after his death, but she'd been too distraught then. She'd been thinking like a grieving widow, not like an investigator.

Given his overall attitude, she gathered there would be little point in asking Detective O'Flannery what names were on the calendar. It wasn't necessary, anyway. Mrs. Fallon kept a duplicate schedule on her desk. A quick glance in the secretary's direction drew a subtle nod, indicating that she knew precisely what Dana was thinking and that she was still in possession of the second calendar.

Dana returned her gaze to the detective. "I assume my husband's calendar was in the middle of his desk, where he always kept it," she said blandly.

He nodded. "I believe it was."

"Then would you mind telling me why the hell you had to tear the office up to find it?"

He regarded her blandly. "We didn't go in specifically looking for a calendar."

"What, then? What else were you hoping to find? What was on the warrant? I assume you had one."

"We had one," he said grimly. "Mrs. Miller, really, why don't you just leave the investigation to the Chicago police? Let them do their jobs."

"If one more person suggests that, I'm going to scream.

If they were doing their jobs, they'd have the killer behind bars by now. Even a halfway decent cop knows that leads start turning cold after a few days. It's been weeks now, and the Chicago cops have done diddly-squat, as far as I can tell. Now, are you going to tell me what you were really looking for in my husband's office, or am I going to have to sue you for violation of his civil rights, trespassing and anything else I can come up with?"

He exchanged another look with Kate, but for once Kate didn't appear overly sympathetic. He sighed heavily.

"Okay, you asked for it. We were looking for drugs, Mrs. Miller. And, yes, indeed, the search warrant mentioned drugs specifically, in case that was going to be your next question."

If the idea had not been so totally preposterous, Dana might have grabbed the vase of flowers off Mrs. Fallon's desk and cracked it over his thick skull. As it was, she laughed.

"You think my husband, a respected minister, had drugs in his office? His *church* office? Are you out of your mind?" she inquired.

"The Chicago police had a tip from a very reliable source that your husband was dealing drugs and that Yo, Amigo was the front for his operation."

Speechless, Dana sank onto a chair.

"You're a liar!"

Rick Sanchez's voice cut through the already charged air like a whip. Dana hadn't heard his approach. She doubted if any of the others had, either. Grateful for once to see him, grateful to have such a vehement ally, she didn't flinch when he put his hand on her shoulder and squeezed reassuringly. In fact, she found the murderous glint in his eyes rather satisfying. Let these two males go *mano a mano* for a while and see which one came out the winner. She'd put her money on Rick.

"Who are you?" Detective O'Flannery asked in a quiet tone clearly meant to defuse the rapidly escalating situation.

"I'm Rick Sanchez, the coordinator of Yo, Amigo. And this source of yours better have a name, or I'll start by suing you personally for slander."

Mrs. Fallon, who hadn't spoken since they'd been seated, rose unsteadily to her feet and walked over to the detective. She barely came to his shoulder, but that didn't seem to intimidate her one whit.

"Young man, I will not allow you to come in here and defame the name of a decent, kindhearted man. It was bad enough that you tore the place apart, but saying such things about Reverend Miller puts you in cahoots with the devil, as far as I'm concerned, and I won't stand for it."

"Amen, Mrs. Fallon," Kate said.

Dana observed that Detective O'Flannery was looking considerably less sure of himself than he had been when he'd walked in. He appeared to realize that he'd lost his sole ally.

"I know that all of you admired and respected Reverend Miller," he said gently. He looked at Dana. "And you loved him. But no one knows everything there is to know about another human being. I've talked to parents whose child has just committed murder, and they will give testament that no child of theirs would ever do such a thing. It's a defense mechanism. We don't want to see evil in those we love."

Dana shot out of her chair at that. "My husband was not evil, Detective. If you think we're biased on the subject, then ask any member of his congregation. Ask the kids in Chicago whose lives were turned around because of him. Ask the patients in the hospital who sat beside their beds when they were ill? Ask some of our elderly parishioners whom they called in the middle of the night when some noise frightened them? It wasn't the police, dammit. It was my husband. If you think that man could ever, *ever* sell drugs, then you are so delusional you're a danger to the community."

"Amen," Kate said again.

Detective O'Flannery looked more distressed by Kate's defection than by Dana's actual tirade.

"I'm just telling you what was in the warrant," he said defensively.

"Was the source named in the warrant?" Rick asked. "I'll bet I already know the answer to that. He wasn't. Because he was too much of a coward to come forward publicly with such ridiculous charges. He would have been laughed out of town. I could give you a list, though. There are half a dozen people in Chicago with the clout to convince a judge that what they're saying should be taken seriously enough to justify a search warrant in another jurisdiction. We could start with the mayor. Now, there's a man worthy of a police investigation."

The detective held up his hands. "Whoa, let's not start throwing mud around."

"Excuse me?" Dana protested. "Did I hear you correctly? You come in here slandering my husband, and now you're worried about a little mud being splattered on some other good citizens?"

"Settle down," the detective said sharply. "All of you. First of all, I don't know who the Chicago source was. Second, I didn't say I bought into the theory. I was just telling you what was in the warrant. That's one reason I came along. The charge didn't match anything I'd ever heard about Reverend Miller. I wanted to see that everything was done by the book."

Dana gestured toward Ken's office. "You call that doing things by the book?"

He shrugged. "Thorough searches get messy."

"Not when I do them," Dana countered.

His gaze narrowed at that. "Meaning?"

She decided it might be best if he didn't know that she was launching her own investigation and that it had gotten more urgent in the past half hour.

"Nothing," she said.

He didn't look as if he believed her, but he apparently decided to let it pass.

"I know you want to believe in your husband, Mrs. Miller. The rest of you, too, but the truth is, it looks as if the Chicago police were onto something."

"What?" all four people in the room chorused in disbelief.

"You can't be serious," Rick said.

Dana felt a huge knot forming in the pit of her stomach. Something was going on here, something dark and dangerous and far more complicated than she'd ever imagined.

"What did you find?" she asked softly.

"Traces of marijuana, a small amount of cocaine and evidence that he'd had crack tucked away, too," he said unhappily. "I'm sorry."

"Oh, sweet heaven," Mrs. Fallon murmured, and sank back onto her chair.

"It was planted," Kate said with absolute certainty.

"You bet your life it was," Dana agreed. She shot a venomous look straight into Detective Dillon O'Flannery's eyes. "You said traces of drugs were found. How much?"

"Not a lot," he admitted. "Just enough to prove it had been there."

"Not enough to cost anyone big bucks, right? Not enough to put a dent into a real drug operation?"

"No."

"Just enough to make him look guilty of some crime," she concluded. "If that doesn't suggest planting, I don't know what would. And I intend to prove it, or die trying."

Despite her trembling knees, she managed to stand and then to walk out the door, head held high. She would not cry in front of Detective O'Flannery. She would not let him see how deeply she was shaken by what he'd said. The thought of so much as a trace of all those drugs in Ken's office made her sick to her stomach.

She felt Kate slip up beside her.

"Are you okay?" she asked in a hushed voice.

"I will be," she said stiffly. "As soon as I see them all in hell for what they're trying to do to my husband."

10

As soon as they were out of sight of Detective O'Flannery, Dana whirled on Rick and slapped him with all of her might. Frustration, blind rage, hurt all went into that slap. The force of the blow felt exhilarating. Rick's eyes widened with surprise, but to his credit he held his temper, even as a red mark in the shape of her hand took form on his cheek.

"Mind if I ask what that was for?" he inquired.

"You're the one responsible for this," she accused, refusing to massage her stinging hand or to apologize for using it to strike him. "If Ken had never gotten involved with you, he wouldn't be dead and none of this would be happening."

She was tempted to smack him again, but Kate apparently sensed her intention and slipped an arm around her waist as they walked into the house and began murmuring soothing reminders about using honey, not vinegar, to catch flies. The comment was practical, so very much Kate, that Dana managed a faint smile. Her temper calmed. A vague hint of embarrassment stole over her. She had never resorted to physical assaults in her life, but she'd slapped Rick twice now. Obviously, the man did not bring out the best in her.

"Okay, okay, no more physical abuse," she promised.

"Glad to hear it," Rick said, gingerly touching his jaw. "Are you ready to go into Chicago now?"

Dana had forgotten all about the plans that had obviously brought him to the church in search of her in the first place. She wanted to tell him that she wasn't going, that she was going to stay right where she was and think about what the detective had told them, but she couldn't. The answers, including those to this latest twist, were still at Yo, Amigo. They had to be. Someone there, possibly even Rick himself, had set her husband up. With the police adding up false information, suppositions and planted drugs, finding the truth was more critical than ever.

"Just let me freshen up," she said to buy herself a few minutes to compose herself. She couldn't spend five minutes alone with Rick in her current frame of mind or, despite her very recent promise, they'd wind up in a ditch somewhere with her trying to pummel him to death.

"If you'd like," she told him, "you can put the cameras and other equipment in the car. Everything's by the front door. I'm afraid I never made it to the drugstore to get extra memory cards, though."

When he saw the gathered photographic supplies, he seemed surprised that she'd done as much as she had. "No problem. We'll stop on the way." He glanced at Kate. "Are you coming along?"

Kate looked toward Dana, as if awaiting some sort of signal. Dana said, "No, she can't. She has things to do here."

Rick nodded. "Good to see you again, Mrs. Jefferson. Dana, I'll be in the car, whenever you're ready."

As soon as he'd gone outside, Kate whirled on her.

"What things do I have to do here? Are you sure you ought to be alone with that man? There are enough sparks flying between you two to light up downtown Chicago. Why can't you just meet the man halfway?"

"I just can't, that's all. I don't trust him," Dana said defensively. Nor was she willing to admit that she feared letting down her guard for so much as a second around him. Right now, thank goodness, she wanted to kill him, not sleep with him. She wasn't so sure that would last forever, though. At the moment, she'd be grateful just to get through the rest of the day without making a fool of herself.

"Okay, so don't trust him. Just be nice." At a sharp look from Dana, Kate held up her hands. "Okay, okay, what do you want me to do?"

"Finish going through that list of church members and check off anyone whose name sets off any sort of alarms."

"Such as?"

"Rumors about a sudden change in lifestyle, nasty tempers, shady business dealings, whatever. Anything you've heard that might seem remotely suspicious. If you finish that, try going to the newspaper morgue to see if any of the names show up in articles related to any kind of corruption, drugs, excessive parking tickets, whatever."

"I take it we can exclude those receiving media accolades."

Dana thought about that. "Not necessarily. If they've gotten any kind of positive publicity, maybe they'd go to some extremes to avoid having their reputation tarnished."

"That's pretty twisted logic," Kate said.

"We're dealing with a pretty twisted mind. This person not only killed a minister, but he's trying to frame him in a drug conspiracy and throw the police offtrack."

"Okay," Kate agreed, accepting the theory. "I've got it. What time do you want to get together?"

Dana thought of the trip to and from Chicago, the class she was scheduled to teach. They were already running late. As much as she wanted to know what Kate learned tonight, she knew she'd be too exhausted to absorb it.

"Unless you stumble on something urgent, come over in the morning," she suggested eventually.

"I'll leave a message for you if I find out anything that can't wait until morning," Kate promised. "Now run along. It's not good to keep an impatient man waiting."

"If it were up to me, he could wait until hell freezes over," Dana muttered. But she turned and left just the same.

She slid into Rick's car without speaking. Despite her earlier fury, she felt a renewed surge of guilt when she saw that his cheek still bore traces of her slap. She had never believed that violence solved anything. She had never, ever resorted to it herself. She'd never even gently swatted one of her kids to make a point.

She could blame her behavior on stress, but that would be excusing the inexcusable. She vowed then and there to do as Kate had asked and force herself to give Rick Sanchez a break. She was lucky that he was still speaking to her after the way she'd treated him. He could have reneged on his promise to help her earn the trust of the kids at Yo, Amigo and she would have had no one to blame but herself. There were plenty of allies in the world who didn't like each other. She supposed the two of them could fit into that category.

Rick pulled out of the driveway and headed toward Chicago, without breaking the silence. He seemed neither angry nor upset, merely thoughtful.

When she could stand the silence no longer, Dana

decided to take the first step in achieving détente. "I'm sorry I slapped you," she said softly.

"I know."

"I wasn't angry with you so much as the circumstances. It was really Detective O'Flannery I wanted to hit."

"I know."

She frowned at him. "You don't know everything, Sanchez."

He glanced toward her and shrugged. "Maybe not everything," he conceded. "But when it comes to you, I think I know quite a lot. I saw the way you kept clenching and unclenching your fists while O'Flannery was talking. Frankly, I wouldn't have minded taking a shot at the man myself."

"I wish you had," she said wistfully.

"We'll get whoever's behind all this, Dana. I promise you that."

She listened to the conviction in his voice and wished she could believe him, wished even more that she could trust him. Unfortunately, she doubted she would ever entirely rid herself of the possibility that he was involved in this investigation only so that he could cover any tracks that might lead back to Yo, Amigo.

If she was wrong, though, then Rick suddenly had motives almost as powerful as her own for wanting to know who was behind not only Ken's death, but the defamation of Yo, Amigo's reputation.

He had to be insane, flat-out, men-in-white-coats insane. From the moment he'd tackled Dana Miller during her middle-of-the-night quest inside Yo, Amigo, Rick had been so aware of her, so aroused by her that he could barely think straight in her presence.

And all the while his body was humming with electricity, his mind was reeling with guilt. This was Ken's wife, for God's sake. Ken's widow, he amended with a sigh. And that, somehow, made the lust he was feeling that much worse.

After each encounter, he vowed to rein in his feelings. He was finally forced to accept that it was like trying to rein in a runaway stagecoach. It could be done, but it required almost superhuman, John Wayne–caliber effort.

Even so, even knowing that he was tempting fate by spending one single second in her presence, here he was, drawing her deeper and deeper into his world. The stupidity of it nagged at him all during the drive into Chicago. His only consolation was the fact that Ken had believed in Yo, Amigo as deeply as Rick did. He would not want to see it brought down as a part of any investigation of his murder.

Ken would also want the people who'd been closest to him—Dana and Rick himself—to work as a team, not as enemies. They needed to be united, if they were going to fight what appeared to be an intricate conspiracy surrounding his death.

The drug charge leveled by that detective was so outlandish that Rick had trouble taking it seriously. But he knew in his gut that it was as serious as a bullet in the chest. Whoever had planted those drugs and leaked their presence to the police was determined not only to sully Ken's name, but to bring down Yo, Amigo. If Rick got to that person before the police did, the court system was going to have to wait in line to mete out justice. After he finished, prison would probably look good to the creep.

He glanced over at Dana as he turned into the tiny parking lot beside a neighborhood drugstore to pick up the supplies she needed. She seemed lost in thought. He was finally coming to realize what Ken had known all along, that she was a loyal, admirable woman. Despite all that crap that Detective O'Flannery had thrown at her, she had never once lost faith in her husband. Rick couldn't help wondering what it would be like to have someone believe in him so thoroughly.

Few people ever had done so. Certainly not the immigrant parents who'd given up on him when he'd turned to gang life because of the sense of power and belonging it gave to him in this strange new country. Surely not the cops, who'd prayed for just one slip, just one charge against him they could make stick. Even his own followers hadn't believed in him with that kind of blind faith. He'd just happened to be the one who'd ascended to a position of power because he was a little bigger, a little tougher than the rest.

Ken, however, had believed in him from the start. Even though he was still struggling to turn his life around when they'd met five years ago, even though Yo, Amigo was little more than an idea, it was an idea that Ken had embraced. He'd had the finesse that Rick lacked to pull the program together. Rick had had the street smarts to attract a few toughened kids into the program, but Ken had been able to handle the power brokers, to squeeze dollars out of empty city coffers. The program existed today because they had trusted and respected each other.

Even so, that wasn't the same as having the trust and respect of a woman. Rick wasn't sure why that was so, only that when he'd seen that firm belief shining in Dana Miller's eyes, he had envied Ken more than he could say.

"What kind of memory cards do you need?" he asked when he'd pulled into a parking space.

"I'll run in and get them," she said at once.

"I'll go," he countered, just as firmly. "My turf, remember?"

The corners of her mouth twitched in the beginnings of a smile. "We'll go together so I can see what they have. Will that suit you?"

Rick nodded. "I'm relieved to see that you can compromise."

"How about you? Can you compromise?"

"Of course."

She regarded him skeptically. "Sorry. I don't see it."

"Don't see what?"

"You ever backing down, once you've taken a stance. You're too arrogant, too bullheaded."

He grinned. "I've grown rather fond of you, too."

She scowled at that. "It wasn't a compliment."

"I know."

They were still bickering as they bought the memory cards and returned to the car. Nonsense bickering. Bickering that to Rick seemed almost to border on the affectionate. There was no more venom in it. It was as if that vicious slap had finally cleared the air between them and made peace possible.

"You know, Dana, if you're not careful, you and I might actually wind up being friends."

"No way," she muttered hastily.

A little too hastily, it seemed to Rick. He wondered how long it would take her to accept the possibility that animosity and distrust could evolve into friendship. He could envision it, just as he could almost envision a day when they would become lovers. No doubt suggesting that would earn him another slap, despite the truce they had declared.

Still, he couldn't help wondering what would happen if he bridged the distance between them and kissed her the way he wanted to, deeply and thoroughly. Would she slap him for that, too, or would she melt in his arms?

The temptation to find out was almost irresistible. Fortunately, though, he had a lot of practice at resisting temptation. He'd had to curb his once healthy appetite for petty theft. He'd had to tame his violent temper, even in the face of provocation like that scene in Ken's office earlier.

Surely, he could resist the compelling urge to kiss a woman whose heart belonged to someone else, a woman who wouldn't even admit to liking him.

Of course, that was the point, he thought wryly. He wanted to force an admission that she wasn't as immune to him as she claimed.

"Are you planning to start the car any time soon, or shall I get out and walk the rest of the way?" she inquired tartly, breaking into his thoughts.

He noticed that she was shifting uncomfortably under his gaze. He found that telling enough, for the moment. The kiss could wait awhile longer, he concluded.

But it wouldn't be too much longer. Minutes, maybe. Hours. Days. A few months at most. Time for him to make sure that more was involved here than his always healthy libido. Not even a saint could be expected to show much more restraint than that. And the word on the street had been pretty consistent about one thing for years now: Rick Sanchez was no saint.

11

Dana had the uneasy feeling that something other than cooperating to find Ken's killer was on Rick's mind. It had been a long time since she had been the subject of a fascinated gaze from a man other than her husband, but she hadn't forgotten the signs. There had been a knowing gleam in Rick's eye, an easily recognizable flaring of pure lust. She had trembled under that look. It was a reaction she wasn't crazy about.

Kate had mentioned the sparks in the air between them. They had both interpreted that as pure friction, but what if it was more? No, she thought quickly, she wouldn't allow it to be anything more. She didn't even like Rick Sanchez very much. She certainly didn't trust him. How could she possibly be attracted to him? The lust, if it existed at all, was completely one-sided. It had to be.

Which didn't mean, of course, that she didn't have to deal with it. If Rick were ever crazy enough to try something, if he dared to risk this tenuous truce between them by putting the moves on her, she would simply explain to him, in no uncertain terms, that he was way, way off base.

She found herself grinning suddenly at the image of the prim lecture she intended to deliver. Yes, indeed, Rick Sanchez was definitely the kind of man who'd respond well to being told that something—or someone, in this case—was off-limits. He'd probably try to seduce her just to prove how wrong she was. She didn't have quite enough confidence in her resistance to put herself to that particular test.

"Has anyone signed up for the class?" she asked, hoping the move to a safer topic would alter the sizzling tension in the car.

Rick grinned. "These kids don't exactly sign up for things. They show up or they don't. You could have one kid there today or twenty."

"Or none?"

"That's a distinct possibility."

Her spirits sank. She was counting on this overture to pave the way for her. Frustrated, she met Rick's gaze. "Okay. What then?"

"You'll just have to find another way to win them over."

His nonchalant response grated. "You really don't intend to cut me any slack here, do you?" she asked.

"None," he agreed as he pulled into his space behind the building.

His attitude solidified her resolve. "Don't look so smug," she retorted. "I've always loved a good challenge."

"Then you ought to be in heaven here," he said, leading the way inside.

Instead of taking her to his office, he continued past it to a small classroom. It was filled with a hodgepodge of desks and chairs of various shapes and sizes. Wood and Formica surfaces alike had been scarred with graffiti. The blackboard bore a similar collection of four-letter words in English, along with what she assumed to be the Spanish equivalents.

"English lessons?" she inquired.

Rick muttered something unintelligible under his breath and grabbed an eraser. The blackboard was wiped clean in a matter of seconds. There wasn't anything to be done about the desks.

He looked around the dreary, cramped room with a critical gaze, then glanced at her. "It's not much, but it's the best I can do."

"It'll be fine," she assured him. "We won't be spending much time inside, anyway."

Alarm flared his eyes. "Why not? Where are you thinking of going?"

Dana thought that ought to be obvious. "Outside," she said patiently. "It's the best place to teach photography. All of the classes I took spent at least half the time outdoors and most of the rest in the darkroom. Outdoors is where you find the interesting faces, the best scenery, the architectural curiosities. It's also the best way to work with lighting, to learn to use the camera's settings for the best effects. It's where I have the most experience. I've never done much indoor or studio work."

Rick was shaking his head before she could finish. "Dana, I've told you how I feel about you being out in this neighborhood. It's not safe."

"I'm not going to be alone. The kids will be with me."

"I don't know," he said uneasily. "You'll be the only *gringa* around, an easy target."

His choice of words startled her, but she saw at once that he was right. It was an unnecessary risk, one she didn't dare take with three sons counting on her safe return.

"Can't you teach the class here, indoors?" he suggested.

"For a week or two, maybe, while I go over the basics. But if you want these kids to really get some experience, we'll have to venture out sooner or later. Do you have any kind of van to take them someplace else?"

"Are you kidding? On our budget, we can't afford bus fare. Look, just make it later. I'll rearrange my schedule so I can come, too."

She found that prospect almost as disturbing as the idea of being a target. She quickly glanced around the empty room. "All of this planning seems like a moot point, at the moment. The room isn't exactly overcrowded with students, and it's already after four."

"Time is another problem," he explained with a grin. "They have no sense of it. Part of that's rebellion, I'm sure. Part of it's because they've never had to adhere to any particular structure in their lives."

"Is there a bell or something?"

"Nope. Around here, when it's time for a class or a meeting, there's only one thing to do—go around the building and round them up."

Dana nodded. "Okay. You do that. I'll get set up."

"Sorry, *querida,*" he said with apparent amusement. "Any rounding up will have to be done by you. I have work to do this afternoon."

She stared at him. "You expect me to go out there and talk those kids into coming to my class?"

He winked at her. "Pick the right kid and the rest will follow."

She scowled at him. "Any hints?"

"Nope. I think I'll let you go with your instincts. I'll see you around five-thirty or so. That should be about as much as you can take, before you start wondering what you've gotten yourself into and whether it's worth it."

With that new taunt left hanging in the air, he was gone. Dana sank down on a chair and stared around her. Even if she thought of this as being some sort of elaborate undercover scheme, it was still, without a doubt, the oddest investigation she'd ever conducted.

Or attempted to conduct, she amended, conceding that she hadn't actually done the first bit of real investigating yet. She'd thrust herself into the midst of potential informants, but until she actually held a conversation with someone, the effort was pretty much wasted.

She could sit here until five-thirty and claim that she'd tried, but Rick would see right through that. Or she could march herself out into the main gym and see who was hanging out. If she ever expected to get any answers, there was only one option. She headed for the gym.

She was barely a few feet from the classroom when she spotted Maria coming her way. The teen beamed at her.

"*Señora* Miller, you did come back. I had to see it with my own eyes. I was sure you would tell Rick to go jump into a stream."

Dana was so relieved to see a friendly face that she didn't bother correcting the fractured phrase. "Hi, Maria. I'm about to go in search of prospective students. Any idea where I should start?"

"Rick said I shouldn't interfere," she said, then grinned. "But if I were you, I would speak first to Marco."

Dana instantly recalled the young man who had surveyed her so insolently on her previous visit. He'd seemed dark and dangerous to her then, even with Rick beside her. He was not the person she wanted most to deal with. Naturally, though, that made him the obvious choice. She sighed.

"Where is he?"

"In the gym, as always. He may have given up the streets, but he cannot live without turf of his own. In the gym, he is king."

"Exactly how did he claim the title?" Dana inquired worriedly.

"As a lion would," Maria said, innocently creating a very worrisome image. "I must run, before Rick misses me and guesses that I've come to see you."

She vanished almost as quickly and quietly as she'd appeared.

"Ah, yes," Dana muttered with a trace of bitterness. "We wouldn't want to upset Rick."

Sucking in a deep breath, she turned into the gym. Sure enough, Marco was sitting on a bench on the sidelines, holding court. At the sight of her, he fell silent. His sensual mouth curved into a smirk as he lazily surveyed her from head to toe as she approached.

"I see the *padre's* widow is back," he said when she drew closer. "I did not expect it."

"Life is just full of unexpected twists and turns," Dana replied.

"What brings you back out of your safe little suburban world?"

As an investigator who frequently faced belligerent, defensive individuals, she knew there was only one way to deal with a man like Marco. She had to stand up to him and refuse to let his sarcasm get to her. Just as Rick had been doing with her, she couldn't help thinking. He probably thought she had a worse attitude than Marco. Now would be a good time to start changing that, she concluded.

"And here I thought you were so tapped into everything that goes on around here," she said, making the taunt light, but hopefully effective enough to catch his attention. "Haven't you heard? I'm teaching a photography class."

"Now, there's something almost as practical as basket weaving," he said, drawing nervous laughter. "Another example of the Anglo notion of keeping idle hands busy."

Dana shrugged off the glib remark. "Who knows? Maybe someone here will have a good enough eye to become a fashion photographer or a photojournalist."

She glanced at the pregnant girl seated next to him. Rosa, wasn't it? Even with the extra weight she carried with the baby, she was a beautiful girl. She had gleaming dark hair, high cheekbones and sparkling eyes that, despite Marco, glinted with interest. "Perhaps Rosa, with the right portfolio to show around, could become a model," she added.

She gave him the same sort of insolent going-over that he'd given her. "Even you, Marco, have an interesting look about you. A bit of attitude…" A massive understatement, she thought. "Strong features. With the right pictures, an agency might take a chance on you. Or with your aggression, you could take your camera into places no one else would dare and become a world-famous photographer."

A little of his disdain faded, replaced by the tiniest hint of interest. She prayed that the limb she was going out on wouldn't get chopped off behind her. She did know a handful of people in the modeling business and at ad agencies in Chicago, as well as a few journalists. She could get pictures into their hands. She had no idea what their reactions would be, though.

She did know, however, that there was a danger in building false hope here. Already, these young people had seen too many dreams dashed—their parents' and their own.

"Don't get me wrong," she added as a deliberate caution. "Either side of the camera, it's hard work. It's not something for a coward to tackle. It's a risk. If it pays off, it could pay off very well. Or it could amount to nothing at all."

"You know people in this business?" Rosa asked, eyes shining with excitement. Clearly she had been intrigued by Dana's words.

"Shut up," Marco ordered her harshly.

"No, you," the girl retorted, undaunted by the order. "It doesn't hurt to listen, to see what she has to say. That is your trouble, Marco, you never want to listen. You are twenty-two and you think you know everything."

Dana waited to see which one would win the argument. To her astonishment, something in Marco's eyes softened as he gazed at Rosa.

"You would want to do this?" he asked. "You would be a model?"

Rosa rubbed her hands over her rounding belly. "When the baby is born, I would like to know I can support her without taking help from anyone."

Marco said something to her in rapid Spanish, but she refused to back down. Chin up, she faced him defiantly. Eventually he shook his head, his expression resigned.

"Take the class, if it will make you happy," he said, his tone indulgent.

Rosa's expression turned speculative then. "You, too, I think," she told him, clearly not satisfied with her own small victory. "We could do this together."

Dana thought she detected a faint hint of wistfulness in Marco's expression, but he refused to accede to Rosa's request.

"I am not wasting my time in this way," he said with finality. "The rest of you may do as you like."

Dana seized the concession as the best she was likely to get. "Rosa, come along. If any of the rest of you would like to join us—even if it's just to watch what's going on—we'll be in the classroom for the next hour."

To her disappointment, only Rosa followed. Inside the classroom, Rosa regarded her sympathetically. "It is a waste of your time to teach for just one, is it not?" she asked worriedly.

"No," Dana said at once. "I would rather have one person who is truly interested than a whole roomful of people who are just killing time." Plus, there would be only one to see how inexperienced she was at this teaching business.

"Now, tell me, would you rather learn how to use the camera or would you rather let me take some pictures and see how they do?" she asked Rosa.

The teenager smiled shyly. "Do you truly think I am pretty enough to be a model?"

"I'm not an expert, but yes, I do."

"Then take the pictures, please. I would like to have one to show the baby someday, even if nothing else ever comes of this."

"Why don't I tell you what I'm doing as I set up anyway? It never hurts to know a little about what the photographer's job is. I don't have all the equipment that a professional would have, but we can make do," she said as she set up her tripod, loaded a fresh memory card into the best of the cameras and mounted it on the stand. "I'll have to use natural light, which puts us at a disadvantage, compared to all those fancy lights in a photography studio, but it may make the pictures more interesting. I'll do a few in black-and-white, then some in color."

Rosa watched what she was doing with obvious fascination. As soon as everything was set up, Dana pointed her toward the teacher's desk. "Let's try something up there," she suggested.

Rosa touched her face worriedly. "My makeup and hair, they are okay?"

"You look beautiful," Dana assured her. "Very natural." She just prayed she could capture that beauty. Though she'd taken more than one photography class for the pure enjoyment of it, she had very little experience with anything remotely like fashion photography. She was far better at catching an errant husband sneaking into his lover's apartment, or an insurance cheat playing volleyball when he should have been flat on his back. Those pictures needed only to be clear enough to prove deceit, not crisp enough to sell a product or lovely enough for a gallery showing.

Rosa sat stiffly where Dana had directed her. She needed to relax, so Dana began talking, asking questions about the baby. At once Rosa's expression became more animated. No matter the circumstances of her pregnancy, it was clear that the baby was going to be very much loved. Only when the talk turned to the future did her brow furrow.

"It is going to be difficult," she said in a whisper. "I have no job. I have not even graduated from high school yet. I dropped out because of the baby, but I will go back when I can. I want my child to be proud of me."

"How old are you?"

"Seventeen."

So terribly young, Dana thought sadly. "What about your family? Can they help?"

"My family has very little extra, and my father is very angry about the baby. Only my mother has been able to keep him from throwing me out into the streets," Rosa responded matter-of-factly, though the shadows in her eyes made it evident how much this hurt her. "He has not spoken one word to me since I told him. He says I have shamed him."

"Where does Marco fit in?" Dana asked as she clicked the shutter, shot after shot, trying to capture the lightning-quick shifts in mood on Rosa's face. "Is he the baby's father?"

Rosa laughed. "No, no," she said at once. "Marco is my brother. You must excuse him for the way he is. Macho is very important to him. Inside, though, he is very soft, especially when it comes to me and the baby. If it comes to that, if my father throws me out, Marco will take me in. It will cramp his lifestyle, he says, but he will do it."

"So Marco has many girlfriends?" Dana asked.

"Very many," Rosa said. "He cannot settle on any one. I tell him he is scared of commitment."

"And what does he say?"

Rosa shrugged. "He says to mind my own business."

"But you don't," Dana guessed.

"Of course not," Rosa said with a grin. "He is my older brother. It is my duty to pester him."

Dana was just wondering whether she had gained Rosa's confidence, whether she dared to venture on to more serious questions, when the girl said softly, "You must miss the *padre* very much."

Taken by surprise, tears sprang to Dana's eyes before she could prevent them. It happened that way sometimes, when she was caught off guard. For a few minutes at a time, she would almost forget that he was gone and then a reminder would come, just like this, and it would shatter her momentary tranquility.

"I do," she said. "Very much. Did you know my husband well?"

"We all knew him well. He was very much loved here," Rosa told her.

"By everyone?"

"Oh, yes," the girl said fervently.

"So no one at Yo, Amigo would have harmed him?" Rosa looked shocked by the question. "Never!"

"May I ask you another question?"

"About the *padre?*"

"Indirectly. Is anyone here involved with drugs?"

Rosa looked uncomfortable, and it was a very long time before she finally answered. "There have been drugs," she conceded with obvious reluctance. "But no more. Rick does not allow it. If one of us is caught in the building with drugs, or even high on drugs, we are out of the program. That is the way it is and everyone knows it. It is very strict."

"Has anyone been kicked out?"

"Not for a long time."

Dana wondered whether they measured time the same way. "What do you mean, a long time?"

"A few months," Rosa said. "It was before Christmas. November, maybe."

"Who was caught?"

Rosa's gaze narrowed suspiciously. "Why do you want to know this? It was a long time ago."

A few months, Dana thought, barely two, in fact, before Ken's death. Could there have been some connection?

"Not so very long ago," she said. "Who was it, Rosa?"

Her expression passive, Rosa stood up then. "I think I have said too much already," she said, heading for the door. She paused. "Thank you very much for taking my pictures," she said politely.

Dana knew she would only lose ground if she persisted with her questioning. She smiled. "I'll bring them in for you to see tomorrow."

Despite her evident uneasiness, Rosa couldn't hide her excitement. "So soon?"

"I'll print them at home tonight," Dana promised, thinking that the time in front of her computer would be more relaxing than many other things she could be doing. "Will you be here tomorrow afternoon?"

"Yes," Rosa said, clearly unable to resist the lure of those photographs. "I will be here."

Then she hurried away, leaving Dana to wonder just who Rosa was trying to protect. Her first guess would have been Marco, the big brother who'd promised Rosa his protection. But Marco was very much involved in the program. If he'd been banished for drug use, he wouldn't be here now.

Or would he? Was any banishment short-term, no more than a few weeks, perhaps? It was a question for Rick. Would he go as tight-lipped as Rosa had, or would he be honest with her? Maybe this would be the first real test of exactly where his loyalties lay—with his dead friend or with his program. Dana feared she already knew the answer.

When push came to shove, Yo, Amigo would win every time.

12

Dana collected her equipment and took it with her to Rick's office. When she entered, Maria glanced up from her work and smiled.

"There you are. How did it go?"

"I had one student," Dana admitted. "Rosa."

"Do not be discouraged. It is a start. Rosa will tell the others and next time, there will be more."

Dana was not so sure of that, given the last words she and Rosa had spoken. "I suppose," she said, trying not to sound too dispirited. "Is Rick free?"

"Actually he had to leave for a bit. There was a meeting he had forgotten. He said for you to hang in." She tilted her head thoughtfully. "Or was it hang out? Anyway, he will be back shortly. You could wait in his office, if you do not mind the clutter. He will not let me touch anything in there. He says he knows exactly where everything is, and if I organize it, he will be lost."

Dana seized the opportunity. At last, she would have free rein to do some serious snooping. "I don't mind at all," she said, trying not to sound too eager.

"Would you like to see a magazine? We have some that were donated. Most are in Spanish, I'm afraid, but there is a *Newsweek* from last December. That is not too old. And a *Reader's Digest*. That is timeless, yes?"

"That's okay. I'll be fine."

Maria's expression brightened hopefully. "Maybe you would prefer to see some information on the program," she suggested. "We have several papers that were prepared for fundraising and for grants. The *padre* helped us to write them."

"Yes," Dana said, careful to disguise her eagerness. "I'd love to see whatever you have about Yo, Amigo. You don't by any chance have a file of articles that have been done about the program, do you?"

Maria nodded. "Oh, yes, we save them all." She wrinkled her nose. "Even the bad ones."

So not all of the media coverage had been positive, Dana thought. Who were the critics? she wondered. Would they provide some clue about the murder? Or was she grasping at straws to think that opponents of the program might kill as part of some Machiavellian plot to force its closing?

Never before had she been involved in a case in which the victim had been so universally loved. Except for those who disagreed with Ken's philosophy regarding the gangs, there simply were no obvious starting points, at least when it came to identifying people with a motive to do Ken harm.

And yet she couldn't accept the possibility that his killing had been random, even in an area known for its drive-by shootings. Why? Was it simply her own need to put a more meaningful label on the crime? A need to fix blame?

With the quick expertise of a very organized person, Maria put her hands on several thick files and handed them to Dana. "This will keep you busy for a while, yes?

Would you like coffee? One of the boys just brought in some *cafe Cubano*. It is very strong, but very good."

"That sounds wonderful." She took a tiny cup of the dark, sweet coffee with her into Rick's office and settled into the chair behind his desk, the file folders spread out in front of her.

Glancing around, she cursed the lack of a copy machine. She'd never be able to read everything in the time she had. Perhaps, though, there would be duplicates of some of the information on the program. She could take a set of those and concentrate for now on the promising batch of clippings.

Sure enough, inside one folder she found several copies of a slick brochure on Yo, Amigo that had been designed for fundraising, along with a printed fact sheet about costs, goals and achievements. She folded up copies of both and stuffed them in her purse. The grant proposals in another were too bulky to deal with, for the moment, but she made a note of foundations and government offices that had been sent applications for funding.

Then she turned her attention to the articles. One by one, she lifted them from the folder. They were in no particular order that she could discern. They hadn't been sorted by topic or by date. She wondered at the latter. Even if the person filing them, presumably Maria, had simply been stuffing them into the folder, wouldn't they be in something close to chronological order, either front to back or back to front?

Instead, she found articles from two years before filed ahead of those from two weeks ago, followed by one from the program's dedication and grand opening. In fact, rather than being neatly filed, they appeared to have been jammed into the folder hurriedly.

Had someone else searched this particular file and perhaps removed something incriminating? Or, once again, was she grasping at straws? Maybe the person filing simply had no particular system. If Maria had recruited assistance from one of the kids Dana had met, it was entirely possible that the filing had been done haphazardly.

For the moment, perhaps she ought to create a log of the articles by source, date, headline and topic. Later, she could compare it to a search of the archives of area papers to determine which clipping or clippings might be missing, if any. It might lead her to a clue. It was a slim hope, but it was all she had.

Snatching a notebook from her purse, she made hasty entries, not even pausing long enough to read more than a cursory paragraph or two to familiarize herself with the article's focus. For the most part, there was nothing remarkable about the clippings. In fact, most were glowing accounts of the successes achieved.

There was an intriguing in-depth profile of Rick that she had to force herself not to at least skim. It would be easy enough to track down a copy on microfiche later at the local library if it wasn't available on the internet.

As she reached the last few clippings, she wondered at the lack of negative press, especially in light of Maria's claim that even the bad articles had been kept. The only article that could be considered remotely derogatory was one in which it was charged that the program had exceeded its budget. Even in that one, however, the critics had found that the excesses were justifiable and could easily be made up with the increased cash flow from the following year's contributions.

Just as she was about to replace the clippings, she spotted one tiny article that had been left in the folder. It was little more than a single paragraph with a two-line headline, probably tucked away in the newspaper's pages, just as it had been virtually lost in the folder. The headline made her heart pound.

DRUG CHARGES DISMISSED
AGAINST PROGRAM FOUNDER
Chicago police today conceded that there was no evidence to support drug allegations that had been made against Enrique (Rick) Sanchez, founder of the highly successful gang rehabilitation program. Sanchez was released after questioning.

Dana's hand trembled as she read and reread the clipping. Rick had been questioned about drugs. Now the police were convinced that Ken had somehow been tied to drug trafficking. Coincidence? She doubted it.

Why hadn't Rick told her about this after their meeting with O'Flannery earlier? Wouldn't that have been the logical time to explain that this wasn't the first time drug charges had been falsely made about someone connected to Yo, Amigo? Or had they been false? Had he just dodged a bullet because the evidence had been too scanty for a conviction?

She was still contemplating the possibilities and clutching the tiny article when Rick walked back into his office. Something in her face must have given her away, because the smile that had been starting at the corners of his mouth faded.

"What's wrong?"

She held out the clipping. "Explain this."

He didn't even reach out to take it. He just sighed. "The article says I was not guilty, does it not?"

"It says there was no evidence," she corrected. "There must have been some reason for the charge being made in the first place."

"As there was in Ken's case?" he asked dryly.

"It's not the same," she argued bitterly.

Rick's expression hardened. "Why? Because he was your husband?"

"Because he was a good and decent man who deplored the use of drugs."

"And I am not so good and decent?" he asked softly.

Her anger fading just as quickly as it had begun, she stared at him in confusion. "I don't know you that well."

"Exactly, *querida*. You do not know me at all."

Querida, she thought. It was the second time he had used the term of endearment with her. She was not his dear one, his darling, his sweetheart or his honey. She was nothing to him. And yet she couldn't bring herself to protest. The word was like a caress, impossible to ignore, even more difficult to undo, once it had been spoken. Its casual use inexplicably tightened the bond between them. She drew in a deep breath.

"Will you tell me what happened?"

The smile came back, but it was gently mocking. "Are you sure you wish to hear the truth? Maybe you would prefer the illusions, especially if they are damning."

"Truth is always better," she insisted.

"Not always," he said. "But in this case, yes." He held out his hand. "Come, I will tell you as we drive."

After a moment's hesitation, she tucked her hand into his and allowed him to gently tug her to her feet. The contact was too fleeting, too tempting. She was glad that she had so many things to carry. Otherwise she might have allowed him to keep her hand clasped in his.

Once they were in the car, however, Rick seemed to forget his promise. Instead of explaining about the drug charges, he asked how her class had gone.

"Only one participant," she said, and told him about Rosa.

"Do not look so sad. If you were able to get Rosa, others will follow. Marco has given it his tacit approval by allowing her to come."

"Then Marco has so much power?"

"He is a natural leader, yes."

Putting aside for the moment her determination to learn about those supposedly falsified drug charges, she focused on the opening he had given her to discover more about Marco. "Tell me about him," she said. "He seems like a very dangerous young man."

"Marco is a product of the streets—tough, smart and far too rebellious to play by anyone's rules."

"And yet he has played by yours, hasn't he?"

"Most of the time," Rick conceded.

"Why?"

"Because I bailed him out of some trouble once."

"With the police?"

"No, with a rival gang. They had him surrounded. I wouldn't have given ten cents for his life at that point."

"Let me guess. You just waded into the fray and evened the odds."

He grinned. "Something like that."

"In other words, you saved his life."

"He believes that I did."

"Which no doubt made it very easy to strike a bargain with him to get him into the program," she guessed.

"Not so easy," he corrected. "But less complicated than it might have otherwise been. He was forced to admit that it is possible to be strong without a gang behind you."

"How many others have you rescued in this way?"

"Fortunately, some of the others have been won over more easily. A few followed Marco. Others came because their parents or a teacher or a priest dragged them."

Dana knew enough about adolescent psychology to guess that those weren't the ones who stayed. "I'll bet Marco's friends have been your greatest successes," she said.

He nodded. "As I said, he is a natural leader. As was Tico."

"Have you ever regretted making Marco part of Yo, Amigo?"

"Why would I regret it?"

Dana tried to feel her way cautiously with her response. "Because of things he has done."

"Such as?"

"Drugs, maybe."

"We are back to that again," he said wearily. "Drugs have no place at Yo, Amigo."

"That doesn't mean that drug use never happens, does it?"

"No, but there are severe consequences."

"Banishment."

"Yes."

"Has Marco ever been kicked out for using or selling drugs?"

"Never."

He said it so firmly that Dana was taken aback. "Oh."

"Why so surprised?"

"It was something Rosa said. I guess I misunderstood," she admitted. If not Marco, though, then who would Rosa have been so quick to protect? The answer flashed as brilliantly as neon. Rick, of course.

"Rick, tell me about the drug charges against you."

"There were no charges," he reminded her. "Only allegations."

It was a distinction she couldn't quite grasp. "The police suspected you, right?"

"Because someone fed them false information," he said with transparent bitterness. "They had no choice but to investigate, just as they claimed with Ken. While they did, I stepped down as director. I had to abide by my own rules. Naturally it got blown all out of proportion in the media. Of course, when the investigation concluded there was no basis for the accusations, it was relegated to a brief item buried deep inside the newspaper."

"There was more in the papers than that clipping I had earlier?"

"Exposé after exposé for a few weeks last year," he confirmed. "It could have ruined us if so many had not had faith in me and in the program."

Dana was puzzled. "Those other articles weren't in the file."

Rick didn't seem especially surprised. "Maria hates anything negative, especially if it's about me. Perhaps she never clipped the articles."

"Do you really believe that?" Dana asked, thinking of Maria's declaration that she had included even the negative press.

"What's the alternative?"

"That someone deliberately removed them."

"Why?"

She shook her head. "I have no idea, but something tells me we ought to find out."

Rick didn't seem nearly as suspicious about the missing articles as she was. "Why take them from the file when anyone interested could easily look them up online?"

"Maybe the person who took them didn't realize that."

"Anyone knows that newspapers keep archives."

Maybe it was as simple as someone like Rosa trying to protect a man she liked and respected. "Even the kids at Yo, Amigo?" she asked.

He seemed startled by the suggestion. "Okay, no," he finally admitted. "They might not be sophisticated enough to realize that, but doesn't that shoot your theory of some sort of conspiracy all to hell?"

"What theory?"

He smiled. "The one you've been putting together in your head ever since the cops started to toss around allegations about Ken and drugs. Anyone capable of masterminding that kind of conspiracy would have a pretty good idea of how the media functions, wouldn't you say? In fact, they would have to have been manipulating it all along."

"I suppose."

He reached over and clasped her hand. "Don't look so depressed, *querida*. We will find the answers. First, though, we will have a good dinner. Seafood, I think. Brain food. Do you like shrimp?"

Dana nodded, though food was the last thing on her mind.

"Good, then. I know the perfect place."

"Only if it's my treat," she said, thinking of how tight the budget must be for the head of a shoestring program like Yo, Amigo must be.

"It was my idea. I will pay," he insisted, scowling at her.

His expression was so intractable that she backed down. She knew enough about machismo not to waste time fighting it.

"Whatever you say," she said.

He chuckled at that. "Ah, I wonder how long I can expect such docility to last."

"If you're very lucky, until dessert," she said.

"Then I will count my blessings until then."

13

Dana had kept her word. There had been no more interrogations over dinner, no snide remarks. It was the most pleasant, nonconfrontational time they had ever spent together, Rick concluded, feeling oddly out of sorts.

Ironically, he missed the quick-witted arguments, the sizzling tension. He missed the flash of temper in her eyes and even the snap of irritation in her voice. In fact, he found the sudden docility worrisome. It was still bothering him when he took her home.

He had just unloaded her cameras and equipment and tucked everything inside the front door when he caught her expression. She looked lost, so lost that he found himself inviting himself in for coffee, even though he knew that to stay was dangerous. Too much proximity and he wouldn't be able to resist stealing a kiss, just to know the taste and feel of her lips beneath his.

When she didn't say a word—not *go* or *stay*—he brushed past her and headed for the kitchen, leaving her no choice but to follow.

Since she seemed to accept him taking over, it was fortunate that the automatic coffeepot was in plain view, along with a bag of the gourmet blend he'd already dis-

covered she favored. He busied himself for several minutes with the coffee. He searched the cupboards for mugs
and the refrigerator for cream, then put it all down in
front of her.

Seated at the table and staring into space, she seemed
startled by the arrival of the steaming cup of coffee.

Rick turned a chair around backward and sat down
opposite her. With an expanse of solid oak between them,
he ought to be able to keep his hands to himself.

"Where'd you go on me?" he asked eventually.

She blinked and stared. "What?"

"You haven't said much since we left the restaurant.
What's going on?"

She attempted to force a smile, but it wavered, then
faded. "Just thinking, I guess."

"About?"

When she didn't respond, he hazarded a guess. "Ken,
right?"

She nodded and lifted her gaze to his. Her eyes were
brimming with unshed tears. "When we drove up here
tonight, for some reason, it finally sank in that this was
the way it was going to be from now on, coming home
to an empty house, living with all this silence. I mean,
intellectually I've known it before, but tonight I really
felt it. I felt dead inside."

Despite his promise to himself not to touch her, he
reached across the table for her hand. It was icy cold in
his. "You have three sons," he reminded her gently as her
skin warmed beneath his touch. "Soon they'll be back
here with you. The place will be so noisy you won't be
able to stand it."

"It won't be the same," she insisted. "And we won't
be here, not in this house, anyway. The church has been
very lenient about letting us stay on, but we'll have to

move eventually. I've already half made up my mind to go to Florida so we can be near my folks. The boys seem to like it there. The school is good. It would be a solution." She said it without much enthusiasm.

"Short-term or long-term?" Rick asked.

"I don't know," she said candidly. "The choice is too difficult. I haven't been able to deal with it. I managed to get the boys enrolled in school in Florida, because it made sense. They couldn't languish in limbo, while I wrestle with the future."

"Figuring out what's right is never easy," he said.

"And it's harder when you're not the only one involved," she said. "I could come back here and cope somehow. I lived in Chicago before I met Ken. I could do it again. The boys will see him everywhere."

"That's not necessarily a bad thing," Rick suggested. "The memories will be important to them. They'll treasure the unexpected reminders."

Oblivious to the tears that were now tracking down her cheeks, she stared at him hopefully. "You sound so sure."

"I am. You'll never forget, but it will get easier. Just don't look too far ahead. Stick with the moment."

"I guess that's what I did tonight," she said. "I looked too far ahead. I saw our anniversary and the Fourth of July and Thanksgiving and Christmas—all of them without Ken. He made them so special." She sighed, her expression wistful. "He made every day special."

Rick felt a sharp stab of something that might have been pure jealousy. It was inexplicable, but he suddenly wanted to be the one with whom she made so many unforgettable memories. He wanted to make her days— and her nights—so special that she could never forget.

And he felt like the worst sort of traitor for thinking it, especially when he was the kind of guy who didn't make commitments, didn't allow anyone to get too close. Hadn't that been his ex-wife's charge when she left, that she'd felt as if she were living with a stranger? He hadn't thought it possible that he could hurt Dana any more than he already had by inadvertently putting Ken in the line of fire, but he saw now that he could. He could offer her something he wasn't capable of delivering.

"I'd better go," he said, and stood up suddenly.

She stared at him in surprise. "You haven't touched your coffee."

"I shouldn't be drinking coffee at this hour, anyway. I'll never get to sleep." Not that he'd be getting much sleep, anyway. He'd by lying awake, tormented by pure lust for a women who wasn't his, a woman who'd lost her husband—his best friend—barely more than a month ago. Sick, sick, sick.

"Rick?" she said, her expression quizzical.

"What?"

"Does it bother you when I talk about Ken?"

It shouldn't, he thought, but, by God, it did. "Of course not," he said, denying the truth in order to clutch one tiny shred of honor.

"Are you sure? I guess I thought of all people, you would understand."

He reached down and squeezed her hand. "I do," he said. "I do understand, and it's okay. Talk about him all you want. I swear to you, I'll be a good listener, just not tonight, okay?"

Though her expression remained puzzled, she nodded. "Good night, then."

Impulsively, he leaned down and brushed a kiss across her forehead. "Sweet dreams, *querida*."

He was almost out the door, almost safely on his way,

when he heard her footsteps tapping rapidly across the wood floors.

"Rick," she called out.

He hesitated.

"Same time tomorrow? You'll take me back to Yo, Amigo? Rosa's pictures will be ready. She's anxious to see them."

He sighed. "Yes. At the same time," he promised, even though it was going to get harder and harder to see Dana and to protect himself and Yo, Amigo from the harm she could do.

For the longest time after Rick had gone, Dana sat in the still-dark living room, staring into space. She was more confused, more lost than ever. She needed to make some sort of progress in solving Ken's murder. That would give her a sense of purpose. It would also bring about closure, tie up all the loose ends and let her move on with her life, get back to her kids and give them the attention they deserved.

A fresh batch of tears leaked out, skimming down her cheeks, until her face and her blouse were both damp. Eventually she grew impatient with herself, tired of feeling vulnerable, exhausted by the uncharacteristic self-pity.

"Just get on with it," she ordered herself. She grabbed the phone and, oblivious to the time, punched in Kate's number.

Kate's groggy hello instantly filled her with regret. "I'm sorry," she apologized. "You're sleeping. I'll talk to you in the morning."

"No, no," Kate insisted sleepily. "It's okay. Is everything all right?"

"Sure," she lied, "I was just wondering what you'd

found out today. I forgot all about the time. I know you like to go to bed early so you can get up at the crack of dawn to see the kids off in the morning."

"It's not a problem," Kate reassured her. "I didn't learn anything earthshaking, though I do have a few people we might want to look at more closely. Do you want me to get the list now? It's downstairs."

"No. We can do it in the morning. Go back to sleep."

"You sure you don't want to talk? You sound upset."

"No, really. I'm fine. I should try to get some sleep myself, as soon as I call the boys to say good-night. Mother will probably be furious because I'll be getting them out of bed."

"No, she won't. She knows it's important that they hear your voice before they go to sleep. Call, sweetie."

"I will. Good night, Kate. I'm sorry I woke you."

"I'll see you first thing in the morning, and I'm going to want a full report on the kids. Give them my love."

Dana disconnected the call, then dialed her parents' number. Though all three boys were half-asleep and yawning in her ear, she was glad she'd made the call. She felt better, reassured that they were fine.

Afterward, still too restless to sleep herself, she took the memory card of the pictures she'd shot that afternoon to her computer. Though she'd intended the activity to be a distraction, she allowed her mind to wander.

Had she already met Ken's killer? Was it one of the ex–gang members at Yo, Amigo? Or did they merely know more than they were saying? She wanted to believe it was someone like Marco, someone arrogant and rude, whose capacity for violence lurked in the shadows of his eyes.

There was no evidence of it, though. Not yet, anyway. Not even a telltale hint of guilty knowledge in Rosa's eyes under Dana's direct questioning.

When she tired of the questions with no answers, she made print after print, stunned by the results. She couldn't help smiling at the Madonna-like quality of the pictures, especially those she'd shot in black-and-white. She had managed to capture the eternal serenity of the mother-to-be in Rosa's expression, as well as an occasional flash of the sexy siren and, in yet another shot, an impish girl.

Pleased with the unqualified success of her afternoon's work, she went back upstairs. She wandered restlessly for a bit, then eventually settled into Ken's chair, the afghan tucked around her. Her body must finally be getting used to the cramped sleeping arrangement, or else she was just thoroughly exhausted. Tonight, for the first time in weeks, she fell right to sleep.

Her dreams, once again, were not of Ken, as they had been ever since his death. Instead, for the second time, Rick Sanchez was there to taunt her. It was one more thing to hate him for, she told herself when she awoke, her body drenched with sweat. He'd stolen the only time she still had left with the man she'd loved—the dark hours of the night.

In the morning, Dana drank two cups of coffee before making another call to Florida to check in on the boys before they left for school. She'd managed to evade most of her mother's questions the night before, but she knew she wouldn't be able to do it forever.

Her mother picked up on the first ring, as she always did, as though she couldn't wait to hear what the caller had to say.

"Darling, how are you?" she asked, her voice laced with unmistakable concern. "I was hoping to get a chance to talk to you last night, after you spoke with the boys, but you'd already hung up by the time Bobby handed me the phone."

"I'm fine. How are the boys doing? Tell me the truth. Are they okay?"

"They miss you," she said bluntly. "When will you be back?"

"Soon."

"How soon?"

"I can't say for sure."

"Darling, you're not a private investigator anymore. Let the police handle the case."

Dana found the familiar refrain irritating, but managed to keep her tone patient. "We've been over this. I have to do whatever I can to find Ken's killer." She thought of the planted evidence of drugs. "It's gotten more complicated, more important than ever."

"I wish there were some other way."

"So do I, Mother, but there isn't. I'll be back as soon as I can. I promise. As soon as the case is solved, I'll get our things packed up and come back there to start looking for a house of our own to rent," she said impulsively.

"Then you are going to move here? You've decided?" There was no mistaking the excitement in her mother's voice. "Darling, that's wonderful. We'll love having you and the boys close by."

"We'll give it a try, at least until the end of the school year. If the boys like it, we'll make it permanent," she amended hastily to give herself an out in case they all hated it.

"Oh, I can't wait to tell your father. He'll be thrilled."

Dana closed her eyes and tried to share her mother's excitement. All she felt was the relief of having made some sort of a decision, set some sort of a timetable. She tried telling herself it was the smart thing to do. What was there to keep them in Chicago, really, now that Ken was gone? Nothing.

Still, it was home. It was where she had begun her family, where memories lurked around every turn, just as Rick had said the night before. Good memories, as well as all these recent bad ones.

"The memories will come with you," her mother said gently, as if Dana had spoken her thoughts aloud.

Dana smiled. "How did you know what I was thinking?"

"Because that's how we all react to change. We fear that we'll lose our link to the past. Don't you think Dad and I worried about that when we first came here after he retired? We don't lose those ties, though. I promise you. You'll be happy here. You'll have family close by. It will be good for all of you, you'll see."

"You're sure you and Dad can handle the boys for a little while longer?"

"Of course we can. You concentrate on wrapping up your investigation and getting down here to join us."

"I'll be there as quickly as I can be."

Apparently satisfied with that response, her mother let the matter drop. "I'll get the boys. They're dying to talk to you."

"Wait a second," Dana said, recalling her unfulfilled promise to Bobby. "I told Bobby I'd tell you that he's allowed to stay up an hour later than his brothers."

Her mother chuckled. "So, he did call you. I thought maybe he had. Okay, I'll bend the rule for him."

"He also mentioned that you never, ever give them pizza to eat."

"I thought home-cooked, nutritious meals were better," her mother said defensively.

"They are," Dana agreed. "But pizza won't hurt them once in a while. Do you mind?"

"If you don't object, I don't. I'll tell Dad to order it on my bridge night. I won't have to cook a meal before I go, and he won't have to worry about getting the food on the table. He'll also get to cheat on his diet. That should make everyone happy. I draw the line at anchovies, though. They give your father indigestion."

Dana chuckled at the thought of her boys asking for those "slimy little fish," as they called them. "That won't be a problem, I assure you," she said. "Thanks, Mom. I don't know what I'd do without you."

"Then isn't it fortunate that you don't have to? Love you, baby. Here's Bobby."

Dana talked to each of the boys, reassuring them again, now that they were wide awake and could understand her, that everything was okay back home and that she'd be back with them soon.

"Love you, Mommy," each one said in a rush.

"Granddad's taking us to the pool before school," Bobby explained, sounding more upbeat than he had during their past conversations. "The squirts have turned into little fish. I don't know what they'll do when we get back home and there's no pool. They'll probably shrivel up."

"Will not," Kevin shouted.

Dana laughed at the sound of the familiar bickering. For too long, right after Ken's death, they had been too quiet and subdued. Listening to them now, she honestly believed for the first time that they were going to be okay. Did that mean that she, too, would eventually be okay?

"Bye, sweetie," she said to her oldest. "Keep an eye on your brothers and mind Grandma and Granddad."

"Did you talk to her about my bedtime and the pizza?"

"Taken care of."

"Thanks, Mom. Bye."

"Bye," she said again, but the connection had been broken. Sensing that she wasn't alone, she glanced up and saw Kate standing in the doorway.

"Good girl," her friend said. "Everybody okay?"

"They sound like they're getting better every day. I can't wait to get back and see for myself."

"Then go."

"Not just yet, but soon. If I don't have the answers I need very soon, I'll make a quick trip just to get a look at them. I could use a couple of hugs and some sticky kisses myself." She stood up, grabbed the coffeepot and poured Kate a cup, then refilled her own. "Okay, let's have it. What did you find?"

"Like I told you last night, not much. I have half a dozen names that triggered some sort of an alarm when I came to them."

Dana's gaze narrowed. "What kind of alarm?"

"That's just it. I'm not sure. Maybe I just have an overactive imagination from hanging out with you. Or maybe there's something in the dim recesses of my mind, a newspaper article or TV report I didn't see yesterday." She shoved her list across the table. "Any of these ring any sort of bell for you?"

Dana scanned the list: Peter Drake, Miriam Kelso, Vincent Polanski, Lawrence Tremayne, Carolina Vincenzi, Gerrold Wald.

"All of these came from the roster of active church members, right?" she asked.

Kate nodded. "Don't you know them?"

"All but one of the women, actually. Who is Carolina Vincenzi?"

"Tall, refined-looking, with an aristocratic nose and

oodles of dark hair. Very good face-lift. She hardly looks a day over thirty-five, even though I know for a fact she's at least ten years older than that."

"Is she on here because you're jealous of her looks?" Dana asked dryly.

"No, she's on there because I overheard her talking about the gang kids that Ken was bringing into the community. She looks very much like a lady, but she has a trashy mouth and a streak of prejudice a mile wide. I wouldn't want to tangle with her. She's a tough cookie."

"What about Drake, Kelso, Polanski, Tremayne and Wald, especially Tremayne? He's head of the church elders, for goodness' sake. Surely he's above suspicion."

"I know," Kate said. "He's the kind of upstanding guy that any church would be proud to call its own. Good businessman. Decent father and husband." She shook her head. "I don't know what it is, but I don't trust him."

"He's been very kind to me since Ken died."

"I know. I can't explain my reaction."

"Has he ever said anything, done anything even remotely suspicious?"

"No," Kate conceded. "In fact, when I ran a check on him at the local newspaper, he had nothing but accolades. President of this, chairman of that, honored for something else."

"Maybe he's just a good guy," Dana said, thinking of the very polite man who'd always been eager to help Ken with any church problems. He'd been an absolute whiz at straightening out the mess the church's financial affairs had been in when Ken first arrived.

"Maybe so. Or maybe he has the kind of reputation a man would do anything to protect. Isn't that the kind you said to look out for?"

"He is, indeed," Dana said thoughtfully. She tried to

picture Lawrence Tremayne, with his thick brown hair, perfect features and expensive wardrobe, tainting his image by committing a murder. She couldn't do it. Still, there was something to be said for finding answers in the least likely places.

She considered the other names on the list. Peter Drake was a mousy, unassuming little man, but she agreed with Kate that there was something a bit odd about him.

Miriam Kelso was outspoken and highly critical of Ken, as she had been of every other minister the church had had, according to those who knew her best.

Polanski and Wald were in the carpeting business together. Despite that union, they fought loudly and often, always patching things up just in time to save the business from ruin. They had quick, flashpoint tempers, but Dana wasn't convinced they would murder in a fit of rage. They were too used to stopping short of that with each other.

"Maybe I should call and invite them over," she suggested to Kate. "Maybe it's time for everyone at the church to know that I'm turning over rocks to see what crawls out."

Kate seemed a little nonplussed by the idea. "Isn't that asking for trouble? What if one of these people does know something? You could be endangering yourself."

"Very little progress comes without risk."

"I thought you were taking all the risks you needed to by going into Chicago with Rick Sanchez. How did that go, by the way?"

"It was a first step, but I have a long way to go before I gain the trust of those kids. I can't wait for that. I have to keep checking every angle. Will you call these people today? Invite them over for tea tomorrow."

"Why not today?"

"I'm going back to Yo, Amigo."

"Will you tell Rick that you're checking out other leads?"

Dana held up the list of names. "Sweetie, these aren't leads, and that tea tomorrow isn't any more than a chance to float a few theories. It's a little too much to hope that someone will fall to their knees and confess."

"Just in case," Kate said, "maybe you'd better vacuum."

14

Rosa had almost driven Rick crazy asking about Dana and those photographs she'd taken. From the minute he'd walked into Yo, Amigo at 8:30 a.m. until the time he had left to pick up Dana, Rosa had pestered him.

"For the last time, she will be here in a couple of hours," he'd explained at least a half-dozen times. "You can see for yourself."

"You could call her," Rosa had pleaded each time. "You could ask if they turned out at all."

"Patience, angel. You will know soon enough."

"Are you sure she did not tell you they were awful?" the teenager asked worriedly.

"She has told me nothing. She hadn't even looked at them the last time I talked to her."

Rosa's face fell. "Perhaps she did not have time to check them. I thought they had to be done at a drugstore, anyway. Perhaps she will not bring the pictures today at all."

For some reason, he had absolute faith that Dana would do as she had promised. He felt confident reassuring Rosa of that. "She promised to bring them, didn't she? She said she was going to do them herself. Even if she didn't have the time, there are many places that make prints. I swear to you that we will stop at one of them, if she doesn't already have the pictures."

"Yes, but—"

"No buts. If she said she would, then you can count on it," he said, praying his instincts were right. Maybe he should call to check, just in case, and look for one of those one-hour services in the Yellow Pages.

And maybe he was just looking for an excuse to hear her voice, he had thought with disgust. He had forced himself to resist the temptation to dial her number. He'd been less successful forcing her image out of his head. Fueled by an impatience he could no longer control, he left a half hour earlier than he'd planned to pick her up.

Even so, apparently Dana was every bit as anxious today as Rosa had been. He found her waiting outside on the front stoop when he drove up. He noted with a sigh of relief that she was carrying a large, flat envelope, along with the camera bag and other equipment she'd had the day before.

He helped her to load everything except the envelope into the trunk.

"Are those the pictures?" he asked as he put the car into gear.

She nodded.

"Rosa's very excited. I hope they turned out okay. I'd hate to see her disappointed."

"Okay? They're beautiful. Even lovelier than I'd hoped. Trust me, she won't be disappointed."

"May I see?"

She grinned at him. "Now who's anxious? Besides, you're driving. You need to keep your eyes on the road."

"We're still in the driveway," he reminded her.

"Which is no way to get these to Rosa in a hurry."

At the teasing tone, he slanted a look at her. "You sound better today."

"I am better," she said. "I think I'm finally beginning to get a grip on things."

Something in her voice alerted him that she was not referring entirely to her own emotions. "Why? Did something happen after I left last night?"

She said no, but her eyes said otherwise. "Dana? What are you keeping from me?"

"Who said I was keeping anything from you?"

"You weren't out snooping around last night, were you?" he asked, envisioning another foray into the streets surrounding Yo, Amigo. He knew she hadn't made it inside, because he'd lain awake all night tossing and turning on that sadistic couch. He would have heard her, just as he had the first time she'd broken in.

She scowled at him. "I don't snoop. I'm an investigator. I investigate."

"Okay. Exactly what did you *investigate* last night?"

"Nothing," she swore. "I printed these pictures. Then I went to sleep."

His gaze narrowed. He guessed that might be the truth, as far as it went. Perhaps the question had simply been too narrow. "And this morning?"

"Kate came by," she said nonchalantly.

"And?" he prodded with the sudden sense that he was onto something.

"We talked."

He had to fight a grin at her determined reticence. "About?"

"This and that," she said, continuing the evasiveness.

"Dana!"

"Okay, okay, we talked about people in the church who might be suspicious."

The relief he felt was out of all proportion to the announcement. It wasn't as if she'd proved conclusively that Yo, Amigo's kids had nothing to do with the murder. But at least she had opened her mind to other possibilities and was exploring them.

"Anybody look especially guilty?" he inquired.

"No, and don't get your hopes up," she retorted. "So far all I have are hunches and wishful thinking about people who on the surface seem very pious and generous."

"Wishful thinking?"

She sighed. "I don't really want anyone at Yo, Amigo to be guilty," she conceded grudgingly, then added hurriedly, "For Ken's sake. I would hate to think he was betrayed by the very kids he'd befriended."

"He wasn't," Rick said vehemently. "I'd stake my own life on it."

"That's very noble, but you're prejudiced."

"I also know those kids better than anyone."

She paused at that. "I hope for your sake that you truly do."

"You'll see," he told her. If she would give the kids a chance, they would win her heart, just as they had won Ken's. And they needed her faith every bit as badly as they'd needed Ken's. Far too few people had ever believed in them. He thought again of Rosa and her high hopes.

"Dana, be careful with Rosa. Don't promise her things you can't deliver."

"I'll only tell her what I see."

"And that is?"

"That she is beautiful and photogenic."

"She really is?"

"Rick, I swear to you that even though she isn't professional and I've never done anything remotely like a fashion shoot, these pictures are incredible. I've already called a friend of mine about them. He's promised to take a look at them if I send them over. As soon as I have Rosa's permission, that's what I'm going to do."

"This friend knows what he's doing?"

"He's with Hanson and Watts. In fact, he's Ted Hanson."

"One of the best ad agencies in Chicago," Rick said incredulously. "I have heard of them."

"The best," Dana corrected. "At least according to Ted."

"You have that much faith in these pictures?"

"I have that much faith in Rosa. If I can shoot pictures like these, a professional would pay a fortune to get her in front of a camera."

He fell silent at that. He couldn't help worrying that Rosa was being set up for a tremendous letdown, but that was one of the risks of dreaming big, and he had always encouraged the kids in the program to dream very big. For too long, most of them had had no dreams at all.

When he pulled into his parking space at Yo, Amigo, Rosa was waiting in the doorway, her eyes bright with anticipation, her expression fearful. The contradictory emotions were all too typical. Hopes were shot down here with distressing frequency.

"You'll be lucky if she lets you get inside," he warned Dana just as Rosa came rushing up to the passenger door and yanked it open.

"Do you have them?" she asked, all traces of her usual shyness gone.

"In the backseat," Dana assured her.

Suddenly Rosa's expression faltered. "They are terrible?"

Dana squeezed her hand. "They are anything but terrible."

"The others are waiting inside to see, even Marco. Maybe I should look at them first, here so I will not be embarrassed if they make me look like a huge whale."

"I don't think you will be embarrassed," Dana said. "But let's not look at them out here. We could take them to Rick's office, if you like," she said, glancing at him for approval.

"Of course." He was as anxious to see them as the others. Thanks to Dana, he might catch one of the first glimpses.

But at his office door, after running past a gauntlet of kids with expressions ranging from eager to sullenly distrustful, she put a hand on his arm. "Not yet," she told him. "Just Rosa for now."

"Hey, it's my office," he protested. "That ought to count for something."

"It does. We appreciate it, don't we, Rosa?"

"Yes, very much," Rosa said distractedly, her avid gaze locked on that large envelope.

Rick sighed and settled for perching on a corner of Maria's desk to wait. He kept his gaze fixed on the door, wishing he had the power to see through it or the skill to eavesdrop. Not that the place was all that soundproof, but Rosa and Dana were keeping their voices low.

The first hint he got of Rosa's reaction was a faint squeal, then another, and finally a burst of joyous laughter. He glanced at Maria.

"She sounds happy, yes?" Maria said.

"That's an understatement." He pinned his gaze on the door and waited for it to turn. At the first hint of a twist, he was on his feet. So was Maria. He noticed then that Marco had edged into the room and was waiting as well, though his expression feigned indifference.

The door opened and a beaming Rosa beckoned to

15

The meal at Tico's had been every bit as wonderful as the first Dana had shared there with Rick. Burritos stuffed with succulent meat and cheese and spicy jalapeños had been washed down with icy beer. The conversation had been pitifully short on answers, though.

Tico had joined them for a time, but he knew no more than Rick claimed to about the murder. Rick had leaned back in the seat across from her and kept quiet as she cross-examined his friend. There was an expression of tolerant amusement on his face that she had hated.

"This just doesn't make sense," she had cried out at one point in frustration. "No one is more likely to be tapped into the underground network around this part of town, but neither of you has turned up so much as a whiff of information. Why is that?"

She noticed that the two men exchanged a significant look at the question, but both remained stubbornly silent. "What is it that you're not telling me?" she asked again, certain that they were holding back, protecting someone or something—Yo, Amigo, for instance.

Both had denied they were hiding a thing, but she knew a cover-up when she saw one. Neither of them could look her in the eye when he said it. She had vowed to take the subject up with Rick again on the way home, but he was prepared for her questions. He fielded them with vague replies that left her feeling more irritable than ever.

She was still trying to make sense of their odd behavior the next day as she prepared for the arrival of the group from the church. She had baked all morning and hauled out her grandmother's silver service, the one she used only for formal occasions. She'd washed all of her best china cups and set them up on the gleaming dining room table, along with platters of triangular, crustless sandwiches, scones, tiny cakes and delicate almond cookies. She had held enough of these formal teas that she was able to do most of it by rote while her mind toyed with interpreting those undercurrents the night before. Unfortunately, no new spin came to her.

She spent a solid hour dressing for the occasion, more time than she'd spent on herself since Ken's funeral. She chose a soft gray suit, a prim white blouse and gray pumps. Her sterling silver necklace and earrings had been a gift from Ken on a trip they'd taken to Mexico to celebrate their first anniversary.

As she touched the cool metal at her throat, tears stung her eyes, and her gaze drifted toward the window overlooking the church cemetery. A huge knot formed in her throat as she looked at the snow-covered gravesite, where long-dead flowers poked through the blanket of white. The sight of the neglected plot saddened her.

Suddenly frantic to see it cared for, she ran downstairs and toward the kitchen door, almost plowing into Kate, who was just coming up the back steps carrying an armful of fresh flowers to brighten the table.

"Hey, where's the fire?" she asked, studying Dana worriedly.

Dana paused and shook her head, unable to get the words past the knot in her throat. Kate followed the direction of her gaze.

"Oh, no," she said softly. "Not now, sweetie. You can't go out there now."

Gently she took Dana's arm and guided her into the house and into a seat at the kitchen table. She set the flowers in the sink and poured Dana a cup of tea, adding lots of sugar.

"Drink this. It'll make you feel better."

Dana realized then that her teeth were chattering, not so much from the arctic air outside, but from the deep chill within. She closed her eyes and sighed as she swallowed the first warm sip. After several more swallows of the overly sweet liquid, she met Kate's gaze.

"I'm sorry. I don't know what came over me. All of a sudden I was frantic to clear away the dead flowers on Ken's grave. It looks so desolate out there."

"We'll do it tomorrow," Kate promised. "I'll help. We'll buy some fresh flowers, too. Or we can take the ones I brought today."

"They'll just wither and die."

"Then we'll get bright silk ones that will last until spring. That's only a couple of months away, you know. By April, there will be tulips and daffodils blooming all over the cemetery."

Dana smiled at the quick, determined responses. "You're a very good friend."

"And why wouldn't I be?" Kate demanded. "You saved me from financial ruin by getting that evidence against Peter. If it hadn't been for you, I'd be working at some fast-food place for minimum wage and struggling to support the girls. College for them would be out of the question. With luck and tenacity, maybe I'd even be a manager by now."

"Who are you trying to kid?" Dana teased. "You'd be running the whole darned chain by now."

"You always did have more faith in me than I had in myself. Speaking of faith, how did yours in those pictures turn out? Was Ted as over-the-moon about them as you were? Have you talked to him?"

"He called me five minutes after the courier put them on his desk. Rosa has a meeting with him tomorrow. Rick and Marco and I are taking her. She's so terrified and excited she's sure she'll faint when she walks into his office and mess up the opportunity of a lifetime."

"How did her friends take the news that she was getting such an incredible break?"

Dana chuckled at the memory of the aftermath of Ted's phone call. "Let's just say that registration for my photography class has gone through the roof."

"Uh-oh," Kate said. "Doesn't that terrify you? What if lightning doesn't strike twice?"

"Rick's worried about the same thing. I told him and the kids that there are lots of things they can do besides modeling. Not all of them will be suited for it, anyway. I'm hoping I can use the class to get a fix on what they will be good at and steer them in the right direction. I'm not sure if I'm qualified to do career counseling, but I'm going to try."

"Rick must be pleased that you're fitting in so well," Kate said, her expression sly.

"Let's just say he's trying very hard not to say he told me so," Dana replied dryly. She glanced at Kate and thought she detected a new glimmer of excitement in her eyes. She suspected it had nothing to do with the kids at Yo, Amigo. "What's going on with you, by the way?"

"Actually, I have a date," Kate said. "That is, I do if it doesn't upset you."

"Why would it upset me for you to go on a date?"

"It's with Detective O'Flannery."

Dana tried not to stare in openmouthed shock. Of course, she shouldn't be all that stunned. She had seen the sparks flying between the two herself. Even so, she felt somehow as if Kate were betraying her, shifting allegiance to the enemy.

"You are upset," Kate said at once, interpreting her silence as condemnation. "I was afraid of that. I'll call him and cancel."

"You will not," Dana insisted, trying to put her friend's feelings above her own. She owed Kate that after all she had done for her the last few weeks. When Kate seemed about to argue, she silenced her. "Besides, you can pump him for information about the investigation the police are supposedly conducting into this drug business."

Kate grinned. "Obviously he's a very smart cop. He told me you were going to say that."

"Did he also tell you whether he was prepared to lie through his teeth?"

"No. Actually, he said he intended to use the occasion to pump me for information about *our* investigation."

Dana stared. "What? Kate, tell me you didn't blab to him about what we were doing?"

"Of course not, but he's no fool. He figured it out. You dropped enough hints yourself over at the church the day we met him."

"Does he know about this afternoon?" she asked, just as the doorbell rang.

"Not from me, he doesn't," Kate assured her as Dana headed for the living room.

"I hope you're right," Dana said. "I'd really rather not

have the cops turning up in the middle of this little tea party of ours."

She opened the front door to admit Lawrence Tremayne and Gerrold Wald. As she greeted them, she noticed the others arriving in separate cars. While Kate took the coats the two men were wearing, led them inside and offered them tea, Dana waited to greet the new arrivals.

"My dear, how are you?" Miriam Kelso asked. "I've thought of you so often the past few weeks."

"Thank you. I'm doing the best I can."

"And those darling boys of yours," a glamorous, middle-aged woman said, "how are they?"

Judging from the tautness of her skin, this had to be the very well-preserved Carolina Vincenzi, Dana concluded. "They're still with my parents in Florida," she replied. "We thought that would be best for the moment."

She led the newcomers in to join the others. "Please, allow me to get you all some tea and you can help yourselves to scones and sandwiches or whatever you'd like."

As the guests chatted in low voices suitable for an occasion in the home of the recently bereaved, Dana went into the kitchen, closed the door and drew in a deep breath. "Courage," she murmured, then plastered a smile on her face and rejoined the others.

When everyone was seated in the living room, she was about to speak but Lawrence Tremayne cleared his throat and regarded her solemnly.

"Mrs. Miller…"

His sudden formality made her stomach clench. She had the distinct feeling she wasn't going to like what he was about to say. He was the kind of man who normally presumed to call every woman by her first name.

"Dana, please," she reminded him.

Color bloomed in his pasty cheeks. "Yes, of course. I know that you invited us here to discuss certain things, but there are a few things that I wanted to pass along to you, on behalf of the elders."

Dana glanced at Kate and saw that her gaze had narrowed suspiciously as she watched the normally slick church leader try to impart some apparently unpleasant news.

"Of course, you first," she said with as much grace as she could manage, when she was overcome with a sense of impending doom.

"It has been several weeks now since…" He uncharacteristically fumbled for words. "Since your loss."

Dana remained silent and waited.

"We don't want to rush you into a decision about the future, of course." He looked to the others for support, but their expressions were carefully guarded. Most had their gazes cast toward the floor or ceiling. "Actually, it's about the house."

"The house," Dana repeated blankly, then realized exactly where he was heading. "This house." She swallowed back panic. Even though she'd known it was coming, it was too soon. They couldn't force her out yet. She needed more time.

"You would like me to move, is that it?" she asked, her voice shaky.

Relief spread over his face. "Yes, that's it exactly."

"How soon?" she asked.

"As I said, we don't want to rush you. We haven't settled on a new minister yet, but we expect to have a decision soon. Of course, he will need a place to live."

"Of course," she agreed, then repeated, "How soon do you anticipate needing the house?"

He glanced at the others, but they continued to avoid

his daze. "A few weeks, a month perhaps, if that wouldn't be too difficult for you to arrange. I know I had told you to take all the time you needed, but it's just not practical to let you stay indefinitely."

"Of course not. I can be out of here by the weekend, if that would help," she said, fighting an unreasonable fury.

Of course, this was the church's property. She had known that sooner or later she would have to leave it, had already begun making mental, if not practical, plans, but she hadn't expected it to be this soon. She hadn't expected this callous announcement in her own living room with others staring on in uncomfortable silence. She especially hadn't expected it coming from a man who had shown her such compassion right after Ken's death.

"Don't be silly," Miriam Kelso soothed, scowling at Lawrence Tremayne. "You take all the time you need. If the new minister arrives, we can certainly make arrangements to accommodate him until you're able to make your plans. Your life has been disrupted enough without us adding to it."

"Thank you," Dana said, all too aware that Miriam Kelso's kindness wouldn't fare well against the grim determination she had seen on Lawrence Tremayne's face. She couldn't allow that to matter, though. She had to remain focused on the reason for this gathering. She had brought them all here to ferret out information, to get their uncensored reactions to the news that the matter of Ken's death was far from over. This discussion about her moving on was untimely, but irrelevant.

"I would like a little more time here," she said, injecting a dutiful note of gratitude into her voice. She deliberately glanced in the direction of the cemetery. She didn't have to feign the tears that formed in her eyes. "I'm not quite ready to move on and leave Ken behind."

In truth, she hadn't even considered that aspect when she had made the decision to bury him right here, rather than somewhere else. The church had offered the burial plot, and she had seized the offer, because it was one more detail she wouldn't have to attend to.

"Of course you're not ready to make a move yet," Mrs. Kelso declared sympathetically. "We understand perfectly. It was all so sudden, so terribly tragic."

The others chimed in dutifully. Dana wondered if they'd heard yet about the latest phase of the investigation. Apparently not, since none of them brought it up. If they'd known about the drugs, they might very well have ordered her off the premises that very afternoon.

She managed a weak, placating smile. "I also would like all of you to know that I am doing everything I can to solve Ken's murder," she said as if assuming the news would delight them. She watched their reactions very closely, as she added, "The police have essentially back-burnered the case, but I have not."

"I thought it was a drive-by shooting in that terrible neighborhood," Carolina Vincenzi said, sniffing as if she could smell the bad odor all the way out here in the suburbs.

"The police are inclined toward that theory," Dana admitted. "I'm not convinced. As many of you know, I was a licensed private investigator for some time before Ken and I married. I am conducting my own investigation."

The guests did gape at that, even Mrs. Kelso, who'd been doing her best, up until that moment, to be supportive of Dana.

"My dear, are you sure that's wise? Isn't it terribly distressing for you?" she asked.

"It's not only wise, it's necessary," Dana said firmly. "For one thing, the reputation of Yo, Amigo has been tarnished in a way that could lead to its downfall. Ken believed in that program…."

"Begging your pardon, Mrs. Miller, but your husband was a fool," Lawrence Tremayne declared so vehemently that everyone in the room gasped with dismay.

All except Dana. She rose to her feet and stood over him. Her voice quivering with barely suppressed rage, she said, "I will not allow you to slander a man who is no longer able to defend himself, and I certainly will not allow it here in his home."

"It's the church's home," Tremayne retorted tightly. "You would do well to remember that."

She stared at him in shock. It appeared the kid gloves had been removed. "Is that a threat?" she inquired. "May I remind you that you hold nothing over me? You've already told me that I'm being kicked out of here. My husband's insurance will see that my family is provided for. The church doesn't owe me one single dime of compensation. So what, exactly, are you threatening to do to me, Mr. Tremayne?"

Peter Drake interceded. "I think we should all settle down," he said in the soothing manner of a man used to dealing with warring factions. "Lawrence, mind your tongue. You always did have a tendency to run off at the mouth, without giving a thought to what was coming out."

"Lawrence was just saying what many of us thought," Carolina Vincenzi stated haughtily. "There were quite a few of us who thought Reverend Miller was crazy for defending those hooligans."

"He was defending young people who'd never been given a chance in life," Dana reminded her, aware that not so long ago she had shared Carolina Vincenzi's attitude. Her resentment had begun to fade, as she had started to put faces to the names Ken had mentioned so often. "Isn't that what Christian charity is supposed to be about? Or haven't you read a Bible lately?"

"Okay, okay," Kate said, giving Dana's shoulder a warning squeeze. "I think perhaps we've all let our tempers get in the way of good judgment this afternoon. Obviously, this is a very trying time for Dana. Perhaps, it would be best if you all leave and we postpone this conversation for another time."

"Not just yet," Tremayne said defiantly. He scowled at Dana. "I would like your assurance that the church will not be dragged into this so-called investigation of yours."

Dana met his gaze evenly. "The first rule of any investigation is not to rule anything out, Mr. Tremayne. I will follow whatever leads are necessary. If that brings me to the church's doorstep, then so be it."

"Surely you don't think anyone here had anything to do with your husband's death?" Vincent Polanski asked in a shocked tone.

"It's not important what I think," Dana told him. "I will go wherever the evidence takes me."

"Then you'll be dead yourself within a month," Tremayne said with a certain amount of satisfaction.

Dana stared at him. "I beg your pardon?"

The others seemed equally startled by the blunt claim. "Lawrence, shut up!" Peter Drake warned in a tone so uncharacteristically fierce that everyone stared at him in shock.

"No, please," Dana said. "Let him finish what he began. Is that another threat, Mr. Tremayne?"

He flushed. "Of course not. I just meant that you'll be

hanging around in that violent section of town, just as your husband did. You're bound to meet the same fate."

After the past hour, Dana wasn't so sure that the real nest of vipers wasn't right here in her living room.

16

Dana was still pacing the living room, ranting and raving at Kate about the gall of their recently departed guests, when the phone rang. She snatched up the receiver and snapped a greeting.

"Uh-oh," Rick said warily. "What has your drawers in a knot, *querida?*"

With his faintly accented voice, the question had a certain intriguing panache. "Sorry," she apologized. "It's been a lousy afternoon."

"What happened?"

She thought about what actually had happened and concluded that none of it was likely to seem so terrible to an outsider who wasn't living the nightmare. "Nothing, really."

"Tell that to someone who'll buy it. Try again, *querida.* The people from the church came to call, yes?"

"Oh, yes," she said, unable to keep a note of bitterness out of her voice.

"And? There were problems?"

"You might say that."

"Tell me," he said.

He spoke in a gentle, patient way that suggested whatever she described would be made better for the sharing. Dana wasn't convinced, but she told him anyway. "They kicked me out of the house."

"What?"

He sounded satisfyingly incredulous. Dana sighed. "They have the right to do that. It is their house. And I was expecting it. Just not so soon."

"I'm coming out there," he announced, and hung up before she could argue that there was no point.

She slowly replaced the receiver in its cradle and turned to find Kate regarding her speculatively.

"Rick, I assume."

"How did you know?"

"Your color's better."

Dana scowled at her. "Oh, go suck an egg."

Kate burst out laughing. "Sweetie, you're going to have to do better than that if you're going to be any match for those jerks who were here this afternoon."

"Believe me, that was just a warm-up," Dana assured her, grinning. "I had a very tart tongue before I married a minister and decided I'd better learn to express myself more politely."

"Spending time with Rick Sanchez ought to help. He is charmingly rough around the edges, wouldn't you say?"

"Meaning?"

"There's an aura of barely leashed, street-tough danger about him," Kate said. "In other words, he's sexy as hell. I love it that he's rushing out here to your defense."

"Who said anything about him rushing out here?"

"Your expression gave it away," Kate explained cheerfully. "You looked very put out when he hung up on you."

"How did you know he'd hung up on me?"

"Nobody said goodbye," Kate replied.

Dana scowled at her. "You really do need to get an investigator's license. You're very good at this."

"It comes from having to be one step ahead of two secretive teenagers." She tilted her head to one side. "Now, what do you intend to do with him once he gets here?"

"I don't intend to do anything. I didn't ask him to come. He invited himself."

"So you intend to toss him right back out on his ear?"

The prospect of that sight seemed to amuse Kate no end. Dana was thrilled she could provide her friend with so much entertainment.

"No. That would be rude," she said stiffly. "You, on the other hand…" She allowed the threat to remain unspoken.

Kate chuckled. "I was thinking of going home, anyway, but I've changed my mind. I think I'll hang around for a while."

"Suit yourself," Dana grumbled.

She really was getting tired of all the bossy, presumptuous people in her life. Rick topped the list, but Kate was a very close second. Not that she normally didn't count herself very lucky to have Kate around. Kate didn't try to placate her the way so many of the other women in the church did. Kate had apparently never bought the ridiculous idea that getting into heaven had anything whatsoever to do with tiptoeing on eggshells around the minister's wife. She viewed Dana as a human being in her own right, rather than one-half of some sort of holy alliance.

None of that mattered at the moment, anyway. She was losing her focus on the investigation again. For several moments, she tried to concentrate, but everything that had happened remained in a muddle. She finally met her friend's still-amused gaze. "Kate?"

"Yes?"

"Did we learn anything here this afternoon?"

"Sure," Kate said, sobering at once.

"Care to share your insights with me?"

"Lawrence Tremayne is a bully. Peter Drake, contrary to all appearances, is a born mediator. Caroline Vincenzi is a biased snob. Vincent Polanski would jump at his own shadow. And Gerrold Wald has been rendered speechless in their presence."

"What about Miriam Kelso?"

Kate's expression turned thoughtful. "She's the strangest one in the bunch. I know for a fact that she criticized Ken behind his back. In fact, she tried to stab him in the back and have him removed, but today she was so warm and understanding it made me want to throw up. With that kind of duplicity, she may well be the most dangerous one in the bunch."

"Who's dangerous?" Rick inquired, causing both Dana and Kate to jump.

"How did you get in here?" Dana demanded as she tried to coax her heart back to its normal rhythm.

"You left the front door unlocked," he chided.

"And how would you know that? Didn't you even consider knocking first?"

He grinned unrepentantly. "Given the dangers that you persist in ignoring, I was doing a very necessary security check."

"And your qualifications for that would be?"

"Concern," he replied.

He said it in a simple, straightforward way that sent goose bumps dancing along her spine. Dana swallowed hard and tried not to let him see how affected she was by that sincere declaration.

"Breaking and entering by any other name is still a crime," she pointed out.

He chuckled out loud at that. "You might do well to remember that yourself, *querida.*"

Dana winced at the reminder of her failed break-in attempt. "Sorry. I lost my head for a moment."

"Would you like some tea?" Kate asked him, obviously seeking to smooth over the awkward moment. "Or something to eat? We have scads of food left over. People seemed to lose their appetites this afternoon."

Dana tried to envision the very masculine man standing before her balancing a delicate teacup and a plate of tiny sandwiches on his knee. She couldn't do it. "Maybe Rick would prefer a beer," she suggested.

His expression brightened. "A beer sounds great."

"I think there's a bag of tortilla chips around here somewhere," she added.

Kate scowled at her. "With all that good food left over? I don't think so. I'll get the beer. Rick, why don't you check out the sandwiches and desserts? There's a plate on the table. Dana never did get around to eating, either."

The last was clearly meant as a very broad hint. Rick took it. He held out a hand.

"Come, then," he urged. "We will all get something and sit in the kitchen, yes? I like the cozy atmosphere in there. A place like that is the heart of a family."

Dana wanted to resist, but her hand seemed to have a will of its own. It slipped into his much larger one and settled comfortably against the faintly calloused palm. He closed his fingers around hers and tugged her to her feet.

"We have been over this before. You have to eat," he chastised her. "You have to keep your strength up."

"You sound like my mother."

"A very wise woman, obviously."

Dana smiled ruefully. "She likes to think so." She regarded Rick curiously. "What about your mother? Is she very wise?"

"She was," he said quietly. "She died several years ago."

"I'm sorry," she said, instinctively squeezing his hand. "You miss her, don't you? I can hear it in your voice."

"Every day," he agreed. "I admired and respected her, even when we were most at odds. I'm not sure she knew that, though. It is my greatest regret."

The admission told her quite a lot about Rick, things she would never have expected from this man who'd once embraced gang violence as a way of life. It proved that even the strength and compassion of a caring parent might not be enough to counter the allure of the gangs. She had always assumed that only those who were unwanted or unloved or disenfranchised would turn to gangs for support and acceptance.

She started to ask Rick why he had chosen the path he had, but held back instead. Why wasn't important. It was because of the choices he'd made that he'd wound up creating Yo, Amigo. That was all that mattered. She cared about him only insofar as he could shed light on Ken's death. Asking for intimate details about his life would only muddy the waters. It would make their relationship into something personal, when it needed to remain adversarial.

As it was, she was already all too aware of the effect of something as simple as having her hand clasped in his. She was drawn to the warmth he offered in ways that she found both confusing and very troubling. Sharing his secrets would only compound the effect.

Reacting to that rush of confusion, she suddenly withdrew her hand from his, using the pretext of gathering food to make the withdrawal seem less abrupt. The amused glint in his eyes told her that he knew exactly why she'd pulled away.

Settled in the kitchen, where, more and more, Rick seemed thoroughly at home and memories of Ken's presence were gradually fading, the three of them examined the afternoon's events and tried to make sense of them.

"Do you suppose this sudden notice of eviction has something to do with panic that you're going to stumble onto the truth about Ken's death?" Rick asked thoughtfully.

Dana shook her head at once. "They informed me they wanted me to go before I ever said a word about the investigation."

"What about Mrs. Fallon?" Kate asked. "She might have said something about you being in Ken's office. They could have leapt to the conclusion that you were snooping for clues."

"I doubt it. There was nothing odd about my being in his office to gather his personal items. The only thing odd was the police tossing the place."

"Maybe they heard about that," Rick suggested.

"If they had, they never mentioned it. Besides, I think Mrs. Fallon would go to great lengths to protect Ken. I'll bet she has the office spotless again already, and she'll never say a word about the drugs they found in there. The church officials won't know, unless the police question them."

"I agree," Kate said. "But I do have to wonder at the timing of today's little bombshell, especially after Tremayne himself had made a point of telling you a few weeks ago to take your time. I agree with Rick that this turnaround came out of the blue. I think somebody wants you gone before you discover the truth, somebody powerful enough to make Tremayne change his tune."

"What truth?" Dana demanded impatiently. "That underneath that smooth facade, Lawrence Tremayne is a pompous ass? Who would dare to try to push him around? He'd make mincemeat of anyone who tried."

"He shut up when Peter Drake told him to, didn't he?"

"That's true," Dana conceded thoughtfully.

"Tell me about Tremayne," Rick insisted. "That name sounds familiar."

Kate listed all of the man's personal and professional accomplishments, as gleaned from the newspaper files. Dana added her own insights from seeing his work on behalf of the church.

"A model citizen," Rick concluded.

"Until he slipped and told me Ken was a fool and that I was likely to wind up dead," Dana said.

"He threatened you?"

"I'd say it was more like a generous warning that I was treading on thin ice."

"How charitable," Rick said with sarcasm.

"Indeed," Kate agreed.

"Yet he would toss three children out of the only home they have ever known," Rick said with derision. "Already I do not like this man."

"That's two of us," Kate said vehemently.

"Three," Dana added.

"Let me see what I can find out about him tomorrow," Rick offered, his expression thoughtful. "Maybe there are some skeletons hidden in the closet we ought to know about."

Dana had the feeling he already knew exactly where he intended to look, which once more aroused the suspicion that Rick was keeping something from her. It was pointless to ask him, though. Maybe she should give some thought to tapping his phone and shadowing him.

"Anybody else strike you as especially suspicious?" Rick asked, bringing her attention back to the moment.

"Oddly enough, Miriam Kelso," Dana said, drawing a startled glance from Kate.

"Why?" Kate asked. "I know I said she was behaving strangely, but suspicious? That's a little extreme."

"Not really," Dana disagreed. "We both know she was being insincere and two-faced the whole time she was here. I have to wonder why she bothered."

"Maybe she was just playing good cop to Tremayne's bad cop," Kate suggested.

"Maybe, but my gut tells me she was overcompensating for something else."

"Maybe she just felt guilty for being such a thorn in Ken's side," Kate said. "She might have wanted him booted out, but she probably didn't want him dead."

"She wanted him out because of the gang issue?" Rick asked.

"No, general principle," Dana told him. "She found fault with every minister the church ever had. That's just the way she is. We heard about her from the last pastor before we ever got here."

"What about this Drake character?" Rick asked then. "You said he ordered Tremayne to shut up and that Tremayne listened, right?"

"Actually, that was a bit of a shock," Dana said. "I've always thought of him as such a mousy man. I couldn't believe it when he snapped at Lawrence Tremayne like that."

"What I couldn't believe was that Tremayne actually shut up," Kate said.

"Maybe Drake has something on him," Rick suggested.

"Oh, please," Dana protested. "We're getting carried away. Kate, you know Peter Drake. Can you envision him virtually blackmailing anyone, much less Lawrence Tremayne?"

"Not before today, I couldn't. Now?" She shrugged. "I'm not so sure."

"That's three people we should check out more thoroughly," Rick said. "And the others?"

"Polanski and Wald said almost nothing. Carolina said nothing today that she hasn't said a million times in public, according to Kate. I may not be crazy about her viewpoint, but I don't think there are any deep, dark secrets there," Dana conceded.

Rick glanced at Kate. "Do you agree?"

"Pretty much."

"That doesn't sound very wholehearted," he said, seizing on the hint of doubt that Dana had also detected. "What's troubling you?"

"Vincent Polanski's reaction to the news that Dana was investigating," Kate said slowly, as if she were still formulating the thought. "Didn't you notice, Dana? He was the only one here who seemed genuinely distressed that you were going to be looking in our own backyard, rather than in Chicago. The minute he spoke up, I had the feeling that he was the one with something to hide."

"Gut instinct?" Dana asked dryly.

"As a matter of fact, yes," Kate retorted defensively.

Dana grinned at her. "Then I guess we'd better pay attention. These days your gut seems to be more reliable than mine."

"That's because you're not feeding anything to yours,"

Rick pointed out, gesturing toward the untouched food on her plate. "Eat."

"Maybe you ought to whip up a batch of burritos for her," Kate said innocently. "I understand she eats well enough when she's with you at that place called Tico's."

Rick regarded Dana speculatively. "That's true. Perhaps I should call and have him send an order out here. In fact, I am sure he would be delighted to bring it personally. He finds you enchanting." The last was said with an intriguing hint of irritability.

"That's ridiculous," Dana objected, focusing on the plan to have Tico come all the way from Chicago to bring Mexican food and leaving the hint of jealousy in Rick's voice for another time. "There's enough food here already to feed an army."

"But perhaps you have discovered that Mexican food feeds the soul as well as the body," Rick suggested.

"I've never heard anybody rhapsodize over tacos before," Dana said.

"Then I should have taped your comments the first time we walked into Tico's," he taunted. "Even the aroma sent you into raptures."

Dana laughed, despite herself. "Okay, okay, he does make delicious food, but that doesn't mean I have to live on a steady diet of it." She deliberately picked up a little sandwich and popped it into her mouth. It tasted like so much sawdust. She made a face.

"Perhaps what it needs is a few jalapeños," Rick suggested.

"It was tuna," she protested.

"You could tell that?"

"Okay, so it was a little bland. My taste buds have just been deadened by all those peppers you've been feeding me the last few days."

"I know of a way to bring them alive again," he said, regarding her mouth so intently that heat climbed into her cheeks.

Kate bounced up. "Well, on that provocative note, I guess it's time for me to go. See you tomorrow, Dana. Nice to see you again, Rick."

"Kate?" Dana stared after her departing friend with a sense of desperation. Kate never even slowed.

"She has quite a sense of timing, wouldn't you agree?" Rick asked, a smile on his lips.

"Oh, yeah. It's lousy," she retorted.

"Not from where I'm sitting."

"Rick, I think you ought to go, too. It's late and you have to drive back to the city."

"Kicking me out? After I came all this way to prevent the same thing from happening to you?"

The reminder of what had brought him dashing out here tonight made her sigh. "You can't stop me from being tossed out of this house."

"Maybe not indefinitely, but I'll bet I can slow the process down."

She chuckled. "Do you always jump at the chance to tackle any old challenge?"

"Only those that matter," he assured her.

His gaze locked with hers in a way that left her trembling. Apparently satisfied that he'd rattled her, he stood. "Come. Walk me to the door."

Her knees felt weak as she stood, but she walked with him, fighting a ridiculous sense of disappointment that he'd taken her at her word. She did want him to go, didn't she? Of course she did. He was just an irritant that had to be tolerated for the moment. No more.

At the door, he paused and looked into her eyes. She thought she detected a hint of uncertainty in his, just as he shook his head. "Ah, *querida*," he whispered. "What have you done to me?"

Dana swallowed. All of a sudden she was having a very difficult time remembering that she hated this man. "I don't understand."

He framed her face with his hands. His thumbs skimmed lightly across her cheeks, leaving fire in their wake. Just when her breath caught in her throat, just when she was all but certain that his mouth was descending to claim hers, he brushed a soft and tender kiss across her forehead and released her with a sigh.

"*Buenos noches, querida.* Sleep well."

He was gone before she could gather her composure. As he disappeared into the darkness, she whispered, "Good night," and wondered why she suddenly felt bereft all over again.

_17_

It was barely dawn when Dana's phone rang. She answered groggily.

"You were sleeping, _señora_. I am so sorry," a soft voice said.

"Rosa?"

"_Sí_, it is Rosa. I did not mean to wake you."

Dana grinned at the barely contained excitement in the teen's voice. "Today's the big day and you're nervous, right?"

"How do you say…petrified? These people, do you think they will like me?"

"Of course," Dana reassured her. "You already have Ted Hanson in your corner, and he is a very important man."

"Are you sure it is okay to wear what I wore in the pictures? Maybe I should find something else nicer. My Sunday dresses no longer fit, but perhaps Mama would lend me the money to buy something."

"It's not necessary. If I thought it was, I would take you shopping myself." She paused, thinking of the endless stretch of hours between now and their appointment at the ad agency. If they would be empty for her, they would be excruciatingly slow for Rosa. Maybe shopping wasn't such a bad idea. It would take her mind off the stalled investigation into Ken's murder for a while, too. Sometimes a distraction allowed the head to sort through the facts and put them into some new order.

"Rosa, let's do it. Let's go find something special for you to wear."

"Oh, no," she objected with feeling. "I could not take a gift from you. You have already done so much."

"No arguments. It would be my pleasure. Think of it ～～～～ contribution to ～～～～ Even as she ～～～～ ed. It was getting more and ～～～～ "You will drive here alone each day worriedly.

"Of course."

"But I do not think that is such a good idea," she protested. "It can be very dangerous here for you. Rick would not be happy if I let you do that."

Rick was not king of the world, not her world, anyway. "It's not his decision or yours," Dana said testily. "I'll be fine. Ten o'clock, Rosa. I'll pick you up in the alley by Rick's parking place."

After she'd hung up, Dana concluded that this was the best thing that could have happened. She needed to prove once and for all that she could operate independently of Rick's influence. Perhaps people who wouldn't open up in his presence would admit things to her if they saw that she wasn't afraid to be in the neighborhood alone. This was not a time to turn into some sort of timid soul. She was intrepid. At least, she always had been before. She just had to hone that side of her nature again.

Of course, she might get her fool head shot off, she conceded. Still, she felt more optimistic than she had in weeks. She felt in charge again. It was a great feeling.

Despite the traffic, she found the drive into the city exhilarating. The air was frigid, but the sky was a brilliant blue, and the sun sparkled on Lake Michigan.

The closer she came to the barrio, the greater her sense of anticipation. Some of that was on Rosa's behalf. More of it was on her own. She would prove to Rick, once and for all, that she was capable of handling herself, even in this dangerous and somewhat alien environment.

Why she felt she had to prove anything to him was beyond her. She didn't care what Rick Sanchez thought of her. He was simply a means to an end. Even as she thought that, though, she sigh̶ more difficult to convince herself of that w̶ that passed. There was an undeniable connection between them, and it seemed to be growing stronger every minute.

Still, she was in a cheerful frame of mind as she cut through the narrow, crowded streets of the barrio. In the daytime, they were alive with activity. It was hard to feel any sense of the danger that darkened the same streets at nightfall.

As she made the turn into the alley behind Yo, Amigo, she saw a large shadow detach itself from the wall. A faint chill of apprehension washed over her, ruining her earlier mood. The test of her newfound determination was coming a little sooner than she'd hoped.

Even so, she forced herself to drive forward. She refused to let anyone intimidate her within a few yards of her destination. She could always scream bloody murder at this point and someone from Yo, Amigo was bound to come running to her rescue.

Just in case, her right hand folded around the grip of the gun she'd brought along. Though it was registered and totally legal, it had been years since she'd had it out of her safe-deposit box. She'd picked it up this morning on her way into Chicago. How fortuitous, she decided, as the shadow ahead began to take the shape of a tall, broad-shouldered man.

She was so intent on him that she never even saw the second man slip up beside the driver's-side door. When it was wrenched open, she gasped with shock and instinctively swerved the car to the right.

The man muttered an oath, but his grip on the door never loosened. Dana was about to hit the accelerator when a hand stretched across and yanked the keys from the ignition, stopping the car in its tracks.

She whirled in the seat, gun in hand. The barrel was pointed directly at the intruder's midsection.

"Holy Mother of God, point that thing some other way."

At the sound of the voice, she glanced up, straight into Rick's furious face.

"You," she said, shocked and furious herself. "I ought to put a bullet through you, just to teach you a lesson about scaring a person to death."

"Let's just call it even," he suggested dryly.

"Was there a point to your little exercise here?" she inquired.

"I was hoping to show that you were no match for the neighborhood."

"So far, the only times I've been threatened and assaulted here, it's been by you," she reminded him. "I'd say you're the real danger to me."

"You bet, *querida*," he said in a way that didn't sound half so much like the endearment it usually was.

He wrapped a hand around the back of her neck and dragged her half out of the car, then delivered a bruising, punishing kiss that both infuriated and alarmed her. Why alarmed? Because she enjoyed it far too much.

She thrilled to the overwhelming passion behind it. Her mouth stung. Her blood roared. And she hated herself for it, hated feeling so alive, hated that another man could make her feel that way.

Still, she couldn't resist. The gun slipped from her grasp as she reached up to touch Rick's cheek. When it did, he released her and seized it before she could blink.

"Never let your guard down with the enemy," he reminded her softly as he unloaded the bullets from the gun, then stuck it in the waistband of his jeans.

"That kiss didn't feel as if it were between enemies," she said, more shaken than she wanted to admit.

"Sex can be as potent a weapon as guns. You would do well to remember that."

An awful lot of people had been handing out free advice to her lately, and she found it incredibly irritating. Backing away, she sank back behind the wheel and gestured up the alley, where there was no longer any sign of the man who'd distracted her.

"Who was your decoy?" she asked.

"Marco," he admitted readily enough. "He told me of the plans you had with Rosa. We decided you should be made aware of the risk you were taking."

"What a pair of sports!" she said derisively. "Are you coming along on our shopping expedition to protect us from the salesclerks?"

"Though I would like nothing more than to spend the day watching you choose the clothes you will put next to your body, I'm afraid I have work to do here. Marco will accompany you. I will join you later, in time for the meeting at the advertising agency."

"I would hate to disrupt your day. If you're busy, you could skip that, too."

His lips quirked at her testiness. "And miss out on

Rosa's big moment? Never. I would not disappoint her that way. Nor would I let you down."

"How sweet!"

"Stick around, *querida*. You will discover there are many sides to me before we are through."

"And not all of them attractive," she retorted.

He grinned. "But the others compensate, yes?"

Dana wouldn't have answered that if an armed mob had demanded it. The man was already entirely too smug as it was. And she was not prepared to give him a totally honest answer. She couldn't even give one to herself.

Rick's stomach still clenched when he remembered the sight of that gun being aimed so steadily at his gut. Dana had surprised him and, though he would have died before admitting it to her, she had delighted him. She was clearly very brave, even if far too impetuous for her own good.

He was not sure yet which of them had learned the more valuable lesson in that alley. He knew, without a doubt, that he could no longer underestimate her. She... well, who knew what she had taken away from the experience? Perhaps an awareness of just how powerful the chemistry was between them.

He would have loved to take the time to pursue the raw emotions unleashed by that kiss he had initiated, but he'd promised Tico he would stop by the restaurant before it opened. He'd said it was urgent and too risky to be discussed on the phone, when anyone might pick up an extension, either at Yo, Amigo or in his own kitchen.

Maybe this was the break they'd been looking for, Rick thought as he walked the few blocks to the small restaurant. Perhaps Tico had found the link they'd sought to some nefarious Chicago politician.

He slipped in the back door, just so he could inhale

the aroma of meat cooking with cumin and other spices. He snatched a jalapeño from a huge bowl as he passed and bit into it as he winked at Tico's mother, who was overseeing the lunch preparations.

"Out," she shouted at him, shooing him toward the door. "You pay, like everyone else." She was laughing, though, as she said it.

"Te amo, Mamacita," he called back. He paused to give her a smacking kiss on the cheek. Other than his own mother, there was no one he adored more than this woman with the graying hair and aristocratic features, which had been softened by age, but blessed with wisdom.

"When are you going to marry me?" he asked.

"You want my cooking, not me," she retorted.

"Not so. Tico cooks as well as you, and I do not wish to marry him."

She laughed. "Out of here with your foolishness. Tico is waiting for you. He is very anxious." Her expression sobered. "There is no trouble for Tico, is there, Rick?"

"No trouble. I promise."

"Muy bien. Vaya. Go. You are in my way."

Rick found Tico in his office, surrounded by mounds of paperwork. He was on the phone, arguing with a supplier in rapidly escalating Spanish. Rick almost pitied the person on the receiving end of the tirade. It sounded as though he was very close to losing Tico's very lucrative business.

"Give the man a break," he mouthed to his friend.

Tico slammed down the phone, with nothing apparently resolved. "A break? He is my cousin, and he is trying to cheat me and you would have me give him a break? I should cut off his *cahones.*"

Rick winced. "That ought to improve family relations

no end. When your mood improves slightly, perhaps you would like to tell me why you had me rush over here. In the meantime, I will remain very quiet. I would prefer not to endanger my own manhood by crossing you."

Tico sighed and slugged back a tiny cup of the thick, sweet Cuban coffee he preferred. The man must live with a perpetual caffeine buzz, Rick concluded, watching him try to get a grip on his temper.

Finally Tico smiled. His shoulders relaxed visibly. "It has been a bad morning. I'm sorry."

"Thanks, but I'm not the one who deserves an apology. In the interest of family harmony, perhaps you should be saying that to your cousin."

"I will," Tico promised, then grinned. "Eventually. In the meantime, he deserves to sweat."

"Now, since your mood seems to be improving, tell me," Rick said. "What have you found out? I assume this has something to do with Ken's murder."

The younger man nodded. "Someone came to me yesterday. He said he had heard that I was interested in information on the *padre*'s death. He wanted money, so at first I wasn't sure whether he was desperate or trustworthy. In the end, we came to terms."

"Did he have information?"

Tico shrugged. "You will have to decide that for yourself. He says that a thug named Carlos Hernandez was involved."

The name meant nothing to Rick. He looked at Tico. "Do you know him?"

"I know of him. He runs a gang of sorts, though it is closer to a ring of criminals, if you ask me. They are for hire to do a variety of jobs that are not exactly legal. They stay away from drugs, but they are very adept at everything else, from arson to murder."

Rick considered the information. Was it possible that someone had hired this Carlos to hit Ken? But why, dammit? Why would anyone want to see Ken dead? He thought of the drugs that he didn't doubt for a minute had been planted in Ken's office. Was there a link there?

"You say this Carlos has nothing to do with drug trafficking, but would he be above planting drugs to turn someone into a suspect?"

"He will shoot a man in cold blood," Tico said dryly. "I doubt he would blink at the thought of framing someone. Why? Did someone try to pin a drug charge on Ken, as well?"

"Looks that way," Rick admitted. "Where can I find this Carlos?"

"I figured you would want to see him, so I asked my contact if he could arrange a meeting. Carlos will be dropping by for a beer around four this afternoon. The restaurant will be quiet then. You will not be interrupted."

Four? Damn, he was supposed to meet Dana at the ad agency at four for Rosa's big meeting. In the meantime, with the two of them chasing from boutique to boutique, he had no way to get in touch with her to let her know that there'd been a change in plans. And he had just promised her that he always meant what he said.

Still, there wasn't a doubt in his mind that she would want him to meet with Carlos if it would offer them any information at all about what had happened to Ken.

"I'll be here," he told Tico. "But this guy better have something for me, because I'm canceling a very important engagement for this."

"With the lovely *señora?*"

Rick nodded.

"You are treading on dangerous turf with that one, *mi amigo.*"

Tico wasn't telling him anything he hadn't already thought a thousand times. "Tell me about it," Rick said with an air of resignation.

"It happens that way sometimes," Tico observed wryly. "All you can do then is hang on for the ride."

Based on the ups and downs so far, Rick was pretty certain it was going to be a roller coaster.

18

"He said he would be here and he will be," Marco insisted as Dana muttered under her breath about Rick's failure to appear at the ad agency at four o'clock.

"I'm delighted you have such faith in him," she retorted, "but it's after four now. Where is he?"

"Caught up in traffic," Rosa suggested distractedly as she peered at her faint reflection in the glass covering a huge poster of one of the agency's hottest current print campaigns. "Are you certain I do not look like a blimp in this dress?"

Though she wanted to rail against broken promises, Dana forced herself to concentrate on the nervous young woman. "You look like a beautiful woman who is carrying a baby."

Rather than being reassured, Rosa sighed. "I do look like a blimp."

"I promise you your figure will come back right after the baby is born," Dana told her.

"Maybe we should make this appointment for then," Rosa said worriedly. "No one will hire me looking like this."

"A maternity clothes manufacturer would," a male voice interrupted with quiet authority.

Dana glanced into the opened doorway and saw Ted Hanson grinning at her. He was an extraordinarily sophisticated man with an eye for beauty and a genius for selling, but he looked like anything but that.

His prematurely gray hair was curly. Blue eyes twinkled mischievously behind wire-framed glasses. When he wasn't making major presentations to stuffy corporate officials, he dressed as he had today—in jeans and chambray shirts over colorful T-shirts. Today's shade was purple. Not mauve or eggplant, but brilliant purple.

He crossed the room in three strides to scoop Dana up into an exuberant bear hug.

"I'm so sorry about Ken," he told her again, his eyes reflecting a genuine sorrow. "When I heard about it, I was just sick. I apologize again for not getting back for the funeral. I was on a photo shoot in Italy. It just wasn't possible."

"I got the flowers and the note. That was more than enough."

He examined her face intently. "You're doing okay?"

She flushed under the knowing scrutiny. "Well enough," she said. "Come, let me introduce you to two friends. Marco, this is Ted Hanson." She put an arm around Rosa's ample waist. "And this is Rosa."

Ted's practiced gaze swept over the teenager, assessing her with an instinct he'd been honing for the past twenty years. "You're perfect," he said. "Every bit as lovely as the pictures Dana sent over. Let's go inside. I'll show you around and then we can talk about your future."

Looking more than a little awestruck by Ted's whirlwind approach, Rosa followed in his wake down a wide corridor covered with thick mauve carpeting. They passed an astonishing array of award-winning print ads immortalized in giant posters that had been lit with a touch many museums would envy.

Marco glanced at Dana as they walked, his brown eyes reflecting his own barely concealed awe. His usual arrogance and distrustfulness were nowhere in evidence. "He is very good, isn't he?" he asked, gesturing toward the posters.

"The best." She glanced sideways at him. "You should consider talking to him in your own behalf, as long as we're here," she suggested casually.

"No," Marco said fiercely. "This is my sister's day. She should have his undivided attention."

Dana appreciated the sentiment, but was almost certain she heard a little wistfulness behind the words. "We'll see," she said.

Fighting her fury at Rick's failure to join them, she forced herself to concentrate on the upcoming meeting. It was mostly up to her to protect Rosa's interests, though she didn't doubt for a minute that Ted would be fair, if only as a favor to her. They had known each other a very long time, ever since she had successfully investigated the leaks of some of his presentation plans to a competing agency. She had caught the insider who was betraying him within two weeks, preventing the loss of yet another major account.

Ted's bouncing energy and enthusiasm were catching, as he took them on the promised tour, showing them the art department, the copywriters, the small studio where some television spots were actually shot, even an animation department, which so captivated Marco that Dana wasn't certain they'd ever get him away from the room. While watching the work going on there, his usual sullen expression vanished, and his eyes lit with an eagerness she found charming. Then and there she resolved to encourage that unanticipated excitement. For the first time, she truly realized the seductiveness of helping someone to discover a new future. No wonder Ken had gone back to Yo, Amigo again and again.

In Ted's office, the talk turned to jobs and fees and all of the mundane contractual details that Rosa really needed an agent or attorney to oversee.

"If she agrees to any of this today, it will have to be on the condition that a lawyer goes through every word and has the opportunity to challenge any aspect of the deal," Dana said.

"Agreed," Ted said at once. He turned to Rosa. "So, young lady, what do you say? Would you like to come to work for us on an exclusive basis, for say three years?"

"One," Dana corrected. "With options."

Ted scowled. "Two," he countered. "We discovered her. We deserve time to make sure our investment pays off."

Dana grinned at him. "Okay, two," she conceded grudgingly. She had expected him to ask for five in an attempt to tie up a potentially hot commodity for the longest time possible. That he'd been more than fair proved her faith in him had been justified.

"Marco, what do you think?" Rosa asked, her eyes flashing with excitement.

He regarded her with an indulgent smile. "Mama and Papa will go ballistic, but I think you should do it if it will make you happy and will secure a future for you and the baby."

Rosa jumped up and threw her arms around her brother, her expression relieved. "Thank you."

Dana knew by now that Rosa would have defied him if she'd had to, but today's thrill was even greater because Marco had joined in with his approval.

Ted looked jubilant. "Then we have a deal?"

"Looks like we do," Dana said.

As if he'd read her mind, Ted turned to Marco. "Now, what about you, young man? You have the same excellent bone structure and interesting look as your sister. Can we sign you up today, as well?"

Even though Dana had told him the same thing, Marco looked stunned at hearing it from a professional for whom he'd already expressed admiration. "Me?" He glanced at Dana, clearly bemused that she had been right about his own potential. "Is it possible?"

Dana nodded at him encouragingly. "You should at least think about it, Marco. It's a golden opportunity." She slid in a suggestion she hoped would prove too alluring for him to resist. "Perhaps, you could even convince Ted to let you train in animation techniques at the same time."

"I could do this?" Marco asked, gazing at the agency president with obvious disbelief. There was no mistaking the hint of eagerness in his expression, though.

Ted picked up on Dana's less-than-subtle hint at once. "Absolutely. We could work it into the deal."

"I was not so good at school," Marco confessed. "I have no college."

"This would be on-the-job training," Ted reassured him. "I've found that it's always easier to learn something that fascinates you. I can't tell you the times I barely scraped by in math and science classes."

"You?" Marco asked, shocked. "But you are a very successful man."

"I could show you the report cards," Ted assured him. "My mother waves them under my nose whenever she thinks I'm getting too big for my britches. It keeps me humble, she says. Think about my offer, Marco."

Marco's shoulders squared proudly. "I do not have to

think, *señor.* I would be proud to accept this opportunity. I hope that I will not give you cause to regret it."

"I'm sure you won't. I look forward to working with both of you," Ted said, coming out from behind his desk to shake Marco's hand. Rosa jumped up and gave him an impulsive hug, then squeezed Dana hard as well.

"You have changed our lives, *señora.*"

"No," Dana insisted. "I have just given you a helping hand. Return the favor someday to someone else."

"That is what the *padre* always said," Rosa said, her expression suddenly sad. "I wish he could know about this."

"He does," Dana said with confidence, thinking it more than likely he had guided her into the lives of these two promising young people. "I am certain that wherever he is, he knows and he is very proud of both of you."

Rick would be proud, too, for that matter. Maybe she would tell him…right before she strangled him.

Rick sat in the most secluded booth Tico's had to offer and kept his gaze fixed on the door. Even though the restaurant was virtually empty except for a handful of men sipping *cafe Cubano* at the counter, he wanted privacy, should anyone else come in while he was talking to Carlos.

He repeatedly glanced at his watch, noting when four o'clock came and went. Dana was going to have his head for abandoning them with no notice, especially if this Carlos person never showed and he had no news to report to her.

It was four-fifteen by the time an obviously nervous young man entered the restaurant. His gaze darted from table to table, assessing the risks, Rick imagined. When Tico broke away from a conversation behind the counter,

Rick knew that the new arrival was Carlos. Tico gestured toward the booth, and the man swaggered down the narrow aisle and slid in opposite him.

His face was pockmarked and a line of tattoos ran up his forearm, but otherwise he was unremarkable. With his olive complexion, black hair and dark eyes, he was interchangeable with half of the twenty-five-year-olds on the streets of the barrio. Even his dress was moderately conservative—chinos and a T-shirt worn under a leather jacket.

"You are Carlos?" Rick asked.

"Sí."

"I'm Rick Sanchez."

"I recognize you."

"Tico tells me you might know something about a matter that is of great importance to me, the murder of a friend of mine."

Carlos shrugged. "I might. Tell me about this person."

"He was a minister from the suburbs. He became a friend to all of us at Yo, Amigo. He helped many of the young people here. He was a good man, Carlos, a decent man. He didn't deserve to die. The police believe he was a victim of random violence, a drive-by shooting that went awry."

Carlos gestured dismissively. "The police are idiots. It is easier to blame chance than to admit they do not control these streets."

"Have they questioned you?"

A smirking grin played about the other man's lips. "I am very careful. They do not even know I exist. I prefer to keep it that way."

Rick wondered about that. In his experience, the police frequently knew—or at least suspected—far more than they were able to act on. He had been surprised to discover just how much they knew about the inside workings of his own gang, once he had eventually broken free of its ties.

"What have you heard about this shooting?" he asked, careful not to imply that Carlos had any direct responsibility for it.

Carlos studied him intently, as if sizing him up and analyzing the dangers he might represent. "You say this man was good, but he had at least one enemy," he said eventually. "Someone was willing to pay a lot of money to see that he died."

"How much money?"

"Fifty thousand."

Rick had to work to cover his astonishment. He had anticipated some penny-ante crime, a quick hit for enough money to buy another supply of crack. Fifty thousand dollars was big business. How the hell had Ken Miller made such a deadly serious enemy?

"Who, Carlos? Who was behind this?"

"I cannot answer that."

Rick's last thread of patience snapped. He reached across the table and grabbed a fistful of the other man's shirt. "Who, dammit?"

Carlos's eyes darkened dangerously as he broke Rick's grip. His fingers dug into Rick's flesh painfully in a duel for supremacy.

"You will never do such a thing again, *comprende?*" he demanded in a tight voice.

For the moment, because it was prudent, Rick backed off. "Sorry. My friend is dead. I'm sure you can see how I might overreact. Tell me everything you know. I will keep you out of it. You and I…" He shrugged. "If anyone asks, we have never met."

"That is very wise, but I am afraid I have no other answers for you. I never saw this person who paid so much for your friend's death. I heard only a voice on the phone. The money was where I was told it would be. Anonymity protects everyone when you conduct business as I do. I am sure you can see that."

Every fiber of Rick's being wanted to grab this slime by the throat and squeeze the information out of him, but he knew it would be of no use. Carlos had told him as much as he would, perhaps even as much as he could.

He knew far more than he did a half hour ago. He knew that Ken had had a powerful enemy, someone who had intended that he die that night. Carlos had confirmed once and for all that Ken's murder had not been an accident, a case of mistaken identity.

And if those drugs that had been planted in Ken's office were any indication, the danger hadn't died with him. It was still very much alive, and that meant that Dana could very well become the next victim.

_19_

It was dark by the time Dana arrived home, but a full moon created eerie shadows on the snow-covered ground. The unsettling atmosphere suited her mood perfectly. Her emotions were all over the place. She was ecstatic for Rosa and Marco one minute and furious with Rick the next, then despondent when she thought of what Ken had missed today, of all that he would miss in the future.

The first was understandable. The two young people were getting the chance of a lifetime, and she knew in her heart that they would make the most of it. She felt a deep sense of satisfaction that she had played some small role in changing their lives.

She could almost feel Ken beside her, reminding her that good deeds built character and made the world a better place. It was almost as if by helping Rosa and Marco, she had given a gift to Ken, as well—an admission that withholding her support from his work at Yo, Amigo had been wrong. Her understanding of his commitment had deepened, and her love for him had never been stronger.

And yet...

She sighed. And yet there was Rick Sanchez, infuriating her one minute, making her feel alive the next.

His failure to show up—more importantly, his failure to keep his promise—had been both disappointing and unnerving. She shouldn't be counting on him so much. He shouldn't even be capable of disappointing her. A few days ago, he had been a despised stranger. Now…

Again, she sighed. Now he mattered in some way she couldn't define, didn't want to define. She feared that to do so would prove her to be disloyal to Ken.

Still feeling that vague stirring of guilt, she put the key into the lock. Then, before she could turn the key, her gaze was drawn toward the cemetery beyond the house. A stronger wave of guilt sent her in that direction. It was an overwhelming, weighty sense of guilt that led her directly to Ken's grave. She desperately needed to connect somehow to the man she had adored, to remind herself of the eternal promise of love that had bound them.

With shaking fingers, she reached out and touched the cold marble tombstone—an open-armed, welcoming angel—that a stonemason in the congregation had worked on lovingly, day and night, to be ready for the funeral. She traced the smooth surface, remembering, as she skimmed each indentation, the words that had been carved there: Here lies an angel of God, a man of faith. Beloved husband. Beloved father.

The dates below spanned a too-brief lifetime, less than forty years. That saddened her more than anything. The world needed men like Ken, men who put others first and themselves second, men who taught compassion and understanding, men who lived by their words.

She glanced toward the bright, starlit sky and asked again, for the thousandth time, "Why?" It was a plea for understanding, a ritual incantation by now.

No answer came, though, no illumination that could

make sense of the incomprehensible. There was just this terrible sense of loss, an ending that had no meaning.

She knelt in the snow, oblivious to the dampness soaking through her slacks, oblivious to the howling wind blowing off the nearby lake. Frantic now, she dug the withered flowers from beneath the snow and tossed them aside. In a motion as old as time, she smoothed the snowy surface as she would the blanket on a child's bed. Tears tracked down her cheeks, freezing in the icy air. Her skin burned with the cold. Her fingers went numb.

"Why, dammit? Why?" she cried, pummeling the ground, the tombstone.

She waited and waited, but only the cry of the wind answered, not God. Never God.

Dimly, she became aware of a muttered curse, then the warmth of arms surrounding her, of soothing words and the whisper of breath against her cheek.

"It's okay," Rick murmured. "Everything is going to be okay."

She felt herself being lifted, held against a solid chest. Instinctively, she snuggled into the heat and clung as she was carried quickly back to the house.

"Keys?"

She struggled to remember. "In the door," she finally admitted, teeth chattering.

Inside, she was deposited in Ken's chair. The afghan was wrapped around her, the fire lit, and still she shivered.

"Don't move," he ordered.

As if she could, she thought, almost numb with the cold. Only when he returned did he turn on the light, as he handed her a mug of steaming coffee. It had been laced with brandy, she realized as she gulped the fiery liquid and felt the heat shimmer through her.

"More," he insisted.

She drank again and the feeling slowly began to come back. First in fingers and toes, then deeper inside, bringing with it an agonizing pain that no amount of heat could salve.

She finally dared to meet Rick's gaze and was stunned by the anger blazing in his eyes. There was so much fury there, fury and something else. Fear, she concluded with some surprise.

She reached out and touched a finger to his cheek. "It's okay. I'm okay."

He shuddered, but the fear didn't disappear as she'd intended. "What were you thinking?" he demanded. "You could have died out there."

"It was just a few minutes," she argued.

"It's nearly midnight."

"Midnight?" It couldn't be. She had gotten home hours ago.

"I've been looking for you everywhere. Your car was in the driveway, but you weren't answering the doorbell. Thank heaven I never opened the storm door and spotted the keys, or I really would have gone nuts. You scared the hell out of me as it was. I've talked to Kate. She's the one who suggested I look in the cemetery. She's frantic, too. I tried to stop her, but she's on her way over."

"Sorry," Dana whispered, teeth chattering. "I had to tend to the grave."

He stared at her incredulously. "In the middle of the night? If I hadn't found you, you'd have been dead by morning. Are you out of your mind?"

Maybe she was, Dana thought. She thought she had reached rock bottom the day they buried Ken, but maybe she hadn't. Maybe this was it, this not caring if she lived or died.

Rick watched her intently. "I won't let you do it, you know."

"Do what?" she asked shakily.

"Kill yourself. You're going to live, dammit. And we're going to find the person who killed Ken, and we're going to go on, both of us."

"I wasn't trying to kill myself," she said, shocked by the suggestion. She might not care if she lived or died, but she would do nothing to hasten the process, not with three sons counting on her. She would find some way to be whole again, for their sake, if not her own.

"Well, you could have fooled me," he said, still furious. "If I have to move in here and stay with you twenty-four hours a day, you will live, Dana Miller, because that's what Ken would want."

As suddenly as the tirade had begun, it ended, and he dragged her into his arms. "It's what I want, *querida,*" he said softly.

Surprised by the admission, Dana pulled back gently and looked into his eyes. "You?"

"Yes, God help me."

He didn't sound pleased about it, she concluded, somehow amused that this tough, streetwise man had finally come up against something he couldn't control, namely his feelings for her. It gave them something in common. Gazing into his eyes, she admitted, finally and only to herself, that she had no more control over her own growing feelings for him.

Since she couldn't—wouldn't—confess as much to him, she settled for going on the attack instead. "Where were you today? You promised to meet us at the agency. You let Rosa down."

"I let you down, too," he pointed out, clearly grasping

the real source of her irritation. "When you hear where I was, I think you'll forgive me."

She wouldn't be persuaded so easily. "Don't count on it," she muttered.

He shrugged. "If you don't want to hear..." he taunted.

She scowled at the teasing. "Of course I want to hear. Tell me."

He examined her intently. "Are you sure you're feeling up to it?"

"I'm well enough to flatten that attractive nose of yours if you don't start talking."

He grinned. "In that case—"

Before he could begin, the doorbell rang and Kate came rushing inside. She tossed her coat over a chair, revealing a mismatched outfit of sweatpants and T-shirt, proof that she'd been in a hurry. Not until she had examined Dana from head to toe and concluded that no permanent damage had been done did they get back to Rick's news.

He described his meeting with the mysterious Carlos. Dana gaped when he told her how much had been paid for the hit on Ken.

"So much," Kate breathed. "We're talking serious money here."

"Which means that we've stumbled into a genuine hornet's nest," Dana concluded, her excitement for the hunt returning. At last there was progress, a hint, if not proof, that Ken's death had been calculated.

"But Carlos has no idea who this person was?" she asked.

"None, or so he claims," Rick said.

"Do you believe him?"

"He's probably telling the truth. Anyone with enough cash to pay for an execution isn't going to want anything to connect him to it. There won't be a paper trail, probably not even phone records. Whoever delivered the payoff is probably so far removed that even he can't identify the person ordering the hit."

"Do you think we're talking drugs?" Kate asked. "Or some kind of criminal organization?"

"Drugs would be my guess," Rick said. "Especially in light of the so-called evidence planted in Ken's office."

"I don't think so," Dana said slowly, her expression thoughtful. "It's too pat, too obvious. Somebody wanted to muddy the waters by destroying Ken's reputation. My guess is it's somebody with something else to hide."

"Such as?" Kate asked.

Dana sighed. She was too exhausted to take the next leap in logic. "I wish I knew," she said wearily.

"So, what's the plan for tomorrow?" Kate asked, putting her coat back on.

Dana glanced at Rick. "I think it's time we began to take a closer look at the people right here, starting with Lawrence Tremayne," she said, knowing that her words were bound to make him happy.

To his credit, he didn't gloat. He merely nodded his agreement. "I'd like to talk to him," he suggested. "I have a few things I'd like to say about his plan to boot you out of this house."

"Maybe not," Dana said, even though she rather enjoyed this fierce, protective streak he'd developed. "This conversation requires finesse, not blazing guns."

"I don't even own a gun," Rick protested.

"It was a figure of speech," Dana told him.

Kate regarded them both with amusement. "I'll let you two wrestle with the semantics and the details. I need my beauty sleep. See you in the morning, sweetie." She glanced pointedly at Rick. "You, too?"

"Go," Dana instructed before Rick could reply. "It's already after two. Try to sleep past six, for a change."

"Sorry. My internal alarm clock can't be reset," Kate said. "But I will call before I come dashing over here." She winked. "Just in case."

When she had gone, Dana looked at Rick. "You can leave, too."

"No way, *querida*. Not tonight. You go up to bed. I will sleep right here on the sofa."

The proposal raised an interesting quandary, though obviously not the one Rick assumed, judging by the determined glint in his eyes. Eventually she shook her head.

"It won't work."

"What won't?" The jut of his jaw suggested he was ready to battle with her, if necessary. "If you knew how many nights I've slept on a far-worse sofa at Yo, Amigo, you wouldn't worry about this."

"It's not that."

His expression puzzled, he waited.

Dana drew in a deep breath. "I haven't slept upstairs since Ken died. I've been sleeping right here."

"In the chair?" he asked incredulously.

She nodded.

"Oh, baby," he whispered, and scooped her up.

Once more, she nestled against him, not even questioning what he intended. He crossed the room in three strides and started up the steps.

"Which room?" he asked at the top of the stairs.

Dana couldn't bring herself to answer, wasn't sure she could bring herself to cross that threshold, even with Rick's strong arms around her. *Especially* with Rick's arms around her.

Ignoring her silence, he simply peeked in room after room, until at last he reached the cramped master bedroom with its awful gold carpeting. He paused in the doorway and gazed into her eyes.

"Okay?"

"I can't," she whispered. "We can't. Not here."

"Shh. Nothing's going to happen. I'll just stay here with you until you fall asleep. You need to do this, *querida*. You need to move on."

"I'll be moving out soon. I'll buy a new bed, something with a frilly canopy that Ken would never have set foot in. Then it won't even matter."

"It will," he said with certainty. "I think you must face the fact that Ken is gone, that he won't ever be back to share the most intimate part of your life."

She understood the symbolism, the need to let go, to accept, but she wanted to protest that it was still too soon, the wound was still too raw. She could never sleep here, not with the place beside her cold and empty.

But of course, it wouldn't be. Not if she understood what Rick was proposing, that he lay down beside her, perhaps even hold her, until sleep claimed her.

No matter how innocent the offer, though, she couldn't accept it. It would be sacrilege to allow another man into Ken's bed, especially a man she wanted as desperately as she wanted Rick Sanchez tonight. She couldn't allow him to displace Ken's memory here, of all places.

"No, please," she protested again. "We can't do this. There's a guest room next door. I'll sleep there." She smiled wryly. "At least I'm up the stairs. It's a start."

Rick's gaze locked with hers and, for a moment, she thought for sure that he would argue, but finally his expression softened, and he carried her to the nearby room.

The decor was spartan, a simple double bed with a beige chenille spread, a small oak dresser with an antique pitcher filled with dried flowers on top.

Rick gently lowered her to her feet, then reached past her to pull down the spread.

"Can I get you a nightgown?" he asked. "A glass of water? Anything?"

Looking directly into his eyes, she shook her head and reached slowly and deliberately for the buttons of her blouse. His gaze locked on her shaking fingers as first one button, then a second and a third came undone. The dawning awareness of what she intended had his breath catching. She stared at him in mute appeal and waited. Eventually he swallowed hard as he pushed aside her hands to finish the task.

When his knuckles skimmed over bare skin, Dana's heart leaped into her throat. She was caught halfway between panic and excitement, but the brush of his fingertips across her silky bra had her nipples tightening and the blood roaring through her veins as it hadn't done in too, too long a time. The thrill of feeling alive again, of feeling whole, overwhelmed her.

She didn't hesitate to weigh right or wrong. She simply gave herself over to sensation, the shimmering heat, the wild ricocheting of her pulse.

She refused to allow herself comparisons as Rick's hands danced across her flesh, inciting passion. There was joy in his touch, a promised ecstasy that came with each quick, deliberate caress.

Clothes magically disappeared right along with inhibitions. There was a surprisingly easy familiarity between them and none of the edginess of first-time lovers.

He made love with every part of his body, with the shifting of a leg, the stroke of his palm, the lingering touch of his lips. And everywhere he left fire and a wicked yearning in his wake.

Dana's soft pleas counterpointed his harsher moans

as they joined, retreated, then came together again in a tantalizing ritual. She blocked out memories and grief, everything but this exquisite present and the man who was making love to her with such life-affirming tenderness and passion.

It was his name she cried out when release came, his name that echoed in her head as sleep finally stole over her.

But tonight, of all nights, it was her husband's face that slipped into her dreams and made her cry.

20

Rick stood in Dana's kitchen, coffee mug in hand, and stared out the window at the destruction she had managed to wreak the night before on her husband's grave. Wilted, frozen flowers were strewn in every direction. The once-glistening blanket of snow was littered with clumps of dirt and brown petals. Tears welled up in his eyes as he thought of his friend buried deep within that cold earth.

"Ah, *amigo,* she is going to hate me this morning," he murmured ruefully. "And you? How would you feel if you knew?"

He wanted to believe that his friend would understand, that he would give them his blessing to go on living, but he wondered if Ken wasn't a man first and a saint second. Could any man forgive so easily what had happened between his wife and another man so soon after his death?

And yet Rick couldn't regret the night before any more than he could stop mourning the loss of his friend. Dana touched something deep inside him, a part of him that he'd thought incapable of feeling. She was fiercely proud, defiantly strong, and yet there was a vulnerability in her, a neediness that reached out to him. He wanted to protect her, even though he knew she would never thank him for it. It was enough to do it because he had to—for himself and for Ken.

He was more troubled than he dared to admit by what Carlos had told him. As badly as he had wanted to protect Yo, Amigo, as desperate as he'd been to believe that no one in the barrio was responsible for Ken's death, he wondered if that wouldn't have been preferable to this callous, unknown villain.

What kind of person paid fifty thousand dollars for the murder of a minister? Someone who was beyond desperation, someone with something evil to hide, something dangerous to protect. And how would such a person react to the discovery that Dana was more determined than ever to ferret out the truth?

He didn't have to think long and hard about the latter. He'd had waking nightmares about it until dawn. Most frustrating was knowing there was nothing he could say that would dissuade her from continuing the search. Pleas, demands, all would fall on deaf ears. She felt she owed answers to her children and to her husband. After spending last night in his arms, he guessed that her fervor would only be magnified. It was an understandable sentiment, but a risky one.

Something of what he felt must have shown on his face. When Dana walked into the kitchen dressed in jeans and a T-shirt, she regarded him warily, far more warily than a woman should a recent lover.

Unless, of course, she was filled with regrets. He gazed into her eyes only to have her look hurriedly away. Despite his anticipation of the reaction, it hurt just the same. Putting his coffee on the table, he reached out and touched a finger to her chin, forcing her to turn toward him.

"Don't," he said, more harshly than he'd intended.

Her gaze met his, then skittered nervously away. "Don't what?" she asked.

"Pretend that nothing happened. Pretend that it didn't matter."

She kept her gaze steady then. "It didn't," she said vehemently. "It was a—"

"No," he protested, cutting her off. He didn't want to hear that it was a mistake, even though he'd mentally prepared himself for her saying exactly that.

She wouldn't let it drop. "I was feeling lost and alone last night, that's all. I needed to feel alive."

He regarded her knowingly. "And you did, did you not, *querida?* You felt very much alive in my arms."

She closed her eyes, as if to block out the truth, but Rick knew that she couldn't deny it. Neither of them could. What had happened in that bed last night had been more than just sex. A bond had been formed. Where it would lead, he had no idea, but it was as strong as any he'd ever felt.

Few people in his life had really mattered to him—his mother, Tico, Ken and now Dana. He would have given his life for any of them. Instead, two were lost to him forever. He was left to honor their memories and to go on.

"There will be time enough to figure out what it all means," he promised her. "Just don't deny that it was important. Don't lie to either of us that way."

She glanced toward the window, then back at him. "How can you?"

"How can I what?" he demanded. "Stand here in my best friend's kitchen, talking to his wife about making love to her? How can I live with the fact that I'm alive and he's dead? How can I look you in the face, knowing that despite last night, despite everything that has happened between us, you still hold me responsible for his death?"

She started to protest, but he cut her off again. "No, if you're being totally honest, you know that you still blame me simply because of where he was when he was killed. It doesn't really matter who pulled the trigger, does it?"

"Of course it does. That's what this whole investigation is all about."

"Really?" he asked doubtfully. "Or is it about punishing me for living, while your husband is dead?"

"This isn't about you, you egotistical jerk," she said with quiet rage. "None of it is about you. It's about justice."

"Justice?" he asked softly. "Or vengeance?"

She hesitated just long enough to prove his point.

"Leave that to God, *querida*."

"I don't believe in God," she insisted. "Not anymore."

Shocked by the response, he said, "You dishonor your husband's memory when you say that."

She slapped him then, her hand connecting with his cheek with such unexpected force that it snapped his head back. His skin smarted, but no more than his pride. She had taken him by surprise yet again, something no one had done since his teens, something no woman had ever done.

When she would have slapped him again, he grabbed her wrist and held it, his gaze locked with hers.

"Once I can forgive," he said. "Not twice."

Her eyes filled with tears. She would have turned away, but his grip on her arm held her in place.

"This is wrong," she murmured.

"What?" he asked, his voice turning gentle at her evident distress.

"That I want you so badly."

He tugged gently until she came into his loose embrace. "No, *querida*. It is not wrong. It is life. You and I are alive. We cannot be blamed for that. Ken would not blame us for that. He, more than most, understood the cycles, the need for the living to hold on to each other and move on. How many times have you heard him counsel others to let go of their grief and live?"

She sighed, acknowledging the truth of his claim, and relaxed against him. Her arms crept around his waist. He could feel her tears on his bare chest and wondered if she knew that his own cheeks were damp with tears that were part sorrow, part relief.

They would survive, the two of them, because they had to. They would go on. Perhaps together, perhaps not. He had never gazed into the future before, because he hadn't dared. Now, with Dana in his arms and his heart pounding in his chest, he wished he could see what lay ahead.

Unfortunately, the only image that came readily to mind was trouble, spelled out in neon and flashing with savage intensity.

As if to confirm his prescience, the phone rang, shattering the momentary calm between them. With lifted brow, Dana informed him it was Maria as she handed him the receiver. He vowed to strangle the woman when he got back to Yo, Amigo. Dana signaled that she would be back and left the room.

"Yes?" he said.

"Sorry to interrupt," Maria said, sounding more amused than apologetic.

"I'll bet. What is it?"

"You'd better get down here right away."

Rick sighed. "Another break-in?"

"Sí."

"What did they take this time?"

"It's impossible to tell. The place has been turned, how do you say, turvy-topsy?"

"Close enough," he said. "I'll be there as soon as I can. Don't touch anything in the meantime."

"But it is a terrible mess," she protested. "I cannot leave it this way."

"You can until I see it," he told her. "Don't call the police yet, either."

"You know they would take forever to come, anyway," she said wryly. "We are not a priority, unless they wish to hustle someone here."

Rick grinned. "Hassle," he corrected.

"Whatever." She paused. "By the way, how is the *padre's* wife this morning?"

"Mrs. Miller is just fine, thank you."

"She did not sound pleased to hear from me. I interrupted something? The two of you are playing toesie?"

He didn't point out that it was footsie, because he didn't want to belabor the direction of her thoughts. "You are entirely too nosy, Maria," he said instead. "I will be very glad when you go off to college."

"You say that now, but I know better," she said confidently. "You would be buried under paperwork in a week and cursing the day I left. That is why I must come back every day."

She was probably right, unfortunately. Rick would have died before telling her that, though. She was entirely too sure of herself as it was.

"I'll be in soon. If you're tempted to clean something, run home and help your mother."

"My job is here. I will be waiting for you."

When he'd hung up, he glanced up to see that Dana had returned. She was watching him curiously.

"Problems?"

"A break-in at the center."

"At least this time you know I had nothing to do with it."

He grinned. "That is some consolation, yes."

"You didn't sound especially surprised when Maria told you. How come? Has it happened before?"

He saw no point in keeping the past problems from her. "A few times."

"Is that why you were there the night I broke in?"

He nodded, without adding that his latest invasion did not appear to have followed the pattern. Earlier thieves had taken whatever valuables they could find. Although it was possible that this one had ransacked the place because there was nothing of value left to steal, he suspected that wasn't the case. This one, he believed, had been looking for something less obvious than computers or DVD players.

"I'd better get back into town. Will you come with me? The sign-up sheet for your class has gotten very long, thanks to your success with Rosa and Marco, and that was even before they heard about the deals that were struck yesterday. Everyone is eager to see you."

"Tomorrow," she promised. "Today I want to see what I can dig up on Lawrence Tremayne. He's the only person I can think of who might be able to come up with fifty thousand dollars for a hit."

"You will take Kate with you?"

She shook her head. "No, this is something I have to do alone." She smiled. "Don't look so worried. I investigated dozens of cases without the people having any idea whatsoever that I was digging around in their lives."

"You'll pardon me if I only recall that I caught you red-handed trying to sneak into Yo, Amigo."

"I was in a rush to do something. I was careless," she conceded. "It won't happen again."

He framed her face with his hands. "See that it doesn't," he said softly. "Before each step you take, think of your sons. Think of me. We are all counting on you remaining in one piece."

She made a face at him. "Gee, thanks. With that in mind, I won't dare to take any risks at all."

"That's the general idea." He pressed a quick kiss against her lips. He wanted to linger for more, but didn't dare. One thing would lead to another and the day would pass. It would be a far more pleasant alternative than his current plan for the morning, but he knew in his gut that they would not find peace in each other's arms until Ken's murderer was behind bars and the past could be well and truly put behind them.

"I will call you later," he promised.

She gave a little shrug of indifference that suggested she would not be counting on his keeping that promise any more than he had kept the one he'd made the day before. Her lack of faith, though well-deserved, stung.

He forced a smile. "You'll see, *querida.* I am a man of my word."

"Whatever," she said, her voice laced with disbelief.

He saw then what he should have seen sooner. As important as that meeting with Carlos had been, he had paid a heavy price for choosing that over keeping the commitment he had made to Dana. In time, she might forgive him. Trust would not come so readily.

21

Dana didn't realize how tense she had been all morning, until Rick finally left and she felt her breath ease out of her in a deep, heartfelt sigh. The cramped muscles in her shoulders relaxed as well. The burning sensation in the pit of her stomach slowly disappeared.

Ironically, she couldn't place the blame for the tension on him. She was the one who'd been tied up in knots, trying to resist throwing herself straight back into his arms. She had awakened in torment, as images of her wanton behavior the night before came back to her.

Rationally, she knew it was not possible to betray a dead man, but in her heart, she felt she had done so. She might tell herself again and again that even the marriage vows said only "until death do us part," but she had always believed they were meant to last through eternity.

Surely they should at least last beyond the first anniversary of her husband's death. What she had done was unforgivable. Ken had been gone less than two months and already she had been with another man. Far worse, it had been a man who had played at least some small role in her husband's death, even if she was coming to admit that the role was only indirect.

If she were ready to be totally honest, she'd have to admit, though, that it had been good. More than good. She had been more uninhibited with Rick in some ways than she had been with her own husband. Maybe that had to do with timing and desperation, or a million and one other things, but she couldn't help wondering if it meant she had always held back subtly with Ken, simply because of who he was...a minister. If that were true, she could come to hate herself for cheating them both that way. Or was it simply that each experience in life, each person, paved the way for the experiences and people to come?

What kind of woman was she? The question tormented her.

Rick would have said she was merely human. Ken, she thought with a rueful smile, would have said the same. He had been exceedingly nonjudgmental about human frailties. There had been no fire-and-brimstone sermons about dire consequences spoken from his pulpit. He had preached compassion and love. His God was a kinder, gentler one than the one she'd been brought up to believe in. As a child, she had sometimes quaked at the images of hell her pastor had managed to evoke on Sunday mornings.

So, where had Ken's God been when someone had pulled a gun and aimed for Ken's chest? she wondered angrily for the thousandth time. What was the purpose of the test He had designed for those left behind? What was the morality lesson when evil triumphed over good?

As ever, no answers came to her. She forced herself to push aside the questions and concentrate on those she could answer. Reaching for the pad of paper she kept by the phone, she began jotting down the background information she wanted on Lawrence Tremayne before she faced him again and confronted him with her suspicions.

She was determined to conduct the remainder of this investigation slowly and methodically. Up until now, the impulsive decisions she had made had skirted disaster by a very narrow margin. No more. From vast experience, she knew what needed to be done and how to do it, so that it would hold up in court. It was time she started acting like the trained detective she was, rather than a grieving widow.

Lawrence Tremayne owned a large company with its own office tower in downtown Chicago. She had no idea what sort of business it was or what its holdings were, and it was about time she found out.

She would start with a broker who had handled investments for her after she had sold off her investigating company and put the money into a joint account with Ken for the future of their children. If Tremayne Industries was traded on any of the stock exchanges, Jean Bragg would know it. Dana picked up the phone and called her.

She waited impatiently through the expected expressions of sympathy and gave terse replies to Jean's questions about the boys. Apparently her abrupt answers alerted the other woman that this wasn't a social call.

"Okay, Dana, what can I do for you?" she asked, her tone changing to brisk formality. "Are you worried about the status of your investments? I can assure you that everything is in order in both your names with right of survivorship. There will be no problems getting access to anything, if you need to liquidate. I'm sure things must be unsettled for you financially now."

"Thanks, Jean. I'm not worried about that. Ken had insurance and I have some savings. We're set, until I can get back into my old business. Actually, I called for some information."

"Sure. If I have it, it's yours."

"What do you know about Tremayne Industries?"

The broker's hesitation was barely perceptible. "Why? You aren't thinking of moving some of your money into it, are you? I can tell you right now, you have far better stock in your portfolio already."

Jean's worried reaction set off alarm bells. "Then it wouldn't be a good investment?" Dana probed cautiously, trying not to arouse suspicion with her questions. It would be far better if the broker merely thought she was checking out a prospective addition to her stocks.

Again, there was the slightest hesitation before Jean said, "It's a local company, as you probably know. It's had some rapid growth in the past. Long-range, maybe it's still a good investment."

She paused, as if she weren't sure how to proceed. "Okay," she said finally. "Here's the deal. I don't like to bad-mouth a local company, but in the short-term, I'd say Tremayne Industries is very risky."

"Why?"

"Tremayne has had some bad luck with a few of its properties lately. A couple of huge development deals fell through in Latin America."

Dana seized on the last. "Tremayne does business in Latin America? Why?"

"Growth. Opportunity. At least, I'm sure that's what he anticipated."

"But it was a bad call?"

"So it seems."

"But how can that be? By all accounts, he's a savvy businessman."

"I honestly don't know. All I've heard is that he's heavily in debt, because these deals went sour. You know I like to support local firms. There's plenty of information readily available. I know the people firsthand. Some of these companies are on the cutting edge, which I find very exciting. But the bottom line is I'd think very seriously before putting a dime into Tremayne Industries right now."

Dana decided she had all of the information she was likely to get without giving away her real interest in the company. "Thanks, Jean. I'll give it some more thought."

"Call if you need anything else. I'll give you the best advice I can."

"I know you will," Dana said. "Thanks again."

As she slowly replaced the receiver, she pondered what she'd discovered. Lawrence Tremayne's business was in trouble, maybe not in dire straits, but trouble enough that a cautious broker was recommending against investing in it.

What was the significance of the fact that the trouble had begun with a Latin American connection? Was that and the fact that Ken had been shot in a heavily Latino neighborhood pure coincidence? Dana didn't believe much in coincidences.

She also knew there was a danger in leaping to conclusions. Fortunately, the ringing of the doorbell kept her from doing just that.

She opened the door to find Detective Dillon O'Flannery on her porch. His expression—never especially cheerful in her brief experience with him—was very grim. He looked as if he'd rather be almost anyplace else on earth.

"What?" she demanded, her heart thudding dully, as she considered what his presence meant.

"I'm sorry. I really am," he began.

She reached out and clutched the door for support. What had happened? One of the boys? Her parents? What? Images from that night just over a month ago flooded back. Two policemen had stood on her doorstep then, their expressions every bit as tormented as O'Flannery's was now.

"Just tell me," she whispered, fighting panic.

He held out a piece of paper. Startled, she simply stared at it. She recognized what it was at once, but she couldn't quite believe it.

"It's a search warrant," he explained, confirming her guess.

"A search warrant?" She almost laughed, giddy with relief that no one else she loved was dead. Then, as the implications sank in, she stared at him. "Why?"

"Probable cause to search for more drugs."

"I don't believe this." Her temper rose. "How dare you? My husband was not dealing drugs. He abhorred drugs."

"We found evidence of drugs in his church office," O'Flannery reminded her, his voice oddly gentle. "Look, I know this is upsetting, but why not let us in and get this over with?"

"No," she said, standing squarely in his path. "Who's behind this?"

"It was the next logical place to look, after what we turned up at the church."

"Logical?" Her voice climbed. "There is nothing logical about any of this. Someone is campaigning to destroy my husband's reputation and I want to know who. More anonymous sources?" she suggested derisively.

Because it was inevitable anyway, she moved aside and gestured expansively. "Go on. Search to your heart's content. You'll be wasting time and taxpayer dollars. You won't find a damn thing."

He turned then and gestured to the uniformed officers waiting behind him, men she'd been too blinded by fury to even notice before.

With O'Flannery on her heels, she returned to the kitchen and sank down onto a chair. He refilled her cup with coffee, rinsed out the mug Rick had left on the counter and poured another for himself. He sat down opposite her.

"I'm not taking any pleasure in this," he said eventually.

"I'm thrilled by your sensitivity," she said bitterly. "Tell me, did Kate know you were coming over here this morning? Does that explain why she hasn't shown up yet?"

He winced a little at that. "No. Obviously, I couldn't say a word to anyone until we had the warrant in hand."

"I'm sure she'll be impressed with your dedication to duty. I'll pass along the word."

Blue eyes locked on hers. "Let me do the explaining, okay? Your spin might be just a little biased."

Dana studied his expression. "Don't tell me she actually matters to you. I thought perhaps she was just a source you planned to pump for information about the evil, drug-dealing pastor."

"She's a nice woman," he said simply. "I don't run across too many of those in my line of work."

"Yes, she is nice," Dana agreed. "Too nice to get mixed up with the likes of you."

He looked offended. "Hey, I'm one of the good guys, remember?"

"I suppose that depends on where you're sitting,

doesn't it? From where I sit, your white hat is decidedly dirt-streaked."

He shrugged. "I guess it is a matter of perspective. I'd still like to have a chance to get to know Kate better. That won't be possible, if you condemn me in her eyes. She cares too much about your feelings. She's already made that plain. I suppose that puts me at your mercy. It's a damned awkward position, one I'd rather not be in, to tell you the truth."

He actually did sound vaguely unsettled by the power she held over him. Dana sighed. Maybe Dillon O'Flannery was a decent guy. Maybe it was just circumstances that were no fault of his own that put them on opposite sides, for the moment. She could be reasonable enough to concede that Kate had the right to make up her own mind about him.

"I won't interfere," she said at last, drawing a relieved smile. "But you upset her and I will personally rip your heart out."

"I'll consider myself forewarned," he said just as one of his men came to the door and gestured for him.

"What?" Dana demanded when the detective would have walked off with his colleague.

O'Flannery met her gaze evenly, then nodded to the other man. "It's okay. What have you found?"

"Two very small packages of what appears to be cocaine."

Dana stared, openmouthed. "No," she protested. "That's not possible. Where?"

"In a small room at the end of the hall upstairs. It was taped behind the dresser."

In the guest room? Dana thought wildly. Where she had spent last night in Rick's arms? Where no one else had been in weeks?

There was no way in hell that her husband had brought cocaine into their home, any more than he had taken it into his office at the church. She would have staked her life on that.

But if Ken hadn't brought the drugs into the house, then who had? The most obvious answer, the one she didn't like one bit better than the one the police were coming up with, was Rick.

Had he used the opportunity she had so eagerly given him the night before to plant more evidence against her husband? If not Rick, if not last night, why the guest room? Who else had had recent access to it?

"Mrs. Miller?"

She blinked and stared at Dillon O'Flannery.

"Has anyone else been in that room lately?"

She thought of the two people who had spent last night discovering passion in that very room. "No," she said slowly. "No one."

She told herself that the lie wasn't meant to protect Rick. If he was guilty, he didn't deserve protection. The lie was only meant to buy time, until she could look him in the eye and make the accusation herself.

And if she didn't like what she read there, she would strangle him with her bare hands. *Then* the police could have at him with her enthusiastic blessing.

22

Maria's neatly arranged stacks of files had been strewn from one end of Yo, Amigo's offices to the other. Rick surveyed the mess and patted the distraught young woman on the shoulder. It had taken her months to get everything organized. The prospect of doing it all over again clearly daunted her.

"It's okay. I'll get some of the others in here to help you straighten everything out," he promised, more irritated than worried about the ransacking, now that he'd seen it. It didn't look like the work of a professional who was out to discover some specific, incriminating piece of paper. It looked more like kids up to mischief.

"What about the police?" Maria asked indignantly, clearly ready to condemn the perpetrator to prison for life.

Rick shook his head. "Not for this. It will only bring us to their attention. We don't need any more unfavorable publicity downtown. I'll get the word out that we don't appreciate this. That ought to prevent a repeat."

"How will you spread the word?" she asked suspiciously. "Will you talk to Tico?"

Something in her voice caught his attention. She had

sounded almost derisive. He studied her intently. "That's what I was thinking of doing. Is that a problem?"

She shrugged. "Not to me. It is your choice, as always."

Her attitude spoke far more loudly than her words. "Maria, what is it between you and Tico?"

She looked slightly flustered at having been caught sounding disparaging about a man she knew was his friend. "Nothing," she declared, though she wouldn't meet his gaze when she said it.

Rick wasn't buying it. "What nothing? It's something. I can hear it. Have you two argued?"

"Never," she said dismissively. "I would not waste my time."

"Has he done something?"

"Nothing," she insisted.

"If you don't tell me, I'll ask him."

"He will only lie," she said. "Leave it alone. I should not have said anything."

"Believe me, Maria, you have said nothing, at least nothing that made any sense."

He shook his head. Women! He would never figure them out. Perhaps his friend could make sense of the mystery. It had been days since he and Tico had played basketball one-on-one. He resolved to invite him over tonight after the restaurant closed. He would grill him until Tico shed some light on this animosity Rick had detected in Maria's voice.

"If you do not need me, I will being cleaning," Maria said stiffly.

"Fine. If you discover that something's missing, let me know."

"Why? You will do nothing about it, except perhaps talk to Tico."

She said it with a reappearance of that same subtle disdain. This time, however, it was directed at him. Rick stared as she left his office and deliberately allowed the door to slam behind her.

"Now, what the hell was that all about?" he muttered.

He was still pondering that when the door whipped open and hit the wall behind it. Dana came in, fury radiating from her in waves he could feel across the room.

"Hi," he said cautiously. "I didn't expect to see you again this morning." He decided not to mention his displeasure over the fact that she had obviously gone against his frequently expressed wishes and made the trip to Yo, Amigo alone.

"I didn't expect to be here," she said. "Then I had a visit from Detective O'Flannery."

Rick stood up. He would have rounded his desk to comfort her, but a warning look stopped him in his tracks. "Okay," he said slowly. "What did the detective want?"

"He had a search warrant to look for more drugs. Imagine my shock when he found more cocaine."

He stared at her. "You're kidding? In the house?"

"In the damned guest room," she said, visibly shaking with rage. "Taped to the back of the dresser. Now, how do you suppose it got there?"

"I have no idea," he said, then stared at her in shock as her meaning sank in. "You think *I* put it there? Is that what you're telling me?"

Her gaze never wavered. "I think it's awfully damned suspicious that you were in that room just last night and now the police have found drugs in there."

"You were in there, too," he pointed out quietly. "You've had ongoing access to that room with no one around to observe your actions, while I was there only with you. You also had access to Ken's office at the church. I did not."

She stared at him in visible horror as he turned the tables on her. "You believe that I...that I could have planted those drugs?" she demanded.

"It is a more reasonable assumption than the one you're making," he said, forcing himself not to shout.

She shivered violently, then covered her face with trembling hands. "Oh, God, I'm sorry. The whole damn world is going crazy. *I'm* going crazy. I didn't want to believe you could do something so despicable, but nothing else makes any sense."

Rick crossed the room in three quick strides and put his hands on her shoulders. He was relieved when she did not pull away. "Are you sure now that it was not me? Do you trust me at least that much?" he asked gently.

She lifted a tormented gaze to meet his. "I want to believe that."

He sighed at the doubts still apparent in her voice. "But you can't be sure."

"Can you blame me?" she asked angrily. "The timing..." She let her voice trail off.

"The timing sucks. I'll admit that. But I swear to you, Dana, I had nothing to do with those drugs. You know what the policy is around here. I instituted it. I enforce it. Where would I even get the drugs to plant them?"

"I imagine that would be easy enough," she said, gesturing toward the window. "You could confiscate them from half a dozen kids right outside the door, more than likely."

Rick couldn't deny that, as much as he wanted to. In fact, she sounded so rational even he began to doubt himself. "But why?" he asked. "Why would I do that?"

"I don't know. I've been thinking about that ever since

I left the house, and I just don't know." She stared at him bleakly. "Did you hate Ken for some reason? Was last night part of some revenge, too?"

"Never!" he practically shouted, then tried to calm down.

He hated having to try to explain away her doubts, hated even more that she still harbored such deep distrust of him. That she would accuse him of sleeping with her as an act of revenge infuriated him, but he couldn't blame her for it, not entirely. The arrival of the police and the discovery of more drugs would have tested the faith of almost anyone.

"You know I didn't," he said very softly. "Ken was the best friend I ever had. If I'd had the choice, I would have given my life for him."

"Someone hated him," she said. "Someone here. It had to be."

"Why?" Rick asked, fighting bitterness that, after all they'd shared, they were back to this. "Because the kids in the program would be able to get their hands on drugs?"

She nodded.

"Dana, anyone can get their hands on drugs if they want them badly enough. They can score right out there in the suburbs if they know where to look. They don't have to come into the barrio. You know that." He leveled a look directly into her eyes. "Don't you?"

"Yes," she admitted finally. She moved away from him and sat down. "Dammit, it's just so frustrating. Rick, I can't for the life of me figure out what's going on. I was one of the best investigators in the business. I could unravel mysteries that stumped my colleagues. But my husband's murder is beyond me."

"You're just too impatient and too involved. You

haven't been able to step back and look at what you know objectively."

"Because I don't know a darned thing."

"Didn't you find out anything about Tremayne this morning?"

"Just that his company is having financial trouble," she said dismissively.

"That's something."

"I thought so, too, at first, especially since the deals that went sour had a Latin American connection. Then I really thought about it. If he was having financial problems, where would he come up with fifty thousand dollars to have Ken killed? And why would he do it? It's not as though Ken might spread the word and ruin him or something. It wouldn't have been a big secret for long, anyway. My broker told me about it. If she knew, then surely others do, too. So what danger would Ken pose to him?"

Rick settled against the edge of his desk, his knees brushing hers. "Maybe that wasn't the danger. There could be more to this than we know. Don't rule Tremayne out just yet. I still don't like him."

"Now, there's an objective opinion if ever I heard one," she taunted.

Rick grinned. "You're the one who's supposed to be objective. I get to react from the gut."

"What an interesting distinction."

He met her gaze evenly. "Are we okay now?"

"Yes," she said, though her voice lacked real conviction. "I'm sorry I rushed down here to accuse you of planting those drugs."

"It's not a total loss. I need to talk to Tico. You can come with me. It's almost lunchtime. He will be happy to see you again. Perhaps that will distract him sufficiently so that I can get some straight answers."

She hesitated, then nodded. "Maybe a little salsa will clear my head."

Rick grinned. "It couldn't hurt. I've always been of the opinion that salsa has hidden medicinal qualities."

"And jalapeños?"

"Better yet." He urged her through the outer office before she could get a good look at the mess that Maria and several helpers were attempting to straighten up. Clearly she had been too upset to pay much attention to it on her way in. It would be just as well if she didn't start asking too many questions about what he'd learned about the break-in. It was possible she would be no more impressed than Maria by his plan of action...or inaction, as Maria saw it.

Though it was after noon, the restaurant was not yet crowded. Most of the customers came later. By one o'clock it would be jammed. Now, though, Tico turned over the hosting job to one of the waiters and followed them to a booth. To Rick's irritation, he squeezed in beside Dana.

"It is a pleasure to see you, as always," Tico told her, deliberately ignoring Rick's scowl, or perhaps choosing to exacerbate his apparent irritation.

"Your chef performs magic. How could I resist coming back? Besides, you refuse to give me the recipes," Dana replied.

"Naturally," Tico said. "Then you would stop coming."

"Okay, okay, you're glad to see her," Rick groused. "She's thrilled to be here. Can we cut the chitchat and get to the point?"

Tico regarded him with amusement. Dana merely looked puzzled by his irritability.

"I didn't know there was a point," she said. "I thought we came for lunch."

"We did. I also told you I needed to speak to Tico."

"I am right here," Tico said reasonably. "Tell me what's on your mind."

"I was hoping we could play a little basketball tonight, after you close."

"*Sí*, I have no other plans," Tico said readily. "And the rest?"

"What makes you think there is more?"

"You do not come here just to see if I can come out to play, my friend. There are phones for something so trivial."

Rick sighed. Tico wouldn't let it rest until he knew precisely why Rick was so eager to see him. He decided to leave news of the break-in for later, when they were alone. Dana might seize on the details of that and obsess on its possible connection to the murder. He was all but certain it would be a waste of her energy.

Instead, he brought up Maria's name, just to see what sort of reaction he would get.

"What about Maria?" Tico asked blandly, his eyes wide with an innocence that Rick suspected was feigned.

"Have you two argued recently?" he asked bluntly.

Tico's gaze narrowed. "Why would you ask such a thing? What did she say?"

"It's what she didn't say that concerns me," he said, watching Tico's expression closely. It gave away nothing. "I always thought you two got along just fine. Today I got a different impression."

Tico laughed. "That is what this is about? One of your

impressions?" He glanced at Dana. "Rick believes he has deeper insights than the rest of us, that he is attuned to the subtleties of conversations. He prides himself on this sensitivity."

Dana's lips quirked, but she managed to keep from smiling. Rick was impressed with the attempt. He was less thrilled with his friend's observation.

"You're avoiding my question," he accused. "Has something happened between you and Maria?"

"If it has, it is personal, *mi amigo,*" Tico said lightly. "It is not for you to interfere."

"I believe it is. I introduced the two of you. Maria is a good girl. I would not like to see anything upset her, *comprende?*"

For just an instant, Tico's expression hardened in a way that startled Rick. It reminded him that Tico had once been one of the street's most dangerous young men. Then he smiled, once more the jovial host. The transformation was so swift Rick thought he must have imagined that momentary flash of pent-up violence.

"No harm will come to your precious Maria," Tico informed him. "I will see to that."

Dana had watched the exchange very closely. As soon as Tico had excused himself to get their meals, she stared at Rick. "What was that all about?"

"You heard."

"I heard what you said, but the undercurrents were extraordinarily tense. I thought you two were good friends."

"We are." He waved his hand dismissively. "It's a guy thing. Don't worry. We're not going to come to blows over Maria."

"Are they dating?"

Rick had wondered that very thing, but he'd never

heard any rumors to that effect. Then again, Tico's private life was pretty much an enigma to him. It might have been a carryover from his days on the streets, when secrecy had been essential. But Tico guarded his privacy fiercely.

"I don't have any idea," he admitted.

She looked straight into his eyes then. "Why didn't you mention the break-in to him?"

Rick swallowed hard and hoped that the fire he felt in his cheeks wasn't visible to the woman opposite him. Unfortunately, she seemed able to read even what he tried hardest to hide. "I didn't want to get into it with him, just yet."

"You've been avoiding the subject with me, as well. What have you learned?"

"Nothing. I am all but certain it is the work of vandals."

"Nothing was stolen?"

"Not that we've discovered so far."

"How are you handling it?"

Apparently there were to be no secrets between them. "I was going to have Tico put out the word on the streets that we're not happy about what happened. The culprit will turn up."

"The culprit or a scapegoat?" she inquired thoughtfully.

He stared at her. "Meaning?"

"That someone hoping to please you or Tico might very well make a sacrificial lamb of an innocent party."

"I hadn't thought of that."

She grinned. "That's why you have me around, for the subtleties."

"Quiet. You'll ruin my reputation. Everyone around here thinks I grasp those on my own."

"Then you would truly be a rarity among men," she said. "The only man I ever knew who could read between the lines so well was Ken."

"Yes," he agreed, reaching for her hand. "He often saw things that the rest of us missed."

She regarded him with puzzlement. "It sounds as if there's a story behind that."

He thought of his initial impression of her as a suburban snob with little redeeming social conscience. He had wondered at Ken's judgment in marrying such a woman. Clearly, though, his friend had known that there was far more to this woman, a rare depth and complexity that Rick was only now discovering for himself.

"Maybe someday I'll tell you," he said.

"Not now?"

He shook his head. "No, it reflects too poorly on me, I suspect. We have reached a rapport, you and I. I don't want to do anything that might cause you to question that. Your faith in me has been shaken enough for one day."

"You want to be sure you can remain a spy in the enemy's camp?" she asked tightly.

"Never that," he said. He grinned wickedly. "So that I might be invited to share her bed again."

Color flamed in her cheeks at that, but she didn't pull her hand away, not even when Tico returned and stared at the two of them with blatant amusement.

"Perhaps I should warn you about my friend here," Tico said lightly.

Rick was about to respond to the taunt when Dana spoke up. "No need," she assured him. "I know exactly what I'm doing."

"I wonder," Tico said enigmatically.

Then, at a harsh scowl from Rick, he retreated and left them alone, but not before a faint shadow of doubt crossed Dana's eyes. Rick vowed to soundly thrash his old friend at the first opportunity. The stakes in this game were far too high for his kind of taunting interference.

23

Dana returned home to find Kate and Detective O'Flannery engaged in full-scale warfare on her front stoop. She gathered that Kate had heard about the drug raid.

"Stay out of it?" Kate shouted.

She poked her finger directly into the man's very broad chest. He withstood the gesture with obvious amusement, which no doubt only served to inflame Kate further.

"With people like you ready to crucify Ken Miller, there's not a snowball's chance in hell that I'm going to stay out of it," she told him emphatically. "In fact, I might just organize a rally, a protest march on the police station. We'll demand your resignation. Maybe that will teach you to have some respect for the decent people of this community."

Telltale patches of red climbed into his cheeks. The show was so good Dana decided to sit in her car and watch the rest of the performance. She leaned back and waited to see what would happen next. She doubted the policeman would allow the threat of his livelihood to go unchallenged.

"Decent people pay me to keep this community safe,"

O'Flannery barked back, taking an intimidating step in Kate's direction. She held her ground as he added pointedly, "That means following up on evidence of criminal activity."

"Criminal activity, my aunt Bessie. It's slander, that's what it is."

They were toe-to-toe now. Unless Dana was very much mistaken, there was enough sexual energy charging the air to send them both up in flames.

"We found drugs," he countered quietly.

"I don't care if you found an armed militia in the basement and enough guns and drugs to supply the entire Midwest. Ken Miller had nothing to do with any of it," she said so emphatically that she was practically vibrating with indignation.

O'Flannery obviously wasn't impressed. "Your faith in him is touching, but compared to the evidence, it doesn't amount to a hill of beans."

"I'm telling you that you don't have any damned evidence," Kate said, her voice climbing another decibel level, "except that someone was out to get him."

"I agree."

He said it so softly that it apparently took several seconds for it to register with Kate. When it did, her furious expression faltered. "You agree?"

O'Flannery grinned and nodded. "I would have told you that if you'd taken a deep breath and listened for half a minute, instead of trying to blast out my eardrums."

Dana had to admit the effect of that grin was fairly devastating. Even she got a tingle, and she was clear across the yard and immune to the charms of all cops. Kate was absolutely no match for it. She flat-out wilted at the sight.

"Oh."

The smile broadened. "Care to apologize?"

"When hell freezes over," Kate said staunchly. "You still conducted the stupid search."

"It was my job," he explained patiently.

"Then it's a stupid job," Kate said, still defiant.

"Remember you said that the next time you're in trouble and need a cop."

"I don't get into the kind of trouble that requires the Gestapo."

He sighed heavily. "I can see there's only one way to shut you up," he said with an air of resignation, just before he bent down and planted a kiss on Kate that generated enough heat to melt the snowdrifts in the front yard.

Dana waited for a full sixty seconds, expecting steam to rise at any moment, before concluding it was time to make her presence known before the elderly neighbors saw more than their hearts could take. She deliberately bumped the horn as she exited the car. Kate jerked out of the detective's embrace, as if she'd been shot. He looked as thoroughly unflappable as ever. In fact, he seemed so thoroughly amused that Dana had a sneaking suspicion he'd been aware of her arrival all along.

"So we're all agreed that someone has been planting the drugs, correct?" Dana demanded, as she opened the front door and led the parade inside.

"Yes," Kate declared firmly.

"Agreed," O'Flannery said.

Dana beamed at them. "Now all we have to do is figure out who's behind it."

"You make it sound as if that will be a stroll in the park," the detective said. "Do you already have some idea of where to start looking?"

She debated filling him in on the preliminary suspect list she and Kate had drawn up, but decided that would be a tactical error. He'd probably laugh his head off if he heard some of the names on that list. Respected community leaders, one and all. And when it came to a lack of solid evidence, she and Kate were in an even weaker position than the police were with regard to Ken.

"Not really," she demurred.

He looked skeptical. "Okay, let me ask a few more questions, then. Who has access to the house?"

"Just me," Dana said. "The boys are in Florida."

He glanced at Kate. "You don't have a key for emergencies?"

Signs of her hair-trigger temper flared in Kate's eyes. "You're accusing me now?"

"Simmer down. I just want to know exactly where we stand, okay? Do you have a key?"

"Yes," Kate acknowledged irritably.

"Is it still in your possession?"

"Yes, dammit."

"You're sure?"

With a defiant scowl, Kate flipped her purse upside down on the kitchen table, dumping the contents into a heap. She plucked the key out of the mess. "Here. Satisfied? See anything else suspicious? Maybe that lipstick is an illegal weapon. Or the comb? I could do a lot of damage with that comb, I'm sure."

He turned on his knee-weakening grin again. "I'm sure you could."

Kate rolled her eyes. Dana gathered the detective's charms were beginning to wear a little thin.

He fixed his gaze on Dana again. "What about the church? Does anyone there have a spare key?"

She almost said no, then paused. Had there been a master key in Ken's office, along with all the others to the parish hall and the main church? It certainly made sense that there would have been. As had been so recently pointed out to her, after all, it was the church's property.

"I'll call Mrs. Fallon to check," she said, reaching for the phone.

The secretary confirmed the existence of a master set of keys. She checked and reported that it was still locked in a small fireproof safe, along with important church documents.

"Who has the combination to the safe?" O'Flannery asked when Dana repeated what the secretary had said.

Dana asked.

"Reverend Miller did. I do. And Mr. Tremayne, of course, since he frequently has to attend to church business."

Dana tried not to react to the mention of Lawrence Tremayne. "I see," she said quietly. "Thanks, Mrs. Fallon. You've been wonderful through all of this."

On an impulse, she added, "I hope you'll come to lunch tomorrow so I can thank you properly." The suggestion wasn't made entirely out of generosity. Dana had the feeling that Mrs. Fallon knew more about church politics than anyone else. She'd been observing them from the inside for years now, longer than Ken had been pastor of St. Michael's.

"Why, thank you, dear. I'd love to."

"About noon, then?"

"I'll be there."

When she'd hung up, she noticed that O'Flannery was regarding her impatiently. "Sorry," she apologized. "That was long overdue."

"Who has access to the safe?" he repeated.

She debated lying to O'Flannery and keeping Tremayne's name to herself, but decided maybe it was time for the police to put a little pressure on the church elder. If they considered him a genuine suspect, they had the means to conduct a far more thorough survey of his background than she could.

She told the detective the three names. "Mrs. Fallon would die before she would let anyone into that safe."

"And Mr. Tremayne?" he asked, watching her intently. "You think he's capable of this, don't you?"

Dana winced. Apparently O'Flannery was a better detective than she'd given him credit for being, or else she was more transparent than she'd prided herself on being. "Let's just say, I don't like him and leave it at that."

"To your knowledge, has he been in the house recently?"

"Actually, he was here for tea, just the other day," she admitted, regretting the fact that she hadn't recalled that herself earlier. In fact, there had been a whole bevy of people right here at her invitation, all of them suspects, for one reason or another.

O'Flannery's expression brightened. "Now we're getting somewhere. Did he ever leave the room, say, to go to the restroom?"

Dana slowly shook her head. "I don't think so." She glanced across the table. "Kate?"

"No," Kate said with obvious regret. "He was in plain view the whole time." Suddenly her expression brightened. "But several of the others used the facilities."

The detective regarded her expectantly. "Who? What others?"

At a subtle nod from Dana, Kate said, "Miriam Kelso, Peter Drake and Carolina Vincenzi. I remember all of them excusing themselves at one time or another." She paused, her expression thoughtful. "Actually, I take that back. Carolina never said a word. She just slipped out of the room, right after Peter Drake left."

"So each of them had the opportunity to have planted those drugs," O'Flannery said. "Interesting."

Dana found it interesting, but far from conclusive. She still thought Tremayne made an excellent prime suspect. "Don't forget, I was out of town for weeks after the funeral. Tremayne had access to the key. He could have come in here undetected at any time and planted those drugs. I haven't cleaned since I've been back. I doubt I would have looked behind that dresser, even if I had."

With Tremayne and the three who had excused themselves during the tea the only ones with probable access to the upstairs bedroom, the suspect list was shrinking. There was still one on it that Kate and O'Flannery didn't know about, and Dana intended to keep it that way.

As desperately as she wanted to believe that Rick had had nothing to do with Ken's death or the drugs, she couldn't help thinking about the access she'd innocently given him to the very room in which the cocaine had been found. Until she had a truly viable alternative, her awareness of that fact would always stand between them.

Tico was charging the basket with far more force than was necessary, Rick concluded, when he'd taken his third elbow to the gut. He backed off.

"Hey, man, what's with you tonight?" he demanded. "You're playing like a spot in the NBA finals is at stake."

Tico grabbed a towel and wiped his face before replying. "Just trying to work off a little steam," he said.

"Is that it, or do you still have a problem with the fact that I asked about you and Maria?"

Tico shot him a look of undisguised disgust. "Not that again. I don't need this. I have a mother who cross-examines me if I so much as frown. I have employees who think they can run the business better than I can. I have a kid brother who'd rather get high than wait tables."

Rick sensed that this last was the real source of Tico's short temper. "Joey's using?"

"José," Tico corrected. "He's discovered his roots. Latino pride has kicked in with a vengeance, thanks to that worm Carlos."

"He's running with Carlos?"

"He thinks he's some kind of god," Tico said. "Nothing I say can convince him that at the first sign of trouble, Carlos will drop him like a sizzling fajita pan. He'll give him up to the cops if it'll save his own sorry hide."

"Is Joey the one who tipped you that Carlos might know something about Ken's murder?"

Tico shrugged. "Not intentionally. I heard him and his buddies. They said enough for me to add two and two. I had a little talk with Carlos and convinced him that he should clear his conscience by talking to you."

"I'm sorry I missed that conversation. I didn't see any war wounds when I talked to him."

Tico shrugged. "There are other ways to convince a man to do what is right."

Rick's gaze narrowed. "You have something on him, don't you?"

"What I know about Carlos is between us, *mi amigo*. I would not tell anyone—even you—unless it became necessary."

"Dammit, a decent man is dead, a man who helped you get straight, a man who put his word on the line to set you up in business," Rick snapped. "Isn't that enough to make it necessary? Carlos is slime, Tico. He doesn't deserve your protection."

"I am not protecting him. I am maintaining my leverage."

Rick muttered an oath under his breath. Tico's expression hardened.

"Up until now, you have been my friend," Tico said, his tone lethal. "Do not say anything to make me regret that."

Rick really didn't like being warned off by a man who owed his salvation to Yo, Amigo. He whirled on the other man so quickly that Tico was forced to back up a step, straight into the wall. Rick crowded in close, a subtle reminder that he had twenty pounds of solid muscle on the wiry younger man.

"Do not threaten me, Tico. There is too much history between us. I would not like to have to remind you who controlled these streets before you."

Fury flashed in Tico's eyes. "That was a long time ago. You are out of practice."

"There are some things a man never forgets," Rick said.

Sweat beaded on Tico's brow, but his gaze remained defiant. "I like threats no more than you do, *amigo*."

"Then do not make them necessary again," Rick suggested, backing away.

Tico snatched up his gym bag and left, without another word. Rick had the feeling that the exchange had just cost him another friend. What he didn't understand was why it had happened in the first place.

Back in his office, he went over the conversation, word by word, trying to see why Tico had gotten so riled and so defensive so quickly. Was it Joey? Was Joey inadvertently dragging his big brother back into gang life, if only to serve as his protector?

And what were the links between Tico and Carlos? At one time, he supposed, they had been kingpins of rival gangs, though Carlos's name had never surfaced in any of the usual street talk. When Tico had walked away from the streets, the rivalry should have ended, anyway.

Or did such things ever end? Perhaps Carlos's recruitment of Joey had been deliberate, a slap at an old enemy. Not even his recent successes in mainstream society would be enough to keep Tico from reacting to such a taunt.

Damn, where were the answers? Rick had been so sure, when he steered Dana's investigation into her own backyard, that he'd been right. Now he was beginning to have doubts. Some kind of turf war was building right here in the barrio, and his old friend Tico appeared to be smack in the thick of it. Had Ken been one of its innocent victims, after all?

24

Dana was awakened by the shrilling of the phone be-fore dawn. Her heart slammed against her ribs, as she an-ticipated bad news. It was always bad news at that hour.

"Mom?" Bobby's voice sounded plaintive.

Back in Ken's chair again—now there were two rooms upstairs she couldn't bear to sleep in—she sat straight up. Her grip on the receiver tightened. She forced herself to keep her voice calm. "What is it, baby? Is something wrong? You're up awfully early."

"I didn't want Grandma and Grandpa to hear. They're still asleep."

"What didn't you want them to hear?"

"Me and Kevin and Jonathan want to come home."

Dana closed her eyes in a futile attempt to block out the image of her son's pitiful expression. When she couldn't, she sighed. "Not yet, sweetie. I'm sorry."

"When?" he asked, suddenly defiant. "It's not fair that we have to stay here and you get to be at home. We miss our school. We miss our friends."

"You have friends there. Grandma told me that kids are running in and out all the time."

"Babies," Bobby said derisively. "There's nobody my age."

"Not even at school?"

"Oh, sure, but they treat me like I'm some kind of weirdo, just because I'm new."

Dana sensed there was more to this sudden desire to return to Illinois than homesickness. Bobby was also the kind of kid who adapted readily to new situations. Of course, that had been before his very stable world had collapsed.

"What happened at school?" Dana asked, virtually certain that something there was at the root of the problem.

The direct question was greeted with silence, indicating that her guess had been accurate. Bobby had always hidden his feelings. He'd taken his role as the oldest very seriously, especially since Ken's death. He would never have called, if this worry, whatever it was, weren't too heavy for his young shoulders.

"Bobby? What happened?" she persisted. "Something must have. Last time we talked, you were okay with staying in Florida for the rest of the school year. Come on, sweetie, tell me. I can't help if you don't."

"One of the kids…" His voice cracked. "Never mind. It's not important."

She'd been through this kind of hurt enough times to guess at the source of it. "If it upset you, then it is important. Did somebody say something mean?" she asked, anticipating some typical remark about an unfashionable, dorky shirt, or her son's thick-lensed glasses. "You can tell me anything, you know that."

"Not this time. I don't want to say."

"It's okay. Please tell me."

There was another long hesitation before he finally began in a voice that faltered, "He said…"

She could hear him swallowing back tears, and it killed her that she wasn't there to gather him into her arms. "Take your time," she soothed.

"He said…he said my dad was murdered because he was a dope pusher."

Dana gasped, stunned not only by the unexpectedly terrible cruelty of the remark, but by the content. How would a child all the way in Florida know about the rumors all the way up here? When she'd left them there, she'd thought her kids would be safe from wild speculation and all the fallout from their father's death. Sure, parents talked, but the discovery of drugs in Ken's office and at the house hadn't been publicized.

Or had it? She realized she hadn't been paying much attention to the papers or to TV news. Whoever had gone to the trouble of planting the drugs might very well have leaked it to the media.

Damn whoever it was to hell, she thought fiercely. She didn't care for herself, but this was different. Her kids were being hurt by the lies now. And when it came to her kids, this sleaze was walking on very thin ice. She would destroy anyone who attempted to hurt her babies.

"Is it true?" Bobby asked in a tiny, scared voice. He was obviously as shaken by her silence as by the original accusation.

"No, baby, it is not true," she said adamantly. "Your daddy was a fine man and he hated drugs. Remember, he talked about that all the time so you and your brothers would know just how bad they were."

"Then why would somebody say that?" he asked plaintively. "He didn't even know my dad."

"People like to spread gossip. They don't care about

the facts. And kids your age can be especially cruel without even meaning to be. Whoever said that about your
dad probably didn't know what he was saying. He didn't
realize how badly it would hurt you."

"He did, too, know," Bobby insisted. "He laughed,
Mom. He told all the other kids, and then he laughed. I
want to come home *now!*"

Suddenly Dana wanted nothing more than to gather
her children close and hug them. She wanted to be there
to protect them from vicious lies, even though she knew
rationally that that was impossible. Maybe leaving them
in Florida had been a terrible mistake, after all.

Even after all the second-guessing, though, she knew
she couldn't bring them home yet. If they were being
taunted hundreds of miles away, then what would happen
to them right back here in their own community, where
gossip was bound to flourish? Life couldn't possibly go
back to being the way they'd remembered it. Even in
Sunday school in their father's church, there would be
subtle, but unmistakable, shifts in attitudes. There was
no way on earth to prevent it. How would they feel the
first time one of their old friends was forbidden to play
with them because of the rumors and innuendos circu-
lating? They would be devastated.

No, this was no safe haven for them now, either. In
the long run, they were better off right where they were,
at least for the moment.

"I'm sorry, sweetie, but you can't come home yet,"
she said, bracing for more tears. "I'm trying really hard
to clear up all these terrible lies about your daddy. All
of my energy has to stay focused on that. I need a little
more time."

"But Kevin and Jonathan and me could help. We could
tell people the truth."

"I know you could, and that would be a huge help, but it's going to take more than just our word. I have to find out who's behind this, and that takes time. I wouldn't be able to be home with you."

"Grandma could come with us. She would if you asked her to. Please," he pleaded.

"Soon," she promised. "I'll be down there before you know it."

Her vow was greeted with shocked silence.

"You're coming here?" he asked eventually. "We're not coming home?"

She heard the panicked note in his voice and tried to reassure him. "That's something we'll all have to de-cide together."

"No, it's not," he shouted. "You've already decided. I can tell. We're never coming home again. I hate you. I hate you. I wish you had died instead of Daddy."

"Bobby," she whispered, shattered by the harsh words. As the phone clattered to the floor, she shouted one last time, "Bobby!"

She could hear his footsteps as he ran away from the phone. Her eyes swimming with tears, she listened to her mother's sleepy attempt to soothe him, to find out why he was so upset.

Sweet heaven, she had made a mess of things. His angry words echoed in her head as she waited, praying that her mother would notice the dangling receiver and grab the phone.

The minutes ticked by. Silence fell on the other end of the line. She could only guess that her mother had taken Bobby back to his room. Was he still sobbing? Had she been able to console him at all?

Eventually she heard the faint padding of bare feet on the tile floor.

"Dana?"

Dana choked back a sob. "Oh, Mom, what have I done to him?"

"It's not you. It's just the circumstances. The teacher told me what that awful child said to him yesterday, but Bobby wouldn't talk about it. I should have called you myself last night, but I thought maybe he was handling it okay. He was so stoic. I didn't want to upset you by repeating such vicious nonsense."

"Was there something about Ken's death in the papers down there? Is that how that child heard about it, from some news report?"

Her mother hesitated. "Now that you mention it, no. There wasn't a word. I was as stunned as Bobby by what the child said. I was sure he'd just made it up to taunt him. Are you saying there's some truth to it?"

"Of course not, but drugs have been planted." She described what the police had found and the theory that she and Detective O'Flannery shared that someone had deliberately set out to destroy Ken's reputation.

"Well, how on earth would a third-grader down here know about that?" her mother asked indignantly.

"That's a good question," Dana said. "Any idea what the kid's name is?"

"The teacher never said. She was protecting the little darling, I suppose. I'll do my best to get it out of Bobby, if you think it's important."

It was a long shot, but Dana was grasping at straws these days. "Please," she said. "Just try not to upset him any more than necessary. He's furious with me as it is."

"He'll settle down, as soon as he sees you again. He's just frightened. His whole world has shifted, and he's struggling to make sense of it."

"So am I," Dana said with a heartfelt sigh. "So am I."

Dana spent the rest of the morning in emotional turmoil, torn between her children's needs and her duty to straighten out this mess and clear her husband's name. Nothing Kate said could placate her, so she finally sent Kate off to do more digging into the backgrounds of their four local suspects—Carolina Vincenzi, Miriam Kelso, Peter Drake and Lawrence Tremayne.

"I want to know if any of them has so much as a parking ticket on their record, okay? Take my laptop and modem. I just reconnected this morning with some of the financial records services I used to use. You can access those and check their credit, too."

Recalling her conversation earlier with Bobby, she added, "And see if any of them has any ties whatsoever in Florida."

"What will you be doing?" Kate asked.

"Mrs. Fallon's coming to lunch. I'm going to call her right now and ask her to bring along Ken's calendar. I want to check the entries for the last few months before he was killed. Maybe there will be something there, a suspicious pattern of meetings or something."

Kate nodded as she shrugged into her jacket. "Okay, sweetie. I'll check in with you later."

"Do you want to have dinner tonight?"

A guilty expression spread across Kate's face. "I wish I could, but I've already made plans."

"With the cop?"

"Don't say it like that, please. He's a good guy. He really is on our side in this."

"You could have fooled me," Dana retorted, then forced a smile. "Sorry. Go and have a great time. You deserve someone special in your life."

"And you? Where do things stand with the sexy Latino?"

"There's nothing between us. How many times do I
have to tell you that?"

"As many as it takes to make it sound convincing.
You're not even close yet."

When Dana would have protested, Kate hugged her.
"Never mind. Go on denying it if you like. Just don't
shut the door on whatever's happening out of loyalty to
Ken. He wouldn't have wanted that. Remember something else, too. He respected Rick. He thought he was a
very decent guy. He would be happy, I think, if the two
of you found something together. He'd give you his blessing, you know he would."

Dana couldn't tell Kate that she was holding back out
of fear. Not fear of commitment. She already knew that
a committed relationship was important. She believed in
marriage with all her heart. Not even fear of leaping so
quickly into a new relationship, even though she thought
that showed evidence of disrespect for Ken's memory.

No, what she was terrified of was discovering that the
man she was falling for might have had a hand in her husband's murder. No matter how many times she told herself that wasn't possible, no matter how badly she wanted
to trust Rick, she couldn't overcome all of the doubts.
The seed of distrust had been planted, and it seemed to
be flourishing, fed time and again by some new piece of
information just when she thought things might be okay.

"Just think about it," Kate pleaded.

"I will. I promise."

After Kate had gone, Dana made a quick call to the
church to ask Mrs. Fallon to bring her copy of Ken's
calendar. No sooner had she hung up than Rick called.

"How's it going out there this morning?"

"Well enough," she said tersely.

"Doesn't sound like it. What's wrong?"

The genuine caring in his voice had her spilling out what had happened with Bobby earlier. "Am I being selfish to leave him down there so I can finish this investigation?" she asked.

"No. You're just doing what you think is best. Parents make that kind of call all the time. Sometimes they're right, sometimes not. You just have to go with your instincts. Even after this incident, his life is more stable there than it would be here at the moment."

She sighed. "I don't know why, but it helps to have you say that."

"You should listen to me all the time. I am very wise."

"You also have a very large ego."

"Confidence," he countered. "I hear most women consider it very sexy."

"And then there are those who consider it a challenge to destroy it," she shot back.

"Which are you?"

"Oh, I think I'll let you worry about that for a while," she teased.

"So, tell me, what are your plans for the rest of the day?"

"I'm having Mrs. Fallon over for lunch shortly. She's going to bring Ken's calendar so I can see what was going on the last few days he was alive."

"Are you sure that is wise? Won't it upset you?"

"Yes, but it may also give me some new leads."

"Okay, then. You will do as you wish, anyway."

"That's true. By the way, how did your game with Tico go?"

"Not well," he said, his voice sobering. "There is something going on with him, but I can't figure it out."

"Maybe he's in love with Maria, and she's giving him fits."

"No, this has to do with his brother. Joey is tied up with Carlos in some way, and Tico is obviously frightened for him."

"You don't think it has anything to do with Ken's death, do you?"

"I'm not sure, *querida*," he said, sounding genuinely distraught. "I wish I were. I will call you later if I learn anything new that might link Tico's brother to all of this. Joey's not a bad kid, but I don't like his new associate one bit. Carlos is not a man to have as an enemy or as a friend. If there's money to be made, he will use anyone."

"Wait a second," she protested. How could he drop a bombshell like that and then hang up on her? Was he beginning to suspect Tico's brother of pulling the trigger for Carlos? Is that what Tico suspected that had him behaving so defensively?

Unfortunately, Rick didn't seem eager to share his speculations with her. The phone connection had already been broken.

"Well, darn," she muttered, putting the receiver back on the hook.

Thank goodness she had lunch to prepare. That would keep her occupied for the next half hour or so, until Mrs. Fallon's arrival. It had been weeks since she'd actually prepared a meal, not that chicken salad in half an avocado was exactly gourmet cuisine, but it kept her attention off the case for a bit.

She had just put the finishing touches on the plates when she glanced at the clock and realized it was already well past noon. By the time she'd filled the coffeemaker and turned it on, it was almost twelve-thirty. It wasn't like the secretary to be late. She had always prided herself on being prompt, even when Ken had told her time and again, especially during blizzards, to take her time getting to work on icy roads.

Dana went to the living room and glanced across the grounds toward the church. There was no sign of Mrs. Fallon on the path. The first faint stirring of concern crept over her as she went back to the phone and dialed the office. The phone rang and rang, unanswered.

Panicking now, Kate grabbed her coat and keys and raced toward the church. The side door to the parish hall was standing wide open, despite the freezing temperature.

"Oh, dear God," she murmured, sure now that something was terribly wrong.

"Mrs. Fallon!" she shouted as she ran toward the office. "Are you here? Mrs. Fallon, it's Dana."

The door to the outer office was ajar. After she opened it wide, a quick, sweeping glance revealed nothing amiss. The room was as tidy as ever. A cup half-full of coffee was cool to her touch. Had Mrs. Fallon left the building, though, that cup would have been rinsed and set neatly into her desk drawer. It was possible she'd gone into the restroom down the hall and fallen ill, Dana speculated, then dismissed the idea. She would have taken the cup with her to wash.

Dana glanced to her left then and saw that the door to Ken's larger office was closed. With a sick feeling in the pit of her stomach, she opened it, then cried out in shock.

Mrs. Fallon was sprawled unceremoniously across Ken's desk. A bloodstain ran down her back from a bullet wound in the center. Fighting back nausea, Dana rushed to her, searching frantically for a pulse. There was none.

She hadn't been dead long, though. Less than an hour, Dana guessed from her body's temperature and based on the last time she'd spoken to her.

Tears welled up in her eyes. Mrs. Fallon would have hated the uproar that would ensue the moment the police came. She would have hated being the center of attention, especially in this undignified position. If she hadn't known how critical it was to leave everything exactly as she'd found it, Dana would have straightened the woman's dress and laid her carefully on her back.

Who would do such a thing? Who would kill a sweet, gentle woman who had never had a harsh word to say to a soul? There was no question that Mrs. Fallon's death and Ken's were linked. Why? Because she had known something, of course, and because she was going to share that with Dana today.

Was that it? Had someone learned that Mrs. Fallon was having lunch with Dana and feared what she might reveal? Only three people that Dana could think of knew about their plans—Kate, Detective O'Flannery and Rick.

It was the last that had her shuddering and weakened her knees so badly that she had to sit down. She calculated the time from the moment she'd spoken to him until she'd discovered the body. There had been time enough for him to make the trip, if only by the skin of his teeth. A desperate man would make sure it was enough time.

25

Dana had to force herself not to think about Rick's possible involvement in Mrs. Fallon's murder. She reminded herself that suspicions and doubts were not evidence, and then tried to push him completely out of her head. If she were to dwell on Rick's whereabouts right now, she would fall apart, and there was no time for that.

With every second that passed, the chances of someone else discovering Mrs. Fallon's body with Dana herself in too close a proximity to it increased. She really didn't want to have to explain her presence to anyone.

Before she called Detective O'Flannery, Dana wanted to see if she could find Ken's calendar, the one Mrs. Fallon had kept for her own record of his daily schedule so she could pencil in appointments for him.

It wouldn't have been in any obvious place in Ken's office. She was confident of that, so she backed out of the room and gently closed the door, leaving it precisely as she'd found it.

To her disappointment a thorough examination of the secretary's desk revealed nothing. Would Mrs. Fallon have put it with her purse to make sure she didn't forget to bring it along? Or was she so fearful of its contents being discovered that she might have hidden it in the safe?

Dana prayed it wasn't the latter. She didn't know the combination, and though she'd had some experience with breaking into safes, it wasn't a skill she'd actually perfected. She didn't have time to try out her amateur technique right now. The purse was her only bet.

She knew that the secretary routinely changed her hiding place for it, from the supply closet to the filing cabinet in Ken's office to her desk. Since she already knew it wasn't in the desk, she took a deep breath and returned to Ken's office to try the drawers in the file cabinet. There was no sign of either purse or calendar tucked behind the neat rows of folders. For the second time, she closed the door carefully behind her as she left.

The supply cabinet in the outer office was next. If the purse wasn't in there, it was also possible that it had been stolen. Perhaps Mrs. Fallon had merely interrupted a thief, who'd panicked and shot her. Thieves were common enough in churches these days, though until now, St. Michael's had been spared. Of course, most of them didn't go out of their way to shoot an old woman in the back—especially when it was fairly obvious that she couldn't have seen him with her back turned toward the outer office.

Dana tried the door to the supply cabinet and found it locked. No doubt Mrs. Fallon had the key in her pocket. Swallowing her distaste for the task, Dana retrieved the key. She was shaking uncontrollably by the time she returned to the cabinet.

She fumbled her first several attempts to unlock the door, but eventually she was able to get it open. Sure enough, there on the bottom shelf was Mrs. Fallon's purse and under it, Ken's calendar. Dana grabbed the daybook and ran.

Only when she was back at home with the calendar safely secreted away under her mattress did she call the police.

"Where are you now?" Detective O'Flannery asked when she told him what she'd discovered.

"At home. I didn't want to touch anything in the office," she explained dutifully.

"Good thinking," he praised.

She might have felt guilty about her lie if he hadn't sounded so darned condescending.

"Stay there," he added. "I'm on my way."

Within minutes, the church and the grounds were swarming with police. Detective O'Flannery, after a brief visit to the church, rang Dana's doorbell. She had seen him coming and reluctantly opened the door before the second screeching chime could sound.

His gaze swept over her. "You okay?"

"Just peachy."

He grinned and took her elbow. "Come on. Let's go into the kitchen. You'll feel better after you drink a nice, hot cup of tea."

"I already have coffee made," she protested.

"And I'll drink that," he said. "You need tea, preferably loaded with sugar."

"When did you go into medicine?" she grumbled, but she found that she sat willingly enough and let the detective wait on her. He found the tea readily, indicating that he'd been observing her very closely on past visits. Just thinking about it made Dana jittery. She wondered how Kate was going to like being involved with a man who noticed every little detail. Maybe to her it would be a pleasant change, after being married to a man who had hardly noticed her at all.

When O'Flannery handed her the sweetened tea, Dana wrapped both hands around the cup, absorbing its warmth. She hadn't realized how very chilled she was, chilled and heartsick.

"Better?" he asked eventually, his gaze steady.

Dana nodded, resisting the desire to squirm under his penetrating observation.

"Tell me what happened."

She took a deep breath, then recited the information she'd been subconsciously preparing ever since she'd found the body. "I'd invited Mrs. Fallon to lunch." She met his gaze. "You were here yesterday when I talked to her."

He nodded.

"Anyway, I spoke to her again just before twelve, actually closer to eleven-thirty. Then I fixed lunch. When I had it on the table, I glanced at the clock and realized that she was almost a half-hour late."

"And that's unusual?"

"Very. We could have a foot of snow on the roads and Mrs. Fallon would be at her desk precisely at 9:00 a.m. She prided herself on punctuality. She thought it was a matter of courtesy and a tidy mind."

He jotted down a note. "Okay. What did you do next?"

"I had a really bad feeling about it, so I called. When no one answered, I ran over to check on her. She wasn't at her desk."

"Was your husband's office door open or closed?"

She thought of her repeated trips into that office. "Closed," she said. "Just the way I left it for you."

He'd been scribbling down her answers again, but his

head jerked up at that. "Closed? It was open when we got there."

Dana's heart thundered wildly at that news. Had the killer still been there when she'd been in the office? Had he or she seen Dana steal the daybook? Or had someone else come along and stumbled on the murder scene, then fled in a panic?

"Think very carefully. Are you sure you closed it again?" O'Flannery demanded.

Again and again, actually. "I'm positive," she said.

He grabbed his two-way radio and barked out an order to the officers at the church. Then he turned back to Dana.

"You didn't see anyone? Hear anything?"

"Nothing," she swore. "Believe me, I was so scared I think I would have jumped if a pin had dropped."

"Did you notice any fresh footprints in the snow on your way over?"

"The snow's been on the ground for days. The kids play out there sometimes. There's no way to tell which footprints might be fresh."

"Okay, then. After you saw the body, what did you do?"

"I checked for a pulse, then ran back here and called you."

Unlike his response on the phone, this time he stared at her with blatant skepticism. "Isn't there another phone around the church you could have used?"

Dana had figured he'd ask that, once he'd had time to think about it. She was ready with another dutiful recitation. "As far as I was concerned, the whole church was a potential murder scene. I didn't want to disturb anything."

He still appeared skeptical, but he let it pass. "Can

you remember anything else? Anything that struck you as odd, before you ever got to that office?"

The question triggered a memory. "The side door was open," she said at once. "I had my key with me, but I didn't have to use it. No one uses that door except those of us with keys. It's a fire exit. It's kept locked from the outside. If it's opened from the inside, it should set off an alarm."

"But you never heard an alarm?"

"No."

"Which means that more than likely whoever used that door before you had a key and used it to enter," he said thoughtfully.

Dana felt as if a tremendous weight had been lifted off her shoulders. It couldn't have been Rick, then. It had to have been someone connected to the church, someone in that group of suspects she and Kate had already been considering. Lawrence Tremayne, for example.

As if she'd conjured him up, the church elder came bursting into the kitchen just then. Apparently he'd seen no need to bother knocking or ringing the doorbell.

"What the hell is going on here?" he demanded indignantly. "I drop by the church to check on things, and I'm told that I can't go inside." He scowled at Dana, as if she'd had something to do with the presence of the police. "Is there some new scandal? Ever since your husband came here, we have been mired in controversy."

Detective O'Flannery shot a sympathetic look at Dana, then slowly rose to his feet. He scowled at the irate man.

"I don't believe I heard you knock," he said quietly. "That's breaking and entering."

"Who the hell are you?" Tremayne asked. "This house belongs to the church, I can come in here anytime I feel it's necessary."

"Oh, really? I think there are a few laws on the books that might say otherwise, as long as Mrs. Miller is in residence."

The detective was doing such a good job on her behalf that Dana saw no need to enter into the fray. She sat back and watched the two men go at it. Tremayne seemed only mildly intimidated by the mention of the law.

"I suppose you're some legal flack she hired to protect her own interests the minute we told her we wanted her to get out. Well, you can just check the terms of the contract we had with her husband. He was expected to be out within thirty days of being dismissed or leaving for any reason. We have been more than lenient with Mrs. Miller, due to the tragic circumstances."

O'Flannery tried hard, but he couldn't entirely mask his disdain. "Actually, I'm Detective Dillon O'Flannery. And while I'm fascinated with the arrangement you had with Reverend Miller, it's hardly any of my business. And you would be?"

The color washed right out of Lawrence Tremayne's face. He seemed to be having a difficult time recalling his name, so Dana supplied it.

"Ah, yes," O'Flannery said. "I've heard quite a lot about you. In fact, I've left several messages at your office. Don't you check in?"

"How I run my business is no concern of yours," Tremayne said scathingly.

"We'll see about that," O'Flannery replied. "In the meantime, perhaps you'd like to wait in the living room while Mrs. Miller and I conclude our business."

The church elder didn't take kindly to being summarily dismissed. He huffed and turned on his heel.

"Mr. Tremayne?" O'Flannery said.

"Yes?"

"In case there's any doubt in your mind, that wasn't a request, that was an order. Don't even think about budging out of that living room."

Tremayne stared at him, practically quivering with indignation. "You're actually detaining me?"

"In a manner of speaking. I'm sure, as an official of the church, you'll want to cooperate, won't you?"

"Cooperate in what? More of this damnable mess that Miller left behind?"

O'Flannery started to reply, but Dana shot him an oh-please-let-me look. He nodded.

"They're investigating a murder," she told him, her gaze locked on Tremayne's smug face for any change in expression that might betray him. "Mrs. Fallon has been killed."

To her deep regret, his shocked reaction seemed genuine. In fact, his eyes practically bugged out of his head.

"Mrs. Fallon is dead?" he asked, his normally forceful tone gone. In fact, he sounded a little lost.

"I found her body earlier," Dana told him.

He stared at her, looking truly shattered. "Oh, my God, this is terrible, just awful," he murmured, then looked at O'Flannery. "Who would do such a thing? I have to tell the others. They'll want to be here."

"No," O'Flannery said. "Any notifying that gets done for the time being will be done by me. If you'll just go into the other room and wait, I'll be with you in a minute."

All of the fight seemed to have drained out of the other man. He simply nodded. "Yes, yes, of course. Whatever will help."

When Tremayne had gone, O'Flannery looked at Dana. "What did you think?"

"I think he was stunned."

"Me, too. Unfortunately, there's nothing on the books that lets me run a man in just because he's an arrogant jerk."

"He does have a key to that exit, though. And he knew the combination to the safe," Dana reminded him. "Maybe he's also a consummate actor."

"Maybes don't win convictions. You sit tight, okay? Let me go see if I can pump any additional information out of him."

"Can't I sit in?"

"Not a chance." He grinned. "Of course, if you happened to be passing nearby and eavesdropped, there wouldn't be a thing I could do about it."

She returned his grin. "You know, you may turn out to be okay after all."

"Put in a good word for me with Kate, that's all I ask."

Dana doubted Kate needed any good words from her on the subject of the sexy detective. She seemed smitten enough, as it was. Besides, the man needed to worry a little about his prospects.

"We'll see," she said.

He frowned at the lack of commitment, but he didn't argue with her. When she rose to follow him, he warned, "Stay out of sight and keep quiet."

"You'll never know I'm there," she promised.

"I will," he said. "Just see to it that Tremayne doesn't."

Dana tiptoed into the dining room and crept along the wall, remaining just out of Tremayne's line of vision from his position on the sofa on the same side of the living room. To her everlasting regret, O'Flannery kept his voice pitched deliberately low. She couldn't hear half of the questions he asked, but she had no problem at all with Tremayne's responses. He bellowed most of them, growing more and more outraged with each apparent hint that he had access to several crucial pieces of information related to both Ken's murder and now Mrs. Fallon's.

He had just leapt up and declared an end to the interview when Dana felt a hand close over her shoulder. She whirled around and came face-to-face with Rick. Her heart ricocheted around in her chest like a Ping-Pong ball.

"You scared me to death," she muttered.

"What the devil's going on?"

She touched a finger to her lips, then led him back into the kitchen. When the door was closed behind them, she explained about Mrs. Fallon's murder and her own discovery of the body. Although it seemed as if an eternity had passed since then, a glance at the clock on the stove indicated it was only midafternoon.

"What are you doing here?" she asked, unable to keep a lingering hint of suspicion out of her voice. "You didn't say anything about coming out when I spoke to you earlier."

"Maybe I just got lonely."

"And maybe you knew about the murder," she blurted without thinking.

He went very still at that. "What are you suggesting?"

His anger was almost palpable. Her suspicions withered under his hard look. "That it had already made the news," she improvised hastily. "What did you think I meant?"

He regarded her silently, as if he was struggling with his temper.

"You thought I was suggesting that you had something to do with it, didn't you?" she asked.

"It wouldn't be the first time," he retorted.

A telltale guilty flush crept into her cheeks.

"You did, didn't you?" he asked incredulously. "You thought I killed her."

"No," she protested, then sighed. It was absurd to try to lie to him. "Okay, for just a minute, it crossed my mind that you were one of the few people who knew I intended to see her this afternoon and what I hoped to get from her."

Before Rick could respond to that, O'Flannery interrupted. She hadn't even heard him return. "And what would that have been, Mrs. Miller? What did you hope to get from Mrs. Fallon?"

"Information," Dana said at once. Her gaze pleaded with Rick not to contradict her, even though she could see how furious he was with her at the moment. "I was sure she would know who Ken had been spending time with lately, if he'd argued with anyone. Secretaries know far more than we credit them with knowing, especially one as observant as Mrs. Fallon. Now we'll never know what she knew," she concluded, her voice breaking.

"Perhaps we will," O'Flannery said, holding out an all-too-familiar black daybook.

"Where did you get that?" Dana demanded, even though she had a pretty good idea. She had placed one just like it beneath her mattress less than two hours earlier.

"You didn't think I bought all that crap about you racing back here to phone us just to avoid contaminating the scene, did you? There had to be another reason you wanted to get back here, such as hiding some piece of information you wanted all to yourself."

Dana couldn't deny it, so she settled for regarding him sourly. She supposed this wasn't the time to mention that he'd found it without a warrant.

"Anything in here?" he asked.

"I haven't had time to look at it," she admitted grudgingly.

"I should just take it down to headquarters and go over it there," the detective said, then grinned slightly. "But, since you went to so much trouble to get it, I won't."

He joined them at the kitchen table, then cast a look at Rick. "I assume you're interested in what's in here, too."

"Of course. I want to find Ken's killer as badly as Dana does." His gaze locked on hers. "I have my own personal reasons for wanting to prove that neither I nor anyone at Yo, Amigo was involved."

O'Flannery watched the byplay between her and Rick, then nodded. "Okay, then let's see what we have."

He flipped the daybook open to January. Meeting after meeting had been entered in Mrs. Fallon's neat, precise handwriting. There was nothing unusual about any of them. As far as Dana could see, they were the usual assortment of meetings necessary to conducting the business of the church, plus the regular weekly notation of Ken's commitment to spend the evening at Yo, Amigo.

Most of the meetings had the time dutifully noted, but toward the beginning of February there were several entries that did not. Just a name had been jotted down.

"What do you suppose this means?" O'Flannery asked. "Are these people who dropped by without an appointment?"

"Exactly," Dana said. "She always found that extremely annoying, even though Ken welcomed drop-in visits. I guess she dealt with her frustration by putting the names down after the fact."

Tremayne's name had been entered repeatedly, indicating his arrogant habit, which Mrs. Fallon's scowls had obviously failed to correct. So had Peter Drake's name and Miriam Kelso's. Mrs. Fallon had always grumbled that people like that should have known better. "No one would walk into *their* offices uninvited and unscheduled," she had protested often enough.

Some of the names entered were kids, including several visits by Juan Jesus in the days right before Ken's death. Since there had been no mention of his dropping by in January, his repeated visits in February seemed especially suspicious to Dana.

"Could he have known something?" Dana wondered aloud. She glanced at Rick. "Maybe he'd heard something on his weekends at home and it worried him."

Rick looked doubtful. He also looked as if he could cheerfully strangle her for dragging the teenager into this.

"Only one way to find out," he said eventually and with obvious reluctance. "He's staying just a few blocks away, isn't he? Let's go talk to him and clear this up right now."

"Fine," Dana said, facing Rick defiantly. It wasn't as if she'd accused Juan Jesus of killing anyone, just of knowing something about Ken's murder.

"Hold on, you two," O'Flannery said as they both stood up. "This is a police investigation, remember? If anybody's going to talk to the kid, it'll be me."

Dana glanced at Rick and suspected he was about to argue, which would only cause O'Flannery to dig in his heels and start citing all sorts of ethical considerations. She jumped in first. "Couldn't we all go? Rick knows him. Maybe Juan Jesus will be less frightened and more forthcoming with a familiar face in the room."

The detective scowled. "I really hate it when civilians make sense. Okay, let's do it."

To her regret, he tucked the calendar under his arm. Apparently he had no intention of letting her hang onto the lone piece of potential evidence she'd discovered.

"Shall we all go in my car?" O'Flannery asked.

"Fine," Dana said, just as Rick said, "No."

She stared at him.

"Dana and I will take my car," he said tightly. "We'll meet you there."

Judging from the tightening of his jaw and the fierce expression in his eyes, Dana had the feeling that for once in her life, she ought to jump at the chance to have police protection. Unfortunately, O'Flannery merely waved his agreement and headed for his car. She shot a tentative gaze at Rick.

"Okay, whatever's on your mind, let's hear it," she said, bracing for a tirade.

He glanced at her. "What makes you think there's something on my mind?"

"You didn't arrange to get me all to yourself, so you could chat about the weather or kiss me senseless."

His lips almost quirked into a smile at that. "Don't be so sure about the kissing. There are times when you do tempt me beyond endurance."

Despite her suspicions, despite everything, she was intrigued. "Really?"

"Really," he confirmed. "Don't let it go to your head, though. There are also many times I'd like to throttle you, *querida*."

"And this would be which?"

He did smile at that. "Perhaps I'll let you think about that for a bit." His expression sobered. "In the meantime, I will try to think how to protect a good kid from the kind of interrogation you've drawn him into."

"You blame me for drawing Juan Jesus into this?" she asked incredulously.

"I didn't hear anyone else suggesting he might be involved, did you?"

"But I was just…"

"Just what? Trying to cast blame on the outsider, yes? You are more like the others than you would care to admit, I think. Maybe worse, because you hide your prejudice."

"No," she retorted defensively, shocked by his interpretation of her actions. "His name was there. I was just speculating out loud."

"To a police officer," he reminded her. "Not to me. Not to Kate. To a cop."

She winced at his accusatory tone. "I want answers."

"Any answers?" he asked. "Or the truth?"

"The truth, of course."

He regarded her with obvious sorrow. "Sometimes I wonder, *querida*. Sometimes I wonder."

26

Juan Jesus Villanueva was a skinny and, at the moment, frightened sixteen-year-old. His eyes widened with alarm, and he literally shook when Rick introduced him to O'Flannery and explained that he was a detective.

"I didn't do nothing, man." He gazed beseechingly at Rick for support. "Ever since the *padre* brought me out here, I've played strictly by the rules. I swear it."

Rick put his hand on the boy's shoulder and squeezed reassuringly. "It's okay. We just wanted to ask you a few questions. Nobody's accusing you of anything," he said with a pointed glance at Dana.

She smiled at Juan Jesus. "Truly, all we want is some help in trying to figure out what happened to my husband. Can you try to remember what was going on back in February, right before he was killed?"

Rick felt him shudder, but the kid bravely forced a nod. "The *padre* was good to me. I'll tell you whatever I can if you think it will help."

"Thank you," Dana said. "Maybe we should go inside, where we'll be more comfortable."

Juan Jesus shook his head. "I'd rather stay out here. There's no point in dragging the Wilsons into this." He gazed at Rick, studiously avoiding making eye contact with O'Flannery. "What did you want to know?"

Rick glanced at the detective for permission to do the questioning. The other man nodded.

"Do you remember back in February if you were stopping in to see the *padre* a lot?" Rick asked.

The boy looked relieved by the question. "Sure," he said without hesitation. "A couple of times a week."

"Why?"

"Is it important?" he hedged.

"That depends on the answer," Rick told him. "Do you have something to hide?"

"Not the way you mean." He looked chagrined. "Okay. You're not going to believe this, but I was having trouble with Spanish. I mean, I can speak it and all. Hell…" He glanced at Dana. "Sorry. I mean, that's all anyone talks at home, but I never learned to write or read the stuff, not the way you have to to pass a class."

"Why didn't you ask your parents or Maria for help?" Rick asked.

Juan Jesus regarded him with disgust. "You gotta be kidding. I'd never have heard the end of it. Mama would have had me at the kitchen table all weekend long with all the old books she brought from Mexico. I didn't want to waste my time like that."

"So you went to Ken for help?" Rick asked.

"He'd told me from the start I could always come to him if I had a problem. Believe me, this was a big problem. He tutored me a couple of hours a week." He grinned. "Brought my grade up to a B-minus, too."

"And that's the only reason you were spending time with him?" Rick persisted.

"Sure." He stared at them all curiously. "Why? What did you think was going on?"

"Never mind," Rick said. "You've been a big help."

"Wait," Dana said. "Could I ask one thing, Juan Jesus?"

Rick scowled at her. "Dana…"

"It's okay. I don't mind," the teen said.

"Thank you. I was just wondering if anything unusual ever happened while you were with my husband."

Juan Jesus looked perplexed. "Unusual how?"

"A phone call that seemed to upset him, maybe, or an argument with someone. Did anyone drop in unexpectedly?"

Rick had to admit the questions were logical ones. Other names had been noted on those days when Juan Jesus had been in Ken's office. Perhaps he had overheard or seen something.

"People dropped in all the time," the teenager said. "It made Mrs. Fallon loco. She used to get this pinched expression on her face, like she'd smelled a dead rat or something."

"So you didn't find anything odd about any of these drop-in visits?" Dana persisted.

"Not really," he said. Then his expression turned thoughtful. "Except this once. I got there and heard somebody inside crying. I figured somebody had died, the way they were wailing. Mrs. Fallon hurried me out of the office. She made up some errand for me to run. In fact, she couldn't hustle me out of there fast enough."

Dana's shoulders sagged with disappointment. "So you never saw who was in the office?"

"Sure I did. She was too rattled to think clearly, so the errand was a snap. It only took me a minute, and by the time I got back, the crying had stopped, but the door was still closed. Just when I thought Mrs. F was going to send me off on another errand, the door opened and this lady came out. She practically knocked me down, she was in such a hurry. I've never seen anybody look so furious in all my life, not even on the streets back home. She looked mad enough to kill somebody."

As if he realized what he'd said, his eyes widened with shock. "You don't think…?"

"We don't know what to think," Rick insisted quickly. He didn't want Juan Jesus to start speculating. The rest of them were doing quite enough of that. "That's why we're exploring all sorts of possibilities. You don't know who this woman was, do you?"

Juan Jesus shook his head. "Nah. I'd never seen her before. And the *padre* had this confidentiality thing. He acted as if it had never happened. So did Mrs. F. I figured it was none of my business."

"What did she look like?" Dana asked.

"It was kinda hard to tell. She was tall and skinny, I remember that, but she was wearing this big, floppy hat. It covered up most of her face."

Rick glanced at Dana to see if the description rang any bells. He recognized a spark of excitement in her eyes and gathered it had, though she was remaining tight-lipped about her suspicions.

"Anything else?" he asked O'Flannery.

"No." The detective smiled at Juan Jesus. "You've been a big help, son. The *padre* would be proud of you."

Juan Jesus glanced at Rick for confirmation. Rick nodded. "He would be, you know."

"I owe him a lot," the boy said, gazing at Dana. "You must miss him a lot, huh?"

"Yes," she said softly. "A lot."

"If you'd ever like me to come by, maybe help out with your kids or something, I could. I hung out with them sometimes at the church, after my lessons. They're pretty cool for little guys. I'm the youngest in my family, so it was kinda fun to be around kids younger than me. I felt like a big brother, instead of being the baby."

Rick saw that Dana was genuinely touched by the offer. Tears sparkled in her eyes.

"They would like that," she said. "And so would I. When they come back from Florida, I'll call you."

"They're in Florida? Awesome. Frankie's down there, too."

All of the color seemed to wash out of Dana's face at that. "Frankie who?" she demanded so harshly that Juan Jesus looked taken aback.

"Frankie Vincenzi," he responded at once. "He's in my class at school, or at least he was until his mom sent him and his kid brother off to Florida to stay with his grandparents."

"When was that?"

"A couple of weeks ago, I guess. Maybe longer."

"Do you know where in Florida?"

He shook his head. "I don't remember. Geography was my second-worst subject. Maybe if I heard the name, it'd come back to me."

"Orlando? Miami? Tampa?" Dana suggested.

Rick stared at her, stunned by the desperation he heard in her voice.

"Nah, it wasn't any place that big."

"Think, please. Was it Clearwater? Fort Myers?"

Juan Jesus's expression brightened. "Yeah, that's it. Fort Myers. I knew it sounded like some military base or something."

Rather than looking relieved that Juan Jesus had remembered, Dana looked as if she might faint. Rick touched her arm. "Are you okay?"

"I have to get home," she said shakily. "Right away."

Rick glanced at O'Flannery, who was watching Dana intently. "Are we through here?" he asked him.

"For the moment."

"Are you coming back to the house?"

"No. I have some things I want to follow up on at the station. I'll catch up with you two later."

The minute they were back in the car, Rick turned to Dana. "Okay, *querida,* what's going on?"

"Just take me home, please. Hurry. I have to call my parents."

Suddenly it all added up. Her panic. The mention of Fort Myers. Frankie Vincenzi. He turned on the engine and sped out of the Wilsons' driveway.

"You are leaping to conclusions again, *querida,*" he said, even though he'd just done exactly the same thing.

"What conclusions?"

"That Carolina Vincenzi's children are the ones taunting your boy."

"It has to be," she insisted. "But it's more than that. You heard Juan Jesus's description of the woman in Ken's office that day. It had to be Carolina."

He regarded her with confusion. "And if it was?"

"Didn't you hear what he said? He said she looked mad enough to kill."

"And from this you've concluded that she was behind Ken's murder?"

"It makes sense," she insisted.

"No," he argued. He tried to inject a note of reason. "What was her motive?"

"I don't know," she admitted with obvious reluctance. "Whatever they were fighting about."

"Do you know a court of law that would permit this as evidence?"

She scowled at him. "I don't give two figs about evidence. I want to protect my boys. She knows where they are."

"So do dozens of other people," he reminded her. "Everyone in the congregation knows that you took them to Florida to be with your parents. It would not be so difficult for anyone to get the address from the church office. I'd be willing to bet you even received condolence notes down there, didn't you?"

She shuddered at that and covered her face with her hands. "Oh, God, why didn't I think of that? I should never have told anyone they were there."

"You weren't thinking clearly."

"But I should have been. From the beginning I believed that Ken's death wasn't an accident. I should have been more cautious. What kind of investigator am I if I can't even think to protect my own kids?"

"You were not thinking as an investigator at the time," he reminded her gently. "You were thinking exactly as you should have been, as a grieving wife and worried mother."

She sucked in a deep breath and visibly steadied herself. "Yes," she said, her tone suggesting a strengthened resolve. "That was exactly what I was doing, but no more." She peered out the window, then pointed. "Take a left at the next corner."

"But that's the opposite direction from your house."

"I know."

He regarded her suspiciously. "Where are we going?" he asked while he made the turn she'd indicated. Apparently he had no willpower at all where she was concerned. Going along with her harebrained schemes was a habit he really should concentrate on breaking.

"Where else?" she said. "We are going to pay a call on Carolina Vincenzi."

That was not exactly what Rick had had in mind when he'd cautioned her against leaping to conclusions, but he could see from the determined set of her jaw that there would be no talking her out of it. She'd decided to go straight to the source for her answers and, unfortunately, he couldn't fault her logic, even if he did question the impetuous timing of her decision.

"Do you have a plan?" he inquired.

"What sort of plan?" she replied testily.

"Do you know what you intend to ask her? What are we looking for?"

"For starters, I want to know what she was wailing about in Ken's office that day, to use Juan Jesus's phrase."

"And if she chooses to lie?"

She sighed at the suggestion. "Hopefully, my gut instincts will kick in, and I'll be able to tell."

Resigned to helping her in this folly, he said dryly, "Just in case, perhaps you should settle for keeping Mrs. Vincenzi occupied while I poke around elsewhere in her house."

She gaped at that. "You're going to search the house while she's in it? No, it's too risky."

"And what you intend is not?"

She had no argument for that. "But how?" she asked eventually.

"You leave that to me," he said, figuring it was best she not know exactly how skilled he was at breaking and entering. Maybe he'd lost his edge, anyway. It had been a long time. Perhaps he would be caught red-handed, just as she had been at Yo, Amigo.

"Does she have a housekeeper?" he asked.

"No. I think she has a maid, but not full-time."

"Well, hopefully the maid will be off."

"And if she's not?"

He grinned. A maid was the least of his concerns. "I can be very persuasive when I put my mind to it."

She scowled. "I'm not so sure I like the sound of that."

"No need to be jealous, *querida*. I will always save my best efforts for you."

"I am not jealous," she insisted indignantly. "For some reason, I'm just worried about your sorry hide."

"You leave the worrying to me. I will drop you at the corner, then circle the block to park in the back. Keep your eyes open. When you see the car in the front again, then you can wrap up your conversation with Mrs. Vincenzi."

"What if she happens to hear you creeping around inside?"

"She won't," he assured her. "Not if you irritate her sufficiently. She will, perhaps, be wailing again. That should cover any noise I might make."

"Not that I doubt your snooping skills," she said, "but do you have a plan? Do you have any idea what you're looking for?"

"Same as you, *querida,* something that would give her a motive to kill."

"Or the weapon," Dana suggested belatedly. "My God, Rick, what if she has a gun?"

"If it's *the* gun, then we're in great shape."

"Not if it's aimed at us," she said, her expression suddenly dire.

"Don't chicken out on me now."

Her chin rose. "I am not chickening out," she insisted. "You're the one who's always preaching caution."

He grinned as he slowed at the corner. "What do I know?" he asked with a shrug. "Go, *querida*."

She opened the door and slid out, casting a worried look back at him as she slowly closed the door.

"Be careful," she said, then turned and marched intrepidly down the block.

Rick watched her go with a renewed sense of admiration. She truly was a remarkable woman. With a sudden flash of insight, he realized that he had fallen in love with her. Despite her infuriating habit of blaming him for murders he hadn't committed, he wanted to spend the rest of his life with her.

Only after he'd driven away did he begin to get that first nagging sense of impending disaster burning a hole in the pit of his stomach. Had he just sent the woman he loved off to get her head blown off?

27

Carolina Vincenzi lived in ostentatious style. The heavily wooded lots in her exclusive development were an acre or more. With the exception of one or two towering old oak trees, which had the audacity to shed an occasional dead leaf, her grounds had been trimmed and manicured as tidily as any formal garden Dana had ever seen on an English country estate. Even the days-old snow looked clean, as if it had been swept free of soot.

The house, which had been built in no discernible style, had touches of art deco, a little taste of country French, and a hint of Frank Lloyd Wright. It was ugly as sin, too big for the lot and every bit as tasteless as Dana would have anticipated, right down to the gargoyle knockers on the double front doors.

To Dana's frustration, pounding on that massive front door with that hideous knocker and ringing the bell drew no response. The place was as silent as a tomb—an image she wished hadn't come to mind.

Foiled in her plan to cross-examine Carolina, she crept behind the bushes to peer in the closest window, a narrow floor-to-ceiling panel of glass beside the door.

The foyer was practically the size of her living room,

with an Oriental carpet in bright reds and blacks covering most of the wide plank oak floor. An Oriental vase, probably from some ancient dynasty, sat atop a gleaming mahogany table in the center. Someone had devoted hours of elbow grease to getting that deep shine on the wood.

Dana had seen exclusive hotel lobbies that had been decorated with less attention to effect. In her house that table would have been cluttered with mail and keys. Not here. She doubted there was so much as a speck of dust on it, or even swirling in the air above.

Just as she was debating whether to try some makeshift means of picking the lock, she saw a stealthily creeping shadow toward the back of the foyer. Rick, no doubt. She tapped lightly on the window to try to attract his attention.

Rather than Rick, however, it was another man who slipped into view. Peter Drake. Dana stared at him incredulously.

Fortunately, he either hadn't heard her tapping or was too absorbed in his own invasion of the place to give it any attention. He edged into a room on the left and disappeared from view.

Dana practically trampled some kind of thorny bush in her haste to get around to the back of the house so she could intercept Rick before he inadvertently joined Drake inside. She rounded the corner in such a rush that she ran smack into the very man she'd hoped to warn.

"What the hell?" Rick muttered, his arms closing around her. "Dana?" He scowled at her "Why aren't you inside? You've had plenty of time."

"Because no one answered the door," she said simply.

"Ah, I see. Well, good," he said, not wasting time on questioning what he obviously viewed as their good fortune. "Then we should have free run of the place."

When he would have moved toward the door, she held him back. "Not exactly."

"What do you mean, not exactly?"

She described what she had seen. "I guess he figured whoever had been ringing the bell had left."

"Or he was trying to get to a window so he could check," Rick suggested.

Just then they heard an engine starting. Apparently there had been another alternative.

"Or he was trying to get to a door so he could beat a hasty retreat," she said. She took off for the front, with Rick right beside her. They were just in time to see Drake's familiar and very expensive sports utility vehicle speed away.

She glanced up into Rick's puzzled eyes. "Curiouser and curiouser, yes?"

"I'll say. What do you want to do now? Shall we leave or check out the inside and see if we can figure out what Drake was up to?"

She regarded him with suspicion. "It's my call?"

"*Querida,* you're the investigator."

"Yes," she said, grateful for the acknowledgment. "Yes, I am." Excitement shimmered through her. "Let's do it. Can you get us in? I don't have my lock picks with me."

"Perhaps we should just try the door Drake used. I doubt he was locking up on his way out."

Naturally, though, that would have been too easy. The house was locked up tighter than Fort Knox, complete with an alarm system that warned Rick off.

"It's too advanced for my skills," he conceded, after studying the wiring.

"Which raises an interesting point," Dana said. "How did Peter Drake get past it?"

"Maybe Carolina let him in."

Dana recalled the weird feeling she'd gotten as she'd approached the house, the image of the place as a tomb. "You don't suppose…" She let her voice trail off, but Rick caught her meaning.

"That she's inside," he said. "Unfortunately, there's only one way to find out. I don't have a problem setting off the alarm to find out if you don't. We can always say Carolina expected us and that we saw someone sneaking around on the property and decided we'd better investigate."

"Think that'll fly with Detective O'Flannery?"

Rick shrugged. "I suppose it depends on whether or not we find Carolina dead."

Dana shuddered. She'd really stumbled upon all the dead acquaintances she wanted to when she'd discovered Mrs. Fallon's body. "Maybe we should look in the garage first, see if her car's here."

Rick grinned. "Turning cautious, *querida?*"

She scowled at him. "You should be pleased."

"I am," he assured her, leading the way to the double garage on the far side of the house.

To Dana's regret, the builder had inconveniently neglected to put any window into the garage. Dana stared at the impenetrable-looking doors while Rick searched for some indication of whether the alarm system extended to this part of the structure.

"Is it wired?" she asked.

"There's no evidence of it, but anything is possible."

The lack of conviction in his voice set off her own mental alarms. That prickling on the back of her neck had once been very familiar. It had alerted her to impending disaster.

"What now?" she asked.

"Now we see if lifting weights has paid off for me," Rick said, grabbing the handle and trying to heft one of the doors up. Apparently locked, it stayed firmly in place. In fact, it didn't so much as creak on its hinges.

"Very solid," he muttered, then brightened. "But no shrieking alarms have gone off because I tried to lift it. I would have expected a very sensitive motion detector."

"A very good sign," she agreed. "Then we move on to plan two." She dug around in the bottom of her purse for a paper clip. She waved it under his nose and knelt down to fiddle with the lock.

"You expect to break in with a paper clip?"

"No, I *hope* to break in with a paper clip," she said, trying to delicately nudge the lock's tumblers. Her fingers weren't nearly as deft as they'd once been, but the skill hadn't entirely abandoned her. She felt the precise instant when everything clicked into place. The handle turned easily and the door began to glide up smoothly. Adrenaline pumped furiously through her veins. Damn, but it felt good to be back in action. Her confidence soared.

"That's far enough," Rick said, bending down to peek through the opening. "No need to have the neighbors wondering why the garage door's sitting open."

"What neighbors? The nearest one is half a block away, behind a quarter acre of trees."

"You're assuming he never leaves the house to walk the dog I hear barking."

Dana frowned. "Okay, your powers of observation are very good."

"Better than yours, perhaps?"

"Don't rub it in. It might make me start to wonder how you honed them."

He chuckled. "Yes, we definitely would not want that."

"So, is there a car inside or not?"

"Two of them. A Mercedes and a very expensive sports car, a Lamborghini, perhaps, though I have never seen one up close."

"That's Carolina's," Dana confirmed. "Which means she could be inside."

"Or in Florida with her children," Rick reminded her. "She would not leave a car like this in the lot at O'Hare. She would take a limo to the airport, yes?"

The reminder that at this very moment Carolina might be near Dana's children frightened her even more deeply than the possibility had earlier. Finding Peter Drake sneaking around inside the house had only confirmed that something very strange was going on and that Carolina was involved in it.

"Are you ready to check inside?" Rick asked. "If the garage alarm was off, then my guess would be that the whole system is down."

"No," Dana said at once, oblivious of the golden opportunity they had to sneak in undetected. "I want to check on my kids. I have to warn my parents to be alert, in case Carolina shows up there."

"Not even a quick peek?" Rick asked. "You could use the phone inside and charge it to your calling card so there would be no record of it on their bill."

Tempted, Dana stared at him, intrigued with the devious workings of his mind. There had been a time when she would have hired an intrepid, quick-thinking man like that on the spot to work for her. Now she couldn't help worrying just a little about all that she didn't know about the darker side of Rick's past. Was he merely indulging her in this quest to keep her from once more focusing on him as a suspect? At the moment, there was enough to intrigue her right here. She would worry about Rick's motives later.

"Okay, you win." She wiggled the paper clip in front of his nose. "Your turn," she suggested when they reached the front door.

To her chagrin, he was even more adept than she had been with the garage door. They were inside that pretentious foyer practically before she could blink.

"You call. I'll look around," Rick said. "Make sure you don't leave any fingerprints on the phone."

She tolerated the warning because it made sense. "Be careful," she whispered. "This place gives me the creeps."

"It is good to know you don't need a mansion to be happy," he said in an enigmatic way that raised goose bumps and some fascinating speculation.

"Not this mansion, anyway." She left the room before he could respond to that. She headed straight in the direction she had seen Peter Drake taking. Maybe he had only been looking for a nearby exit, or maybe he'd been doing a quick scan for something important.

The room she entered was very masculine and, indeed, it did have its own exit. Perhaps so Carolina's husband could slip in and out at night? she wondered. It was an intriguing possibility.

She knew next to nothing about Tony Vincenzi, except that he'd made his money with a string of upscale pizza places. He rarely attended church with his wife, except on special occasions, such as Christmas Eve services. In fact, Dana realized, she had heard once that he and their sons attended the nearby Catholic church, which would explain why Bobby hadn't known the boy who had taunted him down in Florida...if that's who it was.

Although she was itching to poke through the desk, she took a handkerchief out of her purse, picked up the phone and dialed her parents' number, using her calling card to do it, just as Rick had suggested.

Her father answered on the first ring. It was an old habit, indicative of his impatience. He was usually curt to the point of rudeness on the phone, except with her. His greeting now was as abrupt as always.

"Hey, Dad, it's me."

"Dana, baby, how are you?" he asked, his tone softening.

"I'm fine. Are the boys there with you?"

"They went shopping with your mother. Why? You sound worried."

"It's nothing specific, just a mother's intuition, I suppose."

"A mother's or a private investigator's?"

"A little of both," she admitted. "Did Mom ever find out the name of the kid who'd been tormenting Bobby at school?"

"Bobby wouldn't say. She hasn't pursued it with the teacher, as far as I know. Is it important?"

"It could be. I just heard that a couple of kids from the area are down there."

"So you think they picked up that garbage about Ken from home?"

"Exactly."

"But who would say something like that, unless they knew about the drugs being planted?" He hesitated. "My God, you think that that kid could know the person who planted the drugs, don't you?"

She wasn't surprised by how quickly he'd grasped the problem. "It's possible. Please, Dad, don't alarm them, but keep a close eye on the kids, okay? This whole thing really has me spooked."

"What do the police say?"

"They're doing the best they can," she said, feeling more generosity toward them than she had felt when she'd rushed home to pick up their slack. "They agree with me that it looks as if Ken was framed by somebody hoping to destroy his reputation after his death, probably so the police would dismiss his murder as a drug deal gone sour or something."

"Honey, you do what you have to do. I know you're torn about leaving the kids down here with us, but they're fine. They're adjusting to school. Even Bobby's getting along okay now. Ken was the best son-in-law a man could ask for. You clear his name, okay?"

"I'm trying."

"Just don't put yourself in danger. The boys need you safe and sound. We all do."

Dana thought of the man in the house with her and wondered if the warning hadn't come too late. She trusted that Rick wouldn't harm her, at least not physically. But in making him her ally, she had placed her heart at serious risk.

How would her father feel about this man who was so very different from Ken? she wondered. Would he welcome him, as he had the quieter, gentler man she'd married? Or would his old instincts about troublemakers kick in? Would he view Rick as an ex–street kid who'd flouted the law for too many years? Fortunately, the need to answer that was a long way down the road.

"I love you, Dad."

"Love you, too, baby. Take care of yourself. I'll see to it that no harm comes to your sons."

"I know you will," she said. After she'd hung up, she prayed that he could do as he'd promised. Was he any more of a match for a murderer than Ken had been?

Yes, she concluded. Because unlike her husband, who had trusted everyone, her father had no illusions about human nature. He'd been a prosecutor for too many years, seen too many supposedly reformed criminals released back onto the streets to commit more atrocities. He was the one who'd fueled her desire to become an investigator in the first place. On occasion, she had even been fortunate enough to work for him before his retirement. He'd had a cop's instincts and a passion for seeing justice done.

"Dana?" Rick called in a hushed voice.

She went into the foyer and saw him standing at the top of the stairs.

"I think you ought to come up here."

Her heart thudded dully. "It's not Carolina, is it?"

He shook his head.

"Then what?"

"Not what, who. My guess is it's her husband. He looks just like the guy in the wedding picture on the nightstand."

Dana sucked in a deep breath and squeezed her eyes shut. When she opened them again, she forced herself to climb the steps.

"He's dead?" she asked when she reached the top.

"Oh, yeah," Rick said softly. "He is very dead."

In fact, Tony Vincenzi looked as if he'd been dead for some time—a day or two, perhaps—which brought into question who had killed him. It hardly seemed likely that Peter Drake had done it days earlier, then returned to the scene of the crime for another search of the premises—not unless he was a total idiot, anyway.

Had he even seen the body? He'd been downstairs when Dana had spotted him.

She glanced at Rick. "Shall we call O'Flannery from here or tip him off after we make a getaway?"

"Your call."

"My gut is practically screaming that we should

get our butts as far away from this place as possible," she said.

"And your head?"

"For once, it concurs. Let's go." At the foot of the stairs, she hesitated and glanced around wistfully. "I never got to look around down here."

"I think we can safely assume that if there were anything incriminating in the place, your friend Mr. Drake would have found it. Whoever killed Vincenzi, my guess is that Drake was here to tidy up."

"You think Carolina asked him for help?"

"Or whoever ordered the hit in the first place."

"Hit? Why did you say it like that?"

"His hands were bound behind him. It looked to me as if he'd been kneeling on the floor when he was shot. Classic hit."

Obviously she'd been too rattled by the sight of yet another body to analyze the scene. "Of course," she said, recalling the image of the way his body rested against the foot of the bed, almost as if he'd been saying his prayers when he was shot. It didn't surprise her, as it once might have, that his prayers hadn't been answered.

"Two minutes in that den, that's all I ask," she pleaded.

"I don't think so," Rick said.

He suddenly grabbed her hand and practically dragged her toward the back of the house with an urgency that startled her.

"Would you mind telling me what's going on?" she said, balking at the door.

"We're leaving."

"By the back door? We came in the front."

"Just as Detective O'Flannery is about to do," he noted with some urgency. "Apparently your Mr. Drake wasn't quite as oblivious to our presence as we might have hoped. My guess is he gave us time to get well and truly implicated in the crime, then called the police and reported prowlers."

Dana didn't waste time cursing Peter Drake or the possibility of a silent alarm, which neither of them had considered. She raced out the back door, one step behind Rick.

Fortunately, he'd had the foresight to park on an undeveloped piece of land, just beyond the Vincenzis' property line. They disappeared into the woods almost at once, making it a virtual certainty that O'Flannery couldn't spot them, not without bloodhounds, anyway.

Dana's adrenaline was pumping fast and furiously as they pulled away.

"Remind me to take you on a nice, tame date once all this is over and done with," Rick suggested a few minutes later, when they'd both caught their breath.

"You sure you wouldn't get bored with me?" she asked.

He gazed into her eyes. "Never, *querida.* Never."

The wicked desire she saw blazing in his eyes made her tremble. Oh, yes, she thought, she was in this— whatever *this* turned out to be—way, way over her head.

28

There was no time to ponder what they might have done about the desire darkening Rick's eyes, because they found Kate waiting impatiently for them in the kitchen. The aroma of food was in the air and the table had been set for four. Dana had a pretty good idea whom she'd been expecting.

"Where the devil have you two been?" Kate demanded when they crossed the threshold.

"You wouldn't believe me if I told you," Dana replied. "Have you made coffee, by any chance?"

"I've had time to make a whole gourmet meal," Kate retorted irritably. "Yes, there's coffee and a roast and baked potatoes and fresh green beans. I was just thinking of baking a cherry pie."

Dana grinned at Rick's incredulous expression. "Kate cooks when she's anxious," she explained.

"You would not like to visit Yo, Amigo when these attacks come on, would you?" he asked, sniffing the air appreciatively.

Kate frowned at him. "I don't expect another one. I'm demanding that the doctor give me tranquilizers, as long as Dana and I remain friends."

Dana regarded her suspiciously. "Are you sure I'm to blame for this? I thought you had a date with O'Flannery tonight. Did you have this meal planned for him?"

Kate scowled. "Okay, yes, but the dutiful detective got a call, so I hauled everything over here, figuring maybe you could fill me in on what's been happening. O'Flannery is as tight-lipped as a clam. He said he would come by here, when he could, if he could, whatever. I got the distinct impression that there is news."

"You could say that," Dana agreed. She described the assortment of dead bodies that had recently come to light.

"Holy mackerel!" Kate breathed, when she was done. "What do you suppose it all means?"

Dana glanced at Rick, then said, "Actually, I've been thinking about that. As weird and unlikely as it seems, I think maybe Carolina and Peter were having an affair."

"Oh, yuck," Kate said. "He is so…"

"Bland," Dana supplied.

"No, slimy, smarmy, whatever."

"Not a good candidate for an affair with the elegant Carolina?" Rick interpreted.

"Exactly."

"So, if it wasn't romantic, what was it?" Dana asked. "What connected them?"

"The obvious," Rick said. "The church. They were all on the board, were they not?"

"Yes," Dana said. "So what?"

"Have you seen any financial records from the church?" he asked.

Dana stared. A familiar tingle began, and for once it wasn't the least bit sexual in nature. It was the reaction she always had when she finally discovered the thread that would start to unravel a complex mystery. "What exactly are you thinking?"

"Were these two in a position to embezzle church funds?" he asked point-blank.

Dana was at a loss. She had never interfered in that part of Ken's life. "I have no idea how that part of the church's business was conducted. The only person besides Ken who could tell us that would be Mrs. Fallon."

"And she is conveniently dead," Kate said. "I think Rick might be onto something."

Dana held up her hands. "Okay, I see where you're going with this, and it's certainly worth checking out. It would explain why someone planted drugs. They probably figured it would make it look as if Ken embezzled the money to buy drugs, right?"

"Exactly," Rick said.

"Okay, then, why is Tony Vincenzi dead? He didn't even attend this church."

"Wild speculation?" Rick asked. "He found out what his wife was up to and ratted her out to Ken. That's why she was wailing in his office that day, because she'd been caught. In her case, confession apparently wasn't good for her soul."

As badly as she wanted to tie up all the loose ends, Dana couldn't entirely buy Rick's not-quite-far-fetched theory. "Why would they need to embezzle church funds? Carolina's loaded. You saw her house. And Drake does okay."

"Are you sure about that?" Rick asked. "Appearances can be deceiving. Maybe Carolina's husband kept her on a tight budget. Maybe Drake lived beyond his means."

"And Tremayne? Where does he fit in?" she asked.

"Maybe he doesn't," Kate chimed in. "Maybe we've been focusing too hard on him, because we don't like him."

"Or maybe he's behind it all, to get money for his

failed development deal in South America," Dana said slowly.

"We need to see the books," Kate concluded. "Or bank records. Do you have any of that stuff around the house?"

Dana shook her head. "It's all in the church office. Even if we found the books, do either of you know anything about accounting? I certainly don't. It's not the kind of thing I ever investigated."

"I do," Rick said. "I've had to take a crash course since opening Yo, Amigo. The government demands very accurate records for the funding it provides."

Kate cast a resigned look toward the stove. "That roast was destined to taste like sawdust, wasn't it?"

Dana grinned. "Then it will be just right for that cop who stood you up."

Kate visibly perked up at that thought. "Yes, it will."

"Which cop would that be?" a familiar voice asked just as they reached the front door.

They found themselves facing a very disgruntled-looking O'Flannery.

"Oops," Dana murmured under her breath.

O'Flannery didn't wait for a reply to his question. "Now, just where would you all be off to this time?" he inquired cheerfully.

"A walk," Kate said at once. "We were just going for a walk to work up an appetite."

"I thought we had dinner plans," he said.

"We did. You canceled," she reminded him. "Your message said you'd catch up with me here."

"And take you out," he elaborated.

"You didn't say that. Besides, I'd already cooked. I brought the food over here."

He beamed. "Terrific, then we can all eat together." His gaze settled on Dana, then skipped over to Rick and back again. "Maybe over dessert you two can tell me what you were doing sneaking around inside the Vincenzi home just prior to my arrival there."

Dana sighed. Rick scowled.

"Who is this Vincenzi person?" he asked.

"Oh, give it up," O'Flannery said. "I know you were there. I saw you as you made a dash for the woods. I didn't waste time giving chase, because I knew exactly where to find you."

Dana's expression brightened. "Precisely. Would you have felt the same if you'd seriously thought we were fleeing felons?"

"Felons? Maybe not, but you were fleeing a crime scene. How'd you get in and why were you there?"

"Do we have to do this standing in the middle of the living room while my roast dies a little more with each passing minute?" Kate grumbled peevishly.

O'Flannery sent a warm smile her way. "Of course not. I'm sure we'll all be much more relaxed over a nice, hot meal."

"Speak for yourself," Dana muttered.

"Hush, *querida*," Rick whispered as O'Flannery followed Kate toward the kitchen. "You will stir his suspicions."

Dana stared at him incredulously. "His suspicions are on full alert as it is. I don't have any explanations I care to share with him, do you?"

"No, but I am very quick on my feet. There was a time when it was the only thing between me and prison."

"How reassuring."

He caught her hand in his and squeezed it. Oddly enough, she felt better almost immediately. Not relieved exactly, but warmer. Hotter, in fact. No, she corrected at once, that was another reaction entirely, and one that was growing increasingly troublesome.

"Ah, I see the table is already set for four," O'Flannery said jovially. "What good planning. Or were you expecting someone else?"

"It would serve you right if we were," Kate muttered as she began shuttling dishes of food to the table—enough food for an army, which only confirmed her earlier agitation.

His gaze narrowed. "I thought you understood that I had to go out on a call."

"That was before I knew you were going to try to pin a crime on my friends."

"Nobody said anything about locking your friends up for a crime," he protested. "Besides, Tony Vincenzi was long dead by the time they broke in."

Dana exchanged a congratulatory look with Rick. Obviously, she knew more than she'd ever wanted to know about dead bodies. A few more and maybe she'd qualify for a career in forensic medicine.

She was so intent on patting herself on the back that she apparently missed the significance of the rest of O'Flannery's statement. Kate didn't.

"Are you going to charge them with breaking and entering?" she demanded.

"Not if they open up and tell me what they were doing there," he said, then gazed first at Dana and then at Rick. "Well?"

"Do you actually have evidence that we were ever in that house?" Rick queried quietly.

"An eyewitness, namely me."

Dana gathered from the question what Rick's strategy was going to be. She chimed in. "Where were we when you spotted us?"

"Hightailing it across the backyard toward the woods."

She grinned. Rick looked complacent.

"Interesting," she said. "That would be outside the house, then, correct?"

O'Flannery scowled. "Oh, no, you don't. You two were inside. There's not a doubt in my mind about that."

"But you just said that you didn't actually see us inside," she reminded him. "You're making an assumption based on circumstantial evidence."

He didn't look nearly as rattled or as defensive as she might have liked. He turned calmly to Kate, instead.

"Did these two happen to mention anything about Tony Vincenzi when they arrived here?"

"You mean that he was dead?" Kate asked.

Rick groaned.

"Oh, Kate," Dana murmured.

Kate stared at them. "What did I do?"

"They would only have known about Vincenzi if they were in that house," O'Flannery explained gently.

"Oh, hell," Kate muttered, glaring at the detective. "You tricked me."

"I was only able to do it because you're an honest woman. Thank you. You'll make a terrific witness." He paused and stared pointedly from Rick to Dana and back again. "If it becomes necessary."

Dana broke first. "Okay, okay. I'll tell you why we were there."

He chuckled at the belated and very reluctant offer. "No need," he said indulgently. "Remember, I was there when Juan Jesus described the woman who'd been crying in your husband's office. I knew you'd head straight over there to confront her. I parked a block behind Rick and waited to see how things would play out."

Dana regarded him incredulously. "You tailed us?"

"You bet."

There wasn't so much as a hint of repentance in his voice, which irritated her no end. "Well, given the number of reinforcements you obviously called in," she said sarcastically, "did anybody think to tail Peter Drake when he slipped out of the place?"

The detective's smug expression slipped just a little at that. "Who the hell is Peter Drake?"

"He's the man who was inside Carolina Vincenzi's house when we got there," Rick supplied. "Too bad you missed him. I suspect he could tell you quite a lot about who murdered Tony Vincenzi and why."

To Kate's obvious irritation, O'Flannery shoved aside his plate and leaned forward, elbows on the table. "Maybe you'd better start at the beginning," he suggested, glaring at Dana. "And this time, don't leave out any of the significant details, okay?"

Something in his impatient tone suggested that there would be dire consequences for jerking him around again. Dana took the hint seriously. After a quick glance at the others for approval, she elaborated on the skimpy story they'd sketched for him earlier. When she was finished, the detective sighed heavily and stood up. After casting a regretful look at his untouched plate of food, he motioned toward the door.

"Let's go, all of you."

"You're taking us to jail?" Kate asked. She seemed to have lost a little of her righteous indignation.

"Not yet," he retorted. "Right now we're all going over to the church office. While you're in the vicinity, you might want to say a prayer or two that I don't charge the whole bunch of you with obstructing justice and anything else I can dream up."

Her temper clearly revived, Kate planted herself in his path and glared up at him defiantly. "You wouldn't dare."

He scowled right back. "Try me."

Dana had the feeling that a very promising romance was about to go up in smoke unless someone stepped in to prevent it. Against her better judgment, she interceded.

"Kate, he's just doing his job."

"Well, it's a lousy job," Kate grumbled.

"Could we debate the merits of my career choice some other time?" O'Flannery asked. "Or, if you'd prefer, you three can stay here and argue about it while I go over to the church."

"Not a chance," Dana said, heading for the door. She smiled at him smugly. "Besides, I'm the one who has the keys."

"The lack of keys doesn't appear to be a real impediment with this crowd," he retorted dryly. He reached in his pocket. "Besides, I have a set, too. It's a crime scene, remember? Only the police have access for the moment."

Check and checkmate.

Everyone dutifully trailed after the detective. Dana was so irritated, she was oblivious to the biting, bitter cold wind. She was imagining all sorts of dire fates befalling him, and enjoying each and every scenario, when Rick tugged her to a halt.

"What?" she asked, lifting her gaze to meet his.

"You go on. I'm going back into town."

Given the circumstances, the announcement stunned her. She studied his face intently, but his expression was unreadable. "Why? I thought you were going to help us interpret the books."

"I'm sure O'Flannery can do that."

Her suspicions mounted. "And you can't bear the thought of letting another man steal the limelight?"

"Hardly."

"What, then? Why run out now?" She fastened her gaze on his, or tried to, anyway. He continued looking everywhere but directly into her eyes. Either they were getting too close to a solution he didn't like or… She regarded him with excitement. "You've thought of something, haven't you?"

"Maybe," he admitted.

"Then I'm coming with you," she said at once.

"No. O'Flannery's going to be ticked enough when he realizes I'm gone. He'll blow a gasket if you pull a vanishing act, too. He'll come charging into the city, instead of staying out here and examining those books."

"But you don't think he's going to find anything in the books, do you?"

"I honestly don't know."

"Rick, if you know something, you have to tell me."

He touched a finger to her lips to quiet her. "That's just it, *querida*. I don't know anything. I am only guessing. I will call you as soon as I have something concrete. I swear it. Just cover for me now, okay?"

When it became obvious that he wasn't going to relent and tell her a thing, Dana shrugged indifferently, vowing to herself that she would join him the very instant it was safe to leave Kate and the detective. "Fine. Go."

"What will you tell O'Flannery?"

"Let me worry about that. Get out of here, before he realizes that something is up."

"With Kate beside him, I don't think the investigation is all that's on his mind. He will remain distracted for a moment or two longer." He leaned down and brushed a slow, lingering kiss across her lips.

"I will call you," he whispered eventually. "I promise."

As he turned and hurried swiftly out of sight, Dana

sighed. Didn't he understand that that was another thing
Ken's death had accomplished? Ken had left her with
very similar words on the night he'd been shot. She no
longer had any more faith in promises than she did in
prayers. The streets of the barrio almost guaranteed that
even the most honorably spoken vows couldn't be kept.

29

Something had been nagging at him from the minute he'd stumbled on Tony Vincenzi's body, but not until they'd been playing mind games with Detective O'Flannery had it come to Rick what it was. If he was right...

Madre de Dios, he hoped he wasn't. He also hoped like hell that Dana would be able to keep the detective off his tail. She could do it, if she felt so inclined, but he'd seen the doubts in her eyes, the fear that he was about to betray her to save either himself or Yo, Amigo.

Right now he needed luck and time. He needed to buy a few hours to see if he couldn't straighten this mess out on his own...if he was right that there was a mess and that his old friend—Tico, his triumphant success story—was smack in the middle of it.

His first stop was Yo, Amigo headquarters. With any luck, the information he was after would be in the files, files that Maria kept so organized that he should be able to put his finger on it in a heartbeat. Even after the office had been ransacked, she had managed to put everything pretty much back in order by working day and night, with help from Rosa, Marco and the others, who would have walked through fire for her.

He went straight to the alphabetized stacks of files, searching until he found the *G*s. He went through the pile twice before determining that the file for Tico Garcia was missing. Though he knew he would have no better luck there, he also searched the *T*s, in case it had been mis-filed by someone uncertain of correct filing procedures.

In the end, there was only one conclusion. It was gone. And with it, the only solid piece of evidence linking Tico's restaurant and Tony Vincenzi, if Rick's guesswork was correct.

He sank down into the chair at Maria's desk with a heavy sigh. The fact that the file was missing was as much confirmation as he needed that he was on the right track. Oh, he didn't have all of the pieces of the puzzle just yet, but he didn't like what he did have: one chunk with his old friend's angry face on it and another he was all but certain would have Tony Vincenzi's signature on a loan guarantee.

Only a handful of people knew who had been in on that deal. The investors had insisted on anonymity. They had shunned publicity.

Ken had been one of those who knew. In fact, he had been the one who had organized the backers in the first place. Had he subsequently stumbled on something ques-tionable about the operation? Was that what had put his life at risk? Had the killer also suspected that Ken might have duplicates of the loan papers in his Yo, Amigo files at the church?

There was only one place to get answers, and it was the last place on earth Rick wanted to go, the last person he wanted to confront. Feeling bone-weary and heartsick, he walked the few blocks to the restaurant.

At this hour of the night, business was booming. The salsa music was lively, the aromas mouthwatering. Tico's mother greeted him with an exuberant hug.

"Think you can squeeze me in, *Mamacita?*"

"For you, there is always room. I save the best table for special friends." She bustled down the narrow aisle toward a small table for two, where she usually sat herself when business was slow.

"Sit. I bring you chips right away and a margarita, perhaps? You look as if you need to have your spirits brightened. Tequila is very good for that."

"No margarita, *por favor.* Is Tico around?"

"Not just now." She studied his face and frowned. "Is something wrong?"

Rick wasn't ready to answer her questions. "When will he be back?"

Her expression faltered, then turned to worry. "I do not know. He has gone after Joey."

Something in Rick's stomach went ice-cold at that. "Gone after him where? *Mamacita,* this is important. Please, where are they?"

She hesitated, clearly torn between the two sons she adored and the man who had given her oldest a chance at a better life.

"You want to help them?" she asked, a soft, pleading note in her voice.

"If I can."

She sighed. "Florida. Joey went to Florida. Tico went after him. He was a wild man when he heard his brother had gone there. What is happening? I don't understand this."

Neither did he, not entirely. He closed his eyes against the sick sensation that washed over him. Eventually he forced himself to stand. As he stood, he squeezed Mrs.

Garcia's trembling hand. "Don't worry, *Mamacita.* I will do what I can for them."

"This is very bad, isn't it?"

Thinking of Dana's sons, who were now very much in the path of a man on the run, Rick could only nod. "Yes, I think it may be very, very bad."

He debated taking action alone, keeping silent until he had all the facts. He weighed Dana's frantic worry against her right to know, and saw what he had to do. He owed her the truth. Honesty, in fact, might be the only chance at salvaging whatever there was between them. If he kept silent and anything happened, she would blame him forever.

"Can I use your phone?" he asked.

"Of course. It is in the kitchen."

He called the church office, a number he knew by heart from calling so often to talk things over with his old and trusted friend.

O'Flannery answered. It wouldn't have been Rick's first choice, but maybe it was for the best. A lot of things needed to be set in motion in a hurry, and who better to do it than a cop?

He explained his theory and the admittedly sketchy proof he had. "All I do know for sure is that Dana's kids are down there and somebody needs to be alerted to protect them, in case I'm right and Joey's desperate enough to try to grab one as a hostage."

"Isn't that a big leap?" O'Flannery asked.

He sounded so skeptical that Rick was sorry he'd involved him. "Not if he doesn't get what he wants from Carolina Vincenzi," he explained impatiently. "He's going to be after some other way to get money to get out of the country, and kidnapping would sound like a sure bet if you're a scared kid who's not thinking too clearly."

"I suppose I'll have to trust your instincts on this one. I'll get on it right away," O'Flannery said tightly.

"Let me talk to Dana."

"No."

"Dammit, let me talk to her."

"There's no point in upsetting her with wild speculation," the detective countered. "At this point, we don't have squat."

"They're her kids. She has a right to know what's going on."

"What you think is going on," O'Flannery countered.

"Put her on the phone, or I'll just have to drive all the way out there to tell her in person and waste more time, when both of us could be catching a flight to Florida."

"Dammit, Sanchez!"

Rick remained silent until finally O'Flannery sighed heavily. "Fine. Here she is."

"Rick? What's wrong?"

He filled her in as hurriedly as possible. "O'Flannery's going to get police protection for the boys. In the meantime, I'm calling to book seats on the next available flight out. You call your father to warn him and then meet me at the airport. Okay? Have you got all that?"

To his relief, there was no hysterical outburst, just a terse "Fine. I'll be there as fast as I can."

He had never been more admiring of her strength. "Dana, try not to worry. This is just a precaution. I may have gotten it all wrong."

"No," she said, sounding exhausted and terrified. "I think you've gotten it right. It's the only thing that makes sense."

"Querida?"

"Yes," she said in a flat tone.

"I hope to God I'm wrong."

She never said a word. All he heard was the quiet click of the phone disconnecting. He wondered then if she would someday thank him for solving the case, or if she would only hate him forever for inadvertently setting the whole series of tragic events into motion in the first place.

From the moment Rick told her what he suspected, Dana had felt as if her world began moving in slow motion. Realistically, she knew that phone calls were made hurriedly, that the drive to O'Hare took a fraction of its usual time, with O'Flannery's siren blaring the whole way, but it all seemed to take an eternity—too long, by far, when she imagined her boys in harm's way.

Maybe, though, it wouldn't come to that. Maybe Joey would get what he needed from Carolina and be long gone when they got there. Maybe Tico would greet them and fill in all of the missing pieces of the puzzle, ending weeks of terrible uncertainty and speculation.

For one fleeting instant, she thought of the cost to Rick. He had been forced to admit that his shining example of Yo, Amigo's success was at the heart of some kind of scandal that had led to the murder of three people so far. No sooner had the stirring of sympathy come than she angrily dismissed it. It was, after all, because of him that Ken was dead, just as she had believed in the beginning.

And she had slept with him. Worse, she had begun falling in love with him. She sighed. Why not admit the truth now, at least to herself? She had fallen in love with him, against all odds, against all reason.

When this was over, though, she would walk away from him. It was the only choice she had, she concluded with devastating finality.

He was waiting for them outside the terminal at

O'Hare. After a quick glance at her, he stepped away with O'Flannery so the detective could brief him on all of the arrangements that had been made with law enforcement officials in Florida.

Dana felt Kate's hands on her shoulders and dragged her gaze back from the two men to meet her friend's deeply troubled expression.

"Don't blame him," Kate said, reading her as clearly as if she'd spoken her thoughts aloud. "He didn't kill Ken."

"He didn't pull the trigger, but he might as well have. Ken is dead because of the world Rick dragged him into."

"No," Kate said sharply. "Ken is dead because he cared so much for helping others that he took risks. He weighed them and he took them anyway. The risks didn't matter to him."

Dana stared at her incredulously. "You want me to blame Ken for getting himself killed?"

"Haven't you been doing that from the beginning? Rick is just a convenient target, sweetie. The person you're really furious with is your husband."

She couldn't be mad at Ken, Dana thought, as tears stung her eyes. Ken was dead, gone forever. It would be wrong to be so terribly angry with him.

And yet wasn't there a nugget of truth in what Kate said? From the instant she'd been told about the shooting, hadn't she really wanted to shout and curse at the man who'd left her alone with three young sons, who'd put strangers' needs above his own family's?

She pushed aside the anger. What did it matter now? She couldn't think about any of this now, not while events were still being played out hundreds of miles away. Not while her babies were in danger.

Again, Kate squeezed her shoulders. "Promise me you won't slam any doors," she said urgently. "Promise me."

"It doesn't matter now. I have to concentrate on Bobby, Kevin and Jonathan."

Kate sighed. "Yes, of course you do. They're going to be fine. I'll be praying for them every second until I hear from you."

Before Dana could reply, Rick was beside them, his expression serious, his eyes wary. "We have to go or we'll miss the flight."

Dana nodded, then gave Kate a quick, final hug. She gazed up at O'Flannery. "Thank you for everything you've tried to do."

"It hasn't been enough, but everything's in motion. Your boys will be safe and sound when you get to Florida."

"Dana?" Rick said.

"Yes, I'm coming." She turned and walked into the terminal without another backward glance.

"I have the tickets. We can go straight to the gate."

He led the way and she followed, bitterly aware that he hadn't touched her, hadn't really even looked directly at her since her arrival at the airport. It was as if he already knew, as she did, what the future held for them: nothing.

30

Fear overcame despondency very quickly as the flight touched down in Tampa. A connector flight to Fort Myers was available almost at once, but after they were on board, the plane sat parked at the ramp for what seemed an eternity.

"What's happening?" Dana asked. "Why aren't we leaving?" She reached for the call button to summon the stewardess.

"Weather," Rick said, putting his hand over hers to prevent it. "There's a bad storm passing over. I'm sure we'll take off as soon as it's safe."

Until he mentioned it, she had been oblivious to the raging rain and wind and the occasional violent bursts of thunder. "Dammit, we can't wait," she said unreasonably. "What if—"

Rick quieted the question with a touch of a finger to her lips. "Shh, *querida*. Use that brilliant head of yours. We won't get there at all if we take off, only to crash. You know that. We have to rely on the pilot's judgment."

Of course she understood that, but it didn't matter. Not knowing what was happening to her children was killing her. Her own safety didn't matter at all.

She suspected Rick was just as worried about his friends, although, at the moment, she didn't give a rat's ass if Tico and his brother went down in a burst of gunfire. Still, she knew how hard it must have been for Rick to admit that Tico was implicated in the crime. Yet he hadn't hesitated. He had told her at once. She supposed he deserved some credit for that.

"What made you think Tico might be involved in all of this?" she asked eventually, hoping that conversation would keep her mind off the inevitable delay.

Rick sighed, his expression filled with sorrow. "The way he's been acting lately, for one thing. He's been tense and defensive. He said it had to do with Joey, but a part of me wondered if that was all there was to it. Then today, when we were at the Vincenzi place, I started thinking about the consortium of investors that Ken had put together."

"You'd never met them?"

"Never. I'd never even heard their names, because they insisted on anonymity. I wondered about that at the time. In my experience, most people wish to take credit for their good deeds. I went back to Yo, Amigo to see if the paperwork was in the files, to see what, if anything, it might reveal. It was gone, which explained that ransacking. To my regret, too many things added up."

"I'm surprised you didn't fly down here on your own to check it out, without telling me what you suspected," she admitted. "Tico is your friend, after all."

He gave her a rueful grin. "I considered it."

"And?"

"I figured you would never forgive me if something happened and you believed you could have prevented it, if only you'd known the truth about what was going on. You deserved to hear everything from me." His gaze locked with hers. "Don't forget, *querida,* you and I are friends, too. Perhaps even more than friends."

"It really matters to you what I think of you?" She supposed it shouldn't have, but it surprised her.

"This is not news," he said dryly. "It has always mattered, *querida.* You were the wife of a man I respected, a man I thought of almost as a brother. Even before we met, it bothered me that you hated me so."

"How did you even know I hated you?"

"It wasn't too difficult," he said with a sad half smile. "Never once, in all the time your husband and I were working together, did you invite me to your home. Ken grew uncomfortable whenever I suggested we all get together. Since he and I spent a great deal of time together, it didn't require a tremendous mental leap to realize that you were the one who wanted no part of me."

"It wasn't personal," she said. "It was never personal."

"You were afraid for him," Rick said wearily. "I understood that."

"I was right," she pointed out.

"Does that make you feel any better?" he asked softly. "Or did it only create a rift between you when he was still alive, one that you will never be able to heal, now that he is gone?"

The truth of that hurt. "Yes," she acknowledged. "It created a terrible tension and that makes me feel unbearably sad."

"Me, as well. I regret that I inadvertently came between you." He glanced out the window. "It looks as if the storm is over. We will be taking off soon and then all of this will end."

"You don't have any doubts at all about what we will find, do you? Do you think Tico will fill in the blanks once he is caught?"

"Despite what you think of him, he is an honorable man. He is only trying to save his brother. However that turns out, he will tell you what you need to know."

And then, Dana thought, the nightmare would finally be over.

The instant the plane touched down in Fort Myers, Dana rushed for the door. Her father was waiting for her inside the terminal, and she could tell at once from his drawn expression that the nightmare wasn't over, after all.

"Dad, what is it? What's happened?" she asked as he enfolded her in a tight embrace.

When he released her, he met her gaze evenly. "Now, baby, I don't want you to panic. The police assure me that they have the situation well in hand."

She could feel her already frazzled nerves snapping. "Dammit, what situation? Please tell me."

Her father exchanged a look with a man standing quietly nearby. He walked over to join them.

"Mrs. Miller, I'm Detective Rogers. If you'll come with me."

Dana balked. "Not until I know what's going on, all of it."

"Just tell her," Rick said. "She needs to know everything. She's a very strong woman. She won't fall apart on you."

Her father nodded. "That's right, Detective. My daughter is a professional investigator. She's been working on this case for weeks now. She might be able to help."

"It's your son," the detective said, his voice gentle, his gaze obviously watchful for any sign that she was about to fall apart. "He's being held hostage, we believe by a man named José Garcia."

"Where?" she asked, fighting to keep her voice from shaking. She had anticipated this possibility, but the reality of it was devastating. Her whole body suddenly felt ice-cold with dread.

"At the Vincenzis'," her father said, his expression filled with guilt. "It's our fault. We didn't know. Bobby asked to go to play with one of the boys from school. We didn't realize which boy it was until it was too late."

Not again, she thought. *Please, God, not again.* She couldn't bear to lose another person she loved to this kind of insane violence.

And for the first time since Ken's death, she began to pray. It was pure instinct. She didn't know if there was a God, or if He would hear her this time, but at the moment, prayer and faith were all she had.

31

The Vincenzi home in Fort Myers must be a considerably more modest one than the monstrosity they had searched in the Chicago suburbs, Rick thought, as they drove into the neighborhood of small Spanish-style stucco structures on postage-stamp-size lots.

Dana hadn't said a word since they'd left the airport. She had sat huddled between him and her father on the drive, seemingly oblivious to their presence. She hadn't reacted in any way when he'd taken her icy hands in his and rubbed them to restore the warmth. From time to time, he could feel her shivering, even though the tropical air was warm and muggy.

He glanced at her father and saw that he hadn't missed Rick's gesture. It would have been too much to expect approval in his eyes, but there was no censure, either, just questions that would remain on hold for the time being. Rick could respect a man for wanting to wait and see before giving his blessing to a relationship.

If there was to be a relationship, he reminded himself. That was very much in question, for the time being. Dana was allowing his touch at the moment, because she was, quite frankly, oblivious to it. Later, he had no idea what to expect. He prayed for the best and feared the worst.

In the meantime, there was Bobby to worry about. He was convinced that Joey wouldn't harm the boy. No matter how panicked he was, how cornered he was feeling, he was a decent kid at heart. Rick conceded reluctantly that his opinion was based more on desperate hope than facts. Joey had been in a gang for a long time before Tico had forced him out after his own redemption. He'd been in there long enough to become desensitized to violence. Who knew what effect Carlos's ugly influence had had?

There was a crowd gathered on the street just down the block from the Vincenzi home, though the police had done their best to keep neighbors and others drawn by the unfolding drama at a distance.

"You okay?" Detective Rogers asked Dana, after pulling to a stop behind a line of police vehicles.

She nodded, though her complexion was pale and her eyes darkened by fear. Unshed tears made them shimmer like deep blue pools.

"Let's go, then," her father said. "Let's let Bobby know that his mom is right outside."

As Dana and her father made their way to the SWAT team coordinator, Rick held back and surveyed the throng, searching for Tico. If Joey was inside, Tico wouldn't be able to stay away. Nor would he have gone in with his brother. Rick still believed that his friend would fight to the end to prevent a tragedy.

Eventually he spotted Tico lurking in the shadows, two houses down, standing all alone. Rick slipped through the darkness and came up behind him.

"We've got troubles, old friend," he said softy.

Tico jerked at the sound of his voice, but he never turned. He kept his bleak, tortured face focused on the house where his brother was holding an innocent young boy hostage.

"I was too late," he said in a voice quivering with emotion. "As soon as I knew, I came after him, but I was too late. If all of this comes to a bad end, I will kill Carlos with my bare hands."

"It's time for the truth. Did Joey kill Ken?"

Tico's head snapped around at that. "Never!" he said furiously. "It was that gringo, that slime who is inside at this very moment holding Joey and the others hostage."

Rick gaped at the totally unexpected reply. "Gringo? Who?"

"Drake."

"Peter Drake?" he asked, incredulous, even though he'd seen that very man at the scene of another murder.

"Sí."

"How the devil was he involved?"

"From the beginning, he was demanding payoffs," Tico said, obviously aware that it was too late now for denials or evasions. "He said I should be pleased to become a front for a money-laundering operation, since he had made it possible for me to open."

"I don't understand."

"He and the woman were having an affair. She used her influence with her husband and with the *padre* to put the loan deal together for me. As far as I knew, it was a straightforward deal. Then this Drake came to me and explained the facts of life, as he called them. He had this little drug operation, he and some others."

"Lawrence Tremayne?" Rick guessed, thinking of the Latin American connection that they'd never been able to make sense of.

"He was one. There were more, I suspect, though I never met them."

"Did you cooperate?"

"For a while, until I could think what to do." He regarded Rick wryly. "With my past, I didn't think I could go to the police."

"You could have come to me," Rick said.

"No, my friend. I could not involve you. For once, I needed to solve this problem on my own. You were counting on me to be a success story, yes?"

Rick guessed the rest. "You talked to Ken."

"*Sí*. It was the worst mistake of my life. I should have known how he would react. He went loco. He threatened to blow the whole operation out of the water. He was incensed at the betrayal of men he'd thought to be honorable. I tried to calm him, to make him think rationally, but he insisted on doing it his way, on confronting them with what he knew, on giving them a chance to make things right."

"Right how?"

"By turning themselves in." Tico shrugged. "He was a very naive man, yes? It was his charm, but also his downfall."

"How did Carlos and Joey fit in?"

"Drake went to Carlos with his little problem. Carlos decided it would be a fascinating test of Joey's loyalty to him to ask him to shoot the *padre*. Naturally he did not trust him to do it. When Joey refused, Carlos pulled the trigger, then placed the gun in my brother's hand. Do you think the police would have believed that, though?"

"And today? What happened to bring you down here today?"

"Joey told me earlier that Drake had had Vincenzi killed, too, and that he was planning to fly here, get Carolina and leave the country. We concluded, once more, that the police would not believe such a story. We decided to try to stop them ourselves. Joey, however, was too rash. He went in before we could think of a plan. Drake has them all now."

"Including Ken's boy," Rick concluded quietly.

Tico stared at him. "The *padre's* son is in there?"

"Yes." He met Tico's gaze. "Perhaps you and I should do what the police do not dare."

"Go in?" Tico replied, looking doubtful. "I do not think this is such a good idea."

"We don't have a choice, my friend. If we don't, they may harm the wrong man. They think Joey is behind this, and Drake will be eager to serve him up as the culprit."

"You would do that for me? You would risk your life to save my brother?"

"I would do it for you," he said readily. "And for Dana."

"I saw her arrive," Tico said. "I did not guess that you were with her."

Rick shrugged. "Where else would I be?" he said wryly. "Though at the moment I doubt that she appreciates it."

"You have it very bad, don't you, *mi amigo?*"

"*Sí.* Very bad."

Tico grinned at him. "So, you and I are together again. You have a plan?"

"As I recall, we were once very good at improvising."

"True, but there is danger in that."

"There is danger in living," Rick told him. "And even greater danger, sometimes, in doing nothing."

They moved in tandem then, slipping around behind the house, staying in shadows, alert for the presence of the SWAT team that had every door and window under surveillance. Breaking in without being detected, from either within or without, was not going to be so easy.

"Do you know exactly where they are being held?"

"At the far end of the house, I believe. The garage protects it on one side, and the windows are smaller. I have seen no movement through any of the sliding glass doors. It seems to me it would be foolish to hold them where they can be readily seen, and this Drake is no fool."

Rick regarded the house thoughtfully. "Perhaps we can change that. Wait for me here."

He circled to the front of the house and slipped through the crowd, until he could catch Dana's father's eye. The older man joined him at once.

"Tell Dana to insist on seeing her son, preferably through that sliding glass door in the living room. Once he's there, ask her to try to keep him in view as long as possible. Cry, plead, whatever it takes, okay? Make sure she keeps Bobby where he is plainly visible so there will be no mistakes."

Her father didn't waste time asking a lot of unnecessary questions. He seemed to know intuitively what Rick was planning. He, too, seemed to accept the limitations of the police.

He met Rick's gaze with an unblinking look. "Are you sure you can do this?"

"I have no choice but to try."

"You could leave it to the police."

"And while they debate the alternatives, the man inside could begin to get very jittery. I have to do this for Ken's sake."

"And for my daughter's," the older man guessed. "God speed, son. Thank you."

Rick hated expressing any hint of doubt about the outcome, but he needed Dana to know what she had meant to him. He met the other man's gaze. "If anything should happen to me, would you...?"

He smiled and squeezed Rick's shoulder. "I will tell her that you love her very much. I think, though, that you should come back to her safely and tell her yourself."

Rick grinned. "I'm going to do my damnedest to do just that."

Dana's eyes were gritty from staring so hard at the tiny house, trying to catch a glimpse of her son. He must be terrified. So far, though, the police hadn't let her make an appeal to Joey Garcia, nor had they let her speak to her son.

She was dimly aware of her father having a hushed conversation with Detective Rogers, then of several policemen huddling together, as her father returned to her side.

"You doing okay, baby?"

"Dad, I am so scared," she admitted. "I don't think I have ever been more terrified."

"Not even when Johnny Payne locked you in that steel vault?" he asked, referring to a harrowing incident that had taken place while she was an investigator.

"Not even then."

"He's going to get out of there," her father reassured her. "I believe that with all my heart."

"But we've been at a stalemate for hours. I don't think the police are even negotiating for his release."

"That may be about to change."

She stared at him. "What do you know?"

"Here comes Detective Rogers now," he said, evading her eyes. "Let's see what he has in mind."

"Mrs. Miller, we have phone contact with the kidnapper. Do you think you could talk to him?"

The very idea of chatting with the person who was terrorizing her child made her blood run cold, but she nodded. She tried to remind herself that Joey was little more than a boy himself and that he was Tico's brother.

"What do you want me to do?" she asked.

"Ask to see Bobby. Tell him you want to come up to that front window and see your boy. If he agrees, keep Bobby and the kidnapper there as long as you can."

"What if he refuses?"

"Keep at him until you wear him down. Plead. Cry. Whatever it takes."

She nodded.

"Okay, then, let's do it."

He spoke to the SWAT commander, who relinquished the phone to her.

Dana forced herself to remain calm as she clutched the receiver as though it were a lifeline to her son. "Joey?" she said softly.

A sinister laugh made her stomach plummet. Instantly alert, she said, "This isn't Joey, is it?"

"How brilliant of you to conclude that, Mrs. Miller. You were always far too smart for that saccharine husband of yours."

"My God," she murmured, instantly recognizing Peter Drake's voice, even though she had heard him use that tone only once before, at the meeting at her house with the church elders. "It's you."

"Right again. I was afraid you'd put it together. Those stupid policemen don't have a clue who they're dealing with. I've had them on the phone with Joey all evening. I couldn't resist the chance to talk with you, though."

"What do you want?"

"My freedom," he said simply. "Carolina and I want to leave the country and live quietly."

"I can make that happen," she said impulsively. "But first I want to see Bobby."

"Sorry. Not possible."

Terrified of the answer, she asked the obvious questions anyway. "Why? Have you killed him already?"

"Killed my ace in the hole? Perhaps you're not as bright as I thought."

"Then why can't I see him? You could bring him into the living room. I'll stand right outside the window."

"And I will make myself the perfect target for some sniper."

"No," she insisted. "You can stay out of sight. Just let Bobby come where I can see that he's all right." Though she'd vowed not to cry, she couldn't help the sobs that rose in her throat. "Please, Peter. I have to see him. I have to let him know I'm here."

"You can speak to him on the phone."

"No," she repeated. "It won't be the same. Look, I can help you get away from here, but not unless you do this for me."

"What makes you think you can get the police to let us go?"

"I'm a minister's wife. They'll believe me when I tell them you had nothing to do with this, that it was all Joey Garcia. That's what they think, anyway."

"They are idiots, aren't they?" he said, sounding thoughtful. "Okay, I will bring Bobby to the window. Don't try anything crazy, because I will have a gun on him the whole time. You come up to the house alone. If I see anyone else close, the deal's off and your boy is dead. Are we clear?"

She swallowed hard. "We're clear." She handed the phone back to Detective Rogers and gave him a curt nod to indicate that the kidnapper had bought the plan. Then she began moving very slowly across the street and onto the Vincenzi's front lawn. With each step she took, her heart pounded a little harder and sweat beaded across her forehead.

Was she doing the right thing? She had blindly accepted the police plan without asking what their intentions were. Would they be rushing the house from another direction, even as she herself approached? Was she only putting her son into more danger? It was too late for second thoughts now, though. She was only a few yards from that window and a precious glimpse of Bobby.

There was a neatly tended flower bed outside the sliding glass doors, which substituted for windows around most of the house. Oblivious to the destruction, she stepped on bright pink impatiens until she was close enough to touch the glass.

And then she waited. She waited for so long she was certain that Peter Drake had only meant to torture her by making a promise he had no intention of keeping.

Then suddenly Bobby was there, shoved from behind so hard that he stumbled as he came into view. Dana pressed her hands to the glass.

"Mom!"

He sounded on the verge of tears, but he squared his shoulders bravely. He stepped closer to the doors and blinked at her through his glasses. She noticed one lens was cracked.

"Are you okay?" he asked.

Dana's own tears spilled down her cheeks unchecked. "I'm doing just fine, now that I see you." She pressed her hand against the glass and Bobby placed his against it on the other side. "I love you, sweetie. We're going to get you out of there."

Bobby swallowed hard, his chin wobbling. "I'll be okay, Mom. Try not to worry."

Just then the pane of glass between them shattered.

Dana didn't hesitate to consider what had caused it or whether she or Bobby was likely to be cut. As the shards fell away, she snatched him into her arms and ran. Before she'd taken two steps, they were surrounded by half a dozen officers in bulletproof vests.

Even as they escorted her and Bobby to safety, she could hear the two-way radios blaring with confused exchanges.

"What the hell happened?" the SWAT team commander was demanding. "Nobody had an order to shoot."

Dana glanced up then just in time to see Peter Drake being led away in handcuffs as two very familiar men looked on. She guessed then who had come up with the daring rescue plan. She glanced at her father.

"You knew, didn't you? You knew what they were going to do? How did they manage it?"

The color had finally come back into her father's face in the past few minutes, but his expression remained totally bland. "I think you'll have to talk to Mr. Sanchez about that." He leaned down and scooped up his grandson in a bear hug. "Come on, boy. Let's let your mom have a minute of privacy."

Bobby stared as Rick left the house and crossed the yard. A furious SWAT team commander was about to intercept him when Dana stepped between them.

"In a minute," she told the policeman. "I have a few words to say to Mr. Sanchez."

"One minute," the man replied tersely. "Then I get a crack at him."

Her gaze never left Rick's face. "I will never forget what you did here today. I have no idea how you accomplished it, but I don't care. I will always be grateful."

"I owed you one." His eyes locked on hers. "What will you do now that you have all your answers?"

"Not all of them," she replied, "but I'm sure the police will fill me in."

He nodded. "Are you going to stay here?"

She hadn't thought past this moment, but she nodded slowly. "For a while."

His expression blank, he said quietly, "Yes, that makes sense. The boys will need you with them."

Suddenly she felt as if she were talking to a stranger, making small talk, when far more important things remained unspoken.

Before she could say precisely that, the patience of the SWAT team leader snapped. "You'll have to excuse us, ma'am. This man has some explaining to do."

"Where are you taking him?"

"To headquarters for a little chat."

Dana turned to her father, who was waiting nearby. "Dad, go with them."

Rick's mouth quirked into a full-fledged grin at her protective tone. "I do not need an attorney, *querida.*"

"Humor me," she countered. "And if there's anything else I can do for you, *anything,* you can always call."

His dark eyes challenged hers. "Then this is good-bye?"

Tears stung her eyes, and her heart felt like lead, but she forced herself to nod.

Rick's steady, dark-eyed gaze locked with hers. *"Adios, mi amor."*

Only after he had walked away without a backward glance did she reply softly, *"Adios, mi amor."*

32

Dana couldn't seem to let Bobby out of her sight, much to his chagrin. He finally told her to lay off, or he'd wind up being known all over Florida as a mama's boy.

"I won't even be able to show my face on the streets. I'll have to quit school," he warned.

"Okay, okay." She studied him worriedly. "Are you sure everything's all right with you, though? No nightmares or anything?"

He rolled his eyes. "Mom, I've told you and told you, Mr. Drake never hurt me. Mrs. Vincenzi threatened to cut off his—"

"Never mind. I know what she threatened."

In fact, if Peter Drake ever left jail and got together with Carolina Vincenzi, Dana wasn't sure which one she'd pity more. She had heard a few days ago that Carolina had put her house in Illinois on the market, as well as the house in Fort Myers. She and her sons had vanished. Some thought they were living in Grand Cayman on money Tony had stashed away before his death.

As for Rick, he and Tico had flown back to Chicago as soon as they'd been released by the police. Her father had stayed with them the whole time and reported back that both men had been cleared of any possible charges, even though the local police were mad as hell that a couple of vigilantes had jumped into the standoff with a daring rescue attempt. Rick had shattered the window so that Dana could grab her son while Tico had jumped Drake from behind.

Joey had gone back on the same flight, in police custody, until he could make his statements to the Chicago police about Ken's murder.

She had heard from Kate the night before that Lawrence Tremayne was in custody, as well, though the infamous Carlos had conveniently disappeared. When she'd asked about O'Flannery, Kate had been coy, but she sounded happier than she had been since that sleaze of a husband had run out on her.

Her own world should be settling back into something resembling normalcy, Dana thought, as she sat on the beach with the boys playing nearby. It seemed like a lifetime since she had sat in this very spot and made up her mind to go home and solve her husband's murder. She had her answers now, but she was no less restless. The longed-for peace of mind continued to elude her. This time, though, another man was at the center of her thoughts.

She had her eyes closed when she sensed someone standing over her. She glanced up just as her father dropped down to the lawn chair next to hers.

"When are you going to tell me what's going on between you and Sanchez?" he asked.

So much for pussyfooting around the touchy subject, she thought resignedly. "There's nothing between us," she said.

His eyebrows rose skeptically. "Really? I wonder, then, why he told me to tell you that he loved you if anything happened to him when he was playing hero the other night."

She removed her sunglasses and peered at her father. She wasn't sure which stunned her more, that Rick loved her or that he'd told her father. "Rick said he loved me? You're not just putting words in his mouth?"

"No, and even if he hadn't said the words, it was plain as day when he looked at you. I know the signs, baby. The man's a goner." He regarded her intently. "How do you feel about him? No evasions this time."

She sighed. It was a question she had asked herself, repeatedly. "I don't know," she said, being as honest as she could. "For a time, I thought I did. But before that, I had so much anger and resentment where he was concerned. Then, while I was investigating Ken's death, I kept bumping into more suspicions and doubts. How can I get past all that?"

"Maybe you can't," her father said simply. "But you won't find out by hanging around down here on the beach."

She grinned at him. "Are you kicking me out?"

He studied her face for a minute. "I love you, baby, but yes, that is exactly what I'm doing. Go home. Find out what's left there for you."

For some reason—fear, maybe—she was reluctant to make that commitment. She lifted a handful of warm sand, letting it sift through her fingers.

"Mom thinks we should move down here," she said eventually, testing the idea on him. "She thinks it would be good for the boys to have family nearby."

"True, but your mother doesn't know what I do."

"Which is?"

"That your heart's still in Chicago."

* * *

"Where do you want this?" Kate asked, precariously balancing a huge box.

"What does it say?" Dana asked. "I marked everything."

"If I could see what you wrote, do you think I'd be asking?" Kate retorted.

Dana stood on tiptoe to peer at the top of the box. "Kevin's room. I think those are his stuffed animals."

"What does he have, a blessed zoo?" Kate grumbled as she headed for the stairs. "And would you tell me why you had to buy a three-story town house and put the boys in the top floor?"

"Just to torment you on moving day," Dana replied.

She had been back in Chicago for three hectic months. She had spent most of that time settling Ken's legal affairs and house hunting. Though she'd looked at several places within blocks of the church, time and again she had been drawn into the city, into a neighborhood of old town houses that had been gentrified in recent years.

Before she had made the final decision, she had gone into the cemetery by the church to talk it over with Ken, as she had done with any major decision she'd made since they'd married. As she'd planted daffodils and tulips around his tombstone, she'd told him about all of the emotional upheavals that had happened since he'd left them.

"I'm not angry at you anymore," she had said finally. "I've made peace with what happened, though I'll go on missing you until the day I die." And then, after taking a deep breath, she had told him about her feelings for Rick. "I'm scared, though, scared of moving on, scared of losing another person I love. He's right out there, you know, right in the thick of the very neighborhood where you were killed. How will I be able to stand knowing that something could happen to him at any second?"

She touched the cold marble of the angel and, ironically, it was that fleeting contact that gave her the answer she'd been seeking. Soon enough, they would all die, but for now, she and Rick and their passion were very much alive.

She had glanced up at the sky, a smile on her lips. "Thank you," she whispered to Ken, or God, or whoever had led her to the answer she'd been so desperately seeking.

She hadn't told Rick yet of her decision, had made no overtures of any kind to bring him back into her life. She had wanted to get settled in her new home and bring the boys back from Florida first. Her parents would be arriving with them next week. They were bursting with enthusiasm about coming home and about living in the city. She wanted Rick to see that she had made her choice to stay because it was the right one for all of them, and not solely because of him. Soon, though. Very soon.

She caught Kate staring at her curiously. "What did you do with O'Flannery?" Dana asked her. "He's supposed to be hauling the big stuff."

"Last time I saw him, he was sitting in a chair on the sidewalk cursing the day he ever met the two of us."

"Uh-oh," Dana said. "That doesn't bode well for your future."

"Sure it does. He complains about everything he loves—his job, me."

Kate started up the steps with Dana right on her heels. "He loves you? When did that happen?"

"It happened the day he set eyes on me." Kate grinned. "He just got around to figuring it out the other day,

though. Some men have to be blindsided by a bat before they get it."

"If you two would stop gabbing, we would finish this
move a whole lot faster," the man in question announced
from downstairs. "Where do you want this blasted sofa?"

Dana rushed back down. "How did you get the sofa
in here by yourself?" Her voice trailed off when she saw
Rick standing silently at the opposite end of the sofa,
his expression wary. O'Flannery glanced at Dana, then
back at Rick.

"I guess the sofa can wait," he said, lowering his end
to the floor. He brushed past Dana to head upstairs.

"How did you get here?" she asked eventually just to
break the silence. "I mean, how did you know we were
moving?"

"O'Flannery and I have stayed in touch. He filled me
in. I thought maybe you could use some extra help." He
watched her warily. "Do you mind?"

"No, of course not. It's…" Her voice faltered. "It's
kind of you."

He regarded her wryly. "*Por favor, querida,* enough
of the polite small talk. You look wonderful."

She glanced down at her filthy jeans and baggy
T-shirt. "Oh, I'm a beauty, all right."

"Yes," he said fervently, "you are. I've missed you."

It couldn't have been even a quarter as badly as she'd
missed him, she thought, remembering the lonely nights
when all she'd been able to think about was the single
time they'd made love. She had wondered if they would
ever risk a second chance. If she dared.

"I've missed you, too," she said in a choked voice. "I,
um, I saw that Rosa had an ad in the *Tribune* last Sunday."

He grinned. "She was over-the-moon, as they say."

"And her father? What did he say?"

"He bought up every copy he could find and gave them to all his friends."

"Then I guess it was a good thing it was an ad for cosmetics, instead of lingerie."

"Or maternity clothes," Rick said. "Though I think he is coming to terms with her pregnancy. It's just in the nick of time, too. The baby's due any second."

"And Marco? I've been meaning to check on him, too."

"Marco has gone to Hollywood," he said proudly. "You friend sent his pictures out there to a coagent, and he got him a commercial two days later. I think maybe Rosa will join him eventually. You did a good thing for them." He fastened his gaze on hers. "The others ask about you, you know. They are waiting for you to come and help them."

She was surprised by that and pleased.

"Will you come to Yo, Amigo again? Maybe teach another photography class? Ileana has been taking pictures like a crazy woman. She says she wants to have a portfolio ready when you come back."

"Ileana? With the scorpion tattoo?"

He grinned. "She pretty much terrorizes her subjects into sitting for her, but she's actually gotten some interesting results."

"I'd love to see them."

"I could pick you up tomorrow. We could have lunch at Tico's. He's been asking about you, too." He shrugged. "Bullying me, actually. He thinks I've been wasting too much time before coming after you. Was he right?"

She shook her head.

"I thought maybe you needed time to get your bearings," he explained.

"I did," she admitted.

"And now? Do you know what you want, *querida?*"

His hands were shoved into his pockets, as if he feared he might reach for her, only to have her slip away.

She nodded. If she had doubted it before, she would have known it the minute she had seen him in the living room, filling the room with his very masculine presence, just as he had done in the house she had shared with another man she had loved heart and soul.

She realized then that she had bought this town house with him in mind. She had chosen the vibrant colors for the walls and selected huge pots of hibiscus and bougainvillea to sit beside the French doors in her den, because they reminded her of the passionate man who'd brought her senses back to life. She had especially liked the privacy of the master suite on the second floor, far from the prying eyes of little boys.

"You," she confessed softly. "I want you."

A smile began slowly at the corners of his mouth, then spread. His hands came out of his pockets, and he opened his arms. She flew across the room into his embrace. As his arms closed tightly around her, it was like coming home again, finding a safe haven in the midst of turmoil.

For a long time, neither of them spoke. It was enough just to know the comfort of being held. Then he pulled back and gazed into her eyes.

"We'll fight," he warned her.

She laughed. "But you'll let me win."

His expression rueful, he nodded. "Sometimes. Because there is very little I could deny you."

She touched her fingers to his lips. "Making up will be extraordinary."

"You are extraordinary." He stepped backward, deliberately tumbling them onto the couch with her on top. His mouth sought hers, slowly, gently, and then with a passion that made her blood roar. Everything, their surroundings, the noises from the street, the proximity of Kate and O'Flannery, all of it faded away. The only thing real was Rick and the hunger of his kisses, the heat of his body.

"Think they've forgotten that we're here?" Kate whispered.

The softly spoken words broke the spell. Dana chuckled. "A good friend would have slipped discreetly out the door."

"And left all the rest of the furniture sitting in the street?" O'Flannery asked, then added pointedly, "Including the beds?"

Rick sighed, his gaze locked with hers. "They have a point."

"Yes," she conceded. "Especially about the beds."

"The faster we move, the sooner we'll have this place to ourselves," Rick added. He was already lifting her to her feet as he said it.

But as Dana started to follow Kate and O'Flannery outside, Rick caught her hand and tugged her back. "In case I didn't mention it, I love you, *querida.*"

"I love you," she said quietly.

He had been with her in twilight and in the darkest moments of her life. With any luck, the shadows were gone and the rest of their days would be all sunshine. And if that was too much to hope for, at least they both knew with absolute certainty that their love was strong enough to weather the most volatile of storms.

* * * * *

#1 *New York Times* Bestselling Author

SHERRYL WOODS

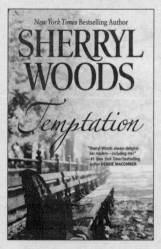

A heartwarming story about a reunion between a mother and daughter and demonstrates that real love knows no limits.

Callie Smith's quest for success has caused a rift with her hardworking family. And with neither her Wall Street career nor her marriage going as planned, she starts to question the choices she's made.

But when charismatic network president Jason Kane pursues her to save a failing soap opera, her life is soon full of more twists than a TV story line. Suddenly she gets to know a whole new side to her mother, and also has the opportunity to save a friend's life. Most unexpected of all, she leaves heartache behind and tunes in to the love of a lifetime.

Available wherever books are sold.

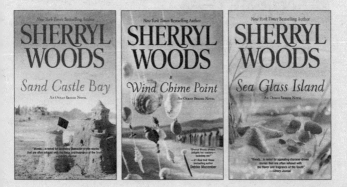

#1 *New York Times* Bestselling Author

ROBYN CARR

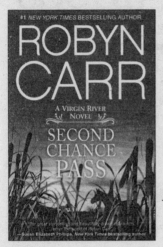

In the space of a few months, Vanessa Rutledge buried her husband, Matt, and gave birth to their son—breaking her heart while filling it with a whole new kind of love. But the one man she longs to share this love with now acts as if she doesn't exist.

Paul Haggerty has done right by his best friend Matt's widow as best he can…considering he's been secretly in love with her for years. Now, just as he's about to make his move, another woman has staked her claim on him—a claim that will be tough to escape.

But with courage and humility, Vanni and Paul might just get a second chance to have the love they both desire and deserve.

Available wherever books are sold.

Be sure to connect with us at:
Harlequin.com/Newsletters
Facebook.com/HarlequinBooks
Twitter.com/HarlequinBooks

HARLEQUIN® MIRA
www.Harlequin.com

MRC1571